Fire Raiser

TOR BOOKS BY MELANIE RAWN

Spellbinder

Fire Raiser

MELANIE RAWN

Fire Raiser

A TOM DOHERTY ASSOCIATES BOOK

New York

This is a work of fiction. All of the characters, organizations, and events portrayed in this novel are either products of the author's imagination or are used fictitiously.

FIRE RAISER

A Tor Book
Published by Tom Doherty Associates, LLC
175 Fifth Avenue
New York, NY 10010

www.tor-forge.com

Tor® is a registered trademark of Tom Doherty Associates, LLC.

Library of Congress Cataloging-in-Publication Data

Rawn, Melanie.
Fire raiser / Melanie Rawn.—1st ed.
p. cm.
"A Tom Doherty Associates book."
ISBN-13: 978-0-7653-1533-5
ISBN-10: 0-7653-1533-5
1. Family secrets—Fiction. 2. Slave trade—Fiction. I. Title.
PS3568.A8553F57 2009
813'.54—dc22
2008046455

First Edition: April 2009

Printed in the United States of America

0 9 8 7 6 5 4 3 2 1

This one is for

Eugena May Fisk

and her daughter

Tracy Sue Lang

and her daughter

Tiffany Amanda Taylor

Fire Raiser

Prologue

June 1, 2004

"HOLLY HONEY, you want to see these kids anytime soon, you better stop planning your next signing tour and get to work."

"I'll sign my name in gentian violet on your shiny bald head if you don't shut the hell up!"

Evan Lachlan, who had by now perfected the art of pacing without actually moving from beside the birthing chair, felt his gut lurch. His wife had been cussing her way through labor for five and a half hours. He'd been coaching her under the assumption that sooner or later—maybe before she ran out of invective, maybe not—he'd be holding a baby.

A baby.

"*Kids*—?" he managed feebly.

William Cutter, M.D., F.A.C.O.G.,[1] P.W.D.,[2] grinned at him. "Surprise."

STEM CELLS CREATE ALL TISSUES, organs, and systems in the body. When a stem cell divides, each new cell has the potential either to remain a stem cell or to become another type of cell with a more specialized

---

[1] Fellow, American College of Obstetricians and Gynecologists

[2] Practicing Witch Doctor

function (muscle, red blood, bone, brain, etc.). Triggering to differentiate stem cells into a desired type could lead to growing neural cells to treat Alzheimer's and Parkinson's, blood vessel cells that would allow a cardiac patient to grow his own bypass, or to producing an entire organ such as a pancreas, liver, or kidney.

Umbilical cord blood stem cells are the "youngest" available stem cells. Freezing these cells essentially stops the clock and prevents aging and damage that may occur to the cells later in life.

"C'MON, HOLLY—PUSH—"

"Lachlan, you tell me that just one more time and I'll make you a goddamned coloratura soprano!"

"Don't worry, Evan," said Dr. Cutter. "They all threaten that."

"I figured. I'm still waiting for how she's never gonna let me touch her again."

"She'll get around to it," was the philosophical reply. "They all do."

Holly growled through a breathless grunt of effort—altogether an interesting sound, though Lachlan wondered whether it was physiologically possible. "What about the one where I string you both up by your balls?"

"Heard that before, too," Cutter scoffed. "Like the man said, honey—*push*!"

AFTER THE UMBILICAL CORD is severed, cord blood can be collected two different ways. In blood bag collection, a needle is inserted into the umbilical vein and gravity drains the blood into a bag. This method of collection is usually done before delivery of the placenta. Syringe collection draws the umbilical blood into syringes containing anticoagulants for storage. This method allows a larger volume of blood to be collected, and can be done before or after delivery of the placenta. The collection process takes less than five minutes and should be performed within ten to fifteen minutes after birth.

"BIG KIDS," DRAWLED DR. CUTTER, stripping off latex gloves as the nurses finished weighing and measuring the babies.

"Yeah," Evan agreed, watching eagle-eyed to make sure nobody dropped his children. "By her fifth month I was walkin' in front of her with a sign: *Oversize Load*."

"Go play with yourself, Lachlan." Holly eased back into piled pillows. "And excuse me, Dr. *Oy-Gevalt*-Holly-You-Look-Like-You're-Carrying-Quints, but *you're* telling *me* they're big? Who's been lugging them around for eight months, anyway?"

"Eh, quitcher bitchin', girl. I got 'em born without a C-section, didn't I?"

"Huh. All you did was play catch. You really think I'd let anybody named 'Cutter' near me with a knife?"

He smiled, supremely unimpressed. "A little more respect for the man with the pharmaceuticals, please."

CORD BLOOD SHOULD BE SHIPPED as soon as possible to the storage facility. Processing should begin within forty-eight hours of collection. Blood will first be tested for infectious and genetic diseases (hepatitis, HIV/AIDS, leukemia, sickle-cell, etc.), and is then separated by centrifuge or sedimentation.

After division into plasma, red blood cells, and white blood cells, the latter are removed for storage. It is essential that all red blood cells be extracted; these can rupture when thawed, compromising stem-cell viability.

Cryopreservation solution is introduced to prevent blood from damage while frozen. Subsequent to gradual freezing to a temperature of –196°C, blood is transferred to permanent storage, remaining frozen via either liquid or vapor nitrogen.

Studies have yet to make a conclusive determination regarding the freezer life of stem cells, but estimates are from ten to fifteen years.

ACCEPTING A BABY into the crook of each elbow, the doctor remarked, "Pretty good work for an old broad."

" 'Pretty good'? 'Old'?" She glared. "Sheriff, where's your gun? I want this man shot at sunrise."

"Too late by about an hour," Lachlan replied, grinning. "Will tomorrow do?"

"The four of you will be home by then," Cutter told him, easing a blue-wrapped bundle into Holly's arms. "In fact, I could probably kick you out tonight, but then you'd miss my five-star room service. I highly recommend the apricot cobbler, by the way. Your turn, Ev."

Lachlan accepted the pink blanket, slightly apprehensive as its contents wriggled. "So when did childbirth become an outpatient procedure?"

"Thank all that tough Irish ancestry," Cutter said. "She probably could've had these kids at Woodhush."

Holly arched her brows. "May I assume, then, that you won't be charging us for the privilege of sitting around doing nothing?"

"I had to listen to you, didn't I? For all the insults, I should tack on hazardous duty pay. But tell ya what—I'll throw in the cord-blood collection process for free."

"You got it already?" She blinked. "When did this happen?"

"You were too busy snarling at your husband to notice. It's already on ice and headed for CryoCache. Here's hoping they never need it."

Nodding fervently, Lachlan contemplated his daughter's auburn hair, thick frowning eyebrows, and rosebud mouth, and completely forgot his self-imposed strictures against making foolish and peculiar noises.

"Mush," he heard Holly accuse. "Absolute marshmallow mush."

Cutter chuckled. "This is your brain. This is your brain as a daddy. Congratulations, Evan. Ready for the handoff?"

"They're not footballs!" Holly griped, clutching her son protectively.

"Oh, shut up," said Evan and the doctor at the same time.

Trading the pink bundle for the blue, Lachlan took his first close look at his son. Tufts of black hair crowned a remarkably self-composed little face that even at five minutes old could clearly be seen to have his nose. He knew he'd started making those noises again when Holly gave a loud snort.

"Double the marshmallow mush," she announced.

"Be glad it wasn't triplets," said Cutter.

That reminded Evan of something he'd been meaning to ask. "By the way, lady love, I'm curious—just when did you find out it was twins?"

She squirmed. "Billy-boy, did y'all say something about pharmaceuticals?"

"One of the sonograms, was it?" Evan suggested brightly.

"Third," said Dr. Cutter.

Holly made a face at him. "We kind of suspected before that, but—it's not unusual at my age, you know. The chances of a multiple birth go up as a woman gets older—"

"No lecture, no statistics," Evan warned. "What I wanted to know is, you kept this information from the father of these twins *why,* exactly?"

"I wanted to surprise you?" she offered tentatively.

"Oh, you did that, all right. Twice the stinky diapers, twice the screaming at three a.m., twice the college educations—God help us." He grinned. "If I wasn't so happy about it I'd probably have a seizure."

STEM CELLS FROM UMBILICAL CORD blood can also be used for cloning.

A human clone is a time-delayed identical twin of another person.

Using scientific techniques, the cloning process has a massive failure rate.

No one has ever succeeded using magic, either.

One

September 3, 2006

THE WATER IN THE BUCKET was meant for the tomatoes. As it cascaded instead over the tousled head and shirtless torso of her husband, Holly felt her knees wobble. She'd been watching him from the parlor window for a few minutes now, still amused after two and a half years that her city boy had taken so enthusiastically to life in the Virginia sticks. The vegetable garden had been all his idea. Tomatoes, squash, onions, corn, peas, and four varieties of chili peppers received his intense devotion every evening when he got home; on Sundays like this one he spent hours out back, babying anything that needed extra attention.

Yep—scratch an Irishman, find a peasant. She grinned to herself. He made quite the bucolic picture in the noonday heat: six feet four inches of summer-tanned Pocahontas County sheriff, wearing frayed old cut-offs and a pair of sneakers, with a battered Yankees cap pulled low over his forehead to keep the sun from scorching his nose. All he lacked was a thin stalk of hay sticking out from between his teeth.

When he took off the cap and stretched wide, her laughter faded; when he reached for the water bucket, the shift of muscle in strong arms and long back brought a little whimper to her throat. Now, with water gliding down his chest and belly, heat curled low in her abdomen and she leaned a little more heavily on the windowsill in deference to her shaky knees.

After a moment she unlatched the screen, pushed it open, and called out, "Hey, farmboy!"

Evan squinted, using both hands to rake back the wet hair dripping into his eyes. The gesture flexed chest, arms, and shoulders to noteworthy effect; he knew it, too, damn him. The grin he gave her made him look half his forty-two years. Holly gulped.

"Yes, ma'am?"

"Don't you think it's time you took a breather?" Breathing was exactly what she wasn't doing very well just now.

"Sounds mighty nice, ma'am," he drawled in his atrocious version of her native accent. "Pardon for askin', but y'all wouldn't happen to be one of them desperate housewives I hear tell about, would you?"

Yeah, he knew what he was doing, all right: knuckles propped just above the low-riding waistband, hips and head in a speculative tilt. Holly's thoughts turned to pillage and plunder—and she'd do it right in the middle of the crookneck squash if she had to. As he showed off a few more moves with an artfully artless scratch to the small of his back, she pretended to consider his question. "Now that y'all mention it . . ." His answering grin was entirely too smug. So, resting one shoulder against the window frame, she folded her arms beneath her breasts. Instant cleavage. Fairly impressive cleavage, too; becoming the primary milk wagon for twins could do that.

His turn to gulp. But he recovered in a hurry—the rat bastard—and said, "Shucks, ma'am, kinda depends on how desperate we're talkin' here."

Holly repressed a sardonic snort. *Evan Lachlan* and *hard to get* were mutually exclusive terms. She hiked the skirt of her cotton sundress up her thighs, hitched herself sideways to sit in the window, and slung one bare leg over the ledge. Dangling her foot, scraping the soft dirt of a flower bed with her toes, she told herself that if the cleavage and the naked leg didn't get him over here within the next thirty seconds, she would go with her original pillage-and-plunder plan, and the squash could damned well fend for itself. Evan cleared his throat and took a couple of involuntary steps toward her. She hid a smirk. *Gotcha!* "Y'all got any ideas, farmboy?"

"One or two," he allowed. The self-confident saunter was back, signaling a tweak in the balance of power. "I'm all sweaty and dirty, though." He rubbed one hand across his chest as if embarrassed by his scruffiness. "And there you are, all pretty and sweet. . . ."

She heard herself growl. She heard him chuckle. She came out of the window like a tackle going for a quarterback sack.

The crookneck squash never had a chance.

MUCH LATER, after a change of venue upstairs to their bedroom, Evan hummed low in his throat as Holly's fingertips stroked his shoulder. His wife knew every one of his buttons and exactly how to push them; the thing was that she never pushed them in the same order. Systematic sequential insanity on a regular basis he could have handled, no sweat. But Holly was way too creative for that. He felt a corner of his mouth twitch, knowing how many husbands would give their left nut to have this problem, and tightened his arms around her.

"You have the most amazing skin," she mused drowsily, hand drifting down his chest. "Not a mark on you—"

He tried to catch her fingers before they reached the center of his breastbone. He wasn't quick enough.

"—except for the scar that's my fault."

Lachlan was quiet for a long moment, spreading his hand over Holly's on his chest. He didn't try to see her face; he knew she wouldn't look at him. Not that he blamed her; his own mind seemed all bruises whenever he tried to think about that night. Finally, he murmured, "We don't talk much about it, do we?"

"I know."

"Three years this Hallowe'en."

"Yeah."

"It wasn't your fault. I know damned well I've said *that* before. I've got a scar. You didn't put it there." He waited, but she wasn't talking. "Holly, I'm *alive* because of—" Something occurred to him, and he drew away from her, turning onto his side. "Why *am* I still alive, anyhow?"

"Evan?" She met his gaze, frowning.

"I never did ask you why I'm still breathing. What you said about how if I ever raised a hand to you again, you'd kill me—"

"We avoid talking about *that* night, too," she muttered.

"At the Hyacinths," he persisted, "I didn't just raise my hand to you. I put a gun to your chest."

He didn't know whether he was more grateful or exasperated when she tried on a smile—not a very good fit—and said, "I thought you were supposed to have amnesia about all that. Or did you forget? To have amnesia, I mean—"

"Knock it off. You know what I'm talking about."

Relenting, she bit her lower lip, then said, "It wasn't you."

"Part of it was."

"No. Whatever Noel called up, it took you—Evan, I watched it, I saw it come toward you and—and *merge* with you. But it wasn't you that night—either of those nights."

"Is that what you've been telling yourself this whole time?"

"What have *you* been telling yourself?"

He lay back flat again and stared at the ceiling. "That I have to be careful. I always knew that. We've talked about my parents before. We both know I have a temper. If—"

"I have a temper, too."

"Ya think?" He smiled briefly, but didn't look at her. "You don't have a family history like mine. If I ever hit you—or one of the kids—"

"Never."

"I know you're sure, Holly. I can't be. I can never be sure."

"What does that mean? That you'll only stop tormenting yourself about it when you're dead? Listen to me, *a chuisle*. The one time, you'd been drunk for a week and you were in martyr mode—"

"You really want to go there?" he asked softly.

"No." Holly took a deep breath. "The other time, you were loaded half out of your skull on that incense stuff to begin with, and then Noel's little playmate came along. I saw it happen, and I was cold sober. You weren't. Not either of those times. Do you remember anything about what happened?"

"Some. Not much." He considered for a moment. "I never knew the flowers on my mother's dress were hyacinths, that day I saw her with the priest. That's what I saw, all those goddamned purple flowers—only it was you wearing the dress. How did Noel do that? What did he tap into?"

"I don't know. That's all the answer I've got, *Éimhín*." Shifting against him, she went on, "We've both had nightmares about it."

"Yeah. I can always tell, because those are the ones you won't talk about."

"And who does this remind us of? My point is that I actually remember both those nights, and you don't, so you're just gonna have to trust me on this, husband mine."

"I am, huh?" He turned his head and eyed her grimly determined face. "Does that mean you're gonna have to trust me about the scar? That it wasn't your fault?"

"Oh, clever man!" she snarled—but her heart wasn't really in it. "Got me that time, didn't you?"

"Yep," he agreed, unrepentant.

Holly sulked for a moment, then settled into his arms once more. "It still doesn't negate the fact that we've never discussed either of those nights in any detail."

"I don't think we want to go *there,* either."

"Just be glad we survived it, and move on?" she suggested.

"It's worked so far."

She kissed his throat by way of apology. "I can't help it. I analyze."

"And you're only turning analytical about *us* because you're not writing a book right now."

She groaned elaborately. "Don't remind me."

"You'll find something. You gotta admit you've been a little busy." Time for a change of subject, he told himself. "Speaking of the offspring, are you sure Lulah's okay with us stashing them with her all afternoon?"

"And tonight."

"That gawdawful politicking party. I'd forgotten."

His grimace gained him no sympathy. "Democracy in action, Sheriff honey."

"I'm still not clear on why I actually have to run for office. Your family—in all its permutations—pretty much runs Pocahontas County, doesn't it?"

"For the last three and a half centuries," she confirmed.

"So—?" he prompted.

"Cousin Jesse was duly elected every four years. You're an interim appointment so he could retire—and, not incidentally, give folks a chance to get to know you and what a staggeringly brilliant law enforcement officer you are. But you still have to be elected."

"And again I ask: why?"

"And again I reply: democracy in action. Labor Day is the traditional start of the campaigning season—something I wish *anybody* running for president would remember," she added crossly. "They seem to think everybody in this country really, truly wants to spend two solid years listening to them yammer."

"I'm no politician," he groused. "I don't do the grip-and-grin thing."

"It's free food and free booze. You'll live."

"Can't we just skip it? That place makes me twitchy. Don't tell me I'm being weird—Lulah doesn't like it, either, and for reasons other than you'd think."

Many and many a year ago, Lulah McClure and Jesse McNichol had cleaned out a houseful of neo-Nazis who had taken over the old Neville mansion. The magical decontamination had taken many days and enough spells to fill a fair-sized grimoire. They hadn't known about Holly back then; unaware that she was a Spellbinder, and that her blood would seal any Work they did, they'd had to return again and again to take care of lingering nasties. One would think that the place had been scoured clean. But Evan got the creeps whenever he even drove past the new wrought iron gates marking the entrance to the access road—and he didn't have a speck of magic in him.

Westmoreland, named (though misspelled, as generations of the truly pedantic had pointed out) for the English title which old Archibald Neville had claimed was in his ancestry before emigration to Virginia, had once spread across a thousand acres. Now it was reduced to about twenty, the rest having been sold off as the Neville fortunes waned. Since they had abandoned the place, back in the '40s, it had changed hands many times—and languished vacant and deteriorating for many years. There had been some talk in the '90s of using it as a field project for the archaeology department of the University of Virginia, digs at old plantations—especially the slave quarters—having yielded fascinating finds elsewhere. A preliminary survey was done, and the engineering students had just ascertained that the central staircase, the walls on either side, the vast cellar, and the back of the house were as sound as the day they'd been finished—when a chimney suddenly collapsed, almost on top of their professor. So much for that plan. In March of 2004 it had been purchased by a German businessman who had turned it into the Westmoreland Inn.

The locals had shuddered, certain that an architectural horror would result. Contractors and craftsmen were imported from outside Pocahontas County—partly because almost everybody in the construction business who lived in the vicinity had been hired to refurbish and expand the old overseer's house at Woodhush. It wasn't until Westmoreland was completed that county residents got a look at it: an extravagant grand opening party that November had introduced the new Westmoreland Inn and its owner, Bernhardt Weiss.

Not as readily seduced by his kitchen or his wine list as he might have wished, PoCo residents nevertheless admitted, more or less grudgingly, that the Inn was an acceptable successor to the antebellum mansion. Greek columns, gracious portico, grand staircase, great wraparound verandah—everything about the house, with its eighteen guest suites and huge ballroom and muraled dining room, was just an eyelash shy of excessive, just a whisker away from overkill.

Herr Weiss had saved that sort of thing for the Spa.

If the house was Greek Revival, the spa facilities were Roman Resuscitation. It was rumored that at Westmoreland one could even get as classically oiled-and-strigiled as if one were at the Baths of Caracalla, although this turned out to be only a rumor.

Since the grand opening event, Evan hadn't set foot on the property. Holly and Lulah, taking advantage of the certificates handed out at the party, had spent a whole day getting massaged, facialed, manicured, pedicured, moisturized, exfoliated, and waxed. Holly reported a lovely experience—while teasing Evan that without at least one spa afternoon at Westmoreland, his New York Metrosexual credentials would expire. But Lulah agreed with Evan: the place was creepy. Further, she told him privately, the whole time there she'd felt blind.

Other men in the county admitted to the occasional massage, and more readily to using the state-of-the-art gymnasium. This was the one reason Evan might have considered driving the long spur road to Westmoreland again; relaxational farming, the occasional horseback venture, and intermittent jogging kept him not quite in shape. Although if he and Holly kept at it as energetically as they'd been doing this weekend, he'd be able to toss the t-shirt his snide little sister had sent him last Christmas: *This is NOT a beer belly. This is protective camouflage for my rock-hard abs.*

As often happened, especially when they were physically close like this, Holly picked up on his thoughts. She rubbed a hand across his stomach and grinned at him. "I keep telling you: I'll ogle Brad Pitt's perfect pecs any day of the week, but who wants to cuddle up to a marble statue?"

Lachlan snorted. "So I shouldn't get all crazy jealous of your old boyfriend?" Who wasn't quite as sculpted as Brad Pitt, but certainly came close.

"Only if it amuses you. And I've told you before, he was never a boyfriend."

He stared at her. "You never did it?"

"No."

Evan began to laugh. "Oh, that poor bastard! No wonder he looks at you the way he looks at you!"

"How does he look at me?"

"You wouldn't understand. It's a Guy Thing."

"Whatever." She dismissed the incomprehensibility with a wave of her hand. "What I want to know is why we're discussing some other man when I've got you naked as a jaybird and ready for more?"

"Who said I'm—" When she gave him a slow, lascivious grin, every nerve below his waist started chanting her name. "Christ, woman, are you trying to kill me?"

"Time I 'fessed up, huh? I'm after the insurance money."

"Why don't you take that smart mouth of yours and do something useful with it?" When she did, he exclaimed, "You *are* gonna kill me!"

"Trust me, lover man—you won't mind."

"FOUR-THIRTY. We gotta get dressed."

Holly hid her face in the curve of Evan's neck. "No."

"C'mon. If we're going to this stupid thing—"

"No." His skin was warm and smooth, smelling of sweat and sex and the jasmine and marjoram their sheets were folded in, and she didn't want to leave here, ever.

"Whatever happened to 'democracy in action'?" He poked her ungently in the ribs. "I've already thought of all the smart remarks you could make about the action in here, so don't bother."

Groaning, she rolled out of bed and grabbed a shirt Evan had dropped on a chair yesterday—or maybe the day before. A housekeeper she wasn't. "Have I mentioned lately that you're an asshole?"

"Ah!" He wagged an admonishing finger. "Five bucks—pay up."

"We're allowed to swear in our bedroom," she protested. "Just not around the kids." They'd made the rule because otherwise, as Lulah had acidly observed, the twins' first words would undoubtedly have been unprintable. The hefty fine had been Lulah's idea as well: financial motivation. For about six months the gallon pickle jar in the kitchen had rapidly filled with portraits of Abraham Lincoln, and the twins' college fund thrived. But it was rare these days that Holly or Evan slipped around the children.

"Door's open," he reminded her sweetly. "Five bucks."

"They're not even in the house!" Padding over to the closet, she started rummaging for clothes. She was Sheriff's Wife tonight, not Bestselling Author, so nothing backless, strapless, or cut halfway down to Argentina. Besides, there was a tropical storm plowing its way to the Virginia coastline, which meant rain here in the Blue Ridge by midnight or so, which meant a jacket for later.

"Okay, then," Evan was saying. "If you get to swear, so do I. Wear the Fuck Me shoes."

Distracted from sartorial musings, she turned an incredulous stare on him. "The what?"

"You know—the choo-choos or the blah-blahs or whatever the hell they are. The stiletto things, with the straps. The Fuck Me shoes."

"It's Jimmy Choo and Manolo Blahnik, you ignorant lout. And I'm assuming you mean these." She held up six hundred bucks' worth of snakeskin sandals with four-inch heels. They were three years out of fashion; had this been New York she would have culled them from her closet long ago. Or maybe not; her husband liked them, and she was ludicrously indulgent of his whims.

He stretched wide, eyeing her and the shoes. "Too bad you can't wear just those and that shirt. There's nothing sexier in the world than a woman wearing stilettos, a man's shirt—and nothing else."

"Sorry, darlin'. The county sheriff would have to arrest me."

"For what? Not indecent exposure. Everything's covered."

"I know the guy, and I'm sure he'd think of something."

"You could probably bribe him." His arching eyebrows and innocent grin told her exactly what the county sheriff had in mind by way of a payoff.

While he showered, she searched her closet in earnest. There was still a whole section of her pre-pregnancy wardrobe she couldn't have squeezed into with a can of axle grease and a crowbar. Evan didn't seem to mind this more voluptuous version of his wife, so she shrugged it off, reasoning that any woman of forty-something who expected to have the body she'd had at twenty-something was out of her mind anyhow. Besides, as Lulah had remarked, "Anytime past thirty-five, you might as well enjoy what you look like now, because in five years you're gonna look worse."

The annoying exception was her husband, Holly mused. He was even more good-looking now than when she'd met him five years ago. It was nothing she could put her finger on—or, rather, it was everything she put her fingers on whenever she got the chance.

"What're you grinning about?"

Startled, she dropped the skirt she'd chosen and turned quickly. He stood in the bathroom doorway with a beard made of soap, a straight razor in his hand, a towel around his hips, and a quizzical look in his eyes.

She considered leering, considered what leering usually led to, and shook her head. "Never mind. Let's stop off and kiss the kids before we head over, okay?"

"Sure. Hey, you wanna grab that long-sleeved t-shirt out of the drawer for me?"

"No." Holly slid past him into the bathroom.

"What, you got two broken arms?"

"No black tonight. You can't wear the cashmere jacket, either."

"The Goddess has spoken?"

"Yup."

"But you always tell me I look hot in the cashmere jacket."

"You do. Just not tonight."

He pondered. "Oh. Too in-your-face New York, huh?"

"Not even in the same league as the Yankees jersey," she teased, and he gave the predictable groan. "It's just that we want people to come up and talk to you, not ask if you want a Zoloft."

"If we don't get out of this party by ten, I'm gonna *need* a Zoloft."

Fifteen minutes later, he was dressed in dark-wash Levi's, white shirt, and leather jacket. And, of course, those miserable old ostrich-hide cowboy boots. Despite the casual outfit, despite two years as sheriff of the smallest county in Virginia—even despite the cowboy boots—*New York* was scrawled all over him. It always would be. He needed a haircut, and he was as tan as any self-respecting country boy ought to be in summer, and the boots should have completed the picture of Sunday-go-to-meetin' rural chic. But he was instantly identifiable as a New Yorker, as unmistakably as Americans were tagged as such in a single glance by Europeans. It wasn't just the clothes—his shirt a shadow-striped silk that fit him to perfection, his jacket tailored to within an inch of its life notwithstanding the fact that it was battered brown leather. It was the way he wore the clothes, the way complete contentment fused with complete confidence—plus an intriguing insinuation of power. Nothing could intimidate him, nothing could scare him. He'd spent most of his life in the greatest city in the world, and more than fifteen years as a law enforcement officer in that city. Deposit him stark naked smack in the middle of Buenos Aires, Bialystok, or Borneo, and New York would still gaze arrogantly from his eyes.

"You're staring again," he remarked as he strapped on his wristwatch and snagged up the leather wallet containing his badge.

"As if this is unexpected," she mocked.

"Back at you, lady love," he chuckled. "Except the skirt's too long."

"No miniskirts after age forty."

"And there are how many precincts of fashion police in this county? Turn around."

She obediently twirled on her toes so that the tulip hem of her skirt flared around her knees. "Okay?" she prompted, knowing very well that the apple green silk dress was a winner—even if it had come from a catalog instead of Barneys, and even if it wasn't hemmed halfway to her ass.

"Oh, very okay." He tucked his Glock into the shoulder holster beneath his left arm. "Married or not, girl, you're going home with me tonight."

"Pretty sure of yourself, aren't you?"

"Nah," he replied breezily, catching her by the waist and pulling her in for a kiss. "You just look easy."

THEIR DAUGHTER HAD BEEN *Susannah* until mid-August of 2004—what would have been Susannah Wingfield's thirty-eighth birthday. That night, Evan had found Holly standing beside the crib, tears on her cheeks. He'd read about the hormones thing, and the postpartum thing, and all the other pregnancy-labor-delivery things, so he wasn't all that surprised that she was crying.

Until she said, "I can't call her that. I just can't. It was a mistake."

Brilliantly, he asked, "Huh?"

"Naming her 'Susannah.' Every time I say it—Evan, I just can't. It's more than two months, but it just doesn't feel right. We have to think of something else."

Slipping his arms around her, he ventured, "Middle name?"

"Maybe."

"We could tack on another one," he said.

Holly nodded against his shoulder. "It's just—she deserves a name of her own, you know? Not have to share it. And we have to remember Susannah as herself, not replace her, not even with our own child. Am I making any sense at all?"

"Shockingly, yes," he teased. "We'll think of something, lady love. Until we come up with a nickname or whatever, we can just call her Hey You. It's not like she'll know the difference."

They'd tried variations for a while, but it turned out she wasn't a Susan, Suzy, Anne, Anna, or any of the usual variations thereof. They experimented with Rowan, shook their heads, then went with Ro for about five minutes—until Lulah started singing, "Merrily, merrily, merrily, merrily," and that was the end of that.

"This is ludicrous," Holly had announced. "I've named hundreds of characters, and I can't come up with a name for my own daughter?"

"It'll come to you," Lulah said serenely.

It did. A couple of evenings later the four of them were sprawled on the nursery carpet, bedtime being a frangible thing at Woodhush, when Holly suddenly announced, "Bella."

"What?"

"Bella." She scooped their daughter up from the floor and held her out for examination. "That's her name."

He looked the baby in the eyes and thought it over. "Bella?"

Holly nodded. "Susannah's middle name was 'Dolcebella'—for which she had as many reasons as you have stories about those damned cowboy boots."

Evan tried it out. "Bella." And damned if the pudgy little arms didn't wave at him. Complete coincidence, of course. "Hey," he said to his wife. "Five bucks."

Both of them were rather unlikely children—and this was clear to Evan even though he was their father. It never failed to amuse him that his genes and Holly's had combined in two such radically different ways—as if their DNA had undergone nothing so organized and stately as the regular process of reproduction, and had instead been tossed into a blender, all the traits of coloring and character whirling around in total chaos until things spliced together and produced these small, amazing persons. He recognized himself and Holly in both kids, plus a lot of stuff uniquely their own. Elias Bradshaw had summed it up neatly during his June visit this year for the twins' birthday party—to which he had brought enough paint to supply an art college, half a library of books, and a closetful of clothing they would grow out of by October. Watching them play with their new goodies, Elias had said, "They're timeless. Practically archetypal. Can't you see them in the ancestral caves? He's happily painting away, creating Lascaux, and she's pacing outside, trying to invent grammar."

Lachlan had to admit that at times it was unsettling to look into his son's eyes. Kirby was completely self-possessed, uncannily self-aware, yet not at all self-absorbed. His smiles were rare and sudden, enchanted with the discovery of some new sight or sound or flavor in his world—or with the rediscovery of his father's arms holding him safe as he was carried up to bed, or his mother's voice singing him to sleep. That the carrying and the singing happened almost every night did nothing to lessen his delight in them, a kind of half-surprised wonder that such good things could happen again and again with only slight variations. It was as if he expected but never took for granted the security of his father's arms and the beauty of his mother's voice, greeting each night's repetition with renewed pleasure and gratitude.

As for Bella—she was an even more unlikely child for a cop and a writer to have produced. Her hands and pockets were always stuffed with one thing or another—from smooth creek stones to mostly dead bugs, all sorts of feathers to samplings of different grasses. A scrap of broken eggshell meant to be compared with a similar souvenir earned equal reverence with the four types of pine cones (and matching needle clusters) conscientiously laid out on a shelf. That she could not yet pronounce the scientific names of things in all their polysyllabic splendor was an inconvenience of youth that frustrated her terribly. It was as if she found nature so compelling that she had to have it with her at all times, so fascinated by the world that she couldn't bear to let go of even its smallest manifestations. Evan called it *collecting evidence*; Cousin Clary Sage avowed that it was the mark of an Apothecary. It would be many years before they'd find out if either prediction was true.

Evan was content to have it so. In spite of all he'd seen and done—and had had done to him—before his marriage, there had yet been a portion of his mind that didn't quite wrap around the magical aspects of his life with Holly. She was a Witch from a long line of Witches, but she had no magic other than her Spellbinding blood. His experiences of magic had not been of the everyday kind. In truth, some of them had been horrific. But then he'd come to live at Woodhush Farm, where Lulah McClure would flick a finger to keep a spoon stirring the spaghetti sauce (always clockwise), or murmur a few words to activate a spell that whisked the dust from the paintings hung along the staircase. All Holly ever did was light a candle or the hearth fire.

So when he contemplated his children, Lachlan felt himself torn. Magic was part of their heritage, and if they were gifted with it, they would have excellent teachers and role models. But magic was also a dangerous thing that could threaten and even kill. So he was never quite sure whether he wanted Kirby and Bella to be Witches or not.

"I'm not walking down to Lulah's in these," Holly warned as she descended the stairs. Evan spared a moment, then a few more, appreciating hair, makeup, dress, and especially shoes; it wasn't often these days that he saw her all put together the way she'd always appeared for a night out in New York.

Not that he was complaining. Nope, not him. He gave her a courtly bow from the waist to make her laugh, then escorted her out the door, down the front steps, and into the dark green Chevy SUV with a five-pointed gold star and *Pocahontas County Sheriff* painted on its doors.

Renovation of the overseer's house at Woodhush should have been easy. Clear out the accumulated junk, have somebody inspect it from shingles to foundation, get the hardwood floors sanded and polyurethaned, paint it inside and out, and hang new curtains. What no one had counted on was that the laws of physics were about to take their revenge for having been toyed with for so many years. Unused since the late 1930s except for storage, the house turned out to be held together with hundred-year-old plumbing, two-hundred-year-old beams, and magic.

Research done during the winter of 2004 had yielded fresh magic that kept the old place upright long enough to fix it. Concoctions, decoctions, gemstones, Holly's blood, and some plain old crossed-fingers wishing were employed throughout the spring and part of the summer as workmen virtually gutted the place. The huge stone sink in the kitchen and the graceful oak banister were all that remained of the original dwelling. The three bedrooms upstairs were transformed into one large and one small, with a bath between. Nothing was kept of the other furnishings, which, after more than sixty years of neglect, consisted mostly of wormholes or rust, and sometimes both.

It became a tidy, creak-free, comfortable little home, finished three weeks after the twins were born, and as familiar to them as their own sprawling house two hundred yards up the gravel drive that meandered among oddly spaced apple, pear, peach, and apricot trees—stubborn leftovers from attempts by various generations to establish orchards. For all the magic in their blood and bones, assiduously applied, farming on more than a for-the-table basis had never paid off for the Flynns. It had taken an infusion of McClures to pay off the last of the mortgages, and this had left Lulah free to pursue horse breeding as a profitable occupation.

She spent a lot of time baby-sitting, too. Before she even moved into the redone cottage, two days of intricate, esoteric magic had made both houses childproof. Or so they had all thought. About half an hour after Bella learned to walk, she figured out how to circumvent the baby gates. Every one installed in both houses had to be spelled so she couldn't do it again and it took Lulah a week to get it right; baby gates were not of her generational experience. When Kirby outfoxed her by scaling instead of unlatching them, their doting aunt was compelled to contribute thirty bucks to their scholarship fund—and respell the gates yet again.

As Evan got out of the SUV, boots crunching on the drive, he heard Holly cussing him and the gravel and the Fuck Me shoes—but under her breath, mindful of her bank balance, because from within the house came two ecstatic little voices: "Mommy!"

The Progeny pelted from the house, alarmingly coordinated and wickedly swift for being only twenty-seven months old, wearing denim pants and t-shirts given by their adored Uncle Elias. Kirby's shirt was green, Bella's was yellow, and each bore the words *Warning: I Am Two.*

His Honor believed in truth in advertising.

"Mommy!"

"Munchkins!"

Steps negotiated at a breakneck pace, Bella and Kirby raced for Holly, four little hands covered in chocolate reaching for her skirt. Lachlan fell in love with her all over again when, instead of leaping back and warning them off, she laughed and crouched down to seize the twins in her arms.

"Chocolate fingers!" she exclaimed. "My favorite!"

By the time they noticed their father, and were duly tickled and kissed, the mess had pretty much been transferred from them to Holly's clothing. But why scold them? The kids were washable; the dress was washable; she was washable; what was the point?

It was a measure of Evan's adjustment to the ambiance of his Virginia home that he didn't jump two feet in the air and draw his Glock when he heard a miniature roar, and then another, and then a high-pitched shriek from inside the house. Lulah was indulging herself again.

All the plants were gathered into a jungle in the parlor. Across a hundred-year-old Moroccan carpet, through cacti and succulents, herbs, flowers, and the two potted palms from the dining room, prowled a throng of dinosaurs. Lulah McClure, past sixty and still as supple as a teenager, sat cross-legged on the floor, flicking a finger here and there to direct a splinter of magic to this or that plastic rendition of an extinct creature, seeming not to notice that her playmates had abandoned her. Evan ducked instinctively as a winged whatsis swooped up to perch on a curtain rod, and heard a frustrated roar from the t. rex near Lulah's right knee. She used a careful finger to coax a lumbering herd of long-necked herbivores toward a pot labeled *catnip*—while Brigand, the plant's rightful beneficiary, watched from an armchair and yawned. The cat had played this game before, and knew from experience that soft, furry prey held infinitely more promise of amusement—not to mention flavor—than cold, hard plastic.

It had come to Evan's attention rather slowly—because nobody talked about it in the open, and he'd had to piece it together from hints and casual remarks—that Lulah was one of the most gifted Witches of her generation. She hadn't turned her back on it, and indeed enjoyed using her talents, but the power she might have had outside Pocahontas County was considerable and she had never pursued it. Principally because of Holly. After Tom and Margaret McClure died, Lulah had been happy to raise their only child. Evan—and not a few others—wondered sometimes if Holly hadn't provided her with the perfect reason not to take a more prominent place within the community.

As for Holly—it must have been like growing up the slight, bookish son of a five-Superbowl NFL-Hall-of-Fame linebacker father. No matter how much you were loved, no matter how much you were valued for your own abilities, no matter how proud you knew your dad was of you, there was always the knowledge that you could never compete in the eyes of the rest of the world. Lulah's prodigious magic was treated quite matter-of-factly within the family; Holly never seemed intimidated by it; but the awareness of it was always there.

Evan grinned suddenly as Kirby scrambled across the rug to pluck a wayward dinosaur from the predatory reach of something with a lot of white plastic teeth. The linebacker-and-son scenario was not one he'd ever worry about: not only was Evan not exactly the intimidating type in any area of endeavor, but if a vote had been held, Kirby would be unanimously elected Least Likely To Be Intimidated In This Or Any Other Lifetime. Certainly not by his parents, and not even by his formidable great-aunt.

At the moment she was admonishing him to pick up the stegosaurus by her bony spine plates *and* spiked tail, please—otherwise the tail would lash out and the spikes would do what they'd been meant to do, and they'd do it to his hand. There was some sort of esoteric follow-up about useful evolutionary adaptations and medieval weapons. Lachlan tuned it out. He'd learned how to do that. Holly on her own was pedantic; put her together with Lulah, and a man could be up to his neck in trivia and swimming for his life before he knew it.

"We'll be back by midnight or so," Holly told her aunt. When Lachlan turned a look of outraged betrayal on her, she added, "There'll be a lot of hands to shake, and you know very well that Mr. Warren will want to talk about putting in a traffic light over in Flynton, and—"

"I thought that was the kind of conversation you're supposed to rescue me from. Don't political wives do that?"

"Nah, we just let the major donors cop a feel." She knelt and finished wiping off Bella's chocolaty fingers with her skirt. "No, sweetie, I don't think the Diplodocus wants a peanut butter cup. She might get a tummy ache."

"But, Mommy—"

"Maybe some of that nice oregano. Go see if she likes it." As Bella set off to investigate, Holly straightened up and surveyed her skirt. "I have to go back to the house and change. You take the SUV, I'll follow in the Beemer."

"It's gonna take you more than five minutes to put something else on?" When she gave him a look, he shrugged. "Yeah, stupid question."

"Yow!"

"Bella!" Lulah admonished. "Did you hear what I told Kirby about the tails on these animals?"

Evan bent to inspect the scratch. "You'll live, Bella mia." His daughter looked up at him with an expression that clearly said, *Thank you, Daddy, but I figured that one out for myself,* reclaimed her hand, and carefully set the steg down. Then she went about coaxing the flying whatsis out from behind a palm frond to perch on Lulah's third-best willow wand.

"Speaking of donors," Lulah said, "Alec and Nicky sent a check. Not a penny over the legal limit, the cheapskates. They know we could've cooked the books. There's a note for you, Evan. On the hall table."

He went to collect it. From within a sealed envelope he drew a note scrawled on dove gray stationery left over from Nick's bookstore days.

Dear Evan:

Alec orders me to mention at the outset that we were only a little drunk at the time. A day or two ago we had the gemstones and teacups out, practicing for our biennial Election Prediction Ritual, and something curious came up. The gist of it is that at some point in early September one of your children will be at risk. At risk for what, of what, why, exactly when, and which one, we have no idea. These things can be maddeningly vague. Alec (who insists that we weren't really that drunk) is asking if perhaps you'd send along a few strands of hair from our niece and nephew so that we can get a clearer read. You probably won't want to mention this to Holly or Lulah.

As ever, with love to all,
Nicholas

Lachlan chewed his lower lip for a moment. Had Nick and Alec been really worried, they would have sped down here from Connecticut. But had they felt it nothing more than an oddity produced by mild inebriation, the letter would never have been sent. So he'd raid the kids' hairbrushes tomorrow, and not tell Holly or Lulah.

"Anything interesting?"

He slid the envelope into his breast pocket and turned to his wife with an easy smile. "They want to know if I want the next check drawn on Simon's account or Kate's. I'm wondering if I'd have a better chance of winning by outspending my esteemed opponent or doing it the way everybody's gonna suspect me of anyway."

"Physical intimidation?" she suggested. "Parking tickets?"

"Magic." He grinned.

She didn't laugh. She didn't smile. "There's not a single person in this county who ever thought Jesse McNichol ever won a single election any way other than merit. We have rules. We stick to them."

"Hey, relax! I was just kidding."

"It's not funny, Evan. I thought by now you'd understand."

"I was kidding!" he repeated. "Geeze, Holly, downshift it from fifth gear, would you? I wouldn't *want* to get elected for any reason other than that the county wants me as sheriff."

"I know. So let's go to this thing and make sure everybody knows what a prize you are." She went back into the parlor to say goodnight to the children—who ignored her, too busy helping Lulah construct a watering hole out of a saucer and some sphagnum moss. The triceratops family looked interested.

On the short drive back to the main house, Evan brought out his olive branch. "Y'know, being a mother agrees with you."

She picked at some of the dried chocolate on her skirt. "Kirby and Bella agree with me. Mothering as an abstract concept, however—let's just say it's a good thing I'm raising Kirby and Bella, and not abstract concepts."

"I forgot to ask—are we getting anything besides nibbles at this thing?"

"You're getting free booze. What more do you want out of life?"

"A great-looking girl to bring home and fuck through the floorboards." He paused. "Oh, and world peace."

Holly gave up and laughed.

THE STEGOSAURUS THAT HAD infinitesimally wounded Bella wandered off unnoticed out a slight gap in the screen door. Being very tiny, it took the creature all night to traverse the porch, drawn by the scent of flowers in the lavishly planted beds surrounding the house. Sometime around dawn, the steg tumbled off the porch and broke its neck.

Thereby was possible ecological disaster averted when a real dinosaur—*a real dinosaur*—might have found its way to the nest of a snake or a lizard or a bird (though this would be unlikely; stegosaurs were not known for climbing trees), fertilized its eggs or had its eggs fertilized (it was unclear whether the formerly plastic animal had been male or female), and all genetic hell would have broken loose.

The dead stegosaurus eventually slid into the mud caused by that night's rain and slowly decomposed in the flower beds. The next spring, when the soil was troweled preparatory to planting more flowers, missed entirely was the tiny skeleton with its unique row of plates like sails along its spine and spiked tail.

More importantly, perhaps, it was *not* discovered that night that Susannah Rowan Lachlan was indeed a Spellbinder, just like her mother.

BACK AT THE HOUSE, Holly set her dress to soak in something Clary Sage swore was the sovereign remedy for stains from red wine to spaghetti sauce to chocolate, and went upstairs in her underwear to dig out something to wear. Remembering what she'd decided earlier about the weather and the venue, and her husband's dictum about the Fuck Me shoes, she made several selections, threw them all onto the bed, and stood there staring at them. Five minutes later she was dressed in nice, conservative, wife-of-the-candidate slacks and a tailored blouse.

On the stairs, she got as far as the watercolor portrait of Bertha Myrtle Cox dressed as Cleopatra for a fancy dress ball in Richmond, *circa* 1803. The hell with it. If Bertha could bare both shoulders and wear sandals at the age of fifty, Holly could show some leg at forty-two.

Besides, anything with a longer hem wouldn't do justice to the shoes.

Which was as good an excuse as any for her real motivation: there would be more than one man at Westmoreland tonight who liked looking at her legs, and she was coming to the age when a woman is more and more grateful to be looked at.

November 2005

"SO HOW'S THE NEXT BOOK coming along?"

Holly supposed Gib couldn't help it. They hadn't seen each other in years, and certainly not since she'd become a successful author; she couldn't expect him to know that he'd asked the Second Worst Question anyone could direct to a writer. (The First Worst was, of course, *"Where do you get your ideas?"*)

Therefore, because he really couldn't help it and she really was fond of him, she smiled across her Cobb salad and replied, "The usual. Late nights and rewrites."

They were having lunch at the Fourth Street Diner, scene of a hundred teenage angst-fests, and catching each other up on their lives had taken them through two rounds of iced tea and half their lunches. Gib Ayala's family had spent only a few years in PoCo during the late '70s, leaving a semester before high-school graduation. He and his two brothers and five sisters were used to moving, and took it all in stride; Air Force brats, the Ayalas always had each other for company. Their father's career had taken them to seven states by the time they got to Virginia, and before his retirement they racked up two more. Gib and Holly had become friends when his siblings Pedro and Rosa started spending Saturdays helping Lulah with the horses at Woodhush in exchange for riding privileges. The Ayalas had two varieties of fanaticism: horses and flying. Horses scared Gib silly.

Oddly, he hadn't followed his father into the Air Force. He'd gone into business instead. After earning his M.B.A., he'd given himself twenty years to build a company that would net him enough on a buyout to fly whenever he wanted for the rest of his life. He'd done it in eighteen—partly because he was his own best advertisement. His chosen field of endeavor had been a chain of upscale fitness centers scattered through Georgia, Florida, and the Carolinas.

So here he was, sitting opposite Holly at Fourth Street as if it were 1979 again. Now, though, he was the new director of flight operations at Shenandoah Regional Airport, and she was a bestselling writer. They were both married with children, they were both getting gray hairs—but in the last twenty-five years Gib hadn't gained a single ounce that wasn't solid muscle, and Holly would have quite cheerfully strangled him for it if his grin hadn't reminded her why she'd always liked him so much.

Until he opened his mouth again and said, "I Googled you a few months ago, before we moved here from Atlanta."

"Oh, I can't wait. Okay, hit me with it. What are they saying?"

Black eyes twinkled at her in a way that, once upon a time, had made her a little fluttery. "That you and your publisher have a new McClure novel all written and ready to go, and you're just waiting for the right moment to release it so it'll make the most money."

Strangling annoyance, she told him, "Actually, I'm waiting for somebody to option it for an ice show."

He grinned the familiar lopsided grin. "They seemed pretty sure about it."

"Delay a book that you're stone cold certain will make money? Now, that's a career move if ever I heard one. Almost as good as the one where you die so your sales—especially the autographed copies—go through the roof." A quick swallow of iced tea did nothing to help her simmer down. "I know about those rumors. In the first place, why anyone should be so anxious to read *anything* is completely beyond me. I love the Harry Potter books, but does my mental health and/or physical well-being depend on reading the final one in the summer of 2007? Not so much, no."

"You're not flattered by the interest?"

"Of course I'm flattered. It's lovely that people are so involved in what I write. It's my job to make sure they do get involved, because ultimately it's my job to sell books. I've got two kids to raise and educate, and a farm that shows a profit about twice a decade, even with all Lulah's hard work. Evan's salary pays the bills, keeps us all fed and clothed, but it's my job to provide the rest of it."

"I thought your job was about art." He paused, and it was more or less a toss-up whether his next words were ironic or not. "With a capital A."

"I tell stories. Sometimes they're true stories, and those are the biographies. The others are called novels, because I make stuff up. Either way, I tell stories. When I'm on top of my game, I'm pretty good at it. They're functional. They serve a purpose. One of the main purposes they serve is to keep my kids in shoes that fit. That means I have to write stories that other people want to read, and therefore want to buy—preferably in hardback. The books are also functional because they serve the purpose of entertaining, or instructing, or just occupying somebody's attention for a few hours."

"Functional, but not Art? Can't they be both? What about Dickens?"

Holly grimaced. "You *know* how I feel about Dickens!"

"'Never trust anybody who gets paid by the word.' Yeah, I've been hearing that one since the last millennium. My point is that his books were mass market, and he sure as hell wrote them to keep his family clothed and fed—"

"And people lined up on the docks of New York by the thousands to find out whether or not Little Nell had croaked!"

"But they also qualify as Art. Well, to everybody but you."

"Anybody who gets paid by the word, it's in their best interests to draw it all out as long as possible. I don't know, maybe it's our information age. People want their popular entertainment the same way they want their news summaries: quick, concise, pared down to the bare bones. Doesn't leave much leeway for nuance."

"Says the girl whose last novel was six hundred pages long!"

Holly thought for a minute about *Jerusalem Lost*—which had started life as *Jerusalem Found*—and what her life had been like when she'd written it. "Six hundred thirty-two pages," she corrected with a little smile.

"Whatever. But that was—what, two years ago?"

"Three."

"So why does it surprise you that people are wondering about the next one?"

"I'm not surprised by anything anymore. Look, whatever I write next, there will be people who'll complain because it's not the book they want to read. It's this sense of—of *entitlement* that's sort of basically hilarious."

"You know what I think? I think they think your books get written by magic."

He laughed, so she laughed. "If only! Unfortunately, it's just me and whatever's inside my head—plus a computer and a halfway decent word processing program."

"Just wind her up and plug her in, tell her what you want, and six months later—"

"—the book *you* want to read!" She spread her hands wide and wiggled her fingers like a good conjurer was supposed to. "Specific to your desires in all details, with explicit regard to your preferences in everything from battle scenes to sex scenes to what the characters eat for breakfast—"

"—delivered personally to your door by the author herself—"

"—on my knees, with a bottle of Dom Pérignon—"

"—and two dozen roses—"

"—with abject apologies in advance for anything that might disappoint your expectations!"

They toasted each other with iced tea and laughed. Even so, Holly realized something fundamental about the way they related to each other. The thing about him was that he let her get away with it. Halfway through her ranting, Evan would have given her A Look: brows slightly arched, mouth quirked in a little smile, head canted just a bit to one side. If that didn't do it, he'd simply tell her, *"Lady love, shut the fuck up."*

And she *would* shut the fuck up. She trusted his judgment. If he'd reached the point where enough was an oversufficiency of enough, he said so. And she believed him. If Gib had said the same thing, if he'd ever said, *"Holly, honey, shut the fuck up,"* she would have had his balls on a barbeque skewer.

And that, she reflected as she managed to shut herself up, was why she was married to Evan and not to Gib.

Well, that and the fact that she'd never been able to keep her hands off Evan.

Holly was distracted from lusting secretly after her own husband (was that even possible, or did the person one lusted after have to be someone other than one's spouse?) when Jamieson Tyler Stirling came into the diner. Jamey, she knew for a fact, had featured in the secret lustings of most of the female (and quite a lot of the male) population of Pocahontas County since his appointment as acting district attorney this September. It was a marvel that anything got done in a courtroom when he was in it.

What made Jamey astonishing was that he didn't have the slightest consciousness of his own looks. Holly, an attentive observer of human nature and a truly dedicated observer of masculine attributes, had watched futilely for signs of narcissism. At last she had been compelled to admit that the man actually could comb that black hair every morning, shave that chiseled jaw, brush those perfect teeth, and perch rimless glasses on that sculpted nose (glasses that, happily, did nothing to obscure those silvery gray eyes) without realizing the effect he had on others. This wasn't even taking into consideration the body, which was in a category all by its lonesome.

"Holly!" Jamey greeted her with a big smile. She suffered through a kiss on her cheek—really suffered, honestly—and then introduced him to Gib. "I'd heard there was an air ace over at Shenandoah Regional,"

Jamey said as they shook hands. "Now for the really important question: Cessna or Piper?"

"Piper," Gib replied. "Wouldn't be seen driving a Cessna any more than Holly would be seen driving a Yugo. You fly?"

"Not if I can help it. My oldest brother's a pilot for Delta. He's a Piper addict, too."

"Join us?" Holly asked.

"Thanks, but I can't. I'm just gonna grab something to take back to the office. I haven't seen daylight since seven this morning, and if I didn't at least walk across the street to stretch my legs, I'd lose what little remains of my mind."

"Which you'll need for the Worthington trial," Holly reminded him.

"Yeah. Evan knows he's testifying next Thursday, right?"

"I'll make sure he's freshly laundered and wearing a tie," she promised.

"He can arrive in a Santa Claus suit for all I care, as long as he's on time. I want to get these people, Holly. They—" His pager and his BlackBerry went off at the same time. One hand fumbled at his belt while the other dipped into his breast pocket. The juggling act became more complicated when his cell phone shrilled from the vicinity of his right hip; he'd run out of hands and was in danger of dropping everything.

Holly silently begged her husband's pardon and reached for the back pocket of Jamey's trousers, sternly forbidding herself to cop a feel while she was at it. The young man nodded gratefully, bless his innocent heart, as she answered the phone while he checked the other two electronic killjoys.

She was astonished to hear her husband's voice. "You're gonna want to get out to First Baptist right now. There's been another fire."

"Evan? Me. The whole church burned down?"

"Almost to the foundation," he affirmed.

"Anybody hurt?"

"Not even a singe. It happened after choir practice ended—" Away from the phone, he yelled, "Luther, get me a list of the choir members, okay? I want to know if any of 'em saw anything last night."

Holly sighed. "Does that fall into the category of 'long shot' or 'just plain hopeless'?"

"You never know. What are you doing answering the kid's phone?"

"Let's just say I was handy," she said, knowing he'd hear the pun in her voice. "And if you don't stop calling him that, eventually you'll say it in court or something and he won't like us anymore. Who reported the fire?"

"Mrs. Clark and the ladies changed their cleaning day this week. They called about twenty minutes ago. So help me, Holly, we gotta get some kind of alarm system set up for places like this. Way out here on undeveloped land—"

"—which they got cheap because nobody wants it," she added. "At night you'd have to be looking really hard to see a fireglow—and smoke wouldn't show up at all."

"Cloudy last night, and no moon," Evan agreed. "You're not half bad at this. Luther!" he yelled again. "Send Charlotte to canvass the neighboring properties!" To Holly: "That's in the 'hopeless' category, too. But if nobody saw or smelled anything—and most people around here get up at the butt-crack of dawn—then the place had burned out by sunrise. Shit! This means I gotta call in an arson guy."

"How about the Fibbies?"

"Do I have to?" he whined.

"Play nice," she advised, grinning.

"Do I have to? Listen, Holly, I gotta go. But could you check around a little? Probably another dead end, but I don't have forty years of being familiar with this area. I'll get Letisha looking into the Sheriff's Office files, and if there's anything similar anywhere in the tri-county area, but—"

She knew what he was thinking. "I'll ask Cousin Louvena over at the *Record* office. What she doesn't know isn't worth knowing, and if she knows something she can get the newspaper articles about it."

"You're beautiful."

"I know."

"Gotta go. Tell Jamey to haul ass, and kiss Kirby and Bella for me. I may be late."

"Wake me up."

"Really late," he warned.

"Wake me up anyhow. 'Bye."

Sorting out Jamey's gadgets and their information took an awkward while. After some more juggling—and an abrupt fall to the floor that could not have been salutary to the pager's electronic health—he finally got the BlackBerry and its little stylus stashed in his jacket and the pager clipped to his belt.

Holly held up his phone. "Why don't I bring sandwiches out to you guys at the site?" she suggested. "I'm sure Evan hasn't eaten, and probably nobody else has, either."

"Would you?" Jamey asked, abjectly grateful.

She thought about making it a condition of delivery that she could slide the phone back into his trouser pocket herself, but managed some restraint. "Sure. Get going."

He started for the door, turned, frowned, felt his right hip, and looked sheepish as Holly dangled his phone by its antenna. He came to retrieve it, grinned, and then hurried outside.

When Jamey was gone, Gib cocked an eyebrow at her across the table. "A little young for you, maybe?"

"Well, there's that," she laughed. "But actually I'm too married—and *way* too female."

Dark eyes widened. "Really?"

Holly regarded him with a mixture of amusement and affection. "You have to be the only man I've ever known—gay *or* straight—who has absolutely no gaydar at all."

He gave a shrug. "I've never seen that gay or straight matters."

"Evan's the same way. *He* can always tell, though, and I can't recall a single time when you've ever—"

"*Does* it matter? I mean, unless you've got ambitions to get a particular person into bed, who the hell cares?" Wadding a paper napkin with a bit more emphasis than strictly necessary, he went on, "Did I hear right, and another church has burned down?"

"This makes three since the end of September. Evan can't figure the motive—I mean, it's not as if there's robbery involved, or insurance fraud. Baptists don't go in for silver candlesticks and gold communion goblets. And neither of the first two churches had enough insurance to be fraudulent about."

"All Baptist?"

"What?"

"Were they all Baptist churches?"

She thought for a minute. In September it had been Old Believers Church, out on Highway 4; in October, Calvary Weekly Fellowship in Silver Rock; and now—

"I'm sure Evan's thought of it," Gib said almost apologetically.

"Y'know, I'm not sure that he has. Two's a coincidence, but three starts to look like a pattern. That's nice detective work."

"I read a lot," he grinned. "You and Evan are coming over to the house soon, right?"

"Please don't let Erika go to any trouble."

"Are you kidding? How many famous writers does she get to entertain for an evening?"

Holly groaned and threw her napkin at him as she slid out of the booth. As Gib left the diner and Holly put in a lunch order with Gertrude, she reflected that if there was anything she hated more than the *"How's the writing going?"* question, it was being treated as if what she could do made her something to be exhibited at the Tri-County Fair. Which wasn't a nice thing to think, and unjust into the bargain. Trouble was, *knowing* that had never enabled her to ditch the feeling that she was expected to perform like Rex the Mathematical Horse.

There were times when she missed Susannah Wingfield for the most ignoble and selfish of reasons.

The circumstances of the arson—for arson it was, as Holly figured out when Evan threw a charred metal can in the back of his SUV—were too similar to the first fires to make this third one anything but connected.

"If they'd all been started in the same place, I'd maybe think it was somebody with a religious grudge. Thanks, babe," he added as Holly handed him half of a tuna-on-sourdough. "But Old Believers started at the front door, and this one where the benches were stacked in the back corner. That's where Luther found the accelerant."

"Calvary was the pulpit," she reminded him. "That's psychologically suggestive, isn't it?"

He shook his head. "The whacko type can't help it—they leave clues whether they want to or not. This isn't even somebody trying to mess with our heads by *pretending* to be a psychopath. Significant dates, same day of the week, same phase of the moon, all that fun-and-games serial-killer stuff they love to do in the movies."

"Was there gas in the paint can?"

"Wasn't paint." He took a long swig of coffee and looked startled. "Gerdie musta cleaned out the percolator—this is actually drinkable."

"Not paint?" she asked, to bring him back to the point.

"Varnish. Jamey recognized what's left of the logo—he spent most of last month sloshing the same stuff all over the bookshelves at his place. Before you ask, it's a common brand, and we can trace the lot number punched onto the can but that only tells us where it was purchased, not when or by who." He held up a finger. "Don't say it. 'By whom.'"

"Hey, Evan!"

They both turned to see Jamey approaching. He really was scandalously gorgeous, Holly reflected. If he had this effect on a woman insanely in love with her husband, what havoc did he wreak when he was actually *trying* to attract someone?

Evan nudged her in the ribs. "Stick your eyes back in their sockets," he murmured, laughter rippling through his voice. "You're took."

"Looking isn't against the law."

"Well, at least stop drooling. It's undignified for a woman of your years, social standing, and reputation."

She was vastly tempted to stick out her tongue at him, but Jamey had reached the SUV by then. "Whatcha got?" she asked, passing over a turkey and swiss.

"Thanks, Holly. I've got absolutely nothing. I was hoping more than that can of varnish would be lying around, waiting for us to find it."

Evan shook his head. "Nope. No footprints, no tire tracks, no torn fabric conveniently flapping on a tree branch." He set aside the rest of the sandwich and scowled at the charred rubble of wood and brick that had been a church. "I'm not liking this, Jamey. Third church fire, no evidence at any of them."

Holly touched his arm lightly. "Gib pointed out that they've all been Baptist churches."

He shrugged. "More Baptists around here than any other denomination. We've got one each of Catholic, Episcopal, Mormon, AME, Lutheran, and Methodist, plus a synagogue that draws from the Tri-County area. And before you ask—none of these churches were exclusively white or black. It's possible this is religious prejudice, but I think we can rule out racism."

"You're forgetting where you live now," Holly said quietly.

"This is the South," Jamey nodded. "Lacking a solid case contrariwise, racism can never be ruled out."

"Yeah, okay," Evan admitted. "That was wishful thinking on my part. But now that you've mentioned it, there's not a square mile in this whole country where bigotry of one kind or another can be ruled out. After all, it's the Constitutional right of every American to hate."

"And the least American thing any American can do is tell another American to shut up."

Holly shifted impatiently. "Now that we've established our liberal credentials by reaffirming our belief that everyone in these United States has the right to be a moron, can we please get back to the point? You don't have any evidence. You don't even have any guesswork. The only thing remotely resembling a pattern is that all three churches were Baptist—but not even the same kind of Baptist. How am I doing so far?"

"How would you write your way out of it?" Evan countered.

"You know I'm hopeless at mysteries."

"Yeah," he said with a smile, "but you make up for it in other ways."

Jamey grinned. "Am I about to be embarrassed by a PDA?"

"Nothing so decorous," Holly said sweetly. "With him, it's always PDL." When Jamey looked confused, she elaborated. "Public Display of Lust."

"You should be so lucky," Evan shot back. "Go see if Louvena can find anything in the archives." He bent and kissed her soundly on the lips. "Thanks for lunch."

By the time she got back to town, she had consulted via phone with Cousin Louvena Cox, and they had devised a plan. Louvena shut the Pocahontas County *Record*'s back office, told the front desk staffers she didn't want to be disturbed, and locked herself and Holly in the archives room.

"Y'all ready?"

"Say the word," Holly replied cheekily, and the old woman made a face.

"Cute don't get you nowhere with me," she warned.

"Yes, ma'am," Holly answered, properly subdued. Cousin Louvena could do that to a person with one twitch of emphatic eyebrows. She belonged to what was discreetly termed a "collateral" branch of the Coxes—which meant she was a descendant of Ezekiel Cox and his slave mistress of thirty-two years, Jubilee. That he had insisted on acknowledging his children, giving them his surname, and teaching them to read and write in defiance of the law didn't begin to compensate for the fact that he hadn't freed a single one of them.

Evan had a lot of trouble with local history, and especially Holly's family's role in it. That first spring at Woodhush, he'd returned from a long walk around the property completely unable to believe what he'd seen about a half mile from the main house: the splintered wooden markers of the slave cemetery and the bare river-rock foundations of the slave cabins. Holly hadn't exactly forgotten that the evidence was there, but it wasn't something she thought about much, either. Nobody ever understood anything about slavery until they stood looking at its physical remnants, the scars it had left on the land that attested to society's still-open wound. That afternoon, watching her husband pace and seethe, Holly had realized she'd stopped seeing what *had* to be seen. And her parents would have been as ashamed of her as she was of herself.

The extended McClure-Flynn-Cox-McNichol-Bellew-Goare-and-so-on clan had a blotchy record: most had owned slaves at one time or another, some had freed all or some of them in the decades before the Civil War. The only thing entirely in their favor, as far as Holly was concerned, was that not one of her ancestors had fought for the Confederacy. She supposed that was something, anyway. Not much, but something.

It was surmised within the family that Louvena's slave ancestor had bequeathed her progeny an African magic totally unlike the Celtic strain. Certainly no one not descended from Jubilee could do what her great-great-great-granddaughter now did with nothing more than a shell, a square of silk, two candles, and a pinch of what looked like plain grayish dust.

A large abalone shell, its iridescence shimmering by candlelight, was balanced on a glass stand atop brown silk. Drops of light shone through the holes punctuating the shell, shifting as Louvena switched the candle slowly back and forth, left hand to right and back again. Holly watched, fascinated, chiding herself for the many years she had spent paying as little attention as possible to other people's magic simply because she had so little of her own. There was beguilement and grace, and sometimes great beauty, in the act of magic—but even more in observing each individual practitioner. The particular tilt of the head, the sure gestures of the fingers, the melodies of whispered phrases, the eyes that might haze over with the intensity of concentration or burn with clear, fierce power—though she had never felt herself to be fully one of them, and probably never would, still she could appreciate and savor their gifts and their expertise, and watch with a smile the individual quirks and flairs.

Louvena was not the sort of ostentatious Witch who not only enjoyed but positively cherished her own cleverness—and wanted everyone who witnessed it to be as enamored as she was. Deliberate, almost businesslike in her work, she went about her spellcasting in near silence until a snap of her fingers startled Holly.

Her turn. She pricked her index finger, squeezed up a drop of blood, and painted it on the interior of the shell as Louvena directed: a slow five-pointed star. Stepping back, she watched the old woman sprinkle fine gray-brown dust across the inner curve of the abalone. Holly wondered distractedly how many hundreds of dead spiders had been ground up to produce this powder—then flinched again when Louvena turned the shell over and slammed it onto the brown silk, almost forcefully enough to break it.

A tall, thin candle, colored gold outside and red at its heart, was lit from the wick of the first. A moment's burning of its end melted enough wax to affix it to the overturned shell. Holly had never seen a candle burn so quickly, the wax sliding down in a steady stream. No impertinent drafts disturbed the flame or pushed the melting wax to one side or the other. Soon it had burned down to a mere inch or so, and the shell was swathed in red and gold wax.

Louvena blew the candle out. Carefully, she lifted the abalone from the silk and set it aside. Then, with exquisite delicacy, she pinched one corner of the cloth between thumb and forefinger and peeled it from the table.

Holly was amazed to see that the underside of the brown silk was printed with black letters and numbers—and that the heat from the melted wax had seeped through the shell to liquefy some of her own dust-thickened blood. This had left tiny marks on the silk: letters and numbers. Months and years.

"Spider-crush," Louvena remarked, "works different ways. What I was after here was the web between past and future. The pattern. The shell and the brown are good for finding things. Red and gold are Fire, of course."

Holly nodded mutely. No, she would never feel herself one of them—but she had at least developed enough wisdom to appreciate her fellow Witches.

Now Louvena's face creased in a shrewd, wonderfully youthful smile, and from a pocket of her skirt produced an unlikely implement. Holly felt her eyes go wide, and couldn't help grinning as she asked, "You like doing that, don't you?"

"Oh, yes." Louvena chuckled as she uncapped the Magic Marker. "Here—take that steno pad and start writing down what I tell you."

ON THE SUNDAY EVENING drive to Westmoreland, Evan checked in with his office, speaking briefly with the deputy on duty about the day's events. Whenever he thought back to his days as a beat cop in New York, he wondered yet again how the hell his father had done it: year in, year out, robberies and rapes and assaults and murders, every single day. His old man had ended up with a worn-out heart, an alcoholic wife, and two kids who'd fled as soon as legally and financially possible. As Evan listened to Luther run through the list of towns and villages in the county—with *nada, zip, nuthin'*, or *zilch* after each one—he tried to imagine his father out here in rural Virginia. Something between a laugh and a cough thickened his throat for a moment.

"Sheriff?"

"Yeah, Luther. Gotcha. Anything comes up in the next few hours, I'm at Westmoreland for the thing."

"Have fun."

"Yeah. That's gonna happen." He pocketed his cell and drove through the open gates of the Westmoreland Inn, where a sign advised him in English, German, French, Italian, Spanish, Japanese, and Arabic that he was warmly welcomed and that to assure the serenity of the establishment, all guests will please to turn off their cell phones and other electronic devices. (The little hiccup in English grammar was, Evan assumed, deliberate—one of those "charming" mistakes Europeans made that would emphasize the international flavor of the place—for surely Bernhardt Weiss could afford a competent translator.) The sign went on to explain that should any calls be anticipated during his visit, all he need do was leave the phone at the front desk of the Inn or the Spa and messages would be taken. Naturally, in an emergency, he would be contacted at once. Thanking you for your cooperation and have a wonderful stay at The Westmoreland Inn.

"Absolutely. Just *wunderbar,*" Evan muttered, braking gently as he caught up with the line of cars waiting to be parked. Something in him that persisted in finding this place creepy wanted to use his status to jump the line, swerve off the gravel, and park right in the middle of the pristine expanse of green lawn. He contented himself with the fact that valets did not park the sheriff's car. Ever. They could point him a place to pull in—with easy access out—but they weren't touching this vehicle any more than they would Holly's BMW, even though the Beemer wasn't the one with the shotgun under the front seat and the locked ammo box on the floor.

As he waited, he wondered yet again what it was about this place that he just plain didn't like. It was pretty enough, no different on the outside from a hundred other restored antebellum residences throughout the South, with its white columns, wraparound verandah, and grounds landscaped with flowers. Across half the south side of the main building was a ballroom with a thirty-foot oak bar displaying every variety of liquor in the known universe. This May the high schools of three counties had merged their proms into one huge party that was counted an awesome success—even if the bar had been denuded of everything but soft drinks and fruit juice.

Out back, invisible from the driveway, were two other buildings that housed offices, a conference room, and dining and dorm rooms for the staff. These had been constructed from salvage of the old stable and barn. Remembering what it had taken to refurbish the house Lulah now lived in, Evan couldn't help but be impressed by Westmoreland.

But that still didn't keep him from thinking it was a peculiar place.

One of the boys on valet parking duty waved him to a spot that had been kept especially for him. He knew this because there were RESERVED signs on wooden stakes in the prime spots, and one of them had SHERIFF on it. Other dignitaries who rated good parking included the mayors or town managers of Flynton, Silver Rock, Azalea, and Prince Rupert. Lachlan slid the SUV into the space indicated, switched off the ignition, leaned his head back for a moment, and wished he could go home to a quiet evening with his wife and kids.

And wondered suddenly if his father had ever wished for the same thing.

"Sheriff Lachlan!"

"Show time," he muttered, and pasted a smile on his face as he opened the door and got out to greet Elliott Rausche, a local judge who had not appreciated *his* sheriff's department being taken over by a former big-city United States deputy marshal. Jesse McNichol had been sheriff for so long that everyone in the county knew what got you ticketed, what got you a night in jail, and what got you prosecuted. Evan had a different perspective on, for instance, drunk driving. No warnings. Instantaneous arrest. Add this kind of adjustment to the hiring of a new district attorney who didn't believe in plea bargains, and the criminal justice system of Pocahontas County got itself shaken up for the first time in approximately twenty-five years. What all this meant, of course, was that the two judges were at the bench eighteen days a month instead of nine. Judge Schaefer didn't much mind; he was recently divorced and just as glad to throw himself even more single-mindedly into the work that had precipitated his marital problems in the first place. But Judge Rausche's golf game had appreciably suffered. So whenever he could, he caused the sheriff and the district attorney to suffer accordingly.

Evan knew exactly what lecture he was about to get. Last week Jamey Stirling had won a significant victory in Rausche's courtroom, quite literally piling up enough damning evidence (gathered by Evan's department) to make lengthy prison sentences inevitable. All thirty-six kilos of crystal meth were stacked on a table before the jury; all forty-nine padded envelopes, addressed and bearing proper postage, were heaped beside them; all one hundred and forty-two color glossy photographs of various members of the Burker clan cooking, packing, transporting, and/or distributing were displayed. Jamey brought in the receipts for purchased chemicals, the tubs where the meth was stored, the crates and shoeboxes neatly labeled with names and locations of deliveries, and if he could have gotten the rickety old Ford pickup used for distributing into the courtroom, he would have done it. "Overwhelming" had only started there. And it had pissed off Judge Rausche.

As His Honor approached across the driveway, leaving his wife and daughters to climb the portico steps, Evan figured he was about to be told exactly why Rausche wasn't happy.

He was right.

"Y'all gotta understand somethin', Sheriff," began the judge without preamble. "That crystal stuff, it's worse than moonshining, no argument on that. But it's a principle we need to deal with here. We been lookin' the other way on this kind of thing for at least three hundred years. Ain't no big-city cop or prosecutor gonna come in and tell us what's what."

"Look in any direction you want," Evan replied. "Half that shit was labeled for delivery to middle schools in two counties."

Rausche stuck a finger into Lachlan's face. "What you made me do, you with your evidence—which took days to process and inventory, by the way, and hours to present in court, and that's not a productive use of county taxpayers' time—you painted me into a corner. I don't like that. It interferes with my judicial discretion. A little less evidence, fewer charges—that Stirling boy, he really knows how to pile on the counts, doesn't he? Chargin' for every piss they took off the side of the road onto some damned protected wildlife refuge! Your way, I had no choice in sentencing."

Lachlan gritted his teeth. "Let's see if I've got this right. If I'd provided only a kilo of meth for evidence, and Jamey Stirling had prosecuted on only a few counts, you could have slapped their wrists, told them not to do it again, and sent 'em home to cook up more."

"I don't much like your tone, boy."

Lachlan wondered if the man knew what a ludicrous cliché of a Southern judge he was, then remembered what Jesse had told him before his first time testifying in Rausche's courtroom. *"Short, sweet, to the point. Don't use any big words, and remember that the judge he replaced was worse. We keep an eye on him."* The trouble was that Witchly ethics prohibited magical interference with the process of the law. Even if every Witch in the county kept an eye on him, when he sat his ass in his chair, as far as the judicial system was concerned he was one rung down from God.

And besides all that, his eldest son, apple of his eye, was running against Evan for county sheriff.

"Tell you what, judge—the November ballots haven't been printed up yet, so why don't you take your name off and let somebody else put up with me and Jamey from now on?"

"What makes you think you're gonna win an honest term as sheriff, runnin' against Rick? This ain't New York, boy. It ain't even Richmond, where that fancy-ass pansy comes from. This is Pocahontas County, where I been the law for thirty-eight years. And I'll be the law for thirty-eight more if the Almighty lets me live that long."

Or if your wife doesn't find out what you do at legal conventions—or, rather, who you do at legal conventions. Evan widened his smile. Rausche was stupid, but he wasn't *stupid*—he recognized the taunt, turned his head a fraction, spat onto the gravel about an inch and a half from Evan's boots, and went to join his womenfolk.

"Well, that was productive," Evan muttered to himself.

"I'd say predictable," said a woman's voice behind him, and he turned to give Louvena Cox a genuine smile. "Politics just ain't your thing, are they, son?"

He leaned down about a foot and a half to kiss her cheek, then offered his arm. "I leave the charm to Holly."

"Nice double meaning in that," she approved. "Where is she?"

"Changing clothes. Chocolate on silk seems to be out of fashion this year." He escorted her toward the steps. "Are you here on or off the *Record*?"

"You're just full of puns tonight, aren't you? I'm here for the champagne and crab quiche. And you."

"Me?"

"Not to pat your pretty butt—though I'll manage it sometime this evening, I'm sure. No, I figured out a little something about those church fires. It's not much—"

He drew her away from the front door and around the corner of the verandah. "I'll take whatever I can get."

"The Methodist one doesn't show up on any of the Look-see spells."

"You mean there's magic involved in the others, but not the Methodists?"

"Not a breath of it. I got to thinking about what Holly and I dug out of the files back in November—the articles we found using the spider crush. Now, I know damned good and well the barn fire over at Silver Rock in nineteen-and-twenty-four wasn't dry lightning the way it got written up in the paper, and I know this because my daddy started it while he was practicing a coupla spells. Grandma whopped him for it, too. Same with the article on the fire here at Westmoreland, back when Jesse and Lulah cleaned the place out. If Old Man Hartford hadn't called in to the Sheriff's Office to report it, we would never have mentioned it in the paper a-tall. But those articles and a few others were about fires I knew for a fact had magic in 'em somehow. So I checked all the ones since last September."

"And all of them except for the Methodists . . ." Evan mulled this over. "Copycat? Nah, couldn't be—there's nothing to copy. Denominations, points of origin, accelerants—or not—there's no pattern at all."

She lowered herself into an ornate white wicker chair. "Lord and Lady, it's hot. That rain can't come fast enough tonight."

Lachlan regarded her in silence for a moment. "Louvena, do you know something I should know?"

"Many, many things," she replied with a deep chuckle. "Where'd y'all like to start?"

"I'll let you pat my ass all night if you just give me a clue here," he grinned back.

"*Let* me?" she snorted. "Now, where's the fun in that? It's when they don't know it's comin' that they jump the best. Timing, Evan. Life is all in the timing."

Because he had long ago acknowledged this as a Truth of the Universe, he applied it to the topic at hand. Seeing his frown, Louvena helped him out.

"Here's how I see it. It's August of last year, and Cousin Poppy Bellew figures out three days ahead of the National Weather Service that Katrina is gonna be worse than the Battle of New Orleans and the New Madrid earthquake rolled into one. She and some of her Calvary Baptist ladies head down there to help, because that's what Poppy's always done. A couple of friends from Gospel Baptist join them. The Old Believers send down two pickups full of supplies the next day."

"But every church in the county sent stuff—"

"Hush up and listen," she snapped. "Katrina hits. Everybody from PoCo gets separated, nobody knows what anybody else is doin'—and the Feds couldn't find their own asses with both hands and a road map. It's more than a week after the hurricanes before our folks start limping back to home, bringing three New Orleans families who end up liking it here and decide to stay."

"The Westlees, the Dumaines, and the Thomsons," he supplied. Latisha Dumaine had, in fact, become his secretary at the Sheriff's Office. "Wait—they're all Baptists?"

"They surely are, and all at Gospel. But I'm not done yet. Everybody makes it back home eventually—except for Poppy."

Evan mulled this over, too. The last time anyone had heard from Poppy Bellew, she was at a rest stop in Mississippi on her way back to Virginia with three teenaged girls and a thirteen-year-old boy. Her brief conversation with Pastor Deutschman of Calvary Baptist had included no information about who the evacuees were or precisely where she had found them, but before the sketchy cell connection had been lost she had asked him to find host families for children who had been victims of human trafficking.

The shock of this revelation was considerable; Poppy's disappearance was even worse. Deutschman had done as much checking as he could—not much, in the chaos after Katrina and Rita—before Poppy's friends had come home with tales of teenaged girls and boys who'd been kept in a New Orleans brothel. Poppy had taken four of them with her; the others had been turned over to the care of local church groups.

Southern Baptists had been on the wrong side of the slavery issue. Deutschman decided neither he nor his flock—nor anybody he could buttonhole long enough to explain things to—would be indifferent to this resurgence of trade in human beings. Allied with most of the other Baptist denominations in PoCo, Calvary had organized a fundraising and awareness campaign.

"It would work," Evan said slowly, "except for two things. It's not just Baptist churches that burned, and the charity didn't get organized until late last October."

Louvena nodded. "Old Believers burned on the ninth of September."

"Timing," he muttered.

"Like I told you, we got four Baptist churches, St. Andrew's Episcopal, and the Lutheran, all magic. Except for the Methodists."

"Could be cover," he mused. "A smoke screen—"

"That's three puns, and that's two too many," she told him severely.

"Camouflage," he corrected himself, bowing an apology.

"I said it wasn't much," Louvena reminded him. "Just somethin' to ponder."

"I will. Thanks. Now, let's go inside and find you that champagne."

"I hope it's Californian, and not that prissy French stuff," she remarked as they headed back toward the front door. "Nothin' good ever came out of France except the books of Mr. Balzac. And maybe a couple of those haystack pictures."

"Most people prefer the water lilies."

"Huh. Very pretty, but what use are they? Haystacks, now—that's the practical beauty of the gifts of the land brought forth by people's hard labor. The water lily didn't do nothin' but grow. You look at those paintings, they're all soft colors and make you feel nice and restful—but they don't make you think because there's nothing there to be thought about."

"Except maybe weeding the pond?"

He sidestepped her slap at his ass, laughing. But mention of Monet coupled with a glimpse of white-blond hair nearby reminded him of the night of the Lutheran fire.

THE SECOND WEEK IN DECEMBER, the Ayalas had invited the Lachlans over for coffee and dessert. Erika's note mentioned that she was trying out new recipes for pie and needed opinions on which to take to her mother's in Atlanta for Christmas, her three boys having all the usual culinary discernment of teenagers—which was to say none at all. They simply inhaled whatever was put in front of them, and occasionally remembered to say thanks.

The house was just outside the county line, and quite a drive from Woodhush. Erika turned out to be a fragile blonde a little younger than her husband, with big hair and too much mascara. Evan hid a grin, knowing that around tiny women Holly always felt like a complete galumph, terrified of stumbling over thin air and breaking treasured family antiques. Sure enough, her body language changed completely as she sidled into the house, her usual caution with long limbs and big feet turning perfectly pathological. Erika's sons by her first husband—Troy, Titus, and Tristan—showed up just long enough to be introduced, then vanished upstairs to their video games in the third-floor attic that Gib had turned into a family room. Much of the first floor had been gutted to make a single barnlike great room with formal dining at one end, kitchen in the middle, and living room that doglegged the southwest corner of the house.

The coffee was Dominican, the cream was real, and the pie crusts were so light they nearly floated off the plates. Evan gleefully pigged out on blackberry, apple-raisin, pecan, pumpkin, and coconut-banana. The only reason there was no lemon meringue was that the boys had hijacked it before dinner.

"Don't worry about it," Holly told Erika after she apologized a second time for the lack. "Evan will be having dreams about this for a week—which will help when all he gets for dinner is half a head of iceberg lettuce and a tomato."

Later, on their way out to the car, Holly smacked Evan upside the head.

"Ow!"

"That's for gobbling up those pies as if you never get a decent meal at home."

He grinned. "I've been trying to remember one."

"Oh, funny man. You just talked yourself out of the tomato."

"You're a cold, cruel woman, McClure." He swung her around and planted a great big sloppy kiss on her mouth. "That," he told her, "is for knowing that framed posters of Monet water lilies don't belong in the same house, let alone the same *room*, with black Naugahyde sofas."

She choked on a giggle even as she glanced over her shoulder to make sure Gib and Erika's front door was closed. "God, you're wicked!"

"Just observant. They do pay me for that, y'know. Which means I heard what she said when you asked if she'd been over to Monticello yet."

Holly cast another guilty glance over her shoulder and slid into the driver's seat. "I'm trying to think up something tactful to say, Lachlan. I'm not having any luck."

"Could there possibly be anything tactful to say about a woman who goes to Monticello and talks about the lawns?"

"Wicked *and* nasty." She switched on the engine and huddled into her coat while waiting for the heater to kick in.

Evan eyed her profile for a moment. "Please tell me you're not going to ask why he married her."

"Gently, Big Guy," she advised. "Gib was the first person with a Y chromosome who, when he said I was pretty, I believed him. Besides, we'll have to invite them to dinner soon. Social reciprocity, Southern hospitality, and all that." When he snorted, she went on, "Yeah, okay, I noticed the Naugahyde. But furniture has to be washable when you've got kids running around the house."

"Teenagers ought to be civilized enough not to destroy stuff."

"Tell me that again in a dozen or so years," she advised wryly. "But—oh wait, I forgot. *Your* children are perfect!"

"Damned right they are," he affirmed.

She unlocked the parking brake and shifted into reverse. "You're just being smug because you know Clary Sage has a foolproof spill spell. Although if we really want to do it up right, I'll have to find out where Cousin Cam is gallivanting around to this millennium—he does things with textiles that you wouldn't believe."

"Are you trying to change the subject?"

"Why would I want to do that?"

"To deflect me away from discussing your old boyfriend."

"He wasn't."

"But he wanted to be. Or at least his wife thinks he wanted to be, and maybe that he still does." As she slanted him a skeptical glance, he shook his head. "Look, Holly, I know he's an old friend or whatever, but let's get real, huh? A guy knows when another guy's pussy-whipped."

She gave a derisive snort. "Is there any woman in the world so incredible in bed?"

"I assume you're asking out of pure intellectual curiosity."

"There's nothing intellectual about the fact that if I ever tried to pussy-whip you, you'd be gone faster than—"

Evan shook his head again. "That's not how it works, babe. It's not just the fucking. I mean, he's her second husband, right? And they've only been married a few years. It's gotta be something about her that makes him panic every time he thinks about losing her. And before you say it, I don't want to lose *you*, ever—but it's not the same. A man like that, he doesn't think any other woman would ever want him."

She laughed. "You conceited son of a bitch!"

"That's not what I meant. Why don't you astonish the world and just listen for a change? Thank you. This kind of guy, he's always scared that somebody else is gonna look better to her than he does. That what he has with her isn't enough to make her stay with him."

"But that makes *him* the controlling one." She braked at the intersection of Highway 3 and Highway 8, and turned to stare at him.

"It makes him create situations to test whether she still wants him enough to be suspicious. He flirts a little, passive-aggressive, nothing overt—just to make sure she still wants to own him."

"I don't understand," she said plaintively. "A man doesn't trust that his wife loves him enough to stay with him, so he tries to make her jealous to prove to himself that she does love him? And this involves flirting with other women, so that his wife thinks other women want him, which makes her jealous—except that he doesn't *really* think other women want him, which is why he has to reassure himself by flirting with other women so they *will* want him, thereby provoking his wife's jealousy that proves other women want him even when he's convinced they really don't?"

He was quiet for a moment. "Y'know, I didn't completely follow all that."

"Neither did I," she admitted. "And I'm the one who said it." Somebody behind them honked, and she hastily shifted back into gear to make the turn. "So what was the point, again?"

"That's just it. I don't see that there is a point."

"To what?" she asked, more confused than ever.

"Jealousy. It's all about possession, right? Ownership? The idea of anybody trying to own *you*—"

"But I'm your wife."

"Because you chose to be. Holly, you made me a promise. I trust your promises. *Jealous and possessive* means *suspicious and controlling* to me—and I just don't see the point. How do you control the thoughts in a person's head? You can't, so why bother trying? Do I go ballistic when you look at Jamey?"

"He's gay. Not a valid example."

"If you look at one guy, you're gonna look at others."

"You look at women, too." She snorted again. "If you didn't, I'd have you hospitalized."

"Look, what are the classic questions? For the man, it's *Did you fuck him?* But the question a woman asks—"

"*Do you love her?* Are we really still that primitive? Men dedicated to making sure their offspring are in fact theirs, and women manipulating a man's emotional commitment so her children are provided for?"

"What would be your first question, if you thought I was foolin' around?"

She thought for a moment. "Evan, I'm trying to imagine it, and I can't. I mean I really *can't*. You made me a promise, too. And I trust you." She lobbed a whimsical smile at him. "Are we evolved, or just kidding ourselves?"

"Do you really want to find out?"

"No. But you've convinced me that the whole jealousy thing is fairly psychotic."

"That's the way a lot of marriages work." He paused, then shrugged. "My parents', for one. Dad was the jealous one, always suspicious. He had good reason to be, of course. She always kept him on edge, just to prove what a catch she still was."

Holly shook her head. "I couldn't live like that," she stated, repressing a shudder. "Always suspicious, always distrustful—trying to control what you think and feel—"

"Seems to work for some people."

"Does it?" she mused. "Partnership or power trip? I know not everybody's lucky enough to have what we have, but—oh, hell, I don't know. Maybe it's that we actually *like* each other?"

"Yeah, I guess I do kinda like you," he teased. "But where'd a nice girl like you learn a term like 'pussy-whipped,' anyway?"

"Whatever gave you the impression that I was a nice girl?"

"Just what I wanted to hear," he announced, and slid his fingers up her thigh.

Holly laughed, then slowed the car and pulled over to the side of the road—but not for purposes of fooling around. Just as the fire truck roared past, Evan's cell phone played the opening guitar riff of "Life in the Fast Lane." He snagged the phone out of his jacket pocket with his right hand while his left delved beneath the seat for the flasher he insisted she keep in the car.

"Don't you scratch up my dashboard with that thing," she warned. "Or scrape the paint off the roof with it, either."

"You want I should roll down the window and hold it outside while you're doin' eighty miles an hour?" He flipped the switch and wedged the flasher against the windshield while hitting the button on his phone. "Yeah, I know there's a fire—the truck just went past. Where at?"

Fifteen minutes later, Evan was surveying the last smoke rising from the Pocahontas County Lutheran Church. Holly stood nearby, sneezing quietly into her coat sleeve. Jamey Stirling had been there to meet them, having been in his courthouse office when the fire department got the call and sent the engine. "Shit," was all he'd said.

This fire totally screwed any tentative theories about the targets being only Baptist churches. The only upside was that this one had been spotted early, and the damage was confined to a closet where the vestments were kept. When the fire chief gave them the okay, they poked around a bit by flashlight, then decided to tape it all off and wait for morning. Evan sternly forbade himself to think about the klieg lights and crime scene unit and dozen officers looking for witnesses that he would have had at his disposal in New York.

"Nothing?" Holly asked when the two men trudged back to the Beemer.

"Nothing," Jamey confirmed. "Less than nothing. If there's a quantifiable amount that's *less* than less than nothing, this is it."

"I'm really starting to get pissed off," Evan remarked. "Getting pissed off is bad for my blood pressure."

"Come home with us, Jamey, have a Scotch, and we'll talk about it," Holly said. "Did you get dinner? I can make you a sandwich—"

"Make your own sandwich," Evan advised the young man. "Trust me on this one, Jamey."

A little while later—Evan having firmly replaced the flasher beneath the seat, telling Holly that she'd had her fun for the night driving really, really fast—he canted a curious glance at her. "Come home with us? Make him a sandwich? Is it middle age, motherhood, or frustration about not having a book to write that's making you so domestic these days?"

"Maybe I just like checking out Jamey's ass."

"Oh. Okay." He settled back in the seat, waiting. Sure enough, not two miles had gone by before she squirmed and glanced over at him. "What?" he asked innocently.

"Are you trying to prove how unjealous you can be?"

"Were you trying to provoke me into being jealous?"

All at once she laughed and leaned over to rumple his hair. "Point taken, lover man."

Five

LACHLAN ESCORTED LOUVENA COX into the ballroom, beckoned to the nearest waiter bearing champagne, and left her happily in possession of a bottle of Korbel while he sought out his host. He'd met Bernhardt Weiss four times, and liked him about as much as he liked Westmoreland.

The first time had been right after the purchase of the property, and Weiss, with a thoughtful regard for decorum, had stopped by on his round of county officials to introduce himself. Jesse McNichol had still been sheriff back then, so Lachlan just sat back and watched, drinking coffee and nodding every so often, as Cousin Jesse made nice. A few words had been said about New York, and a few more words about Evan's lovely and talented wife, and then the man departed.

The second time was in Flynton, just outside the bank. Lachlan had been called out on a domestic disturbance—this was before the county in general had developed sufficient understanding of his attitude toward spouses who hit each other and parents who hit their children—and was coming out of the Dairy Queen with a cold soda that he wished was a jigger of single malt so he could get the taste out of his mouth. Weiss was getting out of his Mercedes and ten or so of his employees were getting out of the Westmoreland courtesy van. Upon seeing Evan, Weiss had paused while his workers entered the bank. A brief conversation about the virtues of saving one's wages and the advisability of shopping around for interest rates ensued. Evan then excused himself to take Polly Henderson to the county lockup for attempting to carve her husband a new one, and the whole drive kept asking himself just what it was about Weiss that raised his hackles. It wasn't as if the man had a comic-opera German accent, a monocle, military bearing complete with heel-clicks, or the blue-eyed-blond Aryan look about him. He was pleasantly spoken, polite, handsome enough in a thin-nosed, sharp-cheekboned way, and seemed genuinely charmed by rural America.

The grand opening of Westmoreland in November 2004 was the third time Lachlan had encountered him. Holly and Lulah were introduced, hands were shaken, and that was it—except that Lachlan felt like he needed a shower.

The fourth time had been in the Sheriff's Office again, the day after the fire at the Lutheran church—which was, in fact, the church Weiss himself attended. After a reasonably subtle but ultimately unsuccessful attempt to learn what Evan knew about the arson, Weiss had issued a personal invitation to the Lachlans to be his guests at the Westmoreland luncheon buffet the following Saturday. Evan declined with a polite smile; they were already engaged, but thanks very much, and so forth. Weiss accepted defeat on all counts and left.

Before Evan could find his host this evening, he caught sight of Holly. She had paused in the ballroom doorway, scanning the crowd. He was the one she was looking for, no doubt of it. He smiled as she found him, both smug and grateful, because he was the only one who could put this look onto her face. To use an old-fashioned phrase, she prided him. She did him honor.

As she approached, he took in the latest version of her Candidate's Wife look. Denim skirt, sort of a dark butterscotch color, off-white silk shirt, and dark green corduroy jacket: sleek, classic, and modest, until your eyes got to the hem of her skirt and followed the legs down to the Fuck Me shoes. As he dragged his gaze back up—was it okay to ogle one's own wife in public?—he noted the usual ensemble of jewelry: engagement and wedding rings, signet ring, and Susannah's diamond bracelet, augmented tonight with small hoop earrings and the *Fortis et Fidus* castle-and-crown brooch at her lapel. As she took his arm and leaned up for a kiss he murmured, "The Lachlan crest on your hand, the Lachlan badge on your jacket—what, the Lachlan hunting tartan's in the laundry?"

Her tongue flicked out to lick his upper lip before she drew back and smiled her sweetest. "I'm making sure everybody knows who I belong to, O Light of My Life."

"Remind me to have your clan badge tattooed on my—Evening, Judge Schaefer," he said hastily.

"Nice to see you, Evan. Holly, you're looking as stunning as ever. How are the twins?"

"Rambunctious," she said. "And don't think you can sweet-talk me into believing you really want to hear about the rug rats, Your Honor—I know very well you're hiding from Dulcie Whittaker."

The judge pulled a mournful face. "I see the good counselor quite often enough in my courtroom, thanks. I swear to you, Holly, two minutes into that woman's opening statements, I expect the CSI crew to come in and lay down the chalk outline around the whole jury."

The schmoozing went like that for about twenty minutes as Holly and Evan worked the room. At last she dug her fingers into his arm and whispered, "If you don't get me ice and vodka—mainly vodka—within the next ninety seconds, I'm going to tell them all the truth about you."

"But there are so many truths to choose from," he murmured.

"Indeed there are."

Evan considered. "Ice," he said. "Vodka. Got it."

The regular staff at Westmoreland—almost all Europeans—had been given the night off. Serving the assembled locals were other locals who had volunteered their time, for tonight was not just a political grip-and-grin, but a benefit for the churches destroyed by fire and the charity that assisted victims of trafficking. Some of the wait staff circulated with bottles and glasses of specific liquors and soft drinks; others were behind the bar. Lachlan gave up trying to find somebody with a tray of iced vodka, and approached the gorgeous thirty-foot polished oak bar.

Along the way he heard snatches of various conversations. Only a few of them were ordinary, everyday, how's-the-wife, enjoy-your-vacation, fine-apple-crop-this-year chats. The good citizens of Pocahontas County were by and large a politically inclined lot, relishing the opportunity to get together and discuss anything and everything. Tonight, as he nodded and smiled at his constituents, Evan made copious notes-to-self about people to keep his wife away from at this party.

"—a big place, and most of it is sand. You don't think there are plenty of places to hide WMDs where not even the United States Army could find them?"

"—five deferments! Five! And as for his sidekick in the Oval Office—I don't know about you, but I just feel so much better in retrospect that Dubya was in the National Guard, flying sorties to make sure the Viet Cong didn't invade Boca Raton."

"Traditional marriage? Oh, c'mon, honey. Traditionally, marriage was between one man and as many women as he could afford."

"—mark my words, in 2006, the Democrats are gonna be the party nobody wants to go to!"

"—Coulter? Oh, you mean the Paris Hilton of the neo-cons?"

"—ask me, that man is living proof that evolution doesn't exist and 'intelligent design' never got off the ground—"

"—we can't just cut and run—"

"—determined on adherence to Levitcal law in the Old Testament, you might want to get rid of that bacon-wrapped shrimp on your plate. Double *treyf*."

"—beg your pardon! 'Mormon' and 'archaeology' are *not* mutually exclusive terms!"

"—gettin' sick breathin' the formaldehyde in those FEMA trailers down in Louisiana—the Katrina victims have been gettin' screwed for a solid year now, and—"

"—administration isn't muzzling scientists! Global warming was invented by Al Gore—"

Definitely keeping Holly away from that one, Lachlan told himself. First on the list, of course, was anything to do with Iraq. Should she happen to be feeling mellow, she'd enter into a reasoned discussion. If not, she might do anything from give a ten-minute lecture on precisely why the entire Bush Administration ought to be horsewhipped by somebody who knew how, to merely singing a Vietnam-era protest song under her breath, usually "Your Flag Decal Won't Get You into Heaven Anymore."

One might have assumed that because her husband was running for office, she would tone it down. The noteworthy thing about PoCo was that everybody knew what everybody else thought about everything, and anybody who backpedaled or prevaricated in the interests of winning votes was looked on with what had to be the prototype of the term *withering contempt*. They liked a good debate, these folks. They considered, rightly so, that the bizness of the USA was their bizness, and had been since the very beginning—certainly since long before independence from Great Britain was even a gleam in John Adams's eye. And they'd kept on arguing through all the issues of war, society, law, politics, ethics, and religion that had come up ever since.

Only in matters of race had violence occurred. In this, the county was truly Southern. There had been murders before the Civil War, and lynchings during Reconstruction, and the resurgence of the Klan in the '20s had intensified the nightmare. The last act of race-related violence had been almost forty years ago: the murder of Holly's parents on their way back from an NAACP meeting. This had shocked the entire community so profoundly that when the Klan abandoned Pocahontas County, nobody mentioned how odd it was that some of the families had been residents for generations. As for how many people knew the departure had been prompted by magic . . . who could say?

"It was Holly's Aunt Lizza," Lulah had explained. "She was that good—and that heartbroke over her sister's death. She didn't care if Mr. Scott took her Measure and then shredded it to bits right in front of her. We couldn't any of us figure out what was goin' on, until one day Griff found her collapsed on the kitchen floor. When she came to, first thing she did was start reweaving—Clary Sage had to knock her out with things you don't want to know about. We all got together and discussed it, and decided if somebody wanted to punish us for usin' magic against these people, so be it. And we finished off what Lizza had started. Hexes, spells, blights and blastings, all sorts of things nobody suspected the girl had in her. She nearly wrecked her health, physical and magical. But one by one the Klan members sold up and left. There was an investigation, of course, but we had precedent—I ever tell you about what a McNichol did to a slavecatcher way back when? Anyhow, Mr. Scott came in to have a look—he was short on deputies like Alec and Nicholas at the time, so he investigated us himself. He wrote the whole thing off as not quite kosher, but none of us had profited materially or magically, so he let us be. Lizza was sick for almost a year after—and much as she wanted to, there wasn't any chance of her bein' able to take care of her sister's child. So Griff took her to California, and I took Holly to raise. And we never from that day had another whisper of trouble. We had equal justice, and we had peace. My brother and Marget bought it with their lives."

Forty years later, the Westmoreland Inn was hosting a county gathering that featured every possible shade of human skin. If anybody had a problem with it, they kept it to themselves. But Lachlan was pretty sure nobody had problems. It reminded him of something he'd sensed when Holly had taken him to a couple of Civil War battlefields during their first spring at Woodhush: it was as if all the violence and hatred and bitterness that could possibly exist in that particular piece of land had simply exhausted itself. Nothing was left but quiet, and a certain weariness—and the grass, doing its work, just as Sandburg had written. Evan had tried to explain what he'd felt on the drive home; Holly had given him an odd look, then patted the growing curve of her belly and said, "Daddy is a very wise man, did you know that?"

Lachlan considered that Elizabeth Amarantha Flynn Griffen had been the general on that particular battlefield, with her rage and her grief as artillery. And after she'd won, Pocahontas County had been left in peace.

At the bar, he smiled at the blonde who usually worked the counter at her family's restaurant over in Prince Rupert, and asked for, "One large glass, two ice cubes, and the rest vodka."

"—Jerusalem artichokes are perfect. Has to be a hundred and ninety proof or it won't do the job. Then—"

Evan turned his head and smiled. "Jerusalem artichokes, huh, Rocky? Quite a change from corn mash."

There was a saying about the various nationalities that had settled Appalachia: the English came and built a house, the Germans came and built a barn, but the first thing the Irish did was build a still. Rocky McDermid and Jordy Conleth were just doing what came natural.

Rocky's big hand wrapped itself around a brown bottle of beer. "How ya doin', Sheriff? Me and Jordy were just talkin' about convertin'."

Jordy nodded. "With gas prices what they are . . ."

Evan nodded thoughtfully. When Bush took office, gas had been about a buck-fifty a gallon. "There's more money in selling something to pour in your car, instead of down your throat?"

"That's the long and the short of it, Sheriff."

If two of the most notorious moonshiners in the county—now that the Widow Farnsworth had gone to her reward—were teaming up to produce ethanol, three hundred years of family tradition had just keeled over with a thud, dead in the dust. Evan said, "Let me know how it works out. Maybe the county would be interested in switching its vehicles over. Thanks, Laura," he said as the bartender slid the very full glass over to him. So full, in fact, that he had to lean down and slurp a little before picking it up.

"I thought that was for Holly," Laura asked innocently.

"Which is why you filled it to the brim," he countered. "She tips pretty good when she's had a few—" Whatever else he might have said was muffled by the pimentoed olive she stuffed into his mouth. "Smart-ass kid," he mumbled around it, and went to find his wife.

Along the way, he kept hearing bits of conversation and hoped everybody was getting all their squabbles out of the way before the liquor had a chance to soak in.

"Cheney can hold a meeting so secret even *he* doesn't know about it—"

"—Clinton handed Bush a healthy economy. The way things are heading, Bush is gonna hand over a pawn ticket written in Chinese."

"—kidding me? Hubbard was the most successful con artist since Joseph Smith with the golden plates!"

Well, soak into everybody but the Mormons, the teetotal variety of Baptists, and the recovering alcoholics in the crowd, anyway. A surfeit of juleps, martinis, or beer was the only thing in his experience that could turn the stately dance of Southern manners into a lurching verbal free-for-all. But it wasn't entirely his problem tonight; Bernhardt Weiss had security guys. Lachlan had met them when they registered their guns. He hadn't much liked them, either.

He could see Holly's russet hair over by the verandah doors, then got stuck in traffic. He heard Lexine Kimball's earnest voice say, "You take care of Mother Earth so that Mother Earth will take care of you? That sounds suspiciously Pagan. It worships the creation instead of the Creator. We were given dominion over—"

"What is this, a starter planet? Fouling our own nest can't be what God had in mind."

"Earth is temporary. Science says that the sun will eventually swell up and fry everything out to the orbit of Mars. Just as prophesied in Second Peter: 'But the day of the Lord will come like a thief, and then the heavens will pass away with a loud noise, and the elements will be dissolved with fire, and the earth and the works that are upon it will be burned up.' There's another and better home waiting for us in the eternal heavens."

Evan heroically refrained from rolling his eyes toward the promised celestial abode. Lexine's retirement plan was called The Rapture. She was more industrious about signing people up than an insurance agent with a monthly quota to fill.

"—European Union and a reunified Germany sounds like prophecy about the 'revived' Roman Empire that'll hold power before Christ's return, so can the End Times really be that far off?"

And we're off to the races, Evan thought.

"The Tribulation's purpose is to punish Israel for rejecting Jesus Christ as the Messiah," Lexie went on. "When the Jews finally recognize Him, Israel will be regenerated, restored—"

He thought about all the Jews he knew, and couldn't see any of them making the sign of the cross. *"We're a stubborn people,"* his old buddy Pete Wasserman had once told him. *"We've had to be, in order to survive."*

"—The Rapture is the glorious event we should all be longing for. We will finally be free from sin and in God's presence forever."

Lexie was looking directly at Lachlan now. He smiled, said, *"Mazel tov,"* and slid past her little group, telling himself irreverently that his definition of "rapture" had more to do with Holly and a bed than Jesus and Judgment Day.

Maneuvering himself and the vodka along the outskirts of the ballroom, he kept a pleasant smile on his face—and kept out of all the conversations.

"—well, being Irish or Welsh or Scots is mostly about being *not* English."

"If the Democrats win in November, Nancy Pelosi's gonna be Speaker of the House. Think of it! A woman, two heartbeats away from the Presidency!"

"You mean one heartbeat and a pacemaker."

"—so the Dunns' rabidly anti-abortion stance is psychologically interesting, if pathetic. Her son's not just a pathological liar and a deadbeat with a criminal record, he's an alcoholic. That's probably about one step up from being gay on their religion's scale of damnation. He was born out of wedlock long before she met her husband. Considering the way he turned out, they both feel hideously guilty that in their secret hearts they wish she'd had an abortion. It's classic overcompensation—and they don't realize it, of course."

"—recommendations of the Iraq Study Group. Can you really see him ignoring a blue-ribbon group like that?"

"I would think that as a Catholic, you would join the outcry against abortion in this country—this holocaust of—"

"You know, Reverend, I find that unbelievably offensive."

Now, how had she migrated around behind him without his knowing it? he wondered, turning to find himself confronted with his wife's back, and over her shoulder the Reverend Wilkens.

"There was only one Holocaust—so we must all hope, anyway—and it involved the state-policy, state-organized, state-run extermination of an entire people, simply because they were Jewish." Though Holly's tone was quiet, conversational, even mild—for her, anyway—Evan heard the danger. Too bad the man she'd spoken to did not.

Reverend Wilkens was the salt-of-the-earth type, the solid backbone and tough sinew of the country. He was a good man, and a good citizen, and his church did good works under his compassionate direction. Six generations of Wilkenses in Pocahontas County had eyed the Papist contingent askance—but on this issue they had united. The Reverend just couldn't understand how anyone from a Catholic family could disobey the Pope. Lachlan wondered how Wilkens would react if he knew he was talking to a Roman Catholic Witch.

The Witch was saying, "To use the term in reference to anything else is an abominable insult to the millions who died. I would be vastly obliged if you didn't use it again."

"It's an accurate reference," Wilkens insisted. "And I use it deliberately. What else is *Roe* but state policy that allows—"

"You're absolutely right. It 'allows'—not demands, not mandates, not dictates. It allows for a choice."

"'Choice'? Mrs. Lachlan, we're talking about *children*! The pre-born! Human life!"

"Again, I absolutely agree with you—human lives are exactly what we're talking about." Her tone was still pleasant, but the serrated edges were beginning to sharpen. "The lives of the already breathing. Even this proposed law in South Dakota this coming election, the one that would make physicians into criminals by forbidding abortion—it has an exception. The life of the mother. The already breathing take precedence over—"

"All life is God-given, and to kill it in the womb is simple murder. Those of us who are pro-life—"

"Y'know, Reverend, I've been meaning to ask somebody who says he's 'pro-life' about that term. If I believe in a woman's right to choose, does that make me 'pro-death'?"

"Mrs. Lachlan!"

"Everyone is pro-life. We just differ on which lives are more important. There's common ground here, you know."

"Common ground, or compromise? The epidemic of promiscuity—"

"You see? We're in agreement on that, too. I don't approve of promiscuity, either. It's not just heart-numbing, it's potentially suicidal."

"You are a mother yourself. How can you countenance the murder in the womb of—"

"I *chose* to be a mother. And that's the second time you've used the word 'murder,' so here's a thought for you. Overturning *Roe* won't stop abortions. It will only stop *safe* abortions. Women will die. Is that murder, too?"

Evan knew every inflection of his wife's voice, and the earnest, spuriously innocent I'm-just-asking-for-information tone was one of her most dangerous. He took a step forward, intending to tap her shoulder and end the conversation.

Somebody beat him to it.

"Holly!" exclaimed Gib Ayala. "I've been looking all over for you—I wasn't sure what you drink, so I got you a glass of white wine—oh, excuse me, Reverend, I didn't mean to interrupt."

Of course you did, Lachlan thought. As Ayala caught sight of him, standing there like an idiot holding Holly's vodka, a strange smile flickered over the man's handsome face. Evan nodded and smiled back, and as Holly accepted the wine with a smile of thanks, he thought, *At least the guy's good for somethin' besides keepin' the bench press from gettin' rusty.*

"Sh-sheriff Lachlan?"

He turned and smiled down at Ben Poulter. The vampire smiled back. He wasn't the nasty kind of vampire: he couldn't fly, or change himself into a bat, or move at lightning speed, or not be reflected in mirrors. He just had to drink a couple of pints of blood every so often in order to stay alive. He was looking well tonight, relaxed and genial, and Lachlan wondered which of the local farmers had recently slaughtered a cow; Ben and his family had an arrangement with them about things like that.

"How're you doin', Ben? How's the book comin' along?"

One thing he did have in common with the more celebrated type of vampire was exquisite night vision. Ben was, in fact, an astronomer, and he was writing a children's book about the planets.

"Very well, thanks. I sh-should have something ready by the time Bella and Kirby can read." His eyes were a deep golden-green, like sunlight through pond water, and they could move at times with an eerie darting swiftness. They did so now, evaluating the crowd, and came to rest on Holly and Gib. The pair had moved away from Reverend Wilkens, and were strolling slowly toward the verandah doors. "I remember that guy from when he lived here before. He looks a little like the Latino who was on *West Wing*."

"Don't say those two words around Holly," Evan pleaded with a grin. "She went into mourning for weeks after the final episode in May."

"I can lend her the DVDs," Ben offered, his strange eyes glinting. "Or I could be bribed not to."

"Be nice, Ben, or I'll go back to the bar and order you a Bloody Mary."

"Oldest joke in the book, Sh-sheriff!"

Lachlan grinned and took a swallow of vodka, figuring it was his now, and turned suddenly as a voice behind him spoke his name. He greeted Erika Ayala with a smile, and nodded at her eldest son. Erika was sleek and fashionable tonight in white skirt and a pink tank top under a flowered blouse, but Helmet Hair would always defeat any attempt at elegance. The elaborate pink crystal chandeliers hanging from her earlobes to her shoulders didn't help. After some small talk about Troy's prospects for the football team this coming semester, Erika placed a languid hand on the boy's arm.

"Troy," she said, "go get me something to drink, won't you, darling?"

He moved off obediently. Lachlan had noted that Erika's gaze had never left the sight of her husband and Holly in conversation over by a potted palm. Something rather evil inside made him say, "Bet they were a cute couple in high school."

Erika's brown eyes flickered toward him. "Haven't you seen the pictures?"

"Are there pictures? Holly doesn't have any that I'm aware of."

She was too polite to say aloud that she didn't believe him. Evan repressed a sigh. What she said next confirmed that tweaking her had not been a good idea.

"I hear that she's as fanatical about her writing as he is about his flying. How do you deal with it?"

"I'm not sure I understand."

Erika slanted a sideways glance at him, then blurted, "I asked him once which he loved more—me or flying."

And—wild guess here—you didn't much like the answer? If you didn't already know the answer, you shouldn't have asked the question. And of all the stupid things to ask—Evan tried very hard not to shrug. "It's like that with the creative types."

"Since when is flying an airplane—"

He knew it was rude to interrupt, but he did it anyway. "When he's flying he's off in his own world, right? Doing something that takes him away from everything else? Makes him feel like nothing else can? Sounds to me like it's pretty much the same. When they're into their thing, whatever it is, they don't think about anything else. And God help anybody who tries to get between them and their work." He smiled suddenly, remembering what Holly was like in the throes of a writing binge. He hadn't seen that aspect of her in a long time, though. Now that the twins were out of babyhood and able to entertain themselves for at least part of each day, maybe she'd find another book to write. He hoped so; there were times when her lack of a focus for her intellect and creativity made her a pain to live with.

"No," Erika was saying bitterly, "he doesn't think about anybody but himself when he's flying. Are you saying that Holly is the same way?"

"Pretty much." He really didn't feel like explaining to this woman that the way Holly loved her work was a goodly chunk of what made her Holly, and if she wasn't the way she was he wouldn't love her half as much.

Erika shook her head. "I don't understand how anything can be more important than the people you love."

"It's important in a different way."

"But if they love other things more than they love us—"

"Think what he'd be like if he didn't have the plane. What would he do?"

"He could go back to running a business—"

Evan restrained a snort. "Look, it's not just what they *want*. It's what they *need*. You have to stand back and let them do their thing, and be there when they come back from wherever it is they go that we can't follow."

"What if they don't come back?"

It had never even occurred to him that Holly wouldn't return to him. He thought about it for a moment, then all at once realized what this woman's problem really was. She hated giving her husband up to anything for even a fraction of a second. When he flew, he belonged to the plane and the sky—not to her. And if she didn't own him every instant of every day, then how could she be sure of him? No wonder she was jealous. Suspicious. Controlling. She could never be certain that her husband really loved her, because her definition of love was total possession.

Evan actually enjoyed seeing that absent, abstracted look on Holly's face, the one that meant she was chasing down an idea inside her head. It meant she was doing what she'd been born to do. Her eyes would darken, and her brows would tense, and sometimes she'd bite both lips between her teeth for a second before seizing the nearest pen and piece of paper. When she finished, and came back to him, she was—what was the word? Fulfilled? Satisfied? More than that. Reassured. Convinced that she was worth the space she occupied on the planet, that she was using what she knew and what she felt and what she intuited and what she was to justify her existence.

He simply didn't understand how anyone could resent that. How anyone could not watch it happen, and smile, and enjoy the creation and the happiness and the peace it gave.

This woman wanted her husband's only happiness, his only satisfaction and reassurance and sense of worth, to come from her. It was bewildering, Lachlan reflected, how some people were bound and determined to make themselves unhappy by wanting something impossible to have.

What a misery her life must be, he thought, then practically sang aloud with gratitude as Troy approached with soft drinks. Evan ended the conversation with, "Well, the thing of it is that when she *does* come back, she's all mellowed out. They're her books, after all. She gets to win all the arguments. 'Scuse me, Erika, I should go rescue her from an argument she *can't* win—she's over there talking to Reverend Wilkens again."

"I DON'T KNOW why you do that to yourself."

Holly gave Lachlan exactly the look he'd expected: narrow-eyed, sidelong, and one spark away from furious. She was, at times—not often, but at times—comfortingly predictable.

He'd removed her from Reverend Wilkens's vicinity and guided her toward the bar, and now told Laura, "Two vodkas on ice, one with a twist, one with olives," before propping his elbows on polished oak and regarding his fulminating wife sidelong with an amusement he knew better than to show.

"What, exactly, is it that I do?" Holly asked through gritted teeth. "Stand up for what I believe?"

"Argue with people whose minds are never gonna change." He accepted the vodkas from Laura, gave her a generous tip and a wink, and handed Holly her drink. "You stand up, yeah—but against somebody who isn't playing by the same rules you are. You're on completely different battlefields, lobbing shots at each other that will never hit anything."

Nudging her with an elbow, he coaxed her toward a side door near a grand piano. A faraway crack of thunder echoed off the hills and hollows, and the wind had picked up in the last hour; he hoped the noise wouldn't wake the twins, and that he'd managed to nail down that loose shutter at Lulah's.

"I feel just as passionately about it as the Reverend does," Holly said.

"But you get there by a completely different process. He hears 'abortion' and sees a dead fetus. You hear 'abortion' and see a living woman. He takes the side of—what do they call it? Oh, yeah—the 'preborn.' You're on the side of the already alive. The individual matters to both of you, but with him it's an abstract concept and with you it's the reality of a living, breathing person."

"He wouldn't call it an abstract concept."

"He can't look it in the eyes, can he? I think it's a whole lot easier to care about a human zygote than it is to care about a human being who can actually look you in the eye when she's talking about how her own father messed with her since she was ten, or that she's had six kids and her body can't survive another one, or when her boyfriend found out she was pregnant he disappeared into the wild blue yonder, or—" He broke off. "I see you get my drift."

"You say you don't know why I always argue with people like him—I don't understand why you *never* argue with people like him!" She sipped vodka and crunched an ice cube, then said, "And 'zygote' is a pretty fancy word, Sheriff."

"Intellectual snob," he accused, grinning down at her. "You want the truth?"

"I'm assuming this truth will have about the same relationship to the real truth as every story you've ever told me about those cowboy boots—but go ahead."

"You're lucky I like you," Lachlan teased. "*Truth* is, last week I took up reading the dictionary." Pause. "Backwards."

Holly choked on giggles and almost dropped her drink. Evan rubbed her back until she stopped coughing. "Christ, Lachlan—don't *do* that!" she said when she could breathe again.

"Teach you to insult my boots, lady. Now, to get back to what I was sayin' before—"

"You mean about how I should keep my mouth politely shut when the discussion turns to politics?"

He laughed aloud, genuinely amused. "Holly, you couldn't possibly keep your mouth shut, and I wouldn't want you to. I love it that you're passionate about what you believe in—because one of the things you believe in is *me*."

Her mouth twisted and her forehead scrunched up and she told him,

"I wish you'd warn me before you say things like that. It makes me want to do things to you that would be illegal in several states if we weren't married."

"Now, *that* sounds promising!" A tall, lanky, redheaded man Evan didn't know sidled up behind Holly and snaked his arms around her waist. Her violent start of surprise ended the instant he said, "Hey, Freckles!"

"Peaches!" she cried, delighted.

"Don't call me that." He squeezed tight and let go. As she turned, he went on, "You gonna call me that?"

"Whenever I feel like it, and definitely while I knock you silly for not coming to the wedding!" She smacked him a good one on the shoulder, and he yelped. "Why didn't you come to the wedding?"

"Because I was in Lithuania?" he offered as he rubbed his abused shoulder.

"Lame," she scoffed and with a glance at Lachlan went on, "This is my sorry-ass excuse for a favorite first cousin. Evan, meet Peaches."

"Don't *call* me that! And I'm only your favorite first cousin because I'm your *only* first cousin." Extending his hand, he added, "Please tell her to stop calling me that or I'll stuff ballot boxes for your opponent in November. I'm Cam Griffen. Glad to meet you."

"Same here." The pair shook hands, and Evan told Holly, "Don't call him that."

"That happened fast!" she shot back. "The masculine solidarity thing, I mean. Doesn't the bonding process usually require a televised sporting event and a six-pack? Maybe a manly belch or two?"

"We smoke the same cigars," Evan said serenely, with a nod at Cam's shirt pocket, from which protruded two sleek cylinders of tobacco, each circled by a Cohiba label with its distinctive solid red O. "And we like hugging the same girl."

"Nice work, Freckles," Cam remarked. "He's more than just a pretty face."

"Be nice to your elders, sonny," Holly admonished. "We've got four years on you." She considered him with a frown. "Although to judge by your hairline, you're working on catching up. Who's running you ragged these days?"

He shrugged. "Just the usual Beltway Follies."

"Cam is a constitutional lawyer," Holly explained. "But don't hold it against him. He's really kind of likable—in a frenetic, unraveling-even-as-we-speak sort of way."

"A ringing endorsement," her cousin shot back. "You forgot to mention that I make the meanest julep north of Atlanta, I'm loved by children and dogs and dirty old ladies, and Republicans crawl into corners and whimper when they hear my name."

Evan said, "And you have a personal interest in watching Rausche Junior give a concession speech in November."

Watching them react, he reflected that they really didn't look much alike. Having seen photographs of both Flynn sisters and their husbands, it was obvious that whereas with Holly the sturdy McClures had dominated, Cam's finer bones were directly traceable to his mother. Bella had the same light build. Neither cousin had inherited the aggressive jawline of the McNichol kin. What they shared was the hair, the eyes, the scattering of freckles, and the ruler-straight nose. At the moment, they also shared an imitation of Thumper, astonished by the headlights of an approaching semi.

Evan smiled his sweetest smile. "More than just a pretty face," he reminded Holly, and toasted her with his Scotch.

"Geeze," Cam muttered. "Ya think? Where'd you find him, eBay?"

"Under a rock in Central Park."

"How do you know that I hate Rick?" Cam demanded of Evan. "How do you even know that I *know* Rick?"

"I know that Rick knows you. He said so a few weeks ago. His exact words were, 'You better tell that cousin of your wife's to mind his manners if he comes back around here, Mr. New York City Liberal. I don't have no soft spot for queers.' "

"To which you replied . . . ?" Holly prompted—knowing him, knowing there was more.

"That I hadn't yet had the pleasure of meeting my wife's cousin, but if he is in fact gay, Rick's soft spots are the last thing he'd be interested in."

Cam nodded slowly. "Okay, Holly, it's official. You can keep him."

"I thought you might like him," she said. "Where are you staying? And you'd better say 'With you at Woodhush, Holly darling,' or—"

"With you at Woodhush, Holly darling," he singsonged obediently. "After I repack my suitcase, that is. I'm about fifty yards over and three flights up. Room 314."

Evan couldn't help a startled blink. "You're actually staying here?"

"No," Holly said, "he's staying with us." To her cousin: "Don't mind him, he thinks this place is creepy."

"As a matter of fact . . ." Cam began thoughtfully.

"Oh, don't encourage him!" Holly interrupted.

"I'm just trying to tell you," he protested. "I got in today around noon, and settled down for a nap—"

"Noon? Why didn't you call?"

Evan gave her ribs a squeeze. "Shush. I want to hear this."

Cam hesitated as if waiting for something, then widened his eyes. "'Shush'? That's all it takes?"

"In public, during an election year. Private's another story. So you couldn't sleep this afternoon?"

"I kept almost drifting off, then jerking awake—"

"*Jerk* is right," Holly muttered.

"—and it was like sparks hovering just off my skin, all along my face and neck, and my hands. Weird."

Lachlan mused for a moment. "You're the one with the fabric thing, right?"

"Yeah. Nothing man-made—no polyester, no nylon, anything like that. Silk, cotton, wool, any kind of natural textiles—plus leather—"

"You were touching the bedspread, the blanket?"

"Bedspread," Cam affirmed. "I was lying on my stomach. I had on a long-sleeved t-shirt, and I took off my shoes but not my socks. You think I was picking something up right through the skin?"

"And your face," Holly said, and looked up at Evan. "He said he felt it on his face. That had to be because of the pillow."

"He was lying on his stomach," Evan objected. "It had to've been just one side of his face, right?"

"Nope. And I'm guessing it wasn't so much your palms as the backs of your hands, right?" When Cam nodded, she looked smug. "He sleeps with his face scrunched right down into a pillow—nobody can ever figure out how he manages to breathe—and his hands tucked against his stomach. He's done it since he was little. Nobody knows why. Well, except that he's weird, of course."

"Bite me, Freckles," Cam said sweetly.

"God, I love my in-laws," Lachlan grinned. "The point to all this is that Lulah did a spa thing with Holly when the place first opened, and she won't come back. Said she felt blind the whole time she was here."

"What?" Holly scowled. "She never told me that."

"She didn't want to freak you out. Lulah Sees pretty good, Cam."

"Yes, she does." He chewed his lower lip. "And she said she felt blind? You discuss this yet with the rest of the family?"

That Cam automatically included him in their massive kin network made him smile. Some of the relatives had been a little dubious about him. Being Irish Catholic had been recommendation enough for most of them, but a few eyebrows had arched over his being from New York. And one or two of the cousins weren't happy that Holly had married outside her magical ethnicity.

She was talking again—big surprise. "I can't believe you two are discussing this! If anything really was strange, one of us would have known about it long before now."

"Nobody's said anything," Lachlan admitted. "But I don't know how many of them have been here."

"Or how many of those went past the front desk to the rooms or the spa," Cam added. "Y'know, Evan, I may need some help with my suitcase later on."

He felt his smile widen to a grin. "I like him, too, Holly. If he follows us home, let's keep him."

"Fine," she retorted, "but you're assuming he's housebroken."

"And this would make him different from the twins how, exactly? Cam, let's say ten or so."

"Meet you by the lobby stairs?"

"I'll just happen to run into you while you're checking out," Evan agreed.

Holly did the follow-the-bouncing-conversation thing. "You guys are really going to sneak around upstairs? You're crazy. Besides, if anybody's going to sneak into a hotel room with my husband, it's gonna be me."

"We won't be sneaking," Cam corrected. "I have a key, legitimately paid for." He paused. "And—meaning no offense, Evan—not only is he not my type, I'm damned sure I'm not his type."

"None taken," Lachlan replied serenely. "So—ten, okay? You have a car?"

"Westmoreland has a courtesy van from Shenandoah Regional—which reminds me, Holly, did I hear right and Gib Ayala is running the airport now?"

She nodded. "Yeah, he moved back into the area last October. He and his wife are here tonight, in fact. If you don't have a ride, then I guess you're going home with me—and don't get me started on why we have both cars tonight, okay? You can help me carry the kids back from Lulah's."

"They'll be asleep," Lachlan said. "Which is the only time they shut up."

Cam grinned. "Take after Holly, do they?"

She gave him another thwack on the arm. "For that, Peaches, you get to baby-sit."

"If you don't stop calling me that—"

"Get over it," she advised. Glancing up at Evan, she added, "It's from when he was little—"

"Aw, c'mon!" Cam whined.

"When he was little," she repeated forbiddingly, "and Aunt Lulah used to say he was all cinnamon curls and a peaches-and-cream complexion and sweet as pecan pie. Of course, he never kicked *her* in the shins. Or tried to spook every horse she got on when he was around—"

"I *was* sweet," Cam protested, blue eyes big and innocent. "I was adorable. I still am. Ask anybody."

She grinned. "Anybody outside the Beltway, you mean?"

"Pretty much. And speaking of your infants, I haven't congratulated you yet."

"Thanks," Evan said. "She did all the work."

"And bitched about it for the whole nine months, right? You don't change, do you, Freckles?"

"Oh, shut up."

"Be nice," Lachlan advised. "I bet he knows things about you that would surprise even me."

As Cam's fiendish grin produced a pair of dimples more or less the depth of the Grand Canyon, Holly gave a superior sort of sniff and retorted, "Not a concern, lover man. *He* knows that *I* know what his real name is."

Lachlan had on occasion simultaneously admired and deplored that his wife showed scant delicacy of feeling for those she vanquished. He wondered if it was cowardly to enjoy the unholy glitter in her eyes as long as it wasn't directed at him. But a glance at Cam did not show him the queasy expression he expected; the next instant demonstrated how vast had been his underestimation of her cousin. And, not incidentally, redefined *unholy glitter*.

"Holly," Cam purred. "Darling. You also know what I can do, and that I don't need potions, lotions, notions, shiny rocks—or even, sugar lump, *you*—in order to do it. Or have you forgotten who I used to practice on?"

Lachlan discovered that watching Holly splutter with incoherent outrage was even more rewarding than watching her win. Stifling laughter as best he could while winking his congratulations at Cam, he wisely excused himself to go schmooze Mrs. Paulet—without whose support nobody in PoCo got elected to anything from prom queen to Congress.

"TWERP," HOLLY SNARLED.

"Cleaned up your language, I see," Cam remarked.

"Asshole," she shot back at once.

"Now, that's the Holly I remember."

"I *will* tell him your real name—see if I don't!" When he stuck out his tongue at her, she succumbed to a fit of the giggles. "Oh, knock it off! You look ridiculous when you do that."

"Not the image of the savvy, sophisticated, ruthless attorney terrorizing all who dare to oppose him?"

"Dream on," she advised, but he was no longer paying attention. She followed his line of sight to Evan, who was charming Mrs. Paulet. "My guy's not bad, huh?"

"Not bad at all. A second ago she was playing hard to get, but look at how he's got her leaning a shoulder toward him, just a little. The way he's tilting his head as he smiles—Holly, that's absolute art."

"Oh, it's nothing to do with art or craft. It's all instinct. He doesn't even know he's doing it." She linked elbows with him and coaxed him on a casual stroll around the edge of the crowded ballroom. "He's male, she's female. What he's actually doing is flirting."

"That's what all politicians do: seduce the voters."

"What is it about a Y chromosome that makes men think everything has to do with sex?"

"I said 'seduce,' not 'consummate.' It's the allure of being around somebody powerful. Somebody who can convince you that he or she can get things done that you can't. Your husband is quite obviously a powerful man. Of course, it helps that the guy's a hunk. Nowhere near my type, but a hunk all the same."

"I reiterate: men think *everything* has to do with sex!"

"And who was the one making salacious advances to her own husband not ten minutes ago? By the way, if you were thinking of doing to him what you were probably thinking of doing to him, it's not illegal in any of the states—unless you're in the military."

"Huh?"

Cam gave a little shrug. "It's a violation of the Uniform Code of Military Justice for a soldier to have sex in any way that isn't genital-to-genital intercourse."

"We're talking about a sexual position usually indicated by a two-digit number?"

"Yep," he replied with a blithe and entirely fake smile. "*The Manual for Courts-Martial* says it's unnatural. It comes under the general heading of 'Sodomy.'"

Holly took a healthy swig of vodka. "Weren't the sodomy laws repealed?"

"*Lawrence* v. *Texas*," he supplied immediately. "Sex between consenting adults ain't nobody's business but theirs. But Article 125, the applicable section of the Uniform Code, means the military can prosecute. The results can be dishonorable discharge, forfeiture of all pay and allowances, and confinement for five years—"

"—in a lovely garden suite at Fort Leavenworth," she finished for him. "But gays are the only ones they apply it to."

"Yep," he said again, with the same smile. "When you sign the enlistment papers, do you also sign away all the rights stipulated in the equal-protection clause of the Fourteenth Amendment? It would appear so."

She thought some more. "Only until somebody challenges it in court. I mean, it's discriminatory—not to mention hypocritical—to apply Article whatever only to gays and not to straights." Suddenly she latched onto his arm. "Cam—"

He nodded. "And the penny drops."

"It won't be a court-martial of a gay soldier that will overturn Don't Ask Don't Tell. It'll be when a married heterosexual couple gets prosecuted—"

"Like that's ever gonna happen." He lifted her hand and kissed her knuckles. "You wouldn't have made a bad lawyer."

"There's no call to insult me," she retorted at once. "So what brings you back home to Virginia?"

"Allergies. Have to breathe some home-cooked air for a while."

Holly gave a knowing sigh. "Where'd you get kicked out of this time?"

"That was Lebanon, and it was a long time ago, and it hasn't happened since. Actually, I've been over in Uncle Nicky's part of the world, advising their lawyers on our laws so they can use the same twisted logic on their own laws."

"And yet she is unconvinced of your cynicism," Holly remarked. "How's the democracy thing working out, anyway?"

"I don't know, you tell me," he retorted. "You live here."

"If you came home because you've been missing it—I have to tell you, so have we." She caught sight of Evan again, working the crowd. More: she saw the glint in his eyes that meant Cute Girl Alert. She recognized the young lady: with her newly minted real estate license, Shawntel had found Jamey Stirling his house last year. She was very cute indeed, with strawberry blond hair and her very own original, perky, twenty-six-year-old breasts. Holly smiled to herself and poked Cam in the ribs with one finger, nodding in Evan's direction. "Watch and learn."

Lachlan leaned over a little, just enough to indicate interest, not enough to intimidate with his height and heft. As Holly had known he would, he smiled a slow, almost lazy smile. The girl responded—a woman would have to be dead for three weeks not to respond to Evan Lachlan in predator mode—and canted a glance up at him through her eyelashes. He looked down her blouse, then into her eyes, then said something that made her smile. It wasn't her professional smile—the one that looked borrowed from a synchronized swimmer. This one was real.

"You gonna let him get away with that?"

She didn't take her gaze from Evan and Shawntel as she answered. "I enjoy watching an expert at work." Evan's smile had widened to a grin; the girl actually gulped. Holly stifled a snicker.

Cam's tone conveyed honest confusion. "You don't get even the least bit jealous?"

"And this would be productive how, exactly? He's having a good time. Why should I spoil it for him?"

"Some men like it when their wives get possessive."

"Some men like it when their wives indicate they remember their existence." She shrugged and sipped at her drink. Shawntel was getting less than the full wattage of those hazel-green eyes; Evan had done his looking and was growing bored. Holly could remember the first time she'd been on the receiving end of the complete treatment—the grin, the eyes, the voice, the leaning in, the glance down her cleavage, plus the throaty chuckle and a quick brush of fingertips across her arm—and decided Shawntel probably wouldn't have survived it anyway. Still without glancing at her cousin, she slipped her arm around his waist and said, "Okay, Cam-my-man, suppose I do huff my way over there and drag him off. This would embarrass me, annoy him, make her insufferably smug that I felt threatened. It would be admitting that she is, in fact, a threat. And that's just not the way it is."

"Well, no," he mused. "I can't see anybody you married being stupid enough to risk not being married to you. What I mean is that any man for whom you wouldn't be enough isn't a man worth having."

"What an adorable thing to say!" She grinned up at him. "Although I have to admit it appalls me that I understood the way you said it."

"I'm still not understanding *you* on this."

"I know he's a hunk, he knows he's a hunk, everybody with eyes to look knows he's a hunk. Flirting with other women only makes him more conceited than he already is—and that's sayin' something, believe me." She laughed to herself as Evan's head tilted slightly to one side, a posture that in anyone else would indicate careful concentration. But with him, when a corner of his mouth did that odd little quirk—yeah, he was bored, and just being polite, waiting for Shawntel to finish talking so he could escape. "Let me put it this way," she told Cam. "How colossally stupid would somebody have to be to pay attention in public to someone they want to sleep with? It's the ones they glance at sidelong—the ones they make a point of not noticing—that their partner has to worry about."

"Most people aren't that smart." He paused. "Wait a minute. If they *were* that smart—"

"—that's a whole 'nother kettle of worms, as Lulah would say. When it gets to the point of actively hoodwinking someone you're supposed to love . . ." She shook her head. "That's dishonorable, and just plain nasty." She watched Evan extricate himself and saunter off to schmooze some more, leaving a misty-eyed Shawntel behind. Shaking her head, she was about to ask if Cam wanted to flag down one of the circling waiters for a drink when she felt him wobble a bit. "Cam?"

"Holy shit," he breathed, wide-eyed gaze fixed on someone near the foyer doors. "Where did *he* come from?"

She squinted a bit, unerringly found the object of his shocked stare, and chuckled. Curling a hand around his elbow, she coaxed him gently toward the nearest waiter and snagged a glass of something. "Easy, Peaches. To quote the bard, 'You're leaving tongue-marks on the carpet.' Or you would be, if this wasn't a hardwood floor. Further, I know 'you'd walk on your lips through busted glass if you could get next to that'—but what good would your lips do you then? Here, drink. *That* is Jamieson Tyler Stirling, Esquire, acting Pocahontas County District Attorney, and candidate in November for same. He's thirty-four, B.A. from William and Mary, J.D. from Yale, and, as may be readily ascertained with a single glance, catastrophically gorgeous."

"Is— is—"

"Come on, drink some more. That's my boy. Is he gay? Oh, yeah. Is he single? Oh, very. Why don't you go talk to him?" She considered his poleaxed expression. "Once you can form semicoherent sentences again, anyway. To continue: he likes motorcycles, The Glenlivet, and Linda Ronstadt—or maybe Warren Zevon, or maybe both. Hard to tell." She waited. Cam just kept staring at what Holly had to admit was a gray-eyed, black-haired, no-man's-eyelashes-should-be-that-thick walking invitation to sin. "How do I know all this, you ask? Well, you didn't ask, but I'm going to tell you anyway. At this very moment he has a pair of leather gloves stuffed in the back pocket of his jeans—which fit him quite delightfully, I might add, and don't tell me not to look, I'm married but I'm not dead. He just now picked up a glass from the tray with The Glenlivet bottle on it. And he's singing along under his breath to 'Poor Pitiful Me.' Of course, the gloves could be just regular driving gloves, but please note that his hair is a mess, which could be either from the wind of a motorcycle ride or from taking off his helmet. I'm hoping the latter, as there *are* helmet laws in this county, and considering he's the Acting District Attorney, he's pretty much obligated to obey them. In any case, you see how simple it is, Watson, once I explain how it's done." She waited again. Cam stayed silent. "Plus when he's not driving something from the county motor pool, he rides his Harley over to dinner at Woodhush. And he went shot-for-shot with us last month with Evan's collection of single malts."

At long last the poor man blinked. "He's changed his drink."

"Huh?"

Cam half-turned—as if that was all the physical movement he could manage, as if his body would not entirely obey him. As he spoke to Holly, his gaze kept slanting to his left, where Jamey Stirling was now being talked to at great and flirtatious speed by a brace of college-age blondes. "He used to drink Johnnie Walker Black. In law school. Yale," he added, as if only now recalling the name of the institution. "It was at Yale."

"I *know* where you went to law school!" she exclaimed. Grabbing his arm, she pulled, then yanked, and eventually he stumbled a bit and followed her. Out a side door they went, and around a corner of the verandah, and all the while she was talking. "You know him? You *do* know him! You have a history! You never told me about him." They fetched up against the porch railing, and Holly glared at her cousin. "You never said a single word—"

"Yeah, I did," he murmured, staring down into his glass. "I told you about him, kind of, a long time ago—it wasn't anything. I mean, it was, but—not the kind of thing you talk about. Just—a thing."

"Eloquent," she snapped.

"Holly," he pleaded.

Recognizing genuine distress, she relented. "I'm sorry. Look, do you want to get out of here? You can, you know. Nobody will mind."

"No. It's okay. I just—I was startled. I'm fine." He slugged back the rest of his drink and glanced around for somewhere to put the glass, at last stashing it under a wicker chair. "He looks good," he said helplessly.

"Yeah. And right now you look like crap on a kaiser roll. Let's go for a walk." Holly steered him resolutely off the porch, down the graveled driveway, and out onto the lawn—cursing her stilettos that sank into the grass with every step. When they were well away from the mansion and its floodlights, she picked a bench before a wall of azalea bushes, pointed, and ordered, "Sit."

"Speak. Heel. Roll over. Good dog." Cam settled onto the painted wood and leaned back, sprawling long legs. "Okay. And this is all I'm ever gonna say about it," he warned. "Him, first-year, twenty-one innocent years old. Me, third-year, a jaded twenty-four. Him, trust fund and brand-new Mercedes. Me, three roommates in New Haven's cheapest apartment building and a six-year-old pickup truck. Him, gorgeous. Me—"

"Hold it right there. You're gorgeous, too, you moron."

"Holly, anybody who looks at him—" He shrugged helplessly.

"Yeah, okay, I get the idea. He walks into a room and chairs beg to be sat in. Get to the real story."

"The first time I saw him . . . all of a sudden I didn't have any knees. I can still remember every damning detail, believe me," he went on, mocking himself. "It was a weekend party at Harry and Michelle's—they married after second year and spent the summer in her grandparents' house—everybody went over to help paint the place, 'cause that was the deal they made, but they'd spent the summer in bed instead of working on the house—"

"Peaches! Get to the point!"

"Yeah. So Michelle's invited this guy she knew at William and Mary. He's only twenty-one—kept skipping grades—and she wants to introduce him around so he's not completely friendless when classes start the next week. I take one look at him and—"

"No knees?"

"I'm standing there in the living room, sweaty, stubble-faced, wearing the oldest clothes I own, spattered in Plymouth Plum or Roanoke Rose or some other paint with a cutesy colonial name. He breezes in looking like he just finished a photo shoot for *GQ*. And I swear on everything we hold sacred, four hours later he doesn't have a speck of paint on him. Like I'd spelled his clothes for him. It was spooky."

"But he still said he needed a shower, right?"

"How did you know?"

"He was at Woodhush a few weeks ago for lunch. I took him out to the tack room to show him the saddle great-great-whatever-grandpa Goare rode to the Revolution, and you *know* what the tack room is like when you're rooting around for the really old stuff. I'm covered in dust and cobwebs, and he's still immaculate, just exactly like he did have one of your wards on his shirt and jeans—but he says he's all grungy, and would I mind if he used the hose to rinse off? You're right, it *is* spooky."

"He took off his shirt?"

"Yeah. It was at least ninety, and we had lemonade on the porch while he dried off—Evan got home about then, and ragged on me the whole evening about tucking my tongue back between my teeth—"

Cam shook his head. "He. Took. Off. His. Shirt."

"Oh." Holly gnawed on that one for a minute. "Do you mean to tell me—? You and he never—oh, Cam!" She cradled his face between her hands, stroking his cheeks with her thumbs. "Does this have to do with trust fund and gorgeous and brand-new Mercedes?"

"Mostly the 'gorgeous' part," he admitted. "Especially back then. People looked at him and thought *six-pack*. They looked at me and thought *beer*."

She simply stared. He'd felt inferior? Him? Cam Griffen of the straight A's and concert-quality piano playing and prodigious magic and big blue eyes and perfectly *lethal* dimples—

Then she remembered an evening featuring a silk dress that split up the back seam and a diamond that fell out of its setting. "*. . . there really ought to be a model or actress or somebody staggeringly gorgeous on your arm. . . .*"

"Yeah, okay—I've been there, too," she admitted. "But you never even gave it a chance, did you? Oh, sweetheart, what am I gonna do with you?"

"Leave it alone. I mean it, Holly. Thanks, I love you—but leave it, okay? You can't fix it, you can't change it. It's just—it's *there*." He sighed, then finished ruefully, "Or I guess I should say it's *not* there."

He sat forward on the bench, elbows on knees, spine in a dejected curve as he stared bleakly at the floodlit white mansion. She rubbed her hands gently across his back like she used to do the summer he was ten years old and trying not to cry after his mother died. "You're a fine, sweet, good man. It's just not fair."

"Fair? Life's supposed to be fair? You've gotten idealistic in your old age."

"I've relearned it."

"For the kids?" He glanced up at her.

"Yeah, now that you mention it. I think that once you become a parent, no matter what's gone on in your life before the kids, you have to believe in things again. Life, love, hope—all the good old clichés. Maybe not in life's being fair, exactly, but at least that there's a chance of it."

"So tell me, Freckles, what's your take on the Pandora story?" He smiled with no humor in his eyes. "All the evils fly out of the box to wreak havoc on humans—but at the bottom is Hope. Is that a kindness? Meant to keep us from total despair? Or is it the cruelest joke of all? That in spite of everything, we're still stupid enough and stubborn enough to hope?"

"You can't mean that. You're not that cynical."

"I'm a lawyer," he reminded her. Something changed in his face and he squinted at Westmoreland. "There's something weird about those windows—"

"What?" Turning to look, she saw only the graceful proportions of a restored antebellum Southern mansion three stories high. "What are you talking about?"

"Are you sure nobody's sensed any magic around here?"

"The place was built more than two hundred years ago, Cam. None of the Nevilles ever had any magic, they never married any of our folk, and if there was any Witchery about the place, somebody would've noticed long before now."

He looked stubborn, then shook his head. "Sorry. For a minute I thought I saw—but it's nothing." Pushing himself to his feet, he wrapped long arms around her and went on, "Do me a favor about Jamey, huh? No lectures, no righteous indignation, no ranting and raving, no hugs, no trying to fix it—"

"If you want to make that 'no hugs' thing stick, you better let go of me."

He pretended to consider. "Nah," he said at last, grinning, and cuddled her closer. "This is nice. You're softer and mushier than you used to be, and it's nice."

"Mushy?! You try having twins sometime, boyo."

"That was over two years ago," he reminded her ungallantly, and patted her backside, making her yelp. "Yeah, if I liked girls, you're the kind of girl I'd like."

"Soft and mushy." Holly narrowed her gaze. "You're gonna want to reconsider your phrasing, there, Peaches. And your next line better be something about the radiance of motherhood."

"Absolutely luminous," he said hastily. "Sparkling. Incandescent, even. You glow in the dark. You're practically radioactive. And *don't* call me 'Peaches'!"

"On one condition."

It amused her that Cam didn't bother with a stop at suspicion; he went directly to certainty, prompted by lifelong knowledge of her character—or lack of same. "No," he announced.

She only smiled.

"How about a compromise?" he pleaded. "If I tell you what went on at Yale, will you—I don't know, *relent,* or something? Maybe?"

January 1994

"SO WHAT HAPPENED TO MORGAN?" Jamey asked, weaving his way through the cramped tangle of furniture in Cam's living room. "Nobody's seen him since we left for Christmas."

"He's gone." Cam spoke to the beer bottle between his palms. "Home."

"What? How come? I know he didn't flunk out—he's smarter than anybody in your whole year."

"He didn't flunk out."

"Well, let's see—what are the usual options? Did he get sick? Break any bones? Piss off somebody at the Dean's Office?"

Cam shook his head.

"Well, he didn't go home to get married because he got some girl pregnant, that's for sure," Jamey said in a tone that invited Cam to smile along with him.

Cam had never felt less like smiling in his entire life. But Jamey didn't deserve his snarl. So he made his tone as calm and gentle as he could. "How about I only say this once, and then we never talk about it again?"

"Okay," Jamey said warily. "But it sounds like I'd better sit down."

Cam felt the far end of the sagging old couch dip, heard the soft scratch of denim against worn upholstery as Jamey scooted deep into the cushions. Cam didn't look at him, because he knew exactly what he'd see. Spine straight; no slumping for Mama Stirling's darling boy. Right arm on the doily Gary's grandmother had knitted or crocheted or whatever it was old ladies did with yarn to make useless ornamentation for antiquated couches donated to keep their grandsons from having to sit on the floor. Left arm close to his side, long fingers resting lightly on his thigh. Knees apart but not too far apart; no vulgar sprawling allowed, either. Feet—what was it today, sneakers or loafers? He snuck a glance, saw brown Italian leather below thick wool socks and the fraying hems of old Levi's. Cam knew that pair of jeans, the way they fit just snugly enough to entice but not incite. He also knew the familiar baggy shape of an old black sweater, too comfortable to toss out but too ratty to wear to class, the kind of sweater rich boys wore because . . . well, because that was just the kind of sweater rich boys wore when they weren't wearing excruciatingly tailored Ralph Lauren.

Cam knew what expression would be on that face with its patrician bone structure and wide, sincere, extravagantly lashed eyes. Jamey would look concerned and curious, and unnervingly patient while Cam found the words. Jamey was always patient. He waited so quietly, he never paced or fretted or drummed his fingers. He simply waited. But the thing Cam knew he was truly waiting for was the thing Cam had resolved never to give him.

Oddly enough, Jamey had taught him patience, too. Or maybe it was restraint. Whatever, it felt like cactus needles in his guts and he didn't much like it. But if it kept him from touching the kid, fine. He'd be patient, he'd be restrained, he'd swallow poisoned thorns with a Sam Adams chaser if only he could live out this last semester of law school without putting a finger on Jamey.

They'd erratically circled each other since last August, like wayward planets searching for a mutual center of gravity. Cam knew the attraction was mutual. Jamey didn't understand that it was also mutually disastrous. They were in law school; they didn't have time for this. Maybe if they were both anticipating a future in private practice, maybe there would have been a hope. But Cam wanted a career in international law, and he didn't want to have to keep paranoid lists of which countries stipulated jail time and/or execution for homosexuals. Jamey was planning a stint as a district attorney on the way to political office—which of course was just the perfect milieu for a guy who liked guys.

Thus what Jamey waited so patiently for, Cam would never give him.

He was bemused and fascinated by this gorgeous kid who had so obviously been waiting all his life to fall insanely in love. But Cam wasn't going to be the one Jamey did the crazy with. He wasn't going to be the one to break Jamey's heart. He didn't want that on his conscience. If Jamey was going to louse up his life, he'd have to do it with somebody else.

Cam would never admit to how many hours he'd spent staring at ceiling plaster or faded wallpaper or the lighted dial of his alarm clock, anxiety gnawing at him. Especially after he realized what a hypocrite he was. Jamey's heart was going to get broken; that was a stone cold fact. And Cam would be the one to do it, because Jamey was in love with him.

"Cam?"

No impatience in the question, just worry. He'd been silent too long, he knew. He'd meant to say it, to tell Jamey the whole thing. Now he just couldn't. "Morgan went home to Idaho. He didn't flunk out. As is indeed obvious to anybody with half a brain, he didn't get some girl pregnant. He's just—he's not coming back. Can we please leave it at that?"

Long pause. "Well—okay."

Mother of All Mercy, how could this kid love him so much that he was willing to accept without question? Anybody else would have been demanding explanations right now. Not Jamieson Tyler Stirling.

No, he had something else in mind. Something infinitely worse.

"So you guys are short a roommate until the end of the year."

"No."

"You don't even know what I'm about to suggest!"

"Yeah, I really do. And no, *you* really don't."

"And the award for Best Obfuscation Using a Single Breath goes to—"

"Knock it off."

"All I was going to say was—"

"No."

"Will you for Christ's sake let me finish?"

"No." Cam put his beer down and pushed himself out of the couch's sluggish clasp. "I need coffee. You're buying."

And you're not moving in with us. That's all I need, my final semester in law school when I'm gonna be insane anyway: you *in the shower down the hall every morning.*

They walked the five blocks in silence. Cam stared down at his own feet practically the whole way, at the same boots he'd brought with him to Yale as a freshman. If the boots had been pristine and virginal back then, they were worn out as a twenty-buck whore now. He sort of felt the same.

Not that he'd been virginal back then. Not quite, anyway. The "not quite" was due to Holly's fixing him up with a guy she knew from grad school at UCLA. He and Mac had lasted from July to the end of August, that summer before Yale, while Mac learned the horse-farm business from Lulah and Cam learned the finer points of the apothecary's art from Cousin Clary Sage, as was traditional in the family. He'd studied what every Witch should know about herbs and spices and flowers and trees—though he was principally interested in anything that would help him get through four years of college and three of law school, which made Clarissa grin and give him the appropriate recipe book. Once Mac entered the picture, Cam had played around with a few other kinds of spells, but being too scared to use them had actually been a good thing. Mac liked him without magic. A long moonlit chat with Holly on the Fourth of July clued him in to the value of being wanted for what you were rather than what you could do. But if, as a going-away present, Cam had secretly spelled Mac's favorite riding boots to keep his feet warm when it was snowing and dry when it was raining, nobody ever knew it but Cam. And Holly, who had contributed a few drops of blood. It was the only magic he could give Mac in exchange for teaching him the magic of skin on skin.

Since then there had been few lovers. He was like Holly that way: neither of them could simply fall into bed with someone. He supposed it had to do with trust; a Witch out in the wider world learned wariness, like it or not. Holly's opinion was that the two of them were just fastidious—or, to put it less delicately, damned difficult to please. Whatever. Cam knew who and what he was, and how he wanted his life to evolve, and his plans didn't include sleeping with anybody who would out him.

Not that Jamey ever would. It was just that Jamey was too young and too innocent and too in love with the idea of being in love to think it all through. So Cam would have to do the thinking for him.

They reached the coffee bar without saying a word to each other. Cam ordered Sumatran, black. He'd go back to sugaring up his caffeine fixes during finals, but for now he was trying to lose a couple of pounds. Jamey indulged himself with a combination of coffee, chocolate, coconut syrup, and whipped cream that should have sent him into insulin shock.

"They should call that the Giant Rat," Jamey said as they chose a table near the back. When Cam gave him a puzzled frown, he explained, "Your coffee. Sherlock Holmes, the Giant Rat of Sumatra."

"You'd get along fine with my cousin Holly—a constant barrage of obscure references nobody but Lit. majors ever understand."

For a moment Cam thought Jamey was going to argue against any reference to Sherlock Holmes being *obscure*. Cam was wrong. What Jamey said was: "Morgan came out to his parents, didn't he?"

Cam blinked, swallowed a gulp of coffee, and coughed.

"Sorry. I just thought I'd try to shock you into admitting it. I mean, not that anybody ever thought the guy was straight—or that you and Gary and Keith are anything *but* perfectly straight—it's just that he—and you and Gary and Keith aren't—and since he didn't flunk out or get sick or anything, it was only logical to assume—"

"Jamey," he asked grimly, "do you have any idea what the hell you're talking about?"

"Um—no, I guess not."

"Then maybe you'd better shut up, okay?" Cam sighed, settling back in his chair. Jazz from a soprano sax seeped from the house speakers, just loud enough to cover conversation. Cam often brought Jamey here: they could talk without being disturbed, while fully aware that any inept reaction would disturb others. Nobody paid any attention to anybody else unless voices were raised above the music. At that point, arching eyebrows and meaningful stares exiled the nuisance. This unspoken etiquette had kept Jamey from coming on to him too obviously. It had also kept Cam honest.

And honesty, he realized, was something he owed the kid.

"Okay, here it comes," he said suddenly. "Yeah, Morgan told his folks. Just the Christmas present they wanted, as you can imagine. I don't know how many people there are in that flyspeck town he comes from, but if any of 'em are gay they don't admit it. Ever. Morgan did. So now he's in a treatment program."

"Excuse me?" Cloud-gray eyes went impossibly wider.

"Morgan's parents sent him to queer rehab. They want to fix him."

"Was he broken?"

Cam chose to ignore the peculiar juxtaposition of innocent inquiry and cynical commentary. "From their point of view, yeah. From what I understand, the claim is that these people can turn gays into ex-gays."

Jamey was silent for a moment. Then: "Does it work?"

Cam stared at him, bewildered anew. "Huh?"

"It would seem unlikely," Jamey mused, stirring whipped cream down into his coffee. "More evidence is found every year that sexuality isn't a choice, it's an orientation. The way a person's brain is wired. I wonder when they'll find a combination of genes that will clinch the deal and shut these people up."

"Even if they did find proof, it wouldn't matter," Cam replied. "It's right there in the Bible, folks. God says no, so even if God made you the way you are, you can't *be* the way you are without God getting pissed off and sending you straight to hell."

"And Morgan's parents believe in the Bible."

"Oh, yeah." He swallowed more coffee, missing the sugar rush, needing the caffeine. "I got an e-mail from his father. Pack up all his stuff, please, we'll send you a check for the shipping costs." He sighed and shook his head. "I wrote back and asked if Morgan was okay. His father then apologized for his son, said he hoped Gary and Keith and I hadn't been tainted, and that he was sure we hadn't suspected Morgan was mentally diseased because, of course if we had, we would've ratted him out."

"'Mentally diseased'? That's what he called it? What did you write back?"

"I haven't yet. I just got that e-mail last weekend and I've been so mad I can't get my hands to stop shaking long enough to type. Spellcheck can only get you so far," he added sardonically. "But I did start packing Morgan's things. He had a couple of pamphlets about how to tell your parents you're gay. One of them said to be sure to have a place to go the night you tell your family, because it's a mortal lock that they'll throw you out of the house. If you don't set up somewhere to go in advance, you end up sleeping on the street."

Jamey said nothing for a moment, then took a long swallow of coffee, put the cup down, and met Cam's gaze. "Is that how it was for you?"

He was twenty-six years and four months old and he was convinced he was having a heart attack. Or a stroke. Or a convulsion or a conniption or a seizure or something not immediately fatal but dangerous all the same.

"Cam, breathe."

Maybe he'd just pass out. Yeah, that sounded good. Give in to the whirring and buzzing and black-speckled haze in front of his eyes, fall face-first onto the table, and not have to deal with this.

Except that the little chunk of amber on its gold chain around his neck felt a bit warmer next to his heart, gift of the eldest son to the eldest son in the Griffen family for over two hundred years. Amber for confidence and mental clarity; a strong memory and power of decision; protection, defense—*"And it even cures hay fever!"* He remembered his father telling him that, and giving him one of his big, light-the-world grins. He missed those grins. He took a deep breath, and felt the amber shift against his skin.

"I'm not gonna ask how you knew." His voice sounded almost normal. He'd put a lot of time and effort into presenting an outward image that was so normal he even bored himself. He dated enough women to make suspicion ridiculous; he slept with enough of them to make his sexuality a non-issue; he went to sports bars with the guys to watch big-screen TV baseball in the spring and football in the autumn; he snickered at the jokes and innuendos just the way a straight guy should. So he wasn't going to ask how Jamey knew. He just knew; there was nothing Cam could do about it.

Jamey said, "You don't fit any of the stereotypes—whatever those are anymore. I just— I suppose I was kind of hoping. If you were, then maybe someday I might be able to—"

"Oh, no. No way. Never. Not in a million years."

Downcast eyes, bitten lip, shamed whisper: "You don't— I'm not your type—"

"Not my—oh, shit." Cam sprang to his feet, his chair tipping over behind him with a discourteous clatter. He could feel the stares. "We gotta get outta here," he said fiercely. "Come on, Jamey. Let's go."

"Cam—"

Everyone was being forced to notice them now. And that was the last thing either of them needed. "Let's *go*!"

A minute later they were back outside. The cold scraped at the skin of Cam's face and hands, scoured his throat and lungs with every breath. Jamey hurried along at his elbow. Cam didn't look at him.

It was colder, and there were fewer people on the street. No one passed close enough to hear Cam as he said, "I know what you want to do with your life—and you're gonna be great. Governor, Congressman, Senator—you can be anything you want, Jamey, but you can't be this. You can't fuck it all up by fucking other men."

A hand locked around his arm. He couldn't shake it off, so he stopped walking, turned, and glared down the three inches that separated them in height.

"Shut up," Jamey ordered, scornfully unintimidated. "Just shut up. Do I look that stupid? I know everything you're going to say, and I don't want to hear it from you the way I've heard it from myself ever since I met you!"

Cam considered those furious gray eyes for a moment, then asked mildly, "Well, whoever was talking, were you actually listening?"

Jamey shoved both hands into his pockets. "No."

"Didn't think so." With a shrug, as if none of this mattered, he lengthened his strides—hoping Jamey would get the idea and just go home or something.

Instead, a soft, wet, freezing load of snow hit the back of his head.

"Hey!" As he swung around, another snowball struck him in the shoulder. Jamey was grinning as if he'd just pitched a no-hitter at Dodger Stadium.

"You really want to bring that to the party, Pretty Boy?" Cam taunted.

"You really want to call me that, Grandpa?"

He sternly reminded himself that he was, in fact, twenty-six, not a hundred-and-twelve; twenty-six, damn it, not eight-and-a-half—

He scooped, packed, and let fly twice before Jamey recovered from astonishment and started retaliatory fire.

When they were breathless and soaked and splattered in white, Cam shook his hair free of snow and glared as fiercely as he could. Jamey's carefree laughter warmed him more thoroughly than one of his own spells set into his socks.

"You were *way* too serious," Jamey explained before Cam could even ask. *"Misce stultitiam consiliis brevem: dulce est desipere in loco."*

Rolling his eyes, he fought a grin. Every law student knew enough Latin to get by; Jamey had taken four years of it in high school and another four at William and Mary. "Okay, who is it this time? Virgil? Livy? Emperor Augustus?"

"Horace. 'Mix a little foolishness with your serious plans: it's lovely to be silly at the right moment.' I had to do it, Cam. You looked like all the Brothers Grimm rolled into one."

"There were only two of them. And are you calling me a fairy tale?"

"One more 'Pretty Boy' in my direction, and you'll be—" Jamey broke off the threat, shaking his head. "I was going to say you'd be singing soprano for the Whiffenpoofs, but that wouldn't suit my plans for you at all."

Before Cam could point out that whatever those plans were, they would require him to be at least marginally cooperative and *that* absolutely wasn't going to happen, he saw that Jamey was shivering. "Let's get to my place before we both catch pneumonia," he said gruffly. And the whole walk back, he wondered why he didn't just spell Jamey's coat and sweater and shoes for warmth—as a good-bye present before telling him to go away and never come back.

They sat on the sofa in Cam's fourth-floor walk-up, right back where they'd started, except that the geophysics had shifted and the laws of gravity—shared or not—no longer applied. Cam sprawled, and Jamey sat straight-spined, and thirty-six inches of upholstery sagged between them—just like earlier, just as if nothing had changed. But there was no balance, no equilibrium between attraction and resistance. It was all wobbly and fluctuating and it scared the shit out of him. Jamey knew, had known forever; it was all out in the open now.

"I went on-line," Cam said abruptly, "and looked into programs like the one Morgan's parents checked him into. It's called 'reparative therapy' or 'conversion therapy.' One place is kind of an Onward Christian Soldiers thing, waging spiritual warfare against homosexuality. Another of them says that it's akin to the whole experience of being 'born again'—that you have to die before you can be reborn as a heterosexual. What they do—nine times out of ten they're not even licensed medical or psychological practitioners, they've had no training except in religion, and it's not just the Evangelicals and the Mormons, it's Catholics and Jews and—"

Jamey was shaking his head. "I don't want to talk about Morgan. I'm sorry for him, and I hope his parents decide they love him more than they're scared of him, but he's not me. My parents know—they knew practically before I did. It took a while, yeah, but they're okay with it. They didn't disown me or tell me I'm going to hell, and they sure as shit would never send me to rehab—"

"All hail the Great American Liberal," Cam snapped. "Your parents, my dad, almost all my relatives—"

"Almost?"

"A few of them are kind of hysterically religious, and we don't have much to do with them anyway except when somebody gets married or buried—but that's not the point," he interrupted himself impatiently. "Our families aren't society at large, Jamey. With all the talking you did with yourself, did you ever ask if it'd be worth it to you?"

"With you, it would be," Jamey replied quietly.

"You can't say stuff like that," he admonished, feeling dizzy as the gravitational constant of the universe shifted again. "You really can't."

"I really can," he answered with a tiny smile.

"Yeah? So I'm worth your whole life being about being gay? Because that's what happens. You become the token queer, the faggot in the corner office that shows how enlightened the partners are—hell, maybe even you become the Gay Congressman. And anything else you are gets subsumed and you get defined by one thing only."

"It has to be that way, does it?"

"Two choices." Two only: give in to the attraction and smash into each other to their mutual destruction, or continue to resist and somehow survive this. "Come out, live openly, maybe find somebody and maybe even be happy. And everything else you want to do with your life, you can kiss it all good-bye. The *only* thing anybody will see about you is that you're gay."

"And the second choice is to live a lie."

He nodded slowly. "And if you find somebody you can love, you both have to be careful every minute of every day." He leaned forward, elbows on knees, hands clasped between them so they wouldn't shake too much. "But, Jamey, that way you still get to do all the rest of it! You get to live the other parts of your life, do the work you were meant to do, have people look at you and see a man, a human being, instead of—"

"I don't have to ask which decision you made."

"Yeah. And for now, I'm gonna make the decision for you."

"How noble. How generous."

He ignored the sarcasm. "For now, during law school and while you figure out your future, you have to keep your mouth shut. Because once you're out, that's it. All other choices and all other definitions vanish." He hunched forward, feeling his finger bones grind together. "Dammit—you're smart, good-looking, articulate—"*—with the most beautiful eyes I've ever seen and a mind that works at hyperdrive—*"—you've got charm to burn, but you've also got something better than that—charisma. You're funny, you think fast on your feet—"*—you're proud and honorable and your smile ought to be declared a National Treasure—*"—you've got so much going for you it's scary. You're Luke fucking Skywalker, only you wouldn't know the Dark Side of the Force if it introduced itself and bought you a beer. I'm not gonna let you screw up. Especially not over somebody like me."

"Like you? What do you mean, like you? Goddammit, Cam, don't you *know*? You think I've been hanging around because I want a head start on my third year when I haven't even finished my first? What's wrong with you? If I'm gonna screw up—and may I remind you here that it's *my* life and if I want to screw it up, I can goddammed well screw it up however I want and with whomever I want and I don't completely accept your premise anyway, but what we're talking about here is—is—"

He'd gotten lost in his own sentence. Cam felt a tiny grin tug one corner of his mouth. "You want to start that one over?"

"Fuck you!"

"You have no idea how much I wish you would. But it's not gonna happen. Not with me. I'd never be able to live with myself."

"So your answer is no."

"I'm not even gonna let you ask the question."

Jamey stared for a moment—and then lunged across the threadbare sofa cushions and kissed him.

Nothing imploded. Nothing smashed into a million pieces. He wondered why he had thought they'd crush each other with the force of this thing between them. Whatever had happened at the beginning, the impulse that had started a spin of matter and energy and spirit that had coalesced into their two separate beings, they had found their center of gravity. It felt entirely natural, completely right.

Slowly, he felt himself begin to change. Hands moved over him, not exploring in the way of a new lover but shaping, polishing, and he responded helplessly as those hands made of his previously ordinary body a work of art. He forgot to remember why all this couldn't happen. He didn't feel as if anything were happening at all—nothing new, anyway, nothing that wasn't true and inevitable and preordained, like middle C and light speed. Not even the most eloquent magic had such power as this man had over him.

The panic was minor, compared to the grief. Neither interfered with what he did next. Very deliberately, he sought out the marker in his brain that very talented Witches had taught him to find and use. He directed that peculiarity to the amber nestled near his heart and bespelled every stitch Jamey wore with bitter, bone-chilling cold.

The younger man lurched back. Cam followed him with his eyes, as if trying to memorize the path he would need to take to return to that mouth, those hands. But he needed to forget that there even was such a place as Jamey's arms. Jamey snagged up the afghan crocheted by Gary's grandmother and wrapped himself in it. Cam Worked on that, too, casually, instinctively—taking bleak satisfaction in his own expertise. Jamey would tremble and shiver until Cam unWorked the magic.

This was the only sin his faith acknowledged: doing harm to another. Hurting Jamey was inevitable. Like gravity. Like magic.

His magic, that could delicately mend a tattered heirloom quilt or subtly deflect raindrops when he'd forgotten to wear his coat—his magic could bind and his magic could repel. He could use it as the opposite of gravity, and he could fend off Jamey as if Jamey was nothing more than inconvenient rain.

Cam looked him right in his innocent, troubled gray eyes. "Something wrong?"

He huddled, shivering. "Don't you feel how cold it is?"

"Maybe you're coming down with something. Maybe you ought to go home." He felt cold, too. Ice water in his veins, wasn't that the cliché? Holly would kick him into the middle of next week if she found out he'd even thought it. Holly would kick him into the middle of the next millennium if she found out what he'd just done. "Yeah, I think you should go home and we won't talk about this again."

"Cam—" He was still clutching the thick wool to him, all previous experience stubbornly insisting that it could warm him, would warm him, if only he waited long enough. "Cam—please, I don't know what's going on—"

If Cam had his way—and the magic pretty well ensured that he would—Jamey would never know. A glancing thought rescinded the unnatural chill. Jamey caught his breath and let the afghan drop to the floor; Cam saw the colors bunch around expensively scuffed loafers. Instinct made him grab Jamey's discarded coat and toss it at him. So easy, it was so damned easy—he finished a new spell while the thing was still in the air. Just the lining, just the thin silk within thick wool, so that when Jamey put it on he would feel the revulsion Worked into it. That had been particularly easy: all it took was redirection of what Cam felt about himself. Just the lining, so no one touching Jamey would sense anything; just for an hour, until he got back to his own place fully convinced that all he felt for Cam was disgust. He had only to put the coat on, and feel what Cam wanted him to feel, and he would be gone within minutes.

But Jamey stood there, fists clenched around his coat, staring at Cam with wide, startled eyes. "I've never known anybody as terrified as you are. It's as if this was the Middle Ages, and the Inquisition would throw you in jail and you'd be burned at the stake like a witch or a heretic—"

"YOU FREAKED RIGHT THEN and there, didn't you?" Holly asked.

"Well, being both a Witch *and* a heretic—twice over, seeing as how I'm a deviant from the One True Faith of Catholicism *and* the One True Faith of Heterosexuality—"

"Stop it."

"Yeah," he said wearily. "Okay. So I took the pilgrimage to Salem a little too seriously right after Mom died. Dad wanted to visit the cousins, and how was he to know a couple of 'em had gotten religion and renounced the ancestors?"

Thereby scaring a ten-year-old boy half to death. Unlike Holly, Cam descended from several New England lines of Witches. A perceptive if not actually prescient forefather had fled Salem for Virginia a few years before the hysteria of the 1690s. Among those of the Craft, Pocahontas County had always been known as a safe haven.

Their slow walk while Cam told the story had taken them around to the back of the Inn. A hundred yards or so from the kitchen entrance was a dormitory, windows on both floors blazing as the staff enjoyed a night off. The other buildings—conference rooms, offices, and so on—were dark but for some security floods.

"Anyway," Cam said, "that's pretty much it. We didn't see each other very often for the rest of the year, and then I got my J.D., and—"

"What happened to Morgan?"

"I shoulda known a novelist would want the whole story. If I tell you I ranted some more and that was the end of it, would you even pretend to believe me?"

"Not a chance."

"Thought so."

April 4, 1994

Dear Cam—

You will have heard the news about me before you get this. I didn't want to use anything other than snailmail because I didn't want you phoning anybody to try and stop me. You can't. Nobody can.

It won't be any surprise to you that I'm gay. I know about you, too. Months of sleeping across a room from each other, and we never said a word about what we really are. Thank you for respecting my privacy. I hope you feel that I respected yours.

He'd read the letter only twice in the week since receiving it. He had expected Jamey to show up the afternoon that the news came about Morgan, but Gary figured that people were mostly staying away, giving them time to cope. Cam stifled a cynical smile; people stayed away because they didn't know whether to console him and Gary and Keith as Morgan's friends and roommates or as his fellow queers and possible lovers.

I got sick of the game and the pretense, and I told my parents. I should have kept my stupid mouth shut. My father's world is white, male, straight, patriarchal, Christian, conservative. His wife and children are supposed to do and believe what he tells them, just as he does and believes what the Church tells him (with a ten percent tithe for the privilege, of course). What the Church tells him is that his son is a pervert who is going to hell if he doesn't get married and have kids and perpetuate the whole sorry tradition. Do you know what he said to me before he took me to this place? Direct quote: "I have beliefs as a Christian and I have rights as a father, and this is the way it's going to be."

So here I am at Straight School—where I've been force-fed a gutful of fundamentalism that makes me vomit almost as bad as the chemicals they make me sniff if I get an erection while they're showing me pictures of naked men. (I'm lucky, I guess, that they don't use electroshock anymore. Or at least that they didn't use it on me.) They say that if I have enough faith, if I pray and fast and sing hymns enough, then my homosexuality will go away. It didn't. It hasn't. It won't. So I am a failure. I am a disgrace to my family, a scandal to my Church, a deviant from orthodoxy.

The three of them played it perfectly. Keith indulged in conspicuous public displays of affection with his girlfriend (and accelerated his planned proposal by several months, leading to rumors of pregnancy that turned out to be untrue). Gary made it known that Rhoda Petrovich had spent the weekend with him through the simple expedient of returning her bra on Monday afternoon at the front desk of the library during her shift (she never spoke to him again, but that was okay—she'd served her purpose). Cam—the only one of them who was gay—was seen with Mariella Marquez at, respectively, a salsa bar, a lecture at the School of Drama, and Sunday mass. He and Mariella had a longstanding understanding: she was his beard when he needed to appear straight, and he did her the same favor when her parents visited from New Jersey (they were willing to gloss over that he was Irish and Welsh in favor of his Catholicism), which neatly distracted their attention from her Hindu boyfriend.

I don't know how much you Catholics know about my Church, but it suffices that the Church is always right, and anyone who disagrees is wrong and therefore evil. Feminists, for example. There's a really choice Pat Robertson quote: "The feminist agenda is not about equal rights for women. It is a socialist, anti-family political movement that encourages women to leave their husbands, kill their children, practice witchcraft, destroy capitalism, and become lesbians." He really wrote that in a 1992 fundraising letter. But I think even the Fundies are finally getting the idea that the ship has sailed on that particular piece of patriarchy. So now the focus is on us. Gays are almost too easy for them, you know? It doesn't take any effort at all to demonize us. It only takes one word. AIDS.

My Church says I should find a nice girl, get married, and have lots of babies, and this would cure me. What they mean is that I should lie to this nice girl and pretend that I never had a single thought about men. The only thing worse, as far as I can see, would be to tell her the truth, with the implication that the responsibility for what I am is now on her, to make sure I'm fucked often enough that I won't want men. If I had a "relapse" it would be because she wasn't woman enough to keep me from being gay.

A few envelopes arrived with notes of condolence and checks for helping out with the flowers everyone assumed had been sent. Cam cashed the checks and made an anonymous donation to the campus gay and lesbian alliance.

My Church says I am evil because of the way I feel love. I am sick because of the way I experience sexual attraction. I am destined for eternal damnation because of what's inside me that isn't the same as what's inside straights. One of the "counselors" here told us poor sick queers that whereas physical death still gives the hope of spiritual resurrection, returning to The Gay Lifestyle (I could hear the capital letters) is spiritual death and there's no recovery from that. I really wanted to ask him what he thought The Gay Lifestyle is. I really wanted to ask him what The Straight Lifestyle is. Do all straight people behave the same way, believe in the same things, listen to the same music, share the same politics (God, how I wanted to mention the Log Cabin Republicans!), and make love only in the missionary position? But of course I didn't ask. Mainly because I'm a coward. They're eager here to provide answers, but they also provide all the questions.

Cam was in daily expectation of Jamey's arrival at the apartment. When he finally did come over, Cam let him in, told him Gary and Keith were out for the afternoon, and handed him Morgan's letter.

Actually, this place did provide one blessed reassurance: that there are so many just like me. But within my Church—within all Fundamentalist Christian denominations—there are only two alternatives: grim determination to succeed at becoming straight, or grim acceptance that our faith isn't strong enough to cure us and therefore we must live celibate and solitary lives. I can't see myself doing either. Did I mention that some of these guys are fifteen or sixteen years old? Did I mention that some of the older guys have been in this "therapy" for years?

He went about making coffee, unable to face their usual walk down to their usual hangout. Stray glances caught a sudden stiffening of Jamey's shoulders, a brief tremor of his hand as he read Morgan's letter.

Eventually society will accept that we're just people. That's all. Nothing more, nothing less. I don't have the strength to wait for "eventually." I don't have the courage to be open about what I am. I can't face years of being told I'm not believing hard enough. I've lost my family and my Church. I'm afraid I'm about to lose my deepest faith in the God of forgiveness and understanding, the God I always knew loved me whatever my doubts and failings. I just want it all to stop.

You can show this letter to whomever. It won't matter to me. I have only one thing left to tell you—and it's not profound or wise, it's just a hope.

Live your life, Cam.

Morgan

By the time Jamey placed the pages on the kitchen table—gently, carefully, as if they were some kind of relic—Cam had finished making coffee. He set out mugs and sugar and milk and spoons, slid into the chair opposite Jamey, and waited for the reaction. Jamey really had taught him patience.

"How did it happen?" he asked at last, head bent over the letter.

"Couple of silk ties and a ceiling fan."

"No, I meant how did it happen that parents could send their own child away to be tortured?" He looked up, his eyes the soft, grieving gray of rain clouds. "They'll never see how wrong they are, will they?"

"Probably not." He leaned back and stared out the small, snow-wrapped window above the kitchen sink.

"Cam? It doesn't have to be like that. Not for us."

"Don't you get it? Are you really that naïve? It's the Age of AIDS. Or, as Pat Buchanan called it, 'nature's revenge on homosexuals.'"

"Conservative Christians changed their minds about slavery," Jamey protested. "And racial segregation, and miscegenation—some have even started acknowledging women's rights. They can change their minds!"

"In whose lifetime? Do you really want to be a poster boy for gay rights?"

Now the eyes turned to steel. "*You* don't even want to try."

Cam didn't answer directly. "I have a couple of honorary uncles—and they *are* a couple. Have been for years and years. Alec is a lawyer with a big firm in New York, and Nicky owns a bookshop specializing in mysteries—you'd love it." He smiled briefly. "Jamey, what they've got is the most they can hope for. It's not a lie, but it's not the truth, either. When I first talked about it with them, they told me that I was so many more things than just gay—"

Alec's exact words had been, *"You're a Witch with a talent for textiles, you play Rachmaninoff the way Rachmaninoff always wished he could, you have a good heart and a fine mind and the best dimples since Shirley Temple. You're lousy at basketball and you can't shoot pool worth a damn, but you're a hell of a softball player. You'll be brilliant at whatever you decide to do after college and law school—but you'll never be a courtroom lawyer because you never shut up and that drives judges and juries insane. You're honorable, honest, funny, your family and friends adore you—and oh, by the way, you're homosexual. Now, what's your life going to be about?"*

"—but 'gay' is all people will ever see," Jamey finished for him. "I get it, Cam. We've had this talk before, remember? You don't have to write it in words of one syllable or less and shove it in my face."

"Words," he echoed bitterly. "You have no idea of the words—" He jumped up and headed for the bedroom he had shared with Morgan—each knowing exactly what the other was and neither saying a word about it. On the bed nearest the window were the last scatters of Morgan's clothing, CDs, framed photographs, books. More relics. Cam grabbed a manila envelope stuffed with papers and returned to the kitchen.

"These came with that letter," he began, pulling out pamphlets and flyers and slick brochures. "Morgan's parents made a real project of it, collecting this stuff from every ex-gay organization in the country, doing the research, making sure—"

"Cam—"

"Dammit, where's—yeah, this one. 'Homosexuality is an unintentionally acquired condition that may have biological, developmental, and psychological causes. It is not a predetermined or unchangeable condition, but one that can be altered.' It's caused by a defective bond with good ol' emotionally distant Dad, which led to incomplete development of masculine identity. We don't *really* want to have sex with men, we want the emotional closeness that Dad withheld from us, and by the time we figure this out we've hit puberty, which of course means we sexualize everything—hey, what do you want to bet Morgan's father went into orbit when he found out that according to this theory, *he's* the reason his son turned out gay?"

"Cam. Stop it."

He ignored Jamey's quiet command, searching for a particular flyer. "This one—I love this one. It advises work, exercise, and prayer—what, no vitamin supplements?—and says we probably wouldn't have become gay if we'd had more rough-and-tumble on the playground, and fights with other kids. As we all know, beating the shit out of other people, especially while we're children, is a well-known method of establishing a really first-rate male identity."

"This has nothing to do with us."

"Doesn't it? Don't you understand how society defines you? Did you know, for instance, that we can't be faithful? There's no real meaning in our relationships because we can't be married, and therefore we can never experience a real commitment, and therefore we have emotional problems because we're insecure about our lover's fidelity, which can't be real faithfulness because we can't get married and have the relationship sanctioned and protected by law. I'd purely love to know why we get held up as examples of promiscuity when half of all straight marriages end in divorce. How many fathers are thrilled when their sons lose their virginity—and not, I hasten to add, on the wedding night? The more women a man fucks, the more of a man he is. He's not promiscuous. Oh, no. Just studly."

"I'm not listening to any more of this."

"Yeah, you are—because I know where you want to take this and this is my only chance to explain to you why it's never going to happen! Did you know that nobody is actually *gay*? Where's the page—it must be here someplace—oh, fuck it, who cares? I can tell you everything it said. We have 'inappropriate' attractions which can be overcome with the help of Jesus. But why do the feelings happen in the first place? Well, it can't be God's fault, because God doesn't make mistakes, and homosexuality is definitely a mistake—so queers aren't queers because God made them that way, but if God makes everything and everybody, then being queer really doesn't exist! It's just 'inappropriate feelings.' Isn't that comforting? You're not really gay, Jamey, neither am I. Nobody is. We're just confused."

"Cam, will you for Christ's sake stop it? You're not telling me anything I don't already know!" Jamey stood, paced the five cramped steps around the kitchen, then turned and confronted him. "It's nothing to do with us. Can't you see that? I'm sorry for Morgan, I wish to God he hadn't— I wish his Church or his parents or this 'therapy' hadn't driven him to—" Suddenly he caught his breath. "You're blaming yourself, aren't you? Cam, what he did isn't your fault!"

"I knew about him. He knew about me. Those closets we're all in, they're deep and they're dark. They're locked, Jamey. We can't even look out of them to see that somebody else is in trouble, let alone sneak out far enough to offer some help, because somebody might be watching—"

"Why do you hate yourself so much? This isn't just Morgan. You're scared and ashamed, and you wish to God you were straight—"

"Wouldn't any reasonable person? That's what's so ludicrous about people saying we 'choose' to be gay. Why do they think that anyone would willingly choose the kind of intolerance and bigotry and discrimination—not to mention there's always the possibility of getting beaten to a pulp—" And the magic in him whispered, *—or burned at the stake.* "I'm one of the lucky ones, Jamey. I've got a family who loves me, supports me—not like Morgan's family, saying it's because they love him and it's for his own good, for the good of his immortal soul, when really they despised him and wanted him to change so *they* didn't have to be ashamed—"

"So why is any of it your fault?"

"We all share the fault!"

Jamey drew back. "Those of us who stay closeted betray those who don't, is that it? And every time one of us gets caught and disgraced—or sent to Straight School to be tortured into heterosexuality—"

"—and the rest of us scramble to shore up the pretenses that allow us to exist in this society. Yeah. Think about it, Jamey—think about it realistically, not the way you want it to be. Why does it never happen that the newspapers say, 'Bill Jones, a thirty-nine-year-old heterosexual, robbed a liquor store last night'? A straight man can beat the living shit out of a gay man and get away with it by saying the queer was coming on to him. A lesbian can get raped and that's actually doing her a favor because it shows her what real sex is like! And all the hysteria about 'recruitment' of young boys—has anyone checked the statistics? By far the majority of child molesters are straight men who go after little girls!"

"What does this have to do with *us?*" Jamey shouted. "What does any of it have to do with what we feel for each other?"

Cam clenched both hands in the pile of papers and bent his head, trying not to be physically sick. A warm hand stroked his back, and in spite of himself he calmed a little—like a skittish colt responding to the touch of the man who was gentling him.

"Listen to me," said the soft voice. "That's an ignorant, self-righteous, terrified minority—"

"—who sit in boardrooms, and state capital buildings, and the United States Congress," Cam interrupted thickly. "They're on school boards. They run city governments. They're cops and firefighters and the girl who makes your cappuccino and the guy who delivers your mail. And they hate us, Jamey. They don't know anything about us, and they hate us."

"So make them know who we are."

"'We're queer and we're here'?" he quoted, shaking his head. "You're still not getting it. You come out, and that's what your life is about for the rest of your life. You're gay. You don't get to do or be anything else. Nothing else you say or do ever matters."

"It matters what we do as men."

"As *gay* men."

After a few moments' quiet, Cam said, "What are you doing to me, Jamey? What do you think is going to happen? We can settle for less than we want and less than we dreamed, and less than we could be—"

"—in order to have each other. So we make a trade. I'd do it in an instant, you know I would. To be with you, I'd—"

"You haven't even gotten a taste of what you can become."

"So we wait a while."

"How long? Five years? Ten? We establish ourselves in the lives we always wanted, and then what? You think people will look at you and still think, 'Hey, potential Senator here'? You know they won't. They'll think, 'Hey, look at the queer who thinks he can be a Senator'—and then they'd either laugh themselves into a coma or start looking around for bricks to throw."

Jamey searched his face long and hard. Then: "I'll live the lie for you, Cam. If that's what you want."

He shook his head. "Denying what I feel for you isn't a lie I could tell."

His eyes shone silver, like—like moonlight, Cam thought helplessly, knowing he should never have said what he'd just said. It wasn't fair to either of them. It trapped them both. "No," he warned, taking a step back as Jamey started toward him. "Not gonna happen. Not any of it."

"You can't say something like that and then expect me to just—Cam, I've been waiting forever to hear you say it, not just since the day I met you—"

It was exactly as he'd originally thought: in love with falling in love. Cam told himself that that was all it was, that he'd been convenient, that it could have been anybody—

"I didn't actually say it, though, did I?" He made himself smile, felt the unnatural curling of his mouth quiver through his nerves. "And I won't. Ever."

"That's not a promise you can make."

"Try me."

Another slight pause. With more insight than he'd expected, Jamey said, "If you hide what you are, if you hide from *me*—aren't you doing exactly what these people wanted Morgan to do? What if we told the truth? Heterosexual kids grow up with examples of good and bad marriages all around them—they learn what they want and what they don't want—why can't it be the same for gay kids? Why can't they see Lucy and Charlotte down the street, who have a tree-decorating party every Christmas? Why can't they grow up next door to—to Cam and Jamey, with their adopted kids and backyard barbeques for the whole neighborhood? If same-sex couples got the same dignity as hetero marriages—if there were gay couples to demonstrate that it *can* be done, and done with love and loyalty—"

"And you want it to be us." He couldn't decide if Jamey was insanely brave or just insane.

"It has to be somebody, Cam. Why not us? How do I live with myself if I wait for somebody else to step up and do what I know has to get done—not when I've got the chance to do it—"

"You have no idea what you're saying, do you?"

"I just want to live my life, and live it with you. Out in the open. Not have to hide how proud I am that it's me you want. Me you love."

"I never said that."

Jamey smiled. "You will."

"I can't. Jamey, I'm so sorry. I'm scared, you're right, and I pretend, and I lie, and I wish by all that's holy that I wasn't gay. I accept it—but I don't have to let it define my whole life."

"You're letting other people define you. What kind of life will you have if you refuse to admit so much of what you really are?"

"I don't know."

"What you want," Jamey said slowly, "is something no one can give you. Cam, there's this whole elaborate game you've got going, this stage show where you play the straight guy consumed by law school, and when you've got your J.D. you'll play the straight guy consumed by work. You spend so much time and energy pretending that being gay doesn't exist—you don't think I could possibly love you—what was it you said that time? That you won't let me mess up my life over someone like you? What does that *mean*? Why do you think that?"

"You don't know what it's like to be Cam Griffen."

"I know what it's like to love Cam Griffen," he retorted. "How do I get you to see what I love in you? How do I get you to respect who you are?"

"You don't. You leave, and let me get on with my dismal little psychodrama," he jeered.

"Maybe you ought to stop lying!"

"And maybe you oughta grow up!"

Jamey gave him another of those long, vivisecting looks. "It just got cold in here again," he said, and turned, and left.

Cam sat and stared down into his coffee mug for a long time. Then he got up, put on coat and gloves, and made his way through the dirty snow to the practice rooms on campus. This one thing went right for him today: there were two pianos available, and one of them was unreserved until eight the next morning. So he shut himself in a room with a scarred black Steinway and played long into the night, played all the pieces he hated, pieces that spiteful teachers had made him learn. Played until his fingers and forearms ached and his shoulders were stiff and his whole body hurt as if every muscle had been individually bruised. Because as much as he needed to escape into music and his own exacting musicianship, he couldn't bear to play any of the music he loved. If he did, he would forever associate it with today.

The next weekend he went home to Virginia. Lulah was throwing a party at Woodhush to celebrate the publication of Holly's first book, which was excuse enough for a tactical retreat from New Haven as far as Cam was concerned. That this excuse had nothing to do with his reasons was nobody's business but his.

Holly was in full-throated Holly-ness. She flung her arms around him, called him "Peaches," told him he'd lost weight, ordered him not to read a single word of her book until he had his J.D. in hand, and asked whether he wanted his graduation briefcase to be black or brown. He hugged her tight, told her to *please* not call him "Peaches," said he wouldn't be caught dead reading her book—J.D. or no J.D.—and warned her that if she gave him anything so trite as a briefcase he'd hex all her underwear and she'd never know which pair would give her hives.

"Ha!" she scoffed. "Empty threat!" All at once she squinted up at him, and her fingers lifted to stroke his cheek. "Cam? What's wrong? Do we need to talk?"

"Nothing's wrong," he said with a smile. "Well, maybe talk a little, and maybe later. I'm proud of you, Freckles. Where the hell's the beer?"

They didn't talk until late Sunday afternoon on the long drive to Dulles for their flights out. Eventually surrendering to her loving, well-meaning, maddening interrogation, he managed a truncated version of events. He didn't tell her about Morgan, knowing it would bring on the kind of ranting and raving that would give her indigestion for a week. He didn't tell her Jamey's name, either, just that there was this guy, and it was mutual, but it wasn't going to work out, and he'd be okay.

"I won't have time to breathe, let alone think, for the next couple of months, so I'll be over it before I know it."

She looked for a minute as if she was going to pull over, stop the car, and demand to know every single detail. Then she sighed. "I'm sorry, Cam," was all she said.

Grateful, he shrugged and nodded. "Yeah. Me, too."

A few miles later: "You should talk to Alec and Nicky."

Cam chuckled. "What, the two guys who ruined my life? They're why I can't do the casual sex thing. After so many years of seeing what they have with each other, I can't just jump in the sack and wave good-bye the next morning. I gotta be in love, and it's all their fault."

"Oh, I see," she said with acid sarcasm. "Condemned to a lifetime devoid of promiscuity and unsafe sex. Whatever will you do?"

"Anybody ever tell you how adorable you are?"

"Thousands. You think you're the only one corrupted by Alec and Nicky's example? I want a marriage just like theirs—"

"Except with kids. Yeah, me, too. The marriage part, I mean. But with kids."

"Cam, they've got twenty kids! We're *all* their kids. And I'll lay odds none of us can just get laid."

"Ooh, wordplay! You're not, like, a writer or anything, are you?"

HOLLY STAYED SILENT on most of the walk back to the Westmoreland Inn's front entrance, concentrating on not sinking into the grass up to her ankles.

At length, Cam observed, "You're not ranting."

"Would you like me to?"

"Not so much, no." He hesitated, then asked, "He never said anything?"

"About you? Not a word. Does he even known we're related?"

"He might."

They walked toward a wisteria-swathed pergola, silent, until Holly said, "The first time Evan brought him to the house for a working dinner, he did the sweetest thing. He asked my permission before he picked up Kirby."

"That's just politeness. Never touch somebody's kid unless they've said it's okay."

"No, that's not what it was—I mean, that's not the only thing it was. He said, 'You know I'm gay, right? I promise you have nothing to worry about, but I'll understand if you don't want me near your kids unless I can prove it.' I think I fell a little in love with him then," she mused.

"But you did know he's gay."

"Of course. I knew about *you* probably before you did," she smiled. "Or at least long before you admitted it. And you never *would* have admitted it, and I never would have said anything, if I hadn't felt it necessary to have the Safe Sex talk with you that I knew very well Uncle Griff wouldn't have done if somebody'd held a gun to his head."

Cam groaned elaborately. "Can we please not mention that talk?"

"Mentioning it and then watching your face turn that color is the only way I can be sure you were listening."

"Stop acting like I'm still sixteen and you're twenty and pretending to be such a woman of the world it made me want to puke."

She unstuck a stiletto heel from the lawn and stepped onto the gravel drive. "Get this grass and mud off my shoes, and I'll consider it."

"Why didn't you just take 'em off?"

"Because my stockings would get muddy and that would be even worse. They're nylon and you can't do anything about them. Hold still," she commanded, and steadied herself with a hand on his shoulder while sliding off her shoes.

"I've never understood how women wear those things," Cam marveled. "Let alone why."

"'How' is practice, and 'why' is inherent masochism and the lunatic whims of their husbands," she retorted. "Ouch," she said as the gravel grew teeth and tried to bite a chunk out of her left big toe. "Well? Do something."

He glanced around to make sure no one was watching, took each sandal by a strap, muttered a few words to himself, and the accumulated muck slid neatly from the shoes to the driveway. "Damn, I'm good," he grinned as she used him for balance again while she put the heels back on.

"Not to mention modest." Looking down as she fastened a strap, she murmured, "I never knew who it was. I never knew his name. That party Lulah gave when *Queen's Tapestry* was published—you were in love with him then and you still are." Shoes secured, she took a step back and searched his face.

He snorted. "*That* stupid I'm not."

"I think you're that stupid and then some."

His gaze shifted as if trying to find an escape. He'd always done that when he felt cornered or threatened. Holly watched as his lips pulled tight and his jaw clenched, and was about to say something to reassure him when the restless eyes fixed on her. She would never have believed him capable of the cold look he gave her now as he said, "I've asked you not to meddle. Now I'm telling you. Leave it alone."

Holly caught her breath on a gasp of surprise. The warmhearted little boy, the gawky teenager, the young man still slightly baffled by his own exceptional mind—her crazy, funny Cam was all grown up. She couldn't provoke him anymore and expect to get away with it unscathed.

But in the next instant he proved that her Cam was still there. He made a rueful face, wrapped his arms around her, and whispered, "Sorry. I just need you to take it a little easier, okay?"

"I'm sorry, too," she offered. "I was wrong. Forgive me?"

"Always."

She hugged him tight, mourning the loss of the boy and the teenager and the young man—and wondered if this was how it would feel when Kirby and Bella grew up for real and for good.

As they neared the house again, music came pouring out the open windows. Holly couldn't keep herself from humming along.

We long for true love—well, we've found it: it's just one belief away—

Cam smiled and nudged her with a shoulder. "I've been meaning to ask—who programmed the music tonight? It's been wall-to-wall Hollywood Cowboys. Raitt, Ronstadt, Eagles, Joni Mitchell, Warren Zevon—Buffalo Springfield, for Chrissakes, as if they didn't break up about a hundred years ago—"

"Don't forget Jackson Browne and J.D. Souther. The whole roster of the Avocado Mafia. Not my doing, but I'm not gonna complain, either. I love this stuff. I thought you did, too."

"Like we ever had a choice? Lulah corrupted us during our formative years."

"I'd say we got lucky," she said as they continued up the verandah steps and back into the ballroom arm-in-arm.

"Lucky that I know the words to every song Crosby, Stills, Nash, and Young ever recorded? Individually *and* collectively, I might add."

"I have one word for you, dear heart: *disco*."

"You have a point," he conceded. "Without a solid grounding in the Beatles, the Stones, the Who, and the '70s California Angst Brigade, we would've been at the mercy of some very scary people."

"And you might have become the quintessential Gay Cliché," she agreed. "C'mon, cousin—buy a girl a drink."

"How many have you had?" he asked warily.

"Not nearly as many as I'm going to."

Not that she really wanted another vodka. Jamey Stirling was over by the bar, and she wanted to conduct a little experiment. It wasn't meddling, she told herself with firm self-righteousness. After all, she hadn't made any promises.

As she and Cam approached, Jamey turned abruptly, as if someone had called out his name. Holly wasn't surprised in the least when gray eyes and blue eyes met, skidded shyly away, then locked with an almost audible click. She hid a smile and ordered her own drink. Cam was in no condition to remember what vodka was, let alone how to ask Laura to pour one. Holly was familiar with the sensation tickling at her mind, the feeling she'd first had about five minutes after Alec and Nicky had made their snowy entrance to Woodhush all those years ago. It was the same as the instantaneous recognition when she'd seen Susannah Wingfield and Elias Bradshaw together for the first time. And now here it was with Cam and Jamey. It didn't surprise her at all. This was it: the real, the one, the only.

Cam and Jamey were staring at each other. No move forward, no smile or nod of greeting, nothing. Just staring. Holly found this annoying and ridiculous. Jackson Browne was in the middle of a song now, and she tried to keep her expression from registering the sudden fiendish glee that fizzed as if the vodka had been champagne. She elbowed her cousin ungently. He reacted not at all. Suddenly glad Evan had insisted on the stilettos, she brought one heel down on Cam's instep. Not very hard. But it got his attention.

"What the—? Dammit, what'd you do that for? That hurt!"

She smiled sweetly.

He squinted down at her, gaze dark now with suspicion. "Holly?"

She sang: "'Well, I may not have the answer, but I believe I got a plan—'"

He actually shrank back. All six feet one-and-a-half inches of him. "I thought you were gonna leave this alone—"

"Oh, I think we both know that's not true." Her fingers went around his bicep like a steel vise. "C'mon, Peaches."

"How did this become my life?" he moaned.

"Shut up." Holly urged him forward. Jamey was still staring. Nobody else was, and she counted on generations of strict Virginia manners to keep it that way as she sang softly, "'Honey, let me introduce you to my redheaded friend.'"

"It's 'redneck,'" he hissed, "and what the hell do you think you're doing?"

"Like the song says, I'm going to introduce him to my redheaded friend."

"'Redneck'!" he corrected more forcefully.

"You want to say that a little louder in this part of the country?"

"Holly, please—I'm begging you. Why can't you just let it alone?"

She turned and looked him straight in the eyes, all laughter gone. "If you'd seen what I've seen," she told him flatly, "you wouldn't let it alone, either. You *couldn't*." She gave him an ungentle push toward Jamey.

And then, just as Cam was about to approach—helplessly, Holly thought, as if something elemental like gravity or particle physics pulled them toward each other—Shawntel sidled up to Jamey. Predatory, intent, obviously not going to take *no* for an answer, she slid her fingers across Jamey's forearm, curling her nails into his sleeve.

Holly glanced frantically over at Cam. No spell or inherent gift needed to read that suddenly vulnerable face; she knew exactly what he was thinking. The hand clawing into Jamey's black leather jacket was female, and therefore socially acceptable. Cam smiled just a little and faded effortlessly into the crowd.

She turned back to Jamey. The girl didn't exist for him. The blank astonishment of a few moments before had smoothed into the professional veneer of the accomplished practitioner of courtroom law—which was, after all, a performance art. But as Cam started toward him, Jamey's eyes had suddenly ignited and a smile quivered at the corners of his mouth in a look that said no one else in the world existed for him. As Cam slipped away, Jamey's face became for just one unguarded instant a dozen years older, a hundred years sadder.

Holly knocked back a gulp of vodka and gritted her teeth. Men were idiots. It was part of their preposterous code that a warrior was said to have died a valiant death when all his wounds were in the front. As though dead could get any deader if your heart got carved out of your ribcage while you were watching it happen.

"Okay, that's it," she muttered. A few long strides caught her up to Cam. She tapped his shoulder and when he turned she grabbed his right hand, planted his left at her waist, and said, "Shut up, we're dancing."

Just like that, and they were doing a strange, eccentric '50s sort of be-bop, with a lot of tricky steps and circling under raised arms and a dip or two into the bargain, while Glen Frey sang about heartaches tonight.

"Goddammit, Holly—"

"Smile," she hissed, and maneuvered them by brute force closer to where Jamey stood, still helplessly staring.

"You're cruisin' for a bruisin', as my daddy used to say," Cam retorted, and swung her under his arm, then back, purposely making her dizzy. He pulled her in for a quick whirl across the floor, making her do it backward and too fast, his eyes saying he was hoping she'd stumble. "What'll it take to get you to stop?"

"You've got nothing I want, Peaches, so don't even bother. And you've got nothing that can scare me, either." She made him duck beneath their upraised arms, dragging him back against her with a steely grip. His back slammed against her front as she went on, "You got nothin', boy," hissed over his shoulder. "You want to go on having nothin' for the rest of your life?" She unspun him like a spool of thread, and they were connected only by grasping fingers.

All at once she lost him, his hand pried out of her grip by a larger, stronger hand. Evan took over the dance, pulling Holly tight against him. "Leave him alone, lady love," he warned.

She caught a glimpse of Cam then. Scrawled all over his expressive face was the fact that he'd decided that Evan Lachlan was only slightly less worship-worthy than God.

Male bonding: the refuge of idiots.

Nine

AS HE WATCHED CAM smile ruefully and fade into the crowd, Jamey thought of several drastic things to do. He did none of them. For himself, he didn't care: anybody in PoCo who didn't know he was gay either hadn't met him or was completely clueless. He didn't announce it and he didn't deny it. But everything Cam had always said about not wanting his life to be about his sexual orientation twisted bitterly through his mind. It wasn't nice to out someone who didn't want to be outed.

So he smiled at Shawntel and the two friends who'd joined her, and kept on with his story about finding his house. "And so Shawntel is driving me around to properties I might be interested in, and I'm thinking how beautiful it is here, how green and peaceful. Then she says, 'There's one place I really want to show you, but the owners are out of town and they prefer it if they're at home when I bring somebody over. We can do a quick drive-by—' And she stops, because I've got this look on my face like she's out of her mind. Then it hits me, and I explain to her that here, 'drive by' means 'drive by and take a look,' but where I've been living it means 'drive by and open fire.' "

The women laughed. Jamey, judging that he had expended enough charm, gently disengaged Shawntel's fingernails from his sleeve, hoped she hadn't put divots in his leather jacket, and pleaded the necessity of finding their host.

What he did instead was go in search of Cam Griffen.

Who proved maddeningly elusive. By his third circuit of the ballroom, Jamey was beginning to worry that he'd simply left the premises when, for the first time in more than twelve years, he heard the gentle voice that had lost most of its native Virginia drawl.

"Of all the gin joints in all the towns in all the world . . ."

Jamey turned quickly. "I always saw you as more of a William Powell type, not Bogie. It's the dimples. How are you, Cam?"

"Unemployed." He took a short swallow of his drink. "So how do you like the old homestead? Holly says you've been to visit quite a lot out at Woodhush."

"Are we really going to do this?" Jamey asked. "Hi, how're you doin', nice to see you, been quite a while?"

"How about, What the hell are you doing here?"

"I got tired of the city, and especially of prosecuting city crimes. Gang violence, murders, witnesses who either get amnesia or get dead—I seem to have run out of youthful zeal. And this job opened up, so . . ."

He'd forgotten that Cam's eyes were that particular shade of blue. He'd recognized a resemblance in Holly's eyes, but hers were sharper, more intense. Though the rest of his face was wary, even suspicious—resentment in the line of his mouth, nervousness in the flush of his cheeks—Cam's eyes were still and always would be soft, translucent, the hint of turquoise in their depths accented by heavy brown lashes.

"So Acting D.A. of Pocahontas County was a career move?"

Jamey shook himself from contemplation of the tiny creases twelve years had etched at the corners of those eyes. "More of a keep-myself-sane move, actually." Then he smiled—and smiled wider as Cam actually gulped. "Why, did you think I moved here because of you?"

The careless shrug took visible effort. "If seeing me again was the goal, you'd've had better luck in Eastern Europe."

"How do you fit that ego into your pants in the morning?" He grinned as Cam blushed. "I told you—I wanted country simplicity and a great place to live that I didn't have to sell the left lobe of my liver to afford." He paused, honesty compelling him to admit, "And I figured that since your extended family pretty much runs the place, I'd see you sooner or later."

"You were looking for me just now." It wasn't quite a challenge.

"I surely was. Why'd you sneak up on me like that?"

"I thought I should get it over with." Another restless shrug. "Holly won't give me any peace, otherwise."

"I like her. And Evan. Their little boy reminds me a bit of you."

"Me?" Cam was overdoing the innocent-and-indifferent act, and obviously knew it. But he couldn't stop, any more than Jamey could stop looking at him—just looking at him, after all these years. "Oh, you mean we both act like we're two years old, except he's the only one with a legitimate excuse?"

"No. What I mean is that he gets the same expression on his face that you used to when we'd go to a concert. Evan had some Mozart on the CD a few weeks ago during dinner, and Kirby got that same look—like here was this wonderful new thing in his life, and he was ready to yell 'Cool!' at the top of his lungs."

"I never looked like that."

"Yeah, you did." Jamey decided it was time to throttle it back a little, and so asked, "So whose laws are you going to help write next?"

Cam was evidently just as glad to talk about anything other than how well Jamey knew him. "They want me to go to Iraq."

"God Almighty!" Jamey exclaimed, earning himself curious glances from a few people standing nearby. He inclined his head toward the verandah doors and after a moment's hesitation Cam nodded acquiescence. Nonchalance was turning out to be hopeless for both of them tonight, Jamey reflected as he turned and nearly bumped into one of the waiters; Cam, sidestepping, knocked an elbow into the grand piano. The smack of bone on wood made Jamey wince in sympathy, but Cam seemed more bewildered than bruised. The look he gave the piano, and the almost involuntary way his fingers reached to touch it, confused Jamey—but he forgot his lawyerly training and didn't follow up with a question, because Cam's other hand came to rest for a moment at the small of his back. To feel this man's touch after twelve years was marvel enough; that Cam had touched him of his own free will stunned him.

They found a pair of wicker chairs and sat, and Jamey cleared his throat. "Sorry. I didn't mean to make a big deal of it, I only thought—I mean, I—" He stopped, sighed, and finished helplessly, "Just please tell me you're not going."

Cam grinned mirthlessly. "At times I'm crazy, and at other times I'm stupid, but I'd have to be both simultaneously to sign that contract. It's a nongovernmental organization that teaches developing countries how to do democracy, and they like my record—despite their neo-conservative leanings and my being the proverbial card-carrying member of the ACLU. But there's no way I'm going over there. What the Iraqi people have been through makes me sick—what we've done to them is horrifying—but George Bush broke it, and I'll be damned if I'll help George Bush fix it." He finished off his drink and set the glass down. Not looking at Jamey, he went on, "It breaks my heart to see pictures of Iraqis holding up their index fingers with the ink-stains, to show they voted. So proud, so hopeful—makes me want to strangle the people in this country who don't bother to vote, who ask what difference can it possibly make—"

"Florida 2000," Jamey said. "Ohio 2004."

"Oh, that wasn't so much the voting as the counting. But we've been at this for over two hundred years, and we *still* get into trouble. Those people with ink on their fingers, do they have any idea how demanding democracy is? That even though voting is absolutely necessary, it's so much more than having the vote?"

As Jamey listened, all the old fascination with this man's mind reasserted itself, all the powerful attraction of intellect to intellect. Yet it was more, now: in law school, they'd discussed ideas, abstracts, issues. This was life experience—Cam's in helping to create laws, Jamey's in applying them to society's benefit.

"Democracy requires certain things," Cam was saying. "One of them is the civic will to encourage debate among differing points of view. Colonial America was ethnically and religiously pretty homogeneous—they could establish principles of free speech and press and religion without having to worry about anything too extreme." He reached for his glass, saw that it was empty, and let his hand fall to his thigh. "With new immigration, those principles were tested and strained, but never abandoned."

"The testing only defined those freedoms more vividly—strengthened them," Jamey agreed.

"Right, exactly. And along the way people figured out how vital they are to a democracy. Where there is no tolerance, there's no debate—and without debate there can be no finding a compromise. A law's not a very good one unless it makes all sides at least a little unhappy." He smiled for an instant, then shook his head.

"I suppose you just have to keep referencing Churchill," Jamey mused. "Democracy is the worst form of government, except for all the other forms of government."

"When you've got a society full of people intent on killing each other for ethnic or religious reasons, none of 'em will stay in the same room long enough for the word 'compromise' to be spoken, let alone understood as being necessary to democracy. It's not enough just to get exactly what *you* want out of a particular piece of legislation—it has to screw the other guy as well. Tolerance is a null concept."

Jamey nodded. "'I'm right and you're wrong and here's why' is very American. 'I'm right, you're wrong, and you're going to die for it' is not."

"And that's why I'm not going to Iraq, no matter how much money that NGO offers me or how guilty they try to make me feel."

"You relentlessly beautiful man." Jamey didn't realize he'd said the words out loud until Cam flinched. "I know you don't understand. You never did. It isn't enough, with the eyes—no, it has to be everything about you, from the way you look to the way you think and feel—your mind, your heart—like I said, relentless." He sat forward in his chair and Cam leaned further back into his—oddly graceful, oddly precise, like a dance move previously choreographed. "You have absolutely no right to still be this beautiful," Jamey accused gently.

Half-strangled, Cam managed, "Me?"

"I wanted you the minute I saw you. Covered in paint, filthy dirty, wearing the rattiest t-shirt on the planet—you don't know what it took for me not to jump your bones right there and then. By the time I got you talking, and I found out the rest of it—how your head works, what you think, your music, the kind of man you are—it's twelve years later and you're even more *you*, and while I'm gratified that my instincts were so perfect, I'm very much afraid you've done it to me again, Cam."

"It *is* twelve years later," he rasped. "Don't do this, Jamey. You have no idea who I am now, you don't know the first thing about—"

"So tell me what you think I need to know. Tell me what you think has changed about you. Tell me—" He stopped for a moment as caution and impatience danced their accustomed fandango between his ears, then shrugged and said, "Tell me none of it matters. Tell me you still want me."

"How the hell do you *do* this to me?"

"You mean I still can?"

"Want you? Just *looking* at you hurts."

"It doesn't have to." He got to his feet and started for the steps leading down to the side lawns. He knew Cam was watching him, and he knew

Cam would follow him. A voice inside berated him for attempting to use sexual attraction to bypass potential problems—but whoever owned that voice had never been presented with the opportunity to kiss Cam Griffen.

"This is crazy," Cam Griffen complained behind him. "Do you really want to talk about all this now?"

Jamey smiled to himself. "Why not?"

"Well, just an observation, but we're both sober."

"Says you."

When they were in the shadows of a white pergola all entwined with flowering wisteria, and before Cam could start objecting yet again, Jamey took full advantage of the opportunity.

HOLLY KNEW she was being manipulated. Judging by the glint in his hazel-green eyes, Evan knew that she knew it—and did it anyway. As they danced, and the Avocado Mafia songs followed one after the other, her annoyance at Cam and Jamey was supplanted by succeeding levels of attraction.

First came Sentimentality. She loved the way Evan looked, the way he held her, the laughter in his dragon's eyes, the smile curving the corners of his mouth. Lover, husband, father of her children—the one and only.

Next up was what she called Romance A—subtitled *Find Us A Staircase and Do Your Rhett Butler Impersonation.*

Romance B was *Forget the Staircase.*

She was currently at the fourth level, otherwise known as *Forget the Romance. Fuck Me. Now.*

Bonnie Raitt seemed to agree: *Gonna get a little risky, baby—honey, that's my favorite part. . . .*

Holly grinned and maneuvered Evan to the foyer doors. On the way, they passed the *hors d'oeuvres* table and she snagged a handful of M&M's. Evan's eyes practically fell out of his head.

"Aren't we a little old for this?" he muttered as she coaxed him through the lobby toward the lighted overhead sign that said LADIES.

"Lover man, you're not anywhere *near* your 'best by' date."

Nobody was in the bathroom washing her hands or touching up her lipstick. Holly gave Evan a push toward the sink counter and flipped the toggle that locked the door. When she turned to face him, she laughed.

"You're amazing, you know that?" she asked. "You're blushing *and* you're hard. I didn't think any man had that much blood."

"When did I agree to explore your kinky side without a road map?"

"When you married me," she replied, and sauntered toward him, popping the M&M's into her mouth one by one.

Twelve minutes later, she reflected that by all the laws of physics, she should have fallen over into an undignified, half-dressed, insensate heap. Evidently there was some Law of Evan Liam Lachlan that at the moment superseded all others. Either that, or her tangled panty hose made any movement impossible.

"You're a lunatic," he muttered into the hollow of her shoulder, catching his breath. "That thing with the M&M's—"

"You like?"

"I'm just tryin' to figure out a way to reciprocate."

Her panty hose were a lost cause. When she stripped them off to stuff into the trash, he groaned.

"Now I gotta think of you all night like that!"

"Good," she said sweetly, refastening the straps of her shoes.

"That thing with the M&M's—" he said again.

"You're really gonna be pissed off if I develop a chocolate allergy, aren't you?"

"You lied to our children." He grinned the grin that made her want to kick him or kiss him, and sometimes both. "You told them chocolate *fingers* were your favorite."

She was spared having to react when someone knocked vehemently on the door, and nearly lost her balance on the stilettos as a familiar voice yelled her name.

Holly sighed. "He always was the most inconvenient child."

When the door was unlocked and opened, they found Cam standing with one shoulder against the wall, arms folded, lips and brows eloquently quirked. Mrs. Paulet gave Holly and Evan a swift once-over, lingering a bit on Evan, murmured, "You missed a button, dear," and sailed on by.

Holly glared at her cousin. "Shut up."

"Did I say anything?"

"Shut up anyway."

As they made their way back toward the ballroom, Cam fell in beside Evan. "Nice work," he remarked. "Not that I have much personal experience in the matter, but I'd say that's a woman who's been well and truly—"

"Did I tell you to shut up?" Holly snarled.

"I do my best," Evan said modestly.

"I've known her all my life," Cam went on, "and I've never seen her look quite like that. Your best must be pretty impressive."

"It's all a matter of timing, priming—"

"—and a handful of M&M's," Holly interrupted.

"Correction," Evan said. "A *mouthful* of M&M's. How'd you track us down?"

Cam was still back at the correction. Holly winked at her husband as the younger man stared, blinked, and nearly choked on laughter.

"You found us how?" Holly prompted.

"I came in from outside and saw Mrs. Paulet kind of loitering outside the bathroom. I asked her if she'd seen either of you and she said—" The dimples made an appearance. "—she said that if you hadn't remembered to lock the door, she would've seen much more of both of you than she ever thought she would."

Holly pretended to worry. "How loud were we, anyway?"

"Not as loud as that time in Charleston, on our honeymoon," Evan speculated. "Probably."

"Oh. Good." Glancing around him at Cam, she went on, "What were you doing outside? And don't say smoking a cigar—they're both still in your pocket."

The curse of a peaches-and-cream complexion was that a blush set off every freckle. Cam looked as if somebody had just splattered his nose, cheekbones, and forehead with sepia ink.

Holly caught her breath. "Jamey? You were outside talking with Jamey? Finally! Come on, tell me everything—"

Evan tapped her shoulder. "Holly, lady love, light of my life, mother of my children—go find Jamey and torment *him* for a while."

"I thought you wanted me to leave them alone?"

"That was before they went outside and didn't smoke a cigar."

"I don't deserve this," Cam whined. "What did I ever do to deserve this?"

She patted his cheek comfortingly. "Don't worry, Peaches. Jamey will tell me all I want to know."

"SHE JUST DOESN'T QUIT, does she?" Cam asked.

"I hope that was rhetorical." Lachlan turned to Cam and went on. "I don't know what the thing is with you and Jamey, but I'll warn you right now that if she doesn't hear things that satisfy her, you're really gonna be in for it."

"Oh, gee, quite a change from the rest of my life!"

"We'll have to trade stories one of these days."

"I think I got the basics of your plotline just looking at you two coming out of the bathroom."

"The basics," Evan agreed. "But y'know, I've been trying for years to figure it out, and I think I finally understand. The thing of it is—" He hesitated, not sure if Cam would believe him. "You're gonna laugh, but—setting aside the fact that I love her and I'm also crazy about her—which isn't the same thing, by the way—it kind of belongs to her. I mean, it sure as hell does things for her that it never did for anybody else—including me. Told you you'd laugh."

"Sorry—really, I'm sorry, Evan, but—"

"Friend of mine at NYU," he continued determinedly, "she'd been playing the violin since she was about six years old. She was good, too. She told me once that a violin's a violin's a violin—until you find the one that listens when you talk to it. It'll do things for you that nobody else can get it to do—and it'll get music out of you that you didn't know was there." Evan shrugged and smiled.

"I have to tell you, I am making no sense out of this at all."

"Wait'll you find the right violin." More merciful than Holly, he changed the subject. "It's about nine-thirty—you still want to wait until ten to get your suitcase?"

"Go schmooze some more. See you in the lobby in half an hour."

Back in the ballroom, Lachlan caught the attention of Laura's brother, who was circulating with a tray bearing an ice bucket, two bottles of Stolychnaya, and glasses. While pouring his own drink, Evan said, "In my day, people who hadn't graduated high school weren't allowed to distribute alcohol—even at a private party."

"In my day," Tim retorted, "we encourage it."

"The collapse of civilization is imminent."

"It will be if I don't get a new cell phone. It was working fine this afternoon, then crapped out on me practically the minute I walked in the door tonight. I still can't make a call, and I still can't figure out why."

"Didn't you obey the sign that asked you to turn your phone off in six different languages?"

"Let's see," Tim said, pretending to consider. "Obeying their rules or talking to my girlfriend. Which am I gonna choose?" He glanced beyond Lachlan's shoulder and said, "Der Führer is coming this way. Escape while you can."

Knowing he had no such option, he took a big swallow of vodka and turned to greet his host. "Mr. Weiss."

"Sheriff," acknowledged Bernhardt Weiss with a nod. "Do you enjoy the evening?"

Evan nodded. "Very generous of you to open up Westmoreland like this. And I saw about a hundred umbrellas in the lobby for later, when it starts to rain. That's thoughtful."

"The small amenities of life are so important, do you not agree? Fresh flowers, silk wallpapers, six-hundred-thread-count sheets . . ." He smiled with perfect self-deprecation, showing off a quantity of large, sincere teeth. "You Southern Americans have exquisite manners, and appreciate such things. Oh, but I am forgetting—you are from New York City. Do you miss it?"

"Only the elevators." When Weiss looked confused, Evan went on, "There are six elevators in this county, and not one building taller than five stories. For somebody who grew up in New York, that takes some getting used to."

"Ah. I understand. I did not know, when I chose this county for my Inn, that I would be living in the same area as the famous Elizabeth McClure. Would she agree, do you think, to my hosting a luncheon here? A literary luncheon—which I don't pretend would not publicize Westmoreland over half of Virginia," he added wryly.

"Nothing my wife likes more than an audience."

"Excellent. I shall ask her. And—another favor—would it be possible for her to autograph the books of hers that I own?"

"The only thing she likes better than an audience is an audience that wants her to sign something."

"Thank you." He looked out over the crowd, his voice quieter as he remarked, "You Americans—so contentious in your discussions. All these different factions, so many points of view. Especially as regards sex."

"Generally speaking, we like it," Evan replied laconically. Europeans, of course, found Americans perfectly absurd in their attitude toward sex. A president could be impeached for a blow job in the Oval Office but when every justification for a pre-emptive war was proved to be false, all that most Americans did was hope it would all go away somehow before too many more young men and women died. Maybe the 2006 election would change things; maybe not.

"Living here nearly two years," Weiss was saying, "and studying your country most of my life, still I think I will never comprehend you Americans."

"We're a puzzle," Lachlan conceded. Then, because he wanted to comprehend this man a little better, he asked, "Anything specific I can help with?"

"Something, perhaps. You are the only country that has ever used the atomic bomb. Never have I understood how Americans live with that knowledge."

Don't do it. He's your host tonight, he's a guest in your country, he brings a shitload of money into the county—

"And twice! Even after evidence of the first bomb, it was used a second time."

Don't go there. Not a good idea. Really not a good—

"Does it ever bother you? What your country did to the Japanese?"

Don't do it? Don't go there? Like hell.

"Well, considering that my granddad would've been in the invasion force if Japan hadn't surrendered, no, I can't say that it's ever really bothered me. But I guess what you mean is that we Americans like to think of ourselves as a good people. You're right, and what happened to Hiroshima and Nagasaki isn't exactly consistent with our view of ourselves as civilized." He paused, telling himself he really shouldn't enjoy this as much as he knew he was going to. "It's the same in Germany, though, right?"

"Excuse me, Sheriff Lachlan? I'm not sure what you mean."

"The land of Beethoven, Goethe, and Mozart—my personal favorite. Germany has produced some of the greatest thinkers and artists in history. But you're kind of in the same place we are, aren't you? Germany killed ten million people in concentration camps. It must be difficult to reconcile that with a view of yourselves as civilized."

Weiss did something then that Lachlan had read about in novels but never seen a real human being do: he actually looked down his nose. How he managed it when Lachlan was at least an inch taller made it even more impressive.

Lachlan hid a smile. "Anyway, I guess a lively exchange of opinions is to be expected when so many Americans get together, right?" He put a startled expression on his face and went on, "Oh—excuse me, I think my wife's cousin just got trapped by Judge Rausche, and that's not a fate I'd wish on anybody."

As he walked away, he told himself he really was the worst kind of chauvinist. *I can criticize anything about my country anytime I like, it says so in the Bill of Rights—but don't you fucking dare* wasn't the most enlightened attitude. Still—Weiss's words had irritated the crap out of him. He'd read somewhere once that the stench of burning human flesh was unmistakable. The Germans had known.

As it happened, he did see Judge Rausche, and gave him a wide berth on his way back out to the lobby. Cam showed up a minute or two later, and they went to the front desk for his room key.

"Did Holly find Jamey?" Lachlan asked as they started for the stairs.

"I haven't heard any howls of anguish or screams of outrage, so I'm guessing not." He slanted a sideways look at Evan. "We just talked. Outside. Just now."

"Hey, I'm not your parents or your priest. What you do or don't do—"

"—is going to obsess Holly until I either give in or leave town."

Lachlan waited until the next landing to say, "Whatever's going on with you and Jamey—any chance of working it out?"

"I don't know. But I can feel my hairline worrying itself back another inch on my forehead," he said with a rueful smile.

"I've been meaning to ask. Is that what Kirby can look forward to?"

"Holly's mom and mine were sisters, and quite often the gene comes through the mother, so—" Cam shrugged and eyed Lachlan's morass of dark hair. "The kid's gonna hate you when he gets to be about thirty-five."

"Well, by that time I'll be seventy-five and it's no fair beating up on an old man, even if he is your father and has a full head of hair that he didn't pass on to you." Evan grinned. "He's gonna hate me anyway for giving him the nose."

They reached the landing, turned, and started up the next half-flight.

"Anything else you want to ask?" Cam invited, as if he already knew the answer.

"Such as?"

Digging a brass key out of his pocket, he unlocked Room 314. "My real name."

Evan hid a grin. "I don't have to. I'll just go look it up in that big family map tucked in the newel post at Woodhush along with the deeds to the house and land."

"The genealogy chart will tell you my name, but not the reason for it." Cam swung the door open and they entered. "Our mothers were named in fits of Anglophilia before the Second World War—Elizabeth and Margaret. That's where Holly's 'Elizabeth' comes from."

"I figured that much," Evan said, following him through the sitting room to the bedroom.

Cam hefted his suitcase onto the bed and unzipped it. "It could've been worse for me, I suppose. At least they didn't try a masculine version of 'Margaret'—I don't even know if there is one. Is there?" He frowned. "Doesn't it mean 'pearl' in Hebrew or something? Yeah, that definitely would've been worse. But not by much."

Evan practically heard the light bulb pop inside his own head. "You gotta be kidding. I thought it was 'Cameron' or 'Campbell' or something—"

"If only." Cam busied himself with shaving gear from the bathroom.

"But I thought it was just the girls who got the botanical names."

"If only," Cam repeated. "Because Aunt Marget had used her sister's name for her child, my mother was bound and determined to do likewise. My dad kept asking what the hell she was gonna do if they had a boy, and she'd just glare at him." With a soft sigh, he finished, "They put it in Latin. Sort of."

"Please tell me they didn't do that to a helpless little kid." He couldn't help it; his lips started twitching and he pressed them tight together so he wouldn't laugh.

Cam saw, of course. "Y'know, Ev, I do like you," he said slowly. "I was prepared to like whoever Holly married, but I really *like* you. But so help me, if you say aloud any combination of syllables that even remotely resembles what my parents afflicted me with, I'm going to have to hurt you. I realize you've got three inches and about thirty pounds on me, but I'm pretty good at what I do by way of the family legacy, if you know what I mean, and I can beyond all doubt promise consequences."

"Gotcha." After a moment, he added, "You have my sympathies."

"Thank you," Cam replied with weary resignation.

"Y'know, I thought Lulah's 'Eglantine' was bad. And there's all those Petunias and Tulips—wasn't there a Buttercup?"

"I'm lucky I didn't get stuck with a masculine version of 'Bluebell'?" Cam asked bleakly. "They would have thought of something." He sighed with a fatalism rooted in boundless faith in his family's inventiveness—and bizarre sense of humor. "Put it in the Latin botanical rendering, for all I know."

"Well, isn't Ca— I mean, it's sort of like an old Roman name, isn't it?"

"Sort of, but not quite." He brooded on this for a moment, then asked, "Do you know what the real kicker is? Are you familiar with flower symbolism?"

"Holly's used it on me once or twice." He smiled, remembering bouquets that other people would have found decidedly peculiar.

"Well, the pink version of this flower means—wait for it—'longing for a man.'" He said it as if the words had been doused with lemon juice—or maybe battery acid.

"Almost like they knew, huh?"

"With our folk, you never know what they're gonna see in advance." Cam locked the door behind him and they started back toward the stairs. Down one flight, turn at the landing—

—and Cam walked right into a wall.

Lachlan grinned. "Don't tell me that being a klutz runs in the family, too!"

The younger man looked dazed—and not because he'd bumped anything vital. The suitcase had, in fact, taken the impact, barely missing a little carved cupboard garnished with a vase of flowers. Cam's frown was one of bewilderment, and then of worry. "There's a staircase here. Not the one you're looking at—the one I can see through this wall."

"A secret staircase? Cool! That happens a lot in really old houses, doesn't it?"

"It does. But not this kind." He set down his suitcase and flattened both palms to the wall. "If you know what I mean."

Lachlan was rapidly afraid that he did. "The old houses it happens a lot in—would they include Woodhush?"

"Holly doesn't know about it. Lulah doesn't even know about it. But, yeah, there's one at Woodhush." He glanced over at Lachlan, chewing his lower lip for a second before saying, "It won't show up on any blueprints. Neither will this one. They're not just secret. They've both got magic all over them."

HE WAS FOURTEEN YEARS OLD when he found it.

It was summer, and his dad was traveling on business, so Cam was staying at Woodhush for a month or two. Holly, having just graduated from high school, was even more of a pain in the ass than usual—obsessing about college and clothes and guys. Cam tuned her out whenever possible. His own life had been getting more interesting lately, as he suddenly seemed to be making quantum leaps in height, musicianship, and magic.

As for the first—Lulah had found some old overalls that had belonged to her brother, and Jesse had contributed some aged Levi's; otherwise, Cam would have been condemned to wearing only cutoffs or pants that no longer had even a speaking acquaintance with his ankles. The overalls made him look like a refugee from the Depression, but they were surprisingly comfortable. The Levi's were a little tight in the seat, but at least he could wear them into town without feeling like a complete dork.

The music was, as always, his comfort and delight. The ancient upright piano had been hauled up from the cellar, tuned, and a couple of the cracked keys replaced so that Cam could practice. For something that dated back almost a century, it had an unexpectedly sweet and mellow voice. In the wobbly bench he'd found sheet music for everything from Scott Joplin rags to *Classic Opera Arias for Piano,* and happily spent most afternoons and evenings sight-reading and then memorizing as he played.

As for the magic . . . Jesse was teaching him smithcraft, and he dabbled every so often over at Clary Sage's whenever Holly could be persuaded to drive him. Mainly he learned from Lulah. And only four days into his stay, they'd finally found out what his specialty was.

Among the family treasures were quilts dating back four and five generations, needlepoint samplers created (possibly at gunpoint) by Flynn girls for at least three hundred years, and a peculiar collection of crocheted and tatted doilies and tablecloths, not one of which matched any of the others. There were saddle blankets and bed blankets, woven with varying degrees of skill at the loom featured in one of the portraits on the staircase, and knitted things ranging from tea cozies to very silly hats for golf clubs. The most interesting, however, had come out of a box found only this past spring: a half dozen pieces of lace. They were fine, cobwebby silk, incredibly fragile, patterned in lilies and roses. It was Lulah's idea to preserve and conserve them under glass in frames, and as the three of them worked on the delicate fabric, Cam found himself nudging the weaving back into place every so often, repairing the lace without even thinking about it.

Lulah noticed first. After a few shrewd questions that he couldn't really answer, she took up the scissors from the table, reached over, grabbed the hem of his t-shirt, snipped—then yanked with both hands. The material ripped halfway up his chest.

"What the—? Are you crazy?"

"Fix it," she ordered.

"You *are* crazy!" He looked an appeal at Holly, who folded her arms and pursed her lips and refused to say a word. "Fix it, she says," he muttered, looking down at the ruin of his vintage *Meet the Beatles* t-shirt, torn right through Paul McCartney's face. He thought about it, then thought some more.

"You're intellectualizing," Holly admonished. "Did you have to think when you mended the lace?"

"So speaks the expert Witch," he shot back, and was instantly ashamed of himself. Holly couldn't work hardly a lick of magic of her own; it was her Spellbinding blood that made her valuable. She was, understandably, touchy about it.

"Fix the shirt, Cam. Don't think. Just do."

Cam thought about the magics he'd learned so far in his life; no help there. Then he thought about music. The printed notes required his attention so he could memorize the piece and figure out how it worked.

But when he knew it, and simply played it, thinking wasn't involved. Instinct was.

He looked down at the cloth, seeing how the cotton yarn was interlocked. Then he bit his lower lip and closed his eyes. When he opened them again, the Cute Beatle was gazing soulfully from the silkscreened photograph once more. There was no sign that the material had been rent at all.

Over the next week or so there were consultations with various of the Witchly relations, and some experimentation. From simple repair work (he learned to look on it as simple, anyway) he moved on to spellcasting directly into fabric. Nobody knew yet how long the workings might last; he wouldn't be trying any using Holly's blood until they got an idea about the natural duration and strength of his magic.

What with helping out around Woodhush, his music, daily rides, and now his new studies, he was exhausted by the time he got up to bed every evening. But one night in late July it was simply too hot and humid to sleep. He did the usual toss-and-turn routine. He lay naked on his stomach under the ceiling fan with a wet washcloth across the small of his back (Lulah would have knocked him silly for courting pneumonia). He thought long and hard about spelling coolness into the sheets, eventually deciding his control wasn't good enough yet and he'd probably end up lying on a layer of ice. He even thought about some of the other distractions that had been occurring more and more often lately, embarrassing things that his body seemed determined to do without his conscious consent. But he shied away from those thoughts almost at once.

So he turned to an older method of self-distraction, one that dated to the year his mother had died. He turned onto his stomach, hands flat against his chest, face scrunched into a pillow, and dreamed himself someplace else.

He never went to real places. Over time he had built up a small library of imaginary ones: mountain lakes, castles, beaches that weren't quite California, where he'd been born. There was a house where the whole second story was crammed with books, and a luxury hotel with a weird elevator that ascended in an impossible spiral through an atrium with redwood trees growing three hundred feet high. Sometimes he was in a sailboat with blindingly white sails, and sometimes he was behind the wheel of a 1930s vintage Rolls Royce, and a few whimsical times he held the reins of a coach-and-four only slightly less ornate than the one

British monarchs rode to Parliament in. When he couldn't fall asleep, he could imagine himself into one of these scenes, and whether he truly slept or simply kept dreaming while awake didn't really matter.

That night he sorted through his mental file, wanting something that would banish the sticky heat and raucous insect chorus from his conscious mind. Someplace cool and pleasant, with music . . . well, of course. His personal version of Sleeping Beauty's Castle as seen at Disneyland when he was about four. It even came complete with a Tchaikovsky soundtrack. He smiled into the pillow, thinking how ironic it was for a family of Witches to visit the Magic Kingdom.

Through the dark, narrow hallways he went, up stairwells, through vast chambers of his own devising, decorated with tapestries and huge heraldic war shields—prominently featuring Irish harps and Welsh griffins, of course. He chose a turning at random, opened a wooden door, started up another staircase. He could feel the thick nap of wool beneath his bare feet, smell the mothballs—

Wait a minute.

Cam flipped over onto his back and sat up. Mothballs?

His gaze unfocussed as he concentrated on the picture within his head. It was a new aspect of the castle, this set of stairs with its heavy flowered Persian carpet. No castle had wallpaper, much less the same wallpaper as the closet in Holly's room: Regency stripes of dark crimson and cream, unfaded in the more than a century and a half since its finely woven silk had been pasted onto the walls. . . .

That wall right over there. The one behind the dresser.

He got out of bed and pulled his boxers on, staring at the wall. The full moon outside was low and bright enough to let him see what he was doing. Hoping Lulah and Holly were sleeping better in the heat than he could, he carefully moved the dresser to one side. He felt quite impeccably stupid as he flattened his hands against the wall—but beneath layers of paint and paper and glue, he sensed silk. He had been working with the lace for a couple of weeks now; he knew exactly what silk felt and tasted and smelled like to his magic. There was an impression of metal that confused him until he realized he was venturing within the wall itself, and the metal must be electrical wires threaded down from the attic directly above his room.

Cam took a step back, chewing on his lower lip. There was no indication from this side that the wall was anything other than a solid wall, plastered and papered, with a layer of sunshine yellow paint on top. But he knew there was a staircase behind it. Running his hands over the slightly rough surface, he searched a long time for a seam or crease that would indicate a hidden doorway.

If there wasn't a way in or out here, there had to be one someplace. If he could find the carpet again with its faint stink of mothballs, he might be able to follow it to . . . where did secret doors hide anyway? Fireplaces were standard in movies, and of course revolving and/or fake bookshelves. There was the ever-popular trap door beneath the rug. Oh, and big portraits of the ancestors that swung out from the wall. . . .

He sat on his bed and considered. There were three fireplaces at Woodhush, using two chimneys: the back-to-back hearths that served the kitchen and dining room, and the big one in the parlor. The shared back wall of the double had been torn out years ago, and redone so that you could look—or yell—through it into the kitchen. Ripping it apart would have revealed anything odd about it. He was pretty sure there wasn't enough room on the north side of the house, where the parlor fireplace and chimney were, for a staircase to be tucked inside the wall. And anyway, exploring would not only cause comment, he'd get filthy.

It was entirely possible that there were about five miles of floor-to-ceiling bookshelves in Woodhush, all perfectly real and solid as far as he knew. There could be trap doors concealed anywhere in the hardwood floors throughout the house. Family portraits were all over the place. And what about all the quilts displayed on the walls? What could be hiding behind them? If there was an architectural drawing of the house, he'd never seen it, so he'd probably have to make his own survey to eliminate those places where it would be impossible to fit a staircase such as he'd seen—how thick was a standard wall, anyhow?

He was being stupid. Why did the hidden staircase have to conform to the laws of physics? After all, he'd originally sensed it with his magic, hadn't he?

Hell's bells, as his dad would say. But he'd only really been at this magic thing for less than a year. Like the majority of his male kinfolk, puberty triggered more than whiskers. The girls were different—Holly had been, anyway, her Spellbinder blood evidently operational since birth. Still, she'd never really learned to think like a Witch, had she? Not the way Lulah and Jesse and Clary Sage did, anyhow. The way he himself would have to learn to do.

So he set himself to it, sitting there on his bed at well past midnight of a sultry, stifling summer night. His only real accomplishment was that he forgot about the heat.

The next morning, after Holly had driven into Flynton for yet more shopping and Lulah was busy in the stables, Cam acted on the results of his first attempt at thinking like a Witch and climbed up to the attic. With his newly discovered sense of silk and wool and magic, he found the upper limit of the staircase. It took some shifting around of trunks and boxes, and some serious sneezing at the dust thus disturbed, but at last he found the plank of the interior wall where a knothole had been punched out of the wood. He felt around with his fingers, then with his magic, and then with both.

The hinge really ought to have creaked and squealed, he thought. No time-honored atmospherics at all to this secret door. It should be ashamed of itself.

Bending almost double, he squeezed through—wondering irritably why he couldn't have found this a year or so ago, before legs and arms started growing to unmanageable lengths. The steps were there, and the heavy flowered carpet. It seemed to have been woven specifically for this purpose, because it took the turns of landings in ways no ordinary staircase runner should. He grinned to himself. Magic carpet.

There was no dust here. The rods securing the carpet to each riser were shiny brass, untarnished. As he stood at the very top, looking down, he smelled the mothballs that had so disconcerted him the night before and wondered why nobody had spelled the wool to protect it. Maybe the reason was simple practicality—why use magic when a nonmagical solution worked perfectly well? Or maybe there was already so much magic at work here that even that little bit more would be too much.

Cam mulled that over, recalling something his father had told him. "Don't mess with physics. Most Witches stick to ordinary things—herbs, rocks, tea leaves, wood, stuff that's perfectly comfortable with itself in the everyday normal world—and juice it up with their magic. Major work, distorting physical space or playing around with gradations of reality, that takes a pile of effort and insane amounts of power. And the laws of physics will have their revenge sooner or later."

So he restrained his natural impulse to see if he could do a banishing spell to keep moths from the carpet, and started down the stairs. Keeping a mental drawing of the house in his head did him no good at all.

Someone had warped the laws of physics pretty thoroughly to make this staircase, which led through most of the house. He paused every so often to put his hands against the wall in an attempt to figure out what room was on the other side. Sometimes it worked. There were quite a few doors as well, most of them locked in ways he couldn't understand. The three he could open led into the kitchen, the Wisteria Room, and the upper landing of the real stairs. Keeping alert for any sound that would mean Lulah had returned, he stepped out of the magic passage and into the real house and back again, making note of where the doors were and how they worked from each side. From the unspelled side, there was no hint that there was anything behind the walls except timber and the wires for electricity and phones. He was intrigued by the wiring, because he knew how old it had to be—the first decade of the century at the earliest—yet there was no place where the sheathing had frayed. Somebody had been efficient with a preservation spell.

At last he climbed back up to the attic door, emerged from the staircase, and slid the opening shut. Two hours of piano practice later, he had decided that the secret passage would remain his secret for now.

Because even if he hadn't heard all the gruesome details of the Salem Witch Trials from kids who were his fellow descendants, he'd had the lecture from Holly—and Lulah, and Jesse—about Witches and secrets.

"Learn to keep your mouth shut, Peaches."

"It pains me to say this, because you're a sweet child without a deceitful bone in your body, but there's just a lot of things we don't talk about."

"You're truly one of us now, and that means we all keep each other's secrets—sometimes from each other."

Okay, he did talk a lot (not as much as Holly). And he did have a tendency to blurt at times. But if what he was beginning to suspect was true about him—something that had nothing to do with magic—he would have to get good at keeping secrets. He figured this would be good practice.

He never did get around to mentioning that staircase.

"THEY'RE NOT JUST SECRET," he told Evan. "They've both got magic all over them."

If he had expected Lachlan to say something like, *"Okay, I am now officially weirded out,"* he had underestimated Holly's husband. There was not a single demand to have things proven to him. Cam wondered what Evan had seen and experienced of magic that had—well, not made him at ease with it, exactly, but at least had swept away the usual skepticism and discomfort.

What Evan said was, "Woodhush and the original Westmoreland were built about the same time, weren't they?"

Cam nodded. "Before 1760—the basic fabric, anyway. There were additions and refurbishings, but the structure stayed the same."

"So why are you sensing magic here? I thought Lulah and Jesse cleaned this place out years ago."

With an elaborate shudder, he replied, "Don't *ever* call her an amateur to her face!"

"I'm not," Evan said mildly. "I'm saying that if they got rid of the magic at Westmoreland, somebody since has put it back. So what do we do with this secret staircase, Cam?"

He hesitated. "I really want to say that we leave it alone—"

"—but you're not gonna say that, are you?" The older man grinned suddenly. "This'll be fun."

"Do me a favor, huh? Don't ever ask me to represent you at a sanity hearing."

"Aw, c'mon. You want to get in as much as I do."

"I concede the point." He ran his hands over the wall again, his magic pushing through it to the passage hidden inside. Once again, as at Woodhush, it was the carpet he sensed most strongly. But it wasn't bespelled, it had never been touched by fire— "Shit!" he exclaimed as he finally got a sense of its pattern. "It's *new*!"

"The passage?"

"No, that's old, probably as old as the first house. I'm talking about the carpet on the stairs in there—it's Berber wool, and it's brand-fucking-new!" He stood back, palms pressed together. "And so is the magic."

"Okay," Evan said. After a glance at his watch, he nodded to himself. "It's ten o'clock, this place should be cleared out downstairs in about an hour. Take your suitcase back up to the room and leave it there. I'm gonna go talk to Holly and phone Lulah—" He stopped, cussed under his breath, and snagged his cell phone from his jacket pocket. A few tries yielded nothing. Cam brought out his own, handed it over. More nothing. Evan looked grim. "Somebody was telling me that he couldn't get his phone to work tonight. The sign at the entrance is just to throw everybody off."

"Isn't that assuming kind of a lot? I mean, I'm pretty sure I saw somebody on the phone this afternoon when I came in."

"One of the staff, or one of the guests?"

Cam thought for a moment. "Guy in a pale blue windbreaker—" He wanted to smack himself upside the head for sheer stupidity. "—with *Westmoreland Inn and Spa* in purple letters on the breast pocket." When Evan nodded, Cam added stubbornly, "But I still think that's a pretty big leap you're making."

"The sign asks people to turn off their cells. Anybody expecting a call is asked to leave the phone at the front desk, and they'll come get you if the call comes through—and how much do you want to bet no calls ever come through?"

"Suppose somebody keeps his phone and keeps it on—"

"Malfunction, dead battery, interference in the signal to a tower—how many ways are there to explain it? Mine doesn't work. I'm the sheriff—I make damned sure all my phones are working at all times. How about you?"

"New battery yesterday," he admitted.

"Phones don't work. Lulah felt blind here. You felt something weird with the bedspread. There's a staircase hidden inside the walls—with new magic. There may be something that blocks magic getting in or out, but obviously inside whatever barrier it is, magic can happen. How does that add up to you?" Evan paused, frowning, and for the first time Cam felt the power behind those hazel eyes as they searched his own. Not magic, but power all the same. "Okay, what else?"

"When Holly and I were outside earlier, I thought I saw something when I looked at the house. I don't know what, so don't ask. Just . . . something about the windows that's not quite right. But why was somebody talking on a phone—"

"I think you got played. 'Griffen' isn't a common name in this county, but anyone who's magically connected would check out the locals pretty thoroughly. No Witch in this county knows anything about this place, which means that whoever's using magic wants it kept secret." He ran a hand distractedly through his hair. "Shit, I *knew* Weiss was hiding something! The guy you saw talking on the phone was doing so for your benefit, Cam. Just in case you might think you sensed something—which you did—when you lay down for a nap. When did you make your reservation?"

"A week ago. That's plenty of time to have me checked out, isn't it?"

"Yeah. Look, why don't you take your stuff back up to your room and meet me downstairs in ten?"

"You have a plan?"

"Since I can't phone Lulah, I'm sending Holly back to Woodhush to get her."

"I like this part of the plan." He brushed his fingertips across the wall one last time. "It may take me a bit to figure out how to get into this thing."

"That's *your* part of the plan."

IT WAS FAST becoming Holly's plan to find her husband and her cousin and get out of here. There had been a brief renewal of her discussion with Reverend Wilkens, which ended rather precipitously when Louvena Cox, bless her, sauntered over and said, "Reverend, y'all got a uterus? No? Then hush up. Holly honey, we have things to discuss. 'Scuse us please."

After Louvena gave her a quick summary of her conclusions regarding magic and the church fires—mentioning that she'd told Evan the same things earlier—Holly promised to tell Lulah at the first opportunity. Louvena nodded satisfaction and went back outside to sit on the verandah with her second bottle of California champagne while Holly went in search of Tim and the vodka tray. But the Pledge of Allegiance's "Under God" coterie tried to draw her into their discussion—on their side. Telling herself she really shouldn't, she asked *whose* God they had it in mind to be under—Jewish, Catholic, Baptist, Mormon, Muslim? While they (variously) gasped, spluttered, marshaled their arguments, or simply stared at her rudeness, she resumed her quest for the Stoly. Tim was nowhere in sight. Damn the boy—

"Hi again," said Gib Ayala, and she turned to find him holding a plate of munchies and a full glass of white wine. He offered both; she regretfully declined the latter—not a good idea on top of two vodkas—but selected a slice of quiche from the former. "Interesting party."

"You could say that." Now that she was back in the crowded ballroom, the ceiling fans creating only a remote and ineffective breeze, she could feel the sweat of earlier activities. She wondered if Evan and Cam had retrieved the suitcase yet and how soon she could get home to a cool shower—or, failing that, if she could sneak into Cam's room and wash. Evan did get enthusiastic. . . .

"I forgot to ask, before," Gib said, "any progress on the book?"

"I need to figure out what book I want to write."

"You mean you don't put up index cards with ideas on them and throw darts?"

She snickered. "It's occasionally a little more complicated, but that's actually not a bad idea."

"Commitment problems? Or writer's block?"

She ignored the first suggestion, and especially the tone it was said in. "The psychoanalyst who coined the term 'writer's block'—and claimed he could cure it, which as every writer knows is absolute bullshit—was also the guy who claimed he could cure homosexuality."

Some emotion crossed his dark face, but before she could analyze it he smiled again. "Did I tell you I was trolling websites the other day?"

"Oh, God. Again? What are they complaining about now?"

"All your characters fall in love at first sight. Nobody is ever just friends and then falls in love. They take one look at each other, and—" He shrugged.

"Thirty seconds, Holly—I bet it's not more than thirty seconds before you want to rip his clothes off!" Gib had no way of knowing that her smile was for Susannah's remembered words, not for him. With Evan, it hadn't even taken thirty seconds.

"I suppose it's true," she said at last. "But I never really thought about it. If the chemistry's not there, it can't be faked."

"Isn't that just sexual attraction? You don't even have to talk to somebody before you know you have that. It's how people end up in bed the next morning, not knowing each other's names."

"Well, granted. But I think there are clues, you know? Whether you're consciously aware of them or not. Everybody's always reading everybody else—it's a survival skill. That guy across the river isn't holding a sharpened spear, but that doesn't mean he's not going to rip your throat out with his bare hands if he gets the chance. You'd better be able to figure out fast what his intentions really are—"

"Do you really think it's that instinctive?" Gib asked.

"Absolutely." Love at first sight—she was of the opinion that people who thought their best and most lasting relationships *hadn't* been love at first sight simply hadn't been paying attention.

"Does it go away?"

"It changes. That's the getting-to-know-you part. The talking, sharing things like a movie or a concert—you find out what you have in common, what you don't, what you can learn from each other—"

"So how many times have you fallen in love at first sight?" he asked playfully.

"Oh, hundreds," Holly replied, hiding annoyance. "For instance, there was a tour guide in Morocco, name of Abdel—I'd still be in love with him if he hadn't already had three wives."

"But the chemistry—that never goes away, does it?"

Holly finished off the quiche and swallowed before saying carefully, "If you're trying to take this where I think you're trying to take this, please let's not go there."

"I'm not trying to take it anywhere. I just wanted to know your point of view."

And now, she thought, *I look like a conceited bitch who'd fuck anything that moved.* "So you can post it on one of the websites?" she asked with a smile.

"I'd never do that. Really, Holly. I just wanted to know."

Jamey came unknowingly to her rescue by tapping her on the elbow and saying, "Sorry, Gib, I need her for a second."

"Take me, I'm yours," Holly muttered as he guided her toward a window.

"Pardon?"

"Nothing. What's up?"

"I'm supposed to give a speech about why we're all here, and I can't find Evan to give me the latest."

"There isn't any 'latest' that I know of." Giving him a long look, she went on, "What you really want to talk to me about is Cam."

"Well, yes. But I do have to give a speech." He glanced around. "*Spectatum veniunt; veniunt spectentur.*"

She sighed, privately bemoaning the day he learned his first Latin declension. "Caesar? Suetonius?"

"Ovid. 'Some come to see; some come to be seen.'"

"What's the Latin for 'You are being a smart-ass; do so no more'?"

He laughed. "I'd have to look that one up. Could you do me a favor and check my facts on the church fires against your famous memory?"

She listened as he summarized. Old Believers Baptist, September ninth, 2005. October ninth, Calvary Baptist. Third was on November eighth, First Baptist. December tenth, the Lutheran church. Then a break until February twenty-first, when the Methodists had been hit. Sixth had been the Episcopal church on April eighth. Finally, on August second, Gospel Baptist.

"So it's a month since the last one," Jamey concluded. "And God grant that it *was* the last one. Has Evan got anything I can use tonight to reassure people? Are we anywhere with the investigation?"

"I'm assuming you won't be discussing the similarities and anomalies—none of which make any sense."

"If any of this made any sense, we'd have somebody in custody right now." Jamey started to chew a thumbnail, caught himself at it, scowled, and stuck his hand in the pocket of his black leather jacket. "None of it makes sense," he reiterated.

"Some of it does," she said without thinking, cursing herself when his eyes lit with speculation. She'd almost told him that Louvena had figured out there was magic at all but the Methodist fire. Sometimes she came close to forgetting that he wasn't one of them, that he didn't know anything about Witchcraft in Pocahontas County. "They almost all started at night—is that significant?" A lame save, but a save nonetheless.

"I thought maybe you or Evan had thought of something," he said, disappointed.

"He's the cop, not me. I keep telling you guys, I'm no good at mysteries and clues and things. If you were thinking of reiterating the facts about the fires, my advice would be *don't.* We all know why we're here."

"Yes, and I'd only be emphasizing that Evan and I are stumped." He shifted restlessly, then glanced at her. "So here's a mystery I'm trying to solve. When I interrupted just now, you were looking rather puckish. Who were you planning to eviscerate?"

"Take your pick. You know the one about the Lord High Executioner?"

Jamey laughed. "He has a little list—and they never will be missed."

"My object all sublime," she agreed. "So what were you and Cam up to in the garden?" As his eyes widened, she grinned. "Gotcha."

"Dear lady," he said pleasantly, "I refuse to become a source of innocent merriment, even for you. Oh, God—there's Mr. Weiss and the microphone. Wish me luck."

Finally catching sight of Tim, she pointed an imperious finger. He looked around with exaggerated innocence as if wondering who she could possibly be indicating.

"Mr. Weiss deserves our deepest gratitude for opening up the Westmoreland Inn tonight for the fund-raiser," Jamey was saying. The crowd duly applauded; Weiss nodded in several directions, a modest smile touching his lips.

Holly fixed Tim with what she liked to consider her most evil glare. He only grinned. Vile, loathsome child—

"I was hoping to bring you some encouraging words tonight about the progress of the investigation," Jamey went on. "There are things we know, and things we're going to learn, and that's really all I can say at present. But this terrible series of fires has taught me something about the place I've made my home, and I'd like to share those thoughts with you."

Holly held up her hands just high enough for Tim to see them, and pantomimed closing her fingers around his throat.

"We have our differences here, just as every community in this country has its differences. The conversations I've heard tonight have been about pretty much every issue and idea current in the national debate. Opinions come from all sides of each question. Tom Brokaw has said, quite rightly, that patriotism is not a loyalty oath. I think the most patriotic thing a citizen of this country can do is question the government. This is the remarkable thing about the United States—and it's exactly what our Founders wanted and indeed demanded of us. The free exchange of questions and ideas. When that freedom is threatened—by the destruction of places in which so many of us meet in order to express our beliefs in company with each other—we come together as we have tonight in order to rebuild those places. Because that's what a community does."

Holly forgot about her drink.

"Now, I'm very new to Pocahontas County. I like to think I've been useful thus far; I guess I'll find out in November, because even though I'm running unopposed—which is a very great honor—I still have to win a majority of your votes. But these church burnings have made me feel pretty damned useless. And that makes me angry. Sheriff Lachlan is just as angry as I am. So you've got two incredibly angry officers of the court working this thing, and that's what we're here for. That's our function. I think, though, that what *you're* here for—contributing to the repair and renewal fund—is even more important in many ways than what a sheriff and a district attorney can do. We're supposed to find these criminals and stop them. You're contributing to the future, making sure it will be built—you're saying that the future is going to happen. And that's the most basic faith a citizen of this country can have."

She was aware of someone standing behind her now, but was so riveted on Jamey Stirling that it took her a moment to recognize Cam's touch on her shoulder.

"America is a work in progress. Yes, I know, it's a cliché—but think about what it means. America, it seems to me, was never *meant* to be completed. We were never meant to be a finished product, a thing that at some point would get a final polish and we could all say, 'Okay, all done!' and hold a champagne brunch to celebrate—and then not bother to think about it anymore.

"We *have* to think about it. We're *not* a finished thing. When somebody calls the Constitution a 'living document,' don't they mean it's supposed to do what all living things do—grow and change? So America is pretty much meant to be unfinished. It's challenging work that puts us through a spiritual wringer, that demands our best—because America is the most important work in history.

"Now, anybody who's ever heard me speechify on the subject—which now includes all of you!—knows that I pretty much go off the deep end when I talk about the Constitution. A lot of people wonder why. After all, it allowed slavery, repression, injustice. It forgot to give women the right to vote until nineteen amendments later. One of the amendments turned out to be such a lousy idea that another amendment was needed to repeal it—and then we could all legally enjoy our bourbon again. But the deficiencies aren't in the document. Mistakes were made by those who interpreted the document, who wrestled with moral, intellectual, and spiritual questions—and sometimes got it wrong.

"The reason I get long-winded about it—I prefer to think of it as 'lyrical,' by the way—is that in the document are found the means for change. For correcting mistakes. For righting wrongs. For doing the work that brings progress. Where do we want to go, and how will we get there? What kind of society do we want to live in—and what are we willing to do in order to establish it? And, yes, to protect it. To form a more perfect Union, establish justice, ensure domestic tranquility, provide for the common defense, promote the general welfare—and secure the blessings of liberty. Not *the* perfect Union, but a *more* perfect Union. The Founders knew we'd never get there—but they provided the means to keep working on it.

"And that's what we're all here doing tonight. Discussing our different views of what this country should be, where it should be going, what it should be doing. How to establish, ensure, provide, promote, and secure. Making certain that those places that were damaged will be repaired and restored, because that's what communities do."

He paused, and all at once seemed to shake himself slightly. A tiny smile curved his lips. "I'm a lawyer and a politician—give me a microphone and I'll talk all night. But there are Labor Day picnics tomorrow all over the county, so I'm guessing you'd all like me to shut up now so you can go home. Thanks for being here tonight."

"Damn," Holly muttered as she joined the applause. "I could just kiss that kid right now."

"Me, too," Cam agreed softly. When Holly looked over her shoulder at him, he shrugged and showed both dimples. "What can I tell you? He's always been like that. You should've heard him practicing opening arguments and summations—even during first year."

"You're an idiot," she told him affectionately. "Where's Evan?"

"Why am I an—no, don't answer that. I thought Evan would be here already."

"Haven't seen him in a while. Go find him, okay, so we can get out of here?"

"That's kind of what I wanted to talk to you about. . . ."

A FEW MINUTES LATER, Holly eyed her cousin sidelong. "I see that Evan wants Lulah here to investigate and can't get hold of her by phone, but did either of you happen to think of the obvious? To wit: just go outside the gates where the jamming probably won't work?"

"Is that your tactful way of saying you're not going home to be a conscientious mother to your children?"

"My children are conscientiously protected, thank you very much. I might not be able to do much of anything practical, but experience has taught me to stick around when there's mag—when this kind of thing is going down."

"Nice save," he murmured. "But you'll admit that somebody has to go home and keep an eye on the kids if Lulah's coming here to help."

"I'd nominate Louvena but I think that's her third bottle of champagne. Send Jamey. And where's my darling husband, anyway?"

"He was supposed to be here when I got downstairs."

"I suppose he'll turn up eventually. Why didn't you ever say anything about a hidden staircase at Woodhush?"

"I forgot?"

"Stash the dimples back in the arsenal," she advised. "I've been immune to them for over thirty years."

People were taking their leave. Weiss stood at the ballroom doors, shaking hands and being charming. Holly wished she had sufficient magic to detect it in others; he certainly didn't *look* like anything other than the businessman he presented himself to be. Then again, what did a Witch look like?

"If this was a movie," Cam mused, "about eighty-five percent of the people in this room would be classified as 'dress extras.'"

"What *are* you on about now? And what's a 'dress extra'?"

"People in a crowd scene with no lines to say who bring their own wardrobe—usually party wear of some kind. They're background. They fill up a camera lens and create ambient noise, but they have nothing to do with the real action and dialog."

Holly stared at him. "What brought this on?"

"I was just thinking that in a film they're dress extras, but in real life, they're witnesses." He nodded toward Jamey, who was listening earnestly to Mrs. Paulet. "There were about three hundred people here tonight. They're going to talk to between five and ten people each. There'll be some overlap, of course. Call it seven—which is over two thousand, which in this county is enough to sway an election."

"In the book business, it's called hand-selling—if the people working in the store get turned on to a book, they give it the best shelf space, make the effort to point it out to customers."

"The personal touch," he agreed. "Voters have gotten cynical about campaign commercials—that's why the 'mute' button was invented—and most of them don't have the patience to sit through one of those so-called debates. They trust personal contact—but when they can't get it for themselves, they'll rely on the word of people they know. In short, unless he does something hopelessly stupid between now and November, Jamey just won himself a full term as District Attorney with upwards of sixty-five percent of the vote."

"But you can't do personalized politics at the presidential level, or senatorial," Holly said. "Maybe it's possible if you're going for a seat in Congress. Anything else, and you'd run yourself ragged."

"Or start running two and half years in advance of the election," Cam added. "Thereby risking voter fatigue."

"Trust me, nobody would ever get tired of looking at *that* face!"

"Well, no," he allowed, blushing a little. She was about to ask what exactly had transpired earlier out in the garden when he asked with studied casualness, "So tell me—just how good *is* Evan?"

"Better than good. Great. Verging at times on the godlike."

Familiar hands clasped her waist and a deep voice murmured in her ear, "'Godlike'?"

She leaned back against her husband's chest and purred, "At times."

"How many times?"

"What makes you think you leave me with enough functioning brain cells to keep count?"

"Excuse me," Cam said, "but I'm going to go elsewhere before I need dental surgery. Or insulin." He gave Holly a mocking little bow and departed.

Holly turned in Evan's embrace and smiled up at him. "Let's take a walk."

"Where to?"

"Whoever's car is conveniently parked to get us past the front gates so you can make your phone call."

"Change of plans. There actually is a working phone in this place. Landline at the front desk. They have to be able to call the fire department or whatever, I guess."

"Aw, you were sneaking around without me!"

"I wasn't sneaking. I don't have to sneak. I have a nice big shiny badge."

"And a nice big shiny Glock with ten rounds ready to go, but that's not quite as subtle. What does Lulah say?"

"To send you home to watch the offspring. Yeah, I know," he said quickly when she scowled. "That's what I told her. So I asked Laura and Tim to head over."

"Works for me." The Houdek kids were familiar baby-sitters and the twins wouldn't put up a fuss. Or so it was to be devoutly hoped. "She'd better get all those dinosaurs coaxed back into the box before they arrive, though. Did you tell her about the Woodhush stairs?"

"Do I look suicidal?"

"And here I thought you *liked* Cam!"

"He's gonna get it anyway for not telling anybody he was coming home, so. . . ." He smirked. "How many times can she kill him?"

"How many times can she leave just enough of him alive to start the process all over again?"

"Not my problem," he said with cheerful ruthlessness. Then, more seriously: "I called the office, too. Luther says a bunch of faxes came in from Richmond."

"Forensics?"

"Finally. Except for the Gospel Baptist, dammit. Reverend Ferrers is already antsy about getting the official report for the lawsuit." When she arched her brows, he elaborated. "The church is suing Louis LaPierre, who installed their fire alarms."

"Not very well, evidently."

"The Reverend gave me twenty minutes last week on how the guy sat in his office and swore on a stack in the name of Jesus the Savior that everything was absolutely perfect—and this was the afternoon before the fire!"

"I think that's called 'irony.' Anything interesting in the other reports?"

"Well, except for the Methodist fire, there was no ignition. No source of fire, I mean. Accelerant in one case—the wood varnish at First Baptist—but no source."

"Louvena's right. These aren't normal arsons."

"Except for the Methodists," he said again. "That one was a Zippo lighter and a gas-soaked leather-bound Bible. Pretty obvious. And it only took them six months to get back to me on that one," he added snidely.

"Regretting your clout as a big, bad U.S. Marshal?"

"Only when it comes to getting forensics within a reasonable amount of time. Say, two hours," he smiled. "Anyway, you're right, and Louvena's right, it matches what she was saying about the feel of the other fires. So I'm thinking the Methodist one was either a copycat for purposes unknown, or completely unrelated to the others and not a conscious imitation, or somebody decided it was just time for another fire."

"Any reason you can think of for choosing the Methodists as a fake-out?"

"Not really. But here's the thing. They must be clearing out the outgoing fax files in Richmond, because Luther also got a report on Poppy Bellew."

Holly drew back. "Oh, God—did they find her?"

"Yeah. In her car. But no sign of the four kids she said she had with her." He hesitated. "Holly . . . her car went off the same road in about the same place where your parents died."

She pulled in a long breath, aware of a sudden silence that was only inside her own head. After a moment, she said, "No wonder it took so long to find her. It's all swamps and—" And a car gone off the road would sink fairly fast, and anyone inside would drown, all the while trying to find a way out, if they were even conscious after the skid and the impact—

Evan gathered her close. "I'm sorry, lady love. I gotta ask—was there anything about their deaths that put up any red flags? You know what I'm talking about."

"You'd have to ask Lulah or Jesse. All I ever heard was that it was a bad stretch of road. I was only—Evan, I was about as old then as the twins are now." And something she had deliberately never thought about demanded now to be recognized: the agony her parents must have felt, knowing they would never see their little girl again. "I don't remember them," she whispered. "I only know their faces from photographs. Everything they knew and loved, the people they were, the way they felt about each other, what they wanted to teach me—I only have other people's descriptions. *A chuisle*—if that happened to our children—"

"It won't. I swear to you it won't."

Holly sheltered for a moment more against him, then drew back a little. "Poppy could have let the four kids off someplace—or maybe they got out before—before the car went under."

"She phoned Reverend Deutschman from a rest stop. There's nothing between there and the place they found the car, no town, not even any houses. She wouldn't abandon them, not when she'd asked him to look for families to take them in."

"I don't like this, Evan." She rubbed her cheek to his white silk shirt, feeling the solid warmth of him beneath it. "If they did get out, they'd have nowhere to go, they wouldn't know anybody—if they really were trafficked, they probably didn't speak much English. They'd just . . . vanish."

He rocked her from side to side for a moment, then leaned back to look into her face. "You want to go for that walk?"

"No, I think I just heard the first thunder outside. It'll be raining in a few minutes. And I want to talk to Jamey—if Cam ever gets finished with him," she added with a little smile, glancing to where the pair were standing oh-so-casually at the bar.

"Invite him to dinner tomorrow. Cam's staying with us and doesn't have a car, so there's no escape."

"Oh, he'd just hide in the barn or the tack room—or this staircase nobody but him ever knew about."

"NICE SPEECH," Cam offered.

"You've heard most of it before," Jamey replied with a shrug.

"It's acquired polish." *Like the rest of you,* he didn't add. The careless, instinctive elegance of the law student with money had become a sophisticated presentation of young professional on the rise. If he'd been beautiful back then, there weren't words for him now.

"What happened out there tonight, Cam?"

He'd been waiting for the question. Not that it was particularly welcome, but at least he was more or less prepared for it. "Nostalgia. Just something we had to get out of the way."

"Bullshit." Jamey leaned back against the bar, propped on his elbows. "And even if that was true, we didn't do anything that would've—"

"—relieved the unresolved sexual tension?" Cam interrupted. "Yeah, that was kind of dumb. It was dark, we were alone, relatively safe, and we weren't in each other's pants. What the hell's wrong with us?"

Jamey gritted his teeth. "There are plenty of guys in the world who can say 'You wanna exchange Hallmark cards or you wanna fuck?' I'm not one of them."

"Me, neither." He laughed briefly. "Maybe that's our problem."

"We want more?"

"We want too much."

"You know what I want? Everything."

Cam shook his head. "I don't know what that is."

There was a small silence before Jamey asked, "You'll be around for a while, won't you?"

"At Woodhush. We could maybe . . . I don't know, talk. . . ."

"Talk like we're doing now, or talk like we did outside?" Jamey smiled, and the complexity of humor and unashamed sensuality caught at Cam's throat.

"Uh . . . both?"

"You look like a couple of gunslingers checking out the crowd at a saloon," said Evan—sauntering up to the bar as if his title and badge empowered him to ride a palomino down the dusty Chisholm Trail instead of a Chevy on the well-paved roads of Pocahontas County.

"There's laws around here against loitering with intent—so get past the loitering and on to the intent part, okay?"

"My God," Jamey exclaimed, "you're as bad as Holly!"

"Takes practice," Evan allowed. "Have you clued him in yet, Cam?"

Cam was so shocked he couldn't even splutter. Surely Evan couldn't mean to include Jamey in exploration of a staircase that according to all the usual laws of reality didn't even exist—

Evidently Lachlan had been taking Fiend Lessons from Holly. He grinned, his eyes saying he knew exactly what Cam was thinking and had provoked those thoughts on purpose. "Lulah's been dealing with the twins since this afternoon. Cam's going to give up his room for the night so she can get some peace and quiet, breakfast in bed tomorrow, a massage, the whole shebang."

Cam rallied enough to ask, "And I'm buying?"

"You are," Evan confirmed. "I gotta say it's awful nice of you—the Westmoreland Inn ain't cheap."

Jamey looked suddenly thoughtful. "Before I forget, I've been meaning to ask for ages—didn't anybody tell Weiss that the name's spelled wrong?"

In all fairness, Cam couldn't accuse Holly of giving Jamey Pedantry Lessons; he'd been born that way.

"HE'S A FAGGOT, isn't he? Jamey Stirling, I mean."

Holly was abruptly glad she wasn't holding a drink; shock would have either sent it flying through the air or shattering to the floor.

"I'm right, aren't I?" Erika Ayala continued. "I've heard things about almost everybody of note in this county—but especially about him."

Guardedly, Holly turned to the woman and looked down about half a foot at the earnest, dainty face below white-blond hair. "Why do you ask?"

"I just don't understand how people can let men like that into their homes, near their children—"

Holly nodded thoughtfully. "With all the diseases and so forth, you mean?"

"Well, of course. And besides that, they don't reproduce, do they? So they have to recruit. Your little boy is still a baby, but just wait until he gets to be a teenager like my three. The worry a mother goes through when she knows people like *that* are around—"

"Oh, but I'm afraid you've got it wrong, Mrs. Ayala." The mild tones of Ben Poulter came from Holly's other side. "Homosexuals don't recruit, but vampires do."

He smiled broadly—and if there was a Lord of the Undead, he was definitely directing the special effects, for as Ben's teeth flashed so did a crack of lightning outside, followed by rumbling thunder and the sudden drumbeat of rain. Holly barely heard it, because for the first time in her life she saw his canine teeth: sharp, pointed, and white as ice. For just an instant she was back in her bedroom at Woodhush, cringing away from a huge looming black bat—

But then Ben was just Ben again, who'd gone to school with her parents and her aunts, who was invited to come by Woodhush when Lulah decided to slaughter a calf or a pig, who had taken her and Cam out on summer nights to stargaze.

Erika faltered a step or two back and turned white to the lips.

Ben nodded politely as she skittered away on shaky legs, then turned to Holly. "Awful woman. Gib was a nice kid, as I recall. I wonder how he ended up with her?"

"You are just *bad*, Ben Poulter," she told him, trying not to laugh.

"In five minutes sh-she'll be telling herself sh-she couldn't possibly have seen what sh-she saw. It's how we all stay safe, isn't it? Your folk, and mine." His shoulders hitched dismissively. "By the way, it's just a guess, but I think sh-she thinks her eldest boy has a crush on Mr. Stirling."

Holly felt her mouth gape unattractively open. "Troy? Really?"

"You didn't notice him watching during the speech? Like he'd been thirsty for years and suddenly found—" He paused and smiled—not quite widely enough to display all his teeth. "Well, water, I suppose, to the rest of you."

This time she did giggle. Ben patted her on the hand and went to join his sisters on their way out the doors.

Departures had slowed due to the rain and the chaos of parked cars. On the one hand, Holly told herself, this was a good thing—she and Cam and Evan would have an excellent excuse for lingering—but the mess outside would also delay Lulah's arrival. She'd seen Tim and Laura leave as soon as they'd discarded their aprons, and figured they might be about halfway to Woodhush by now. Another forty-five minutes, she thought, and then they could all troop up to Cam's room using the silly excuse Evan had dreamed up, and after that—

"Shit," she muttered, seeing Gib making his way toward her. Why the hell didn't he take his wife and her kid and just go home?

"Hi," he said, not at all shy about strafing her bare legs with his gaze. "There seems to be a traffic jam out there. Let's go onto the verandah and watch the rain."

She asked herself Ben's question. How *had* Gib ended up with Erika—who was close enough to be watching but not close enough to hear. When Gib's dark eyes sought and found his wife, and a little smile twitched a corner of his mouth, Holly knew Evan had been right about the pair of them.

"I don't think so," she said in quiet tones.

"Holly!" His smile got wider—for his audience. "Are you still riled over what I said before? I didn't mean anything by it. All I want—"

—is for me to make big eyes at you right under your wife's nose so you can go home and fuck each other's brains out because her jealousy really gets you both going?

"Don't," she snapped. "I don't care what you want. Whatever game you've got going, I won't be a part of it."

"I don't understand." His eyes had kindled with restless anticipation, flickering from her to Erika and back again. "Oh, wait a minute—you think she—?" He gave her his most disarming smile. "Well, I admit she *is* the jealous type. But, hey, come on, Holly, how long have we known each other?"

"We knew each other for a couple of years a long, long time ago. I'm telling you again, Gib, whatever you're playing at, leave me out of it."

"I can't help it that she's like that. Besides, that's just marriage."

"Not *my* marriage, it isn't."

"Do you really think it works like that?" he asked, his smile expanding.

She wanted to slap him. She came so close to doing it that she had to turn away, almost shaking with anger and insult—and disappointment, that he had turned out to be so much less than the man she had once thought he would become.

EVAN WATCHED THE LITTLE BYPLAY with increasing interest, and no small amount of apprehension. He knew what Gib was doing. It was the kind of thing guaranteed to detonate Holly's temper. As much as the man deserved it, Evan quite selfishly needed her calm and focused for whatever they'd have to do later, when Lulah arrived and applied her substantial experience to that magical staircase.

As he kept one eye on Holly and Gib, and the other on Erika, he thought over what the woman had said about jealousy and possession—although she hadn't used those words. If Gib was single-minded about flying, Holly was perfectly ruthless about writing. Uncompromising, as only a committed craftsperson can be; so completely self-centered when she was working that she didn't even realize it.

Work came first. He'd recognized that a long time ago. It never bothered him that much, because he figured she'd scrunch things around until there was room enough for him, and then the kids when and if they came. He had discovered during their first months together that when she worked, she *worked*. She ate, slept, thought, dreamed to the rhythm of her book. This happened for days on end, sometimes as long as a week; then she'd come back from wherever she'd been. But when it came time for work again, she took herself off to her interior landscapes. And at such times she became ruthless again, self-centered again, totally alive only when totally alone within herself.

To be honest, he missed that about her. She needed to find a book. He couldn't imagine being jealous of it; he did love that she was passionate about things, because he was one of the things she was most passionate about.

And right now she was passionately pissed off at Gib Ayala. Lachlan touched Cam's arm, nodded in the appropriate direction, and the two of them set off—not to Holly's rescue, but Gib's.

"—Holly, we've always been friends—"

"Hey, Freckles!" Cam said brightly. "How're you doin', Gib? You won't remember me—Cam Griffen, Holly's cousin. I hear you've been running Shenandoah Regional lately. Nice gig for a frustrated fighter pilot, right?"

He kept up the inane spill of chatter as Evan coaxed Holly a few paces away. "Do I need to challenge him to a duel?"

"No, my liege lord. My honor wasn't impugned—no, I take it back. It *was*. He was using me to make her think—and *she* thinks that if I got the chance I'd—"

"I know," Lachlan interrupted gently. "I was right about them, huh?"

"I owe you an apology."

He slung an arm around her waist. "I woulda been good at a duel. Swords, pistols, a good swift kick in the balls—"

She snorted. "He could bench-press your weight without breaking a sweat."

"He can bench-press my Glock."

Her brows drew together in a long, slow frown. "Evan . . . he said 'that's just marriage.' But it isn't. That's—possession. Ownership."

"Well, I kind of hate to bring it up, but—seems to me you used to get jealous every so often."

"Yes, I did," she replied. "But that was before we were married."

"You put that much trust in a license from city hall, a Handfasting, and your own blood?"

"If you'd been spelled six ways to next Imbolc, it wouldn't have mattered, because I'm the one the spell would concentrate on and my blood doesn't work on me. I put that much trust in *you.* Evan, we promised each other certain things. Did you mean them?"

"Yes!" he exclaimed, stung that she could even ask.

"I know. You gave me your word. There aren't many people who understand what 'honor' is anymore," she mused. "It's more than keeping a promise. It's that any promise you make, you never would have made it in the first place if the truth and the emotion behind it weren't as much a part of you as your own heartbeat. Do you see what I mean? Your honor is a fundamental truth of who you are, the way you think and the way you live your life."

He nodded, and waited, knowing she wasn't finished.

"We belong to each other because we choose to. Neither of us bought and paid for the other. What we paid for, what we went through hell to get and hold onto, was to be together and make a life with each other."

He smiled and hugged her closer. "And here I thought you only wanted me for the sex." Looking over her shoulder, he added, "Nice work, Cam."

Holly turned. "Yeah—thanks, Peaches. Have we got our story—you should pardon the expression—straight?"

"I'm being a sweet, adorable, thoughtful, generous nephew and giving Lulah my room and my spa certificates as a respite from you and your *enfants terribles.* Will she remember to bring an overnight bag?" Not waiting for an answer, he went on, "You realize that this is going to be damned tricky, right?"

"How tricky?" she asked.

"Those magic stairs are mucking about with reality on a scale most of us never dare. Dad always said that when it comes to magic and the laws of physics, the latter will get their revenge, no matter how thorough the spells or how careful you are with them." He paused a long moment. "And it'll take a lot of power. I'm not sure I'm up to it."

"Between you and Lulah, we'll do just fine," she predicted with confidence. "She's got the spellcraft, you've got strength to add to hers, and I'll just do what I usually do—"

Lachlan tickled her ear with one finger. "Stand around looking cute with your thumb stuck in the air?"

"I may not be much by way of the family heritage, but I have relatives I can threaten—and they can transform you into any kind of toad I want."

"Out of luck, lady love. I already figured out Cam's real name."

They had been speaking quietly, not in the furtive whispers that always attracted attention but not loudly enough to be heard above the music. Nobody could have overheard their conversation, unless she had deliberately approached to listen.

"Mrs. Lachlan," said Erika Ayala. "May I have a word?"

The three of them swung around. She stood there, fragile and pretty, square-shouldered as a West Point cadet on parade. Evan glanced at Holly, then at Cam. He knew his expression must mirror theirs: *What the hell did we say?*

"I have a favor to ask." She looked briefly at the two men. "In private."

"Holly?" Cam ventured.

"It's all right," Holly said, not taking her eyes from Erika's grimly determined face. "Evan, it's all right."

He nodded and took Cam's elbow in an uncompromising grip. "We'll be around." As they walked a few yards away, he muttered, "Please, God, don't let her rip the woman's throat out."

"At least not without a drop cloth on the floor."

HOLLY GESTURED TOWARD THE PIANO alcove with a commendably steady hand. When they were at a reasonable remove from the thinning crowd, she asked bluntly, "Favor?"

"I know what you are. My husband has hinted at it. So have some other people—they let things slip, thinking nobody will understand or believe. I'm not sure I do believe it, but the evidence does seem to add up."

"To what?"

"I don't know what you call it among yourselves. Conjuring, witchcraft, Satanism—casting spells or consorting with spirits, I don't care. I don't have any interest in you or your kind, except for one thing."

"The favor."

Erika was silent for a moment. Then, the words almost torn out of her: "Make my son not be a queer."

Holly didn't react. She couldn't. It wasn't physically possible to react.

"You can do some kind of spell or incantation and make Troy change. I've seen him looking at other boys in school, and tonight at Mr. Stirling—I tried to tell you earlier that I was worried, I was hoping I could appeal to you as a mother. But then I heard what you were saying about power, and I realized what you are—" She gulped a breath. "He's only seventeen, he's too young to know anything about—"

"No." Was that her voice, so soft and quiet?

"You have to." She stated it as simple fact. "I will *not* have my son be a queer. I just won't allow it. But I *will* let everyone know exactly what you are."

"No," Holly heard herself say again.

"I'll do it. I'll find a way to prove it. You were so sure of yourselves, so smug—talking about such things right out in the open—how many other mistakes have you made? Someone knows. And not everyone in this county thinks you and your family are the next best thing to the Second Coming! You, especially, trying to steal my husband—" She got hold of herself. "But we're not talking about that right now. I'll forget about that if you do what I want."

Holly could only shake her head.

"You *have* to," Erika insisted. "I won't stop until I get proof—and if you were stupid enough to talk here, tonight, what about the last twenty or thirty years?" She looked down at her tightly clasped hands for a moment, then back up into Holly's face. "The rumors alone would—"

"What makes you think you'll be *allowed* to spread rumors, let alone find this 'proof' you're talking about?"

Erika didn't flinch. Holly smiled thinly, awarding points for sheer stubbornness.

"If I am what you seem to think I am," Holly went on, "then surely you have some idea what 'my kind' are capable of. Do you really want to risk it?"

"For my son—of course. Change him. Make him normal."

"He *is* normal. You're the one who's sick. Appeal to me as a mother? You want him to be straight for your sake, not his."

"Help my son."

"He doesn't need help. He doesn't need to be fixed or healed or changed—"

"You slut," she breathed. "I'll ruin you. Everyone will see you for the filthy witch you are—"

"Take your best shot," Holly invited coldly. This wasn't the first time she'd been threatened with exposure as a Witch—but this was the first time she'd ever made threats in return, and it horrified her. She forced herself to calm down. "Erika, this isn't necessary. You don't have to—"

"It won't be necessary if you cure my son of being a fag!"

"I wouldn't even if I could!" Looking down at the exquisite little face, the perfect little body, all at once she understood everything. "You can't stand it that you can't control everything that doesn't fit with your idea of perfection. You don't want people to look at your gay son, and then look at you, and whisper, 'Poor dear, she produced a defective.' You want him to be your idea of perfect—because otherwise what would people think of *you?* You love the idea that other women want your husband, because that means he must be a real catch, so if he's married to you then you must be pretty terrific as well. And lucky you, you get to prove it over and over again, because he's really good at making you jealous—is that the only way he can get himself laid? When you get freaked out and reassert ownership?"

"Shut up. Just—shut up!"

"You stupid, pathetic— I'm warning you, Erika, right here and now. Let Troy be. He's your son. At least pretend that you love him enough to accept him as he is. Because if you make him hate himself, I'll hear about it. I'll hear any rumors you try to spread and I'll know if you ask any questions you shouldn't be asking. And I will make your life a hell you can't possibly imagine. Do you understand me?"

Holly didn't wait for an answer. She walked as quickly as her trembling knees would allow to where Evan and Cam stood watching. When she got to them, she sought the shelter of her husband's arms.

"Don't ask," she said when Cam drew breath to speak. "Not now. Just get me out of here."

Twelve

HOLLY VAGUELY HEARD EVAN telling Cam to take her upstairs, that he was going stay and wait for Lulah. Whatever; she was climbing stairs with her cousin's arm strong and fierce around her, and then walking down a corridor of lush dark scarlet carpeting and Regency-striped walls, and then inside a sitting room with a desk in one corner and an arrangement of two sofas and a chair around a low coffee table. Cam guided her to one of the sofas, shifting his embrace to her shoulders, and pulled her against him as they sat down. She stared out the window at the rain for a little while, until a blast of lightning made her flinch.

"Talk to me, Freckles."

"It's not so much what she said," Holly began. "I mean, it is, but it's so many other things besides that."

"Start with the easiest."

She sorted through disgust and disappointment, worry and outrage, and came up with what was not exactly easiest but certainly the most selfish—and therefore least important. "I threatened her, Cam. I've never threatened anybody in my life with retaliatory Witchcraft. It's not as if it's ever been an option for me. But I told her if I heard anything I didn't like, I'd—"

"You admitted what you are?"

She thought back. "Not really. But I didn't deny it, either. I let her think what she wanted. And I told her I'd make her life hell."

"But you didn't actually use words like—"

"—like *magic* and *Witch*? No."

"Then don't worry about it. What did she want?"

"IS THERE SOMETHING WRONG?" asked Bernhardt Weiss, and Lachlan turned from watching Cam escort Holly to the stairs.

"She's always forgetting that as much as she likes crab, it doesn't much like her," he lied easily. "Her cousin's taking her up to his room for a little while."

"I'm so sorry. Perhaps someone on our staff might be of assistance?"

"She'll be okay in a half hour or so. I'll keep it in mind, though, thanks." He scanned the remaining guests, all waiting for their cars—or for umbrellas so they could get to their cars without drowning. "Man, it's really comin' down out there, isn't it?"

"Quite spectacular, the thunderstorms in the Shenandoah Valley. So different from hurricanes—" He stopped, then continued smoothly, "I find these storms most stimulating."

"So do my kids, unfortunately. My daughter wants to stay up all night and watch every raindrop, like she expects them to be all different, like snowflakes. My son goes for the crayons and starts drawing on anything handy—sometimes the floor." He chuckled. "And then there's the dog, who just hides under whatever he can scrunch himself beneath."

"Ah, brave children, are they? And interested in the world. In a child these are very good things."

Evan nodded, trying to get a fix on his expression—complacency?—when a very familiar and very unexpected voice called his name. He looked over the crowd and at the main doors saw a wet blond head beside a wet red head. "Nicky?" Rudely abandoning Weiss, he threaded his way to them. "Lulah, where the hell did *he* come from?"

"Connecticut, of course," she drawled.

"How are you, Evan?" Nicholas Orlov shook his hand, smiling, but worry furrowed his brow. "Alec and I arrived about an hour after you and Holly left. I'm afraid we got rather distracted by the children—*te jó Isten,* they've grown! Just since June!" He ran his fingers through his sopping hair. "You wouldn't happen to have a towel handy, would you?"

"Upstairs, in Cam's room." He turned to Lulah, who was wringing rainwater out of her ponytail. "Why didn't you tell me on the phone that Alec and Nicky were here?"

"Because I didn't want to waste time. I have a powerful and immediate need to skin that boy alive for not bothering to mention he was coming home. A hotel, for the love of all the saints! And *this* hotel, too!"

CAM SHOOK HIS HEAD. "I don't know why anything surprises me anymore. Will she bully the boy, or do to him what Morgan's parents did?"

"I don't know. I think—I think Jamey's example is a good one, that maybe Troy will compare Jamey's life and the way people respect him to what his mother's attitude is, and—oh, shit, I don't know."

"But she's his mother. Whatever happens, he'll always hate himself in some way for disappointing her." He sank back into the cushions. "Why do people do these things to each other?"

She waited until he looked at her again, and then waited some more until a tiny smile quivered at the corners of his mouth.

"Yeah," he said, "I know. Ours not to reason why—because reason has nothing to do with it." Grasping a pillow to his chest, he started picking at its crimson silk fringe. "If Erika hadn't overheard us talking about magic, she wouldn't have said anything—but if she hadn't said anything, you wouldn't know to look out for Troy."

"What was it your father always said? That there are no accidents, just opportunities disguised as coincidences."

"I never did think that made any sense."

Holly stretched out her legs to prop her feet on the coffee table. "Do you know how much I hate being a Witch but not being a real Witch? I don't hate what I am, I hate what I'm not. Listening to Erika threaten to accuse us all of being what we are—and then listening to myself threaten *her* and knowing I've got nothing to back it up—"

"I always wondered how you stand it, frankly. I can do things, I can be—proactive, I guess. How did Evan put it? You get to look cute and stick your thumb in the air."

"It's a good thing I have talented friends and relations, then, isn't it? Just what an otherwise helpless Spellbinder needs."

He glanced over at her. "You're whining again."

"Play nice, or I won't let you have any of my special high-octane blood tonight, and you can fumble around your secret magical staircase on your own."

Another voice, gently shaded with the vowels of the Virginia Tidewater, said behind them, "So that's why you're all still here."

Holly squeezed her eyes shut and muttered, "I swear by everything holy, if I get eavesdropped on one more time tonight, I'm going to start taking hostages." She looked at Cam. "You left the door unlocked, didn't you?"

"He did," Jamey confirmed.

Cam sighed. "Evan and Lulah are coming upstairs, of course I left the door open. Also, I'm an idiot. As has been pointed out at least once tonight." He stood and turned, facing Jamey. "Hi."

Holly scrunched around to kneel on the sofa, arms folded over its back. "How're you doing, Jamey?" she asked with her brightest smile.

Black brows arched eloquently.

"Is this where we ask what you heard? Or do we just assume it was kind of everything?"

"Pretty much from the part about what a good example I am. I think I can guess most of the rest." He took a few steps forward. "Well, except for the Witch part, and whatever a Spellbinder is. You know I have to ask."

Holly traded looks with Cam. "Your call."

"Your secret," he retorted.

"Yours, too. You know enough so that with my help, he doesn't have to be told anything."

"Holly! You think I'd do that to him?"

"Good boy." She smiled. "That's exactly what I wanted to hear."

Jamey shifted restlessly. "If somebody doesn't tell me something soon—"

"What do you think, Cam? Words or deeds?"

"How'd Evan find out?"

"Accidentally—and then I demonstrated with Nicky's vodka glasses, not having the wherewithal to establish my bona fides more directly." She watched Jamey's gaze cut from one to the other of them, gray eyes darkening below an ever-deeper frown. "I think we need to show him, and I think we need to use me." She surveyed the young man head to heels—a rewarding occupation in and of itself, but she was looking for something that would convince him, something Cam could spell in such a way that Jamey would believe what they were about to tell him.

"It's raining," Cam said suddenly.

Holly rummaged in her skirt pocket for the little pouch containing needle and alcohol wipes she was never without. Cam's lips moved, and Holly pricked her thumb. He touched his left index finger to her thumb, then walked around the sofa to where Jamey stood, slack-jawed and wide-eyed. Quickly, before Jamey could react, he drew an inch-wide circle on the cuff of his shirt where it protruded below the sleeve of his leather jacket.

"Stick your arm out the window," Cam instructed.

"You're kidding, right?"

"Do it," Holly ordered.

"Do you trust me?" Cam asked at the same time.

Holly smiled to herself as Jamey obeyed—because he was obeying Cam, not her. He paced warily toward the window, unlatched it, pushed open the screen, and extended his arm. When he stepped away, his cuff was dark and wet, except for the little circle Cam had drawn. He looked down at it, then at the two of them.

"And this proves—?"

Cam murmured something under his breath, and the rainwater leached from Jamey's shirt, turning to droplets that slipped onto the floor.

"He's very good, is our Cam," Holly remarked. "The material isn't permanently waterproof except for that one little place on your cuff. For permanent, he needed me."

"Spellbinder," Cam murmured.

"Spell—" Jamey looked down at his sleeve, then back at Cam, and gulped.

"Uh-huh," Holly said. "My blood. His talent is for textiles—linen, silk, wool, cotton, and so forth. Remind me to tell you sometime about the prickly heat he inflicted on this evil little troll he had for geometry, until Uncle Griff caught him at it and grounded him—magically speaking—for a month. And then there was the time he kind of overdid a linen napkin wrapped around a bottle of white wine. Instead of nicely chilled—"

Jamey interrupted, "The afghan. At your apartment that day—it was wool."

Holly waited for Cam to say something. When it was apparent that he wouldn't—or maybe couldn't—she went on, "Any kind of natural fiber, really—I don't actually know, because the only talent I have is the blood thing. What did he do to the afghan?"

"I'm sorry," Cam said. "I had to."

"Just to keep me from kissing you?"

Holly felt her eyes widen, and decided it was way past time for her to leave. She was almost to the door when Cam blurted out, "I *had* to!"

And she couldn't help telling him, "No, you probably didn't—but you can discuss that without me. And Jamey—maybe the kissing thing would go over better this time?"

With that, she slipped out the door, wishing it locked from the outside.

"YOU'RE HERE BECAUSE OF WHAT was in that letter, aren't you?" Lachlan asked as they passed the front desk, heading for the main stairs. "And I'm not talking about the check." He smiled sidelong at Nicky, aware that Weiss was in the vicinity, unsure if he was watching, presenting a pleasant front in case he was.

"Indeed," Nicky replied. "Alec and I made further enquiries, and decided we'd pay you a little visit."

Evan interpreted this to mean that more conjuring with rocks or tea leaves or candle wax or whatever had yielded a more urgent warning about Kirby or Bella. He consciously unclenched his fists and traced one hand up the polished mahogany banister as they started the climb. "All of which you've mentioned to Lulah."

"Of course. We left Alec back at the house for a reason."

Lachlan touched Lulah's elbow. "Laura and Tim hadn't arrived before you left?"

"I told Alec to let them in and then lock up behind them, if you know what I mean."

He did. They reached the first landing, skirted the central display table with its gigantic arrangement of fresh flowers—one of Weiss's amenities-that-meant-so-much—turned, and started up the next flight. At the place where Cam had walked right into the wall, Evan paused, looking for a reaction. Both continued on up the stairs. "Damn," he muttered, and followed.

They made the turn into the hall, heading for Room 314, and almost ran into Holly.

"What in the world—? Nicky?"

DESPITE HOLLY'S ENCOURAGEMENT, the kissing thing didn't happen. Jamey's mind, in fact, was so far from anything of the sort that all he could do was stare at Cam, who started by looking apologetic, then uncomfortable, and finally defiant.

"Well?"

"Well, what?" Jamey snapped.

Cam flapped a hand in the air as if trying to grab a coherent word or two. At last he managed, "I don't know what you're thinking!"

"That makes two of us."

"Dammit, Jamey—"

"What do I call you? What's the correct term for—for whatever it is you are?"

"Witch. Capital W, please."

"I'm not going to ask why you never said anything. It's obvious why not. You never even trusted me enough to admit that you're gay until I confronted you with it," he said bitterly, "how could I expect—"

"That's not—"

"—but what really pisses me off is that everybody in this fucking county seems to know about your family, and I work with Evan on an almost daily basis, and I'm over at Woodhush at least once a week, and I feel like a complete fool!"

"It's not an uncommon reaction. Think about it from our side of things for a minute. Or—no, think about when you first figured out you were gay. It isn't exactly something you run around announcing to the whole world."

"It isn't something to be ashamed of, either!"

"They call it a Witch Hunt for a reason, Jamey." Cam shrugged and turned away. "Why do you think there are so few of us left?"

Jamey looked down at his sleeve. There was no difference in the cotton where Cam had drawn the little circle in Holly's blood. No lingering evidence. For a moment he was tempted to go into the bathroom and run water from the sink over his cuff again, just to make sure. He was a lawyer; he liked evidence that didn't vanish on him. But to do such a thing would indicate he didn't believe Cam, which would be a lie. Every instinct he possessed—nothing to do with the trained intellectual legal mind—had trusted Cam at first sight.

"Okay," he said slowly. "You're just exercising a little self-preservation. I can understand that."

"Can you? Oh, imagine my relief."

"Stop it. I'm just wondering what it takes and how long it takes to earn some trust from you people."

"You heard Holly. Evan found out by accident, just like you. It's not something we put on billboards on Sunset Boulevard."

"But this is *me,* Cam! Did you think I'd—I don't know, blackmail you? Betray you? Does everybody automatically get thrown into the same category as Erika Ayala?"

A soft but emphatic knocking on the door interrupted him. Cam flung his arms wide in a *Fuck it, I give up* gesture and called loudly, "Come on in! Join the circus!"

Jamey watched with escalating bewilderment as Holly, Lulah, Evan, and a slight-shouldered blond man aged maybe fifty-five entered the room. There were hugs and exclamations, smiles and kisses, and Jamey felt even more of a fool than before.

Evan sauntered over during the reunion festivities. "It's a shock," he remarked, "but you'll get used to it."

"How long did it take you?"

"Less time than you'd expect. Me, I was more pissed off because she didn't tell me how much money she makes."

"You people are all insane," Jamey announced.

"Yep. Like I said, you'll get used to it."

"Or run shrieking into the night," said the blond man. "Hello, Mr. Stirling. I'm Nicholas Orlov—Cam and Holly's Uncle Nick. I understand you've learned our little secret."

"Uh—yes. Nice to meet you." He shook the man's hand. "And please call me Jamey."

"Lulah was right—lovely manners." He slanted a look upward at Evan. "Do you want to guide him through this using your own experience, or just throw him into the deep end and see how he swims, the way Holly did with you?"

"Oh, I'm sure he can handle it."

Looking around to find that all eyes were on him, Jamey met Cam's worried, wary gaze, and deliberately called up the kind of smile he used in the courtroom when counsel for the defense had just blindsided him. "I can handle it," he said to the world at large, hoping he wasn't telling the biggest lie of his life. And then he looked at Cam again. All the gentle whimsy had fled that expressive face, leaving a man who was a little tired, a little scared, and a lot alone. "It's okay," Jamey added. "I can handle it." It wasn't a lie at all.

NICK TOOK THE DESK CHAIR, straddling it with his arms folded across its back. Holly perched on the arm of the chair where Evan sat with long legs negligently sprawled. Lulah sat between Cam and Jamey on one of the sofas. This was by her own design. Nick wondered why for a moment, then decided it was consideration for Cam's obviously raw state of nerves. Proximity to the gorgeous young man with the troubled gray eyes was probably difficult enough. If touch, or even the prospect of touch, affected Cam the way Alec had always affected Nicky . . . well, it was better if Lulah sat between them.

Cam had very kindly dried off their clothing and removed the mud from their shoes. He couldn't do anything about their hair. Nick ran his fingers one more time back through the damp mess on his head, spared an interior sigh for the slow, inexorable retreat of his hairline, and wondered where to start.

Holly beat him to it. "Not to be ungracious, Nicky, but why are you here?"

"I'll tell you, but we don't have time for you to throw a fit. I know—saying that is the quickest way to guarantee it, but I'm telling you we don't have time. Alec and I, through various methods—all of which we checked at least twice—have come to the conclusion that one of your children is in some kind of danger, and it's going to happen in the next few days."

She fixed her husband with an angry glare. He arched a brow and shrugged. "No fits," she muttered.

"Thank you," Nick said, meaning it; he had longer experience of Holly in rant-and-rave mode than anyone here but Lulah and Cam. "We couldn't get anything specific—not which child, or where, or what would happen. But that's a separate problem. Lulah and I are here right now to investigate Cam's discovery."

"The staircase inside the walls." Jamey said it as if he dealt with such matters every day of the week.

"Yes," Cam said to his own hands, which were clasped schoolboy-prim in his lap. "Like the one at Woodhush, it's originally architectural, but it also reeks of magic. I think the staircase here is as old as the first house, but the spells are recent."

"Jesse and I worked for weeks on—" Lulah stopped, fixing her nephew with a long, dangerous look. "*'Like the one at Woodbush'*?"

"Long story, tell it later," Evan suggested.

"I think we can count on that," Lulah snapped.

Cam gave an audible gulp. "Anyway, that sign outside, about cell phones—it's there to take care of probably eighty percent of the questions that might come up about why there's no reception here. If your phone's off, you're not going to get any incoming calls. There's a barrier of some kind, but whether it's magical or electronic—"

"I'll be able to find out," Nick told him. "If I can't sense Alec, even at this distance, then it's spellcraft."

"Okay. But whichever, and I'm betting it's not technology, the other twenty percent could be explained by dead batteries or something—if people keep their phones on anyway and don't leave them at the front desk like it asks—"

"Cam!" Evan chided. "Breathe. What he means is that Lulah felt blind here—"

"Still do," she said. "It's magic. I'm convinced of it now. You won't sense Alec at all, believe me."

Nicky didn't like to explore the feelings this provoked in him. He rested his chin on his folded arms for a moment and wished his partner were here. "Then we're dealing with Witches who don't want to be discovered as Witches—and if they're hiding from the legitimate practitioners in Pocahontas County, then—" He glanced over at Cam, who had suddenly sat up very straight. "What is it?"

"The piano. I sensed magic, I'll swear I did."

"In a piano?"

Jamey Stirling, Nick observed, hadn't quite gotten the hang of this yet. "All manner of things can take and hold a spell. There are formulae that determine the strength of a particular working of magic, how long it will last, even who can be affected and who gets a free pass, as it were. Just as Cam works with fibers, some people specialize in wood, gemstones, herbs, fire, water, weather—"

"The piano tuner," Holly interrupted. "Sorry, Uncle Nicky—but there was a little Polish guy who was making the rounds just before Westmoreland opened—he'd been brought in special to deliver and tune the pianos here, and Weiss was courting the county, so he sent him around to tune everybody's pianos. We had him look at the upright in the parlor—"

Lulah was shaking her head. "I would have known. I never sensed any magic about that piano."

"You're not Cam, either. You don't know pianos inside and out. Music is part of his magic. And the upright," Holly concluded, "hasn't gone a hemidemisemiquaver out of tune since. Not in the heat or the cold or the damp or the dry."

Lulah's gaze flickered from niece to nephew. "All right. I'm convinced. But mainly because I still feel blind."

Nobody said anything for a minute or so. Nicky used the time to reach for his partner, miles away at Woodhush. Their connection was as real, as unique, as inexplicable as the one between Holly and Evan—which had nothing to do with magic at all—and the one he sensed was forming or perhaps strengthening between Cam and Jamey. The linkage was comfort and warmth, safety, *home*—and not there.

Even knowing why, he was shaken.

"Let's get this done tonight," Evan was saying. "I don't feel like leaving and then making up an excuse for getting all of us back in here. Besides that, Weiss keeps looking at me kind of funny. I don't like him. The chances that he doesn't know about the magic in this place are slim to none—and it seems to me that 'slim' just left the building."

Pushing aside the feeling of emptiness, Nick said simply, "I agree."

"There's a pretty large staff to get past," Holly mused. "The spa people, chambermaids, waiters, kitchen crew, security—but a lot of them will be occupied with cleaning up downstairs, won't they?"

"People are *still* slipping and sliding around in that mud rodeo they've got going out in the parking lot," Lulah added.

"So by the time it all gets sorted out, it'll be pretty late and they'll all be tired." Evan checked his watch. "It's almost eleven. I'm hoping that except for a few regular guards or whatever, they'll all just go to bed. But it's the 'whatever' that bothers me."

Cam shook his head. "Nothing set off any alarms when I was checking out the staircase behind the walls."

"No alarms that we know of."

Holly bumped Evan with her elbow. "Just the perfect ray of sunshine, aren't you?"

Jamey held up a palm. "Um . . . I don't mean to spoil the fun, but has anyone given at least a passing thought to the Fourth Amendment?"

Evan nudged Holly in return. "Pesky thing, the Bill of Rights. We really ought to get a warrant."

"Picky, picky."

"Grounds?" Cam prodded.

"I don't need any," Nick informed them.

"I thought you and Alec were retired," Holly said. "Besides, *your* mandate doesn't cover officers of the court."

Jamey was trying very hard not to look confused, and succeeded only in looking rather forlorn. Nick opened his mouth to explain. Evan beat him to it.

"They have rules, and a tendency to police themselves. Think of Nicky as an officer of a somewhat esoteric court. Another long story I'll save for later. Okay?"

"Okay," Jamey agreed warily.

"I don't know what you're worried about," Holly said. "We're all reasonably bright. I'm sure we'll think of something."

"If all else fails," Evan conceded, "I can always say I caught Nicky breaking and entering."

"Were I ever to do anything so crass," he replied with a sniff, "you would *never* catch me at it. Holly's right. Worry about it later. Now, what about other guests? Did anybody check the register at the front desk? Do we even know how many people are in residence tonight?"

"I can fix it so they won't hear anything," Cam volunteered. "All the wallpaper is silk. No expense spared."

Lulah nodded her satisfaction. "A silence spell and some coercion on the locks will keep them all safe enough. How many rooms?"

"Six on each floor," Evan said. "Varying sizes. Eighteen total."

"It'll take a while." Cam's frown cleared swiftly. "But I can explore walls for hidden entrances while I'm at it."

"Okay," Evan announced, "here's how it'll work. Cam, Nicky, we'll start from wherever we can get in, and head up. Lulah—"

"And Holly," Holly stated flatly.

"—and Holly," he acknowledged with an exasperated glance at his wife, "you head down. Jamey guards the entrance."

"From outside or inside?" Lulah asked.

"How would he warn us if he's outside? It's got to be within the staircase."

Cam scowled. Nick watched Holly try and fail to hide a smile.

"Not a word," Jamey warned. "I'm useless, but I won't be left out any more than Holly."

"We're real pains in the ass, aren't we?" She grinned at him.

"A lifelong aspiration. It's gratifying to know I'm fulfilling it at so critical a juncture in the proceedings—"

"Stash the *sesquipedalia verba,*" Cam admonished.

Jamey leaned around Lulah and glared at him. "'*Quid de utilitate loquar stercorandi?*'"

"Oh, shut up."

Nick waited what seemed a decent interval before asking, "Where's Herr Weiss likely to be after the ballroom empties out? Where's his office, his quarters?"

"Map," Cam said, "top desk drawer."

Turning, he rummaged and came up with a full-color brochure. As he fished for his glasses in his jacket pocket, he remarked, "I suppose you've noticed that they don't spell 'Westmorland' correctly."

"No!" Cam exclaimed with a sudden grin. "You're kidding!"

Nick eyed him dourly over the rims of his glasses, but forbore comment. "Hmm. I think we may assume that the staff dorm won't be of much interest. The main house is rather large, isn't it?" He studied the layout. Ground floor: restaurant and kitchen, ballroom, library, six smaller guest rooms. Second and third floors: six suites each, identical layouts. In the huge cellar was the spa, with the usual facilities for massage, workouts, sauna, steam; locker rooms, whirlpool, lap pool, and Olympic-sized pool. Also, interestingly enough, cold and hot plunges, like a Roman bath. He spared a moment's nostalgia for the Russian *bania* his stepfather Sergei Maximovich Orlov had built long ago in Hungary, then returned to the diagram. Outside the main house were two more buildings, one labeled CONFERENCE ROOMS AND OFFICES and the other one STAFF. He glanced at Cam. "Do we dare take the time to sneak over and put lock and silence spells on the outbuildings?"

"Cars," Holly said suddenly.

Evan nodded his understanding before Nicky had entirely comprehended the import of the word. "Lulah's the only one who can legitimately stick around. Eventually the place will clear out, and somebody will notice all our vehicles. Can we move them, hide them, without being seen?"

"It's a muddy mess out there," Lulah said. "Nobody will count heads. Stash Jamey's motorcycle in the back of my pickup."

Holly nodded. "Better than my Beemer."

Evan eyed his wife sidelong. "How come you have to think of this stuff when we've got other things to do?"

Succinctly: "I plot."

Nick repressed a smile and scrubbed his fingers back through his hair again. "All right, somebody go take care of the cars. Jamey, find a back door and let them in—"

"Not in those white shirts," Lulah pointed out. "And Holly honey, you ain't goin' noplace in those ridiculous shoes."

"I *like* those shoes," Evan said in wistful tones.

"So do I," Jamey seconded. "But she'll break an ankle for sure. And the skirt isn't all that practical, either. What's in your suitcase, Cam?"

Nick expected Holly to whine at least a little. Instead, she smiled and said, "I will consent to looking like a refugee from a trailer park yard sale only if somebody translates Jamey's Latin for me."

"It's one you ought to learn," Cam replied with equal sweetness. "Cicero might have had you in mind." Striking a pose, he declaimed, "'What shall I say about the usefulness of spreading manure?'"

Evan nudged Holly in the ribs. "You asked."

THE ONLY PAIR OF PANTS Cam had with him with even a remote chance of making it up over Holly's ass were part of a navy blue Armani suit. The three inches separating them in height were all in his legs. She sat on the edge of the bathtub and rolled up the hems, cussed under her breath, rolled them up some more, cussed a little louder, and—Armani or no Armani—thought seriously about finding a pair of scissors.

From the other side of the bathroom door she heard Evan say, "I'd never get it buttoned. You got any sweaters in there?"

"This one might work—it's pretty big on me."

Holly shouldered into Cam's dark green dress shirt and tied the tails around her waist. Turning up the cuffs to her wrists, she surveyed her reflection—gold rings, diamond bracelet, and all—and winced. The lipstick, car keys, leather folder with her driver's license, and her needle-and-alcohol-wipes kit that had been in her skirt and jacket pockets were transferred to the pants. Perched again on the tub, she unrolled a pair of socks, then looked at Cam's sneakers. A dozen layers of socks wouldn't make them fit. "Screw it," she muttered, deciding to go barefoot, and opened the door.

Oh, my.

Three shirtless men were arranged ornamentally around the room. Two of them were trying not to look at each other. Holly could scarcely decide where to look first.

Jamey was all lean, luscious muscle covered in nut-brown skin that just begged to be drizzled in sage honey. Cam, more lightly built but just as powerful, was peaches-and-cream dusted with cinnamon. Very nice indeed, the both of them—but while sweets were all very well, she preferred the main course. Taller than either of the younger men, stronger through the shoulders and arms, sun-bronzed and solid—if Jamey made her think of honey-smeared baklava and Cam was peach pie, Evan was . . . prime rib. Flank steak . . . rump roast . . . tenderloin . . . .

A WOLF WHISTLE TURNED all three of them toward the bathroom door. Lounging there, shoulder against the doorframe, looking preposterous in Cam's clothing, was Holly—smiling as if she'd invented them.

"I do purely love the sight of a long-legged man in blue jeans. And now here's three of 'em, right before my poor dazzled eyes. I declare, a girl could get spoiled."

Lachlan watched Jamey blush and Cam stick out his tongue at her. Both of them grabbed for their shirts like teenaged girls caught in just their bras.

"Oh, don't hurry on my account," Holly drawled. "In fact, take your time."

"You know what you are, McClure?" Evan asked. "You're a dirty old broad."

Cam snorted. "She's been a dirty old broad since she was fifteen years old."

"And I've loved every scenic second of it," she shot back. "But this, I have to tell you, will rank right up there among the culminating moments of my life."

"Yeah?" Evan started toward her, still shirtless. "And the ones that rank above it are . . . ?"

"Careful, Holly," Jamey laughed suddenly. "Appease the beast."

"The beast knows very well they all have to do with him."

"Yeah?" Lachlan said again, looming over her now. "Name one."

She curled her fingers into the low-slung waistband of his jeans. "First orgasm you ever gave me. I think I'm still shaking from that one."

"Jesus!" Cam exclaimed as his head emerged from the neck of a black long-sleeved t-shirt. "Don't you two ever stop?"

"I do my best," she said in deliberate echo of what Evan had said earlier that night, and he leaned down to kiss her. A few moments later, she drew back a little. "Get dressed, or I won't be held responsible."

The plum cashmere sweater would indeed be large on Cam. It fit Evan like bark on a tree. Having stashed her clothes and shoes in Cam's suitcase, Holly was happily ensconced in the desk chair by now, ogling at her leisure.

"Black does absolutely nothing for you, Cam. What were you thinking? And I don't know how you could have made a mistake like that charcoal shirt, although I like what it does to Jamey's eyes. In fact, he should wear your shirts more often."

"Lady love," Lachlan said, "you'll excuse my saying so, of course, but right now you're in no position to give fashion advice."

Jamey snorted. "What is this, *Project Runway*?" When all three stared at him, he blushed. "I confess. I watch that show. I conform to the gay fashionista stereotype. Pillory me later. Is everybody set?"

Evan gave them all a once-over, his gaze lingering at Holly's bare feet. She looked down, and grimaced.

"Mine are big," she said. "His are bigger."

Evan took a pair of balled-up socks from her hands and tossed them to her cousin. "Do something to these, will you?"

Cam thought about it for a second, then squeezed the socks between both hands. Lobbing them back at Holly, he smiled a smile of pure sweet wickedness.

"All right, what'd you do?" she demanded.

"Something. Just like he said."

She eyed the socks, then pulled them on. "As long as they don't set me to dancing maniacally like the princess in the fairy tale, I'm good with it."

"You actually trust me?"

"Hell, no. But I remind you, darling dear, that whereas Evan seems to have figured out certain things of a—shall we say—floral nature, Jamey remains unaware of—"

"Warm and dry," Cam interrupted in haste. "Silent. Impervious to punctures. Sorry, didn't have time to include a pedicure."

"Unaware of what?" Jamey asked. Everyone, particularly Cam, ignored him.

"I suppose," Evan asked, "it'd be too much to ask you to keep her from tripping over her own two feet?"

"It would." Watching as she bent to fold up the hems of his pants again, Cam intoned, "'I grow old . . . I grow old . . . /I shall wear the bottoms of my trousers rolled.'"

"Nobody likes a smart-ass," Evan informed him. "Especially a *literate* smart-ass."

Holly straightened up and smiled her sweetest at him. "You just wait. First pair of scissors I see—"

"My best Armani suit? Don't you fucking *dare*!"

Thirteen

FOR A WHILE Lachlan actually thought they were going to get away with it.

As Lulah and Nicky went after the brass locks on the third floor, with Holly trailing along looking as useless as she probably felt, he and Cam and Jamey made their way downstairs to take care of the cars. Weiss, still in the ballroom doorway bidding good-bye to his guests, had his back turned to them, and that was good. Gib, Erika, and Troy were right ahead of them, and that was bad.

Just how bad, Lachlan wasn't going to let Cam open his mouth to let everybody else find out. He glimpsed the younger man's clenched profile, groaned inwardly, and put a grin on his face wide enough so that a even casual observer could have counted his molars.

"Hey, Gib! There you are! Holly's upstairs—Lulah's had it with baby-sitting, wants to get herself spa'd tomorrow, so she's spending the night—Holly said be sure to find you and say goodnight for her. Let me hold that umbrella, Erika. Troy, get the door for your mother. Geez, I hope this rain lets up or all the outdoor barbeques tomorrow are gonna end up as picnics on the rug. Where's your car? Troy, do me a favor and help Jamey load his motorcycle into that red pickup over there. Thanks. Cam, here's the keys to the Beemer—you and Jamey head back to Woodhush, we'll be there in a while. Don't let the kids con you into milk and cookies—the sugar rush will keep them up until dawn."

He knew very well where he'd gotten this overflow of frivolous chatter. No one could live with Holly as long as he had and not pick up the knack of piling on the words until anyone within range simply collapsed from the weight of them. Sending Troy off with Jamey had earned him a barrage of icicles from Erika's pale blue eyes. Gib looked mildly confused. Cam was still seething—but after a brusque nod he set off to find the black BMW.

Lulah had been right about the mud. Cars, trucks, and SUVs spun their wheels and slewed across the lawns until tires found purchase on the gravel drive. Lachlan grinned to himself, relishing in advance the fun of an official four-wheel-drive vehicle he could steer right past everybody else with or without lights and siren. Cutting more gouges in Herr Weiss's manicured grass would be a satisfying bonus.

"Watch out, Erika, that's more like a sinkhole than a puddle." He slid a hand around her waist to steady her, and saw her gaze flicker to Gib to make sure he was watching. Lachlan resisted the urge to grimace. Evidently suspecting him and his of Witchcraft didn't interfere with using him to tweak her husband. "There you go—Troy will get back in a second, I'm sure. Watch your head—whoa, don't slip!" He used both hands at her waist to boost her up into the passenger seat of the family Bronco, then really laid it on by saying in a more intimate voice, "Oh, you've gotten splashed all over your legs," and touched a finger to the mud-spatter on her knee.

She reacted exactly the way he'd known she would. She took her time swinging her legs into the car, and thanked him in a tone even cozier than the one he'd used on her. Not that she smiled; she was a woman who took good care what she smiled at, as if humor was rationed. Then again, maybe she was just scared of getting wrinkles.

Gib was already behind the wheel and firing up the engine. The look he gave Evan was not one of brotherly love. Lachlan pretended not to notice it as he said, "I'll go find Troy," and escaped. Yes, he knew the kind of woman Erika was. He'd almost married someone just like her—the memory was uncomfortable even at ten years' remove—and his mother had been the same type. Out at the front counter, she sold sweet femininity and wide-eyed deference—and really great pie, he reflected with some regret—to the big brave smart how-do-you-ever-think-of-such-things men. Scarlett O'Hara wouldn't melt in her mouth. But back in the warehouse, her stock was a flashing of tits and a swaying of ass and the implication that more would be forthcoming if the guy could scrape together the price of admission—whatever it might be at any given moment. If not, he was welcome to come back when he could afford her. And if he did manage to come up with the scratch, imagine his surprise when he had to keep paying and paying and paying.

"Partnership or power trip?" said Holly's voice in his head, and he smiled to himself, shaking rainwater out of his eyes.

It wasn't easy finding anything more than ten feet away in this downpour, but the outdoor floodlights picked out Lulah's old Ford with its brand new candy-apple red paint job and *Woodhush Farm* in small, tasteful black script on the driver's side door. Kirby had wanted her to put flames down the sides, or a row of galloping horses; Bella had urged lots of big five-pointed gold stars like on Daddy's car. Evan felt an unexpected yearning to be with his children, to forget his disgust with all this adult bullshit in laughing at their innocent mischief. The mischief would linger—Holly and Cam were proof enough of that family trait—but the innocence? Kids grew older and grew up; he couldn't protect them. No parent ever could.

As he approached Lulah's truck, where Troy was leaping down as Jamey slammed the gate shut, he felt renewed anger that Erika wasn't even trying to protect her son. So he paused, and waited for Troy to get to him, and put a hand on the boy's shoulder. "Look, if you ever need a place to hang out and chill for a few days, you come see us at Woodhush, okay?"

Troy looked startled. Then he looked grateful. Lachlan smiled at him and watched him disappear into the rain.

"Nice kid," Jamey remarked.

"Yeah. Hey, is there a way to interpret any existing laws to arrest his mother for malicious stupidity?"

"Evan!" Jamey looked scandalized. "You're the sheriff. I'm the district attorney. We can arrest anybody!"

CAM DRUMMED HIS FINGERS on the steering wheel of his cousin's BMW. Somebody ahead of him was stuck in the mire. He hated traffic jams. He was pissed off anyway—that Ayala woman was lucky she wasn't demanding to be taken to the ER for crotch-rot (nothing so benign as prickly heat would do)—and a glimpse of the son helping Jamey load the motorcycle hadn't improved his temper. People had been looking at Jamey like that all his life. Anybody who *didn't* look at Jamey had been dead for three days.

He hit the button that activated the sound system, wanting some background noise. Half a song later, he freely blasphemed Holly's tastes in music when Don Henley advised that *You get the love that you allow.*

"Christ on a crutch! What wouldn't I give to hear 'Brick House' about now—" He jammed his index finger punching the damned CD player off, and swore again as he cradled his injured hand.

"You have wonderful hands."

Not now—he didn't want to think about Jamey and the wisteria—

"I always loved to watch you play the piano. I've missed that. I don't think I've ever seen anything more elegant—like magic sparking from your fingers when you make music—"

An unpleasant bark of laughter escaped him. Those few hours ago, Jamey hadn't even known—

"Your hands talk all the time, even when you don't say a word out loud. They're good hands. Strong and kind. They've never hurt anyone—"

Jamey hadn't known then what his hands could do, how the magic really could spark through his fingers and bespell things, touch wool or linen or cotton or leather to banish, restore, reweave, warm, soothe, unravel, chill, preserve, destroy—

Silence, he was supposed to be working out ways to spin silence into the silk covering the walls of Westmoreland, use his magic for something of greater consequence than drying rain-soaked clothing. He had never been called on to do this kind of work before. Here he was, almost thirty-eight years old, and he'd probably been part of fewer Workings than Holly, who had no magic at all except her blood.

Coming home had started off okay—watching the familiar landscapes from the back seat of the courtesy van, recognizing most of it, surprised by some of the changes. There'd been that weirdness when he'd tried to take a nap, the not-quite-fiery prickles on his skin that he hadn't wanted to admit felt like magic. Seeing Holly and meeting Evan had been good, too. But then Jamey showed up. And Holly pestered him, and he hadn't had enough to drink, but it turned out he *had* swallowed enough vodka to let Jamey kiss him—

Somebody even more impatient than he leaned on a car horn. He barely restrained himself from following suit.

He felt like an onion somebody had decided needed peeling. Without his permission. With a very dull knife. Brittle outer skin being sliced off; thick layers gouged into, snapping off all the way to the core; fine membranes teased off with a sharp fingernail; poked and prodded for weaknesses—

Another horn galvanized him. He swung the Beemer out of the line-up and onto the grassy side of the road. A quick Y back-and-fill, and he was driving in the opposite direction, between the row of trees and the row of unmoving cars, around the gentle curve back toward Westmoreland. Coming right at him across the grass through the rain was a big green SUV with a gaudy display of police lights on the roof. He swerved and stopped the car, and hit the window button on the armrest.

Evan rolled down his window, already yelling. "What the fuck—? Cam? Are you crazy?"

"Everybody's stuck! I'm going back up to the house and wait until the rain stops! If I have to, I'll get another room for the night!"

Lachlan drew breath to argue, then narrowed his gaze. "You know, that actually works! Let me get this thing out of the way and I'll drive back up with you!"

So it was that Evan parked behind a clump of rhododendrons and dogwood that by daylight wouldn't hide a damned thing but that by night, in punishing rain, rendered the SUV invisible. Cam waited, drumming his fingers again, thinking about silence.

"Take it around the side drive," Evan said as he got into the BMW. "Lulah's truck isn't parked close enough for a quick getaway, and moving it would look odd. I want something a little more accessible, just in case."

"'Quick getaway,'" Cam muttered. "Oh, excellent." As he steered the car across the sodden lawn, he kept glancing up at the house he would soon bespell. Aware now of what was hidden within the walls, remembering the oddity that had chafed at his mind earlier, he leaned forward and squinted at the rows of narrow windows. Some were lit, most were not. All were veiled by the same cobwebby sheers as in his own room. But there was still something he couldn't quite—

"Cam! Pay attention, will you?"

He veered further from the main road and stopped the car in the middle of the front lawn. Wiping a circle in the windshield condensation, he said, "It's the windows. Something in them? Behind them?" He chewed his upper lip, then exclaimed, "Count them! Can't you see it? Look—my room is in the front, right up there." He drew the layout in the moisture still on the windshield. "Three windows in the sitting room, two in the bedroom, one in the bathroom. The suite below is identical. So are the second-and third-floor suites on the other side. Six windows on each floor for the guest rooms, two to light the main staircase and hallways—"

"No, there are nine windows on the right-hand side of the building." Evan seemed to hear what he'd just said. And repeated the important word, very softly. "Nine."

JAMEY WAITED FOR THEM BESIDE Lulah's truck. When the black Beemer drove slowly past him, he jogged through the rain behind the car, following the service road. He was ready with the pertinent question when Cam and Evan got out.

"What happened to being sneaky? Dark clothes, pretending to leave the premises—"

"Traffic jam," Evan explained. "If anybody asks, we're waiting here until the rain slacks off, and spending the night if necessary."

"Who thought *that* up?" he demanded as they crunched across waterlogged gravel to the kitchen door.

"Me," Cam offered tersely.

The door opened, spilling light onto the walkway. A pair of weary young women emerged, wearing the Westmoreland livery—pale blue shirt, black slacks, purple vest, silver nametag—to huddle together under an umbrella. Cam leaped to hold the door for them, oozing charm.

"Ladies, allow me. Be careful where you step. In fact, may I drive you over to your housing? That umbrella's no protection at all. You're going to get drenched."

"Nein, danke," said the blonde, eyes downcast.

The other girl was staring at the dimples as if she'd never seen the like before. Cam said something in German that made her laugh. She eyed his long, lanky frame, cast a yearning glance at the car, and was in the middle of something that sounded like an acceptance of his kindness when the other girl snarled at her for a good ten seconds. Cam backed off, apologizing, and they went on their way.

"Ursula was amenable, Hadwisa was not," he said mournfully. "And though the kitchen has closed for the night, I was offered cocoa—"

"I'll bet," Jamey muttered, leading the way inside.

"—before Hadwisa reminded Ursula that the dormitory would be locked and alarmed at midnight and everybody else was already in bed."

"Nice work," Evan approved, pausing to let his eyes adjust to the dimness of the kitchen. "How good is your German?"

"I know enough not to get arrested. In fact, I can not get arrested in seven or eight languages."

"Congratulations," Jamey said. "Can you do something useful, like dry us off?"

The requested service was performed, the runoff soaking into a mat by the back door. As Cam worked on Evan's boots—it wouldn't do to leave muddy footprints on the carpet—Jamey scanned the kitchen. Nothing out of the ordinary. All the usual accoutrements of a restaurant: massive Sub-Zero refrigerators, pristine metal counters, two huge Wolf stoves, pots and pans and utensils gleaming in tidy rows. Whiteboard with the next day's specials scrawled in red; cautionary signs about handwashing and hair nets and so forth, the usual Health Department placards in English and Spanish with computer-printed additions in other languages. Jamey recognized German script and Russian Cyrillic characters, but the three others defeated him.

"Polish, Hungarian, and Romanian," Cam said at his shoulder, startling him.

"How did you know?"

"German and Russian are easy to recognize. Polish, Hungarian, and Romanian use the same alphabet as the rest of Europe, with their own accent marks and—"

"Mr. District Attorney," Evan cut in, "do you think we need to look into the immigration status of those two young ladies?"

"I beg your pardon?" He blinked.

"Ursula and Hadwisa," Evan said, with emphasis. Then, responding to Jamey's frown: "Those two young ladies named Ursula and Hadwisa who were speaking German and who probably weren't born in Kansas City?"

"Oh." He considered. "Well, Sheriff Lachlan, now that you mention it, perhaps we ought to check the papers of every worker at this establishment."

"Excellent. How about we start upstairs?"

Cam shook his head. "And we bid a fond farewell to Fourth Amendment protections against unreasonable search and seizure."

"You really haven't been back in the States for a while, have you?" Jamey led the way down the central aisle between aluminum counters.

"Don't make any phone calls you wouldn't want the FBI to hear," Evan seconded.

"'Work in progress,'" Cam muttered. "Right."

"DOORS ARE ALL taken care of," Lulah said as Cam, Jamey, and Evan rounded a hallway corner on the third floor. Unable to help himself, Cam blinked a couple of times in surprise; his aunt gave him one of her scathing little smiles. "A lock is a lock in this place. Work on one, find the rest, link all of them together, and now I'm standing around waiting for you to get on with it."

"Using the same principle? Hmm." He thought about it—a little too obviously. Lulah reached up and flicked a finger against his temple. "Ow!"

"I brought some toys," she whispered, as if imparting the grand secret to all magic. "So did Nicholas. You want help?"

"No," he replied, stung. "I don't need Nicky's shiny rocks or your concoctions. I can do it."

"All by your lonesome," she approved. Turning to Jamey, she continued, "You're getting the full razzle-dazzle tonight, aren't you? I'll apologize later for not telling you about us—"

"No need to apologize. I quite understand your caution. What sort of toys?"

"Oh, this and that."

"Can I get a little silence here?" Cam asked.

"Was that a rhetorical question," Holly muttered, "or are you inviting them to become awestruck at the speed and precision of your work?"

He distributed his sunniest smile among them all, complete with dimples. "Actually, it *is* rather pretty."

And it was. Taking Lulah's cue, he'd done what was necessary to a panel of silk wall. Using it as a pattern, he encouraged it to spread, fingering its way from one expanse of oyster-and-burgundy stripes to another. It looked like a computer model of flight paths weaving their way across the globe—and all at once he remembered how eerie that map had looked in the days following 9/11, when nothing flew across North America except planes belonging to the United States military. This was different. Tendrils of light curled down the corridor and curved down the stairs, decorating the walls in silence. From the third floor down to the second the white-gold brightness wove and spread, then descended to the ground floor, sliding around the cold dead steel of fire doors to find more silk. In front of him the upper hall was a tunnel of glittering interlocked lines, delicate and twinkling. It really was too bad Holly couldn't see it.

Nicky could. He gave a slow, approving nod. "Clever."

Holly and Evan knew better than to expect anything spectacular—or maybe they were relieved that nothing spectacular had occurred. Cam reminded himself to badger them for the full story of Evan's encounters with magic. Jamey, on the other hand, looked like someone watching a French art film: waiting for a plot, chafing at the uncertain focus, wondering when—or if—something would happen.

At last Jamey said, "That's *it*?"

"You expected phantom dragons breathing fire?"

"An *abracadabra* or two would've given it some atmosphere."

Evan laughed. "As a friend of ours says, magic is within. Everything else is just props. Anything you'd care to share with the class, Nicky?"

He was sorting through a handful of gemstones. Props or not, they were useful, as Cam well knew. He fished the amber from beneath his t-shirt, warmed it in his palm for a moment, then saw Jamey frowning at him. "It was my dad's, and his dad's, on back about two hundred years."

"And to think I used to worry that you might have arthritis," Jamey muttered.

"Oh, it's good for that, too. Also eases stress, cures hay fever, protects against evil spirits, is an antidote to poison, and heals ear infections." As Cam rattled off the list, he became aware that Nicky's face was wearing its own version of *scathing*.

"Amber," the older man intoned, "also encourages eccentric behavior. Settle down, children. I know you don't think you need this, Cam, but use it anyway." And he passed over a smooth, irregular lump of bloodstone. When Cam just stared at it, resting in the hollow of his palm, Nicky hissed, "*Az Istenért!* It opens doors and loosens bonds—and it also topples stone walls, as some of us have reason to know. Holly, if you would?"

Cam appreciated the sympathetic look she gave him; being scolded by Lulah *and* Nicky in the same five-minute period was not a prescription for enriched self-esteem. When a drop of her blood was smeared onto the rock, Cam nodded his thanks and closed his fingers into a fist. The stone warmed to his hand much faster than it seemed it should. And he was reminded that not only had it been a very long time since he'd done any real work with gems—let alone with Holly—he had never done this kind of thing at all.

As they descended to the second-floor landing where Cam had sensed the doorway—cautious and alert for any stragglers among the guests or any staff on patrol—Cam wondered how many times he had used his magic for aggression. Aside from that afternoon with Jamey, practically none. A Witch learned early on that certain things were acceptable and many things were not. He'd gotten away with the prickly heat on his teacher's shirts for three gleeful days before his father found out—and a month living in a world muted of magic had taught him his lesson. Some people required more stringent lessoning in the ethics of Witchcraft—there were rumors about the boyhood exploits of great-grandpa Flynn, for instance, and nobody had ever let one of the Kirby cousins forget the time she'd tried to cheat on a chemistry lab final and nearly blown up the whole high school. By adulthood one was expected to toe the line without exterior prompting. Some people didn't, of course, which was why Alec and Nicky had been kept so busy for so many years.

Cam had known excellent mentors and fine examples all his life. He remembered with squirming shame every single instance when he'd behaved with less than scrupulous deference to the moral imperatives of his kind. Opening a door into a hidden staircase wouldn't be added to the list—but it was entirely possible that somewhere in their explorations tonight he'd have to make some aggressive moves.

He wondered suddenly how Nicky and Alec had justified doing some of the things they'd undoubtedly done.

"Magic is a tool like any other," Alec had told him once. *"Well, not* quite *like any other, but you know what I mean. You can use it like an elevator to get where you want to go faster and easier—but stairs are better for your heart."*

"An elevator?" Nicky rolled his eyes. *"You have the most remarkable talent for obscure and semi-meaningless metaphors—"*

"Ha! 'Semi' means 'half,' so you just admitted I'm at least half right!"

"I've admitted no such thing. Alec," Nick explained to Cam, *"is a glass-half-full kind of person."*

"Whereas Nicholas isn't of the glass-half-empty persuasion. No, his outlook is that the glass is almost certainly cracked and won't hold water at all!"

Cam knew how the glass felt.

They had reached the landing. The bloodstone was almost uncomfortably warm in his hand now. They were all watching him, expecting him to do something. Remembering the windows, he turned to his right, then realized that because he was facing the front of the building, he should be looking left. Rattled, he marched over to the place where he'd tried to walk through the wall, trying to let the stone guide him. Loosen bonds, open doors—

Would there be a knothole with a hidden catch, like in the attic at Woodhush? A nearly invisible seam somewhere, a knob, a pressure-sensitive panel, a certain nail in the wainscoting—

The bloodstone was cooling in his palm.

"Stop trying so hard," Lulah murmured from behind him. She grasped his left hand and pressed a small, smooth oval into it. Glancing down, he saw a bit of wood about the size of an apricot pit, banded with silver. A letter had been burned into it with a metal die. Turning it over, he smiled suddenly, for the obverse was a different wood, white and fine as ivory, with a different rune—and this one was lightly touched with blood. Though it had been years since Leander Cox had taught him about different kinds of wood and Clary Sage had made him memorize the tree alphabet, these two came back without effort. Rowan and Holly: *Luis* and *Tinne*.

Why this would help wasn't something he had time to ask, because the bloodstone and the wooden charm were both warming in his hands. He smelled wool, and tasted the chill of brass on his tongue, but beneath both was the feel of water. He didn't understand it, but he used it. Confident now, he faced the wall, laid his fisted hands against the silk, feeling the stone in his right hand quiver even as the wood in his left hand seemed to become liquid and then solid metal and then liquid again.

Slowly he slid his hands down, letting the warm certainty permeate his knuckles and spread through his fingers to his palms. At the wainscoting, he stretched out his thumbs, and smiled. The catch was just behind a vase of flowers on a small carved wooden cupboard. Awkwardly, without unclenching his fingers, he used his thumbs to shift the vase. On the underside of the wainscoting he found the little button.

A chink of darkness etched his bright web of white-gold silence. It widened, lengthened, and became a doorway. Beyond was a landing, carpeted in eggshell-colored wool, hung with burgundy silk, adorned with a needlepoint-cushioned footstool and another small cupboard with polished brass handles on which rested a tall crystal vase full of flowers.

HOLLY HEARD NICKY'S QUICK INTAKE of breath, saw Lulah smile, and reasoned that something had happened. Jamey was staring with splendid intensity at the same area of wall the two Witches were staring at. Holly didn't bother. Neither, she noted with a sideways glance, did Evan.

"Not bad," Lulah allowed, a deep note of gratification in her voice giving the lie to her words. She reclaimed the talisman and stuffed it into a pocket of her jeans. "Everybody in before some jackass wanders up these stairs. Come on, you too, Jamey."

Holly made a mental note to ask more closely about that wooden charm, handed to her for Blooding without a word of explanation. She caught her aunt's eye with a meaningful frown; Lulah smiled and looked innocent.

"Come on *where?"* Jamey was asking.

"Through here," said Nick—and walked through the wall.

"Goddamsonuvabitch!"

Holly patted his arm. "You remember the scene in that Indiana Jones movie where he takes the 'leap of faith' and steps out onto the rock path he's convinced isn't really there?"

"So which one of you works for Industrial Light and Magic?"

She couldn't help noticing that when she'd said *leap of faith,* Cam frowned. *Yes, dearest—faith in you, just like Evan has faith in me. We all have to believe in each other, or nothing works.*

She shut her eyes and walked through the wall.

It was crowded on the landing. Holly pressed her back against Evan, his arms around her waist, as six people crammed into a space comfortable for perhaps three. She stifled an ill-timed giggle as Jamey pressed up against Cam's side and Cam tried to edge away—and Jamey only moved closer.

The stairwell was of dizzying depth; Holly felt a twinge of vertigo as she peered downward. There were landings every so often, but no turnings—which made the stairs incredibly steep. She was reminded of the time she and Susannah had ventured down into the pyramid of Menkaure in Egypt, thigh muscles groaning at the awkward incline. At least in this stairwell there was room to stand upright, and it was lit by reflection from the outdoor floodlights through three narrow windows, one above the other, delicately curtained in white.

Lulah tapped her shoulder. "Holly, unglue yourself from that man and come with me."

She sidled away from her husband, knocking over the footstool. "Do we have a way Jamey can warn us if anything happens that we need warning about?"

Evan hauled out his Glock. "Makes a nice, loud noise."

Cam's blue eyes went wider than ever and he glanced at Jamey. "You know how to use that?"

Jamey unchambered the clip, checked it, snapped it back home, and flipped off the safety. He cocked a brow at Cam.

"Oh . . . kay . . . ."

"See ya," Lulah said, and started down the stairs.

One landing, and another, each with its little footstool and cabinet and cut-crystal vase of flowers. White roses, lavender roses, and snapdragons; posies of blue violets clumped at the base of tall, stately papyrus that reminded her of Egypt again. Holly waited for her allergies to kick in; when they didn't, not even a tickle, she frowned.

"Lulah, I'm not sneezing. I can't even smell the flowers. Are they real?"

A touch to a single petal of a lavender rose made Lulah catch her breath. "That's not just magic, it's some kind of focal point. The bowl's real, and the water—so are the flowers, for that matter. But they're in stasis." She ventured another delicate touch and snatched her fingers back. "That's Master Class work. Whatever's spelling the flowers fresh is connected to whatever's spelling this staircase. But how was it done?"

"And the flowers have all been different," Holly mused. "Roses, violets, gladioli—" She caught herself with a hand on the wall, startlement making her clumsy, as usual. "Lulah, all these bouquets are seriously magical flowers. White rose for secrecy, snapdragon for deception—"

Lulah stared at the vase of lavender roses. "And those, for enchantment. They've been in every vase thus far. What have we gotten ourselves into here?"

Holly had heard that note of worried perplexity in her aunt's voice perhaps five times in her life. Before she could ask something stupid and useless, Lulah started down the stairs again.

After two more landings—decorated with various combinations of flowers, but always featuring white and lavender roses—Holly asked, "Are we level with the first floor yet?"

"Oh, we're below the real cellar. I know you can't feel it, but we are."

"I should have counted the number of steps."

"What for? You know that thing people say sometimes when they're casting a Circle? A place that isn't a place and a time that isn't a time? Well, a distance isn't a distance, either. In fact, I'd be surprised if there were the same number of steps going up as there were coming down. This much magic packed into this restricted a space—people probably tramping up and down all the time—"

"So why isn't there anybody here?"

"You want to thank our luck or chase it away by insulting it with questions?"

"You sound like Jesse in his 'never look a gift dragon in the mouth' mood." Holly hiked up Cam's pants. "Did he make that wooden thingy?"

"The silver that binds it, yes. But the talisman is Leander Cox's work. He's been experimenting with combinations, and thought you and Bella would be a good place to start. Rowan is good for dowsing for metals as well as for water. I was guessing Cam would sense the former. Didn't know there'd be both."

"So gratifying to know my daughter and I are inspirational." She thought about Bella and Kirby, tucked up in their beds—no, their beloved Uncle Alec was at Woodhush, they'd be clamoring for stories and games, or sitting in his lap as the thunderstorm rolled from valley to mountains. It felt odd, not being able to hear it anymore. Outside was lightning and rain, but within this stairwell all was hushed. Perhaps the white roses ensured that, as well.

Holly wondered what the hell she was doing here, gallivanting around a magical staircase, looking for who knew what, when she ought to be at home. It wasn't as if she was all that much use. Besides, she wasn't a free agent anymore, with responsibilities to no one but herself. She had a husband and children. And never mind that investigating this place had been her husband's idea; that was his job. It was hers to . . .

. . . to write books. Only she had no idea what she wanted to write next, and no book had shoved its way to the front of her mind, demanding to be written. She'd done some short stories, a few articles, but that was all. It was her job and she hadn't been doing it for more than two years and sooner or later it was going to make her crazy.

Back in the day, had she snagged up like this, she probably would have taken a trip somewhere. Florence, London, Athens—even a quick driving tour of New England or a week in D.C. spent wallowing in the Smithsonian and the Library of Congress—but there was no place she wanted to be except home with her family. She didn't miss taking off whenever she felt like it—and the next time she did, it would be with Evan and the children, to show them the places she loved. It was always more fun when there was somebody along to share it with, like the long, lovely summer she and Susannah Wingfield had spent in Europe years ago—God, how she missed Susannah.

She touched the diamonds on her wrist, swallowing the sudden upsurge of grief. It never got easier; sometimes she thought she might be getting used to it, but—

She bumped up against Lulah and nearly sent them both sprawling. She was framing an apology when she saw what had startled her aunt into an abrupt halt.

They had reached the bottom of the stairs. To their left was a door. A hospital door. Complete with a push-pad on the adjoining wall and a rectangular window and a single word in orange script.

"Surgery?" Lulah wondered.

"As in 'plastic'?" That would fit with a spa hotel.

"Why put it at the bottom of a magical staircase?" Lulah snorted.

Grimacing agreement, Holly slapped the metal pad. The door swung inward with a *whoosh.* A half-circle desk centered the room, with all the usual nurse's station trimmings: chart rack, computer, monitoring screens. But no telephones, and nothing resembling an intercom. The only sign of occupancy was a pink-and-blue coffee mug (CRYOCACHE—FOR CONSTANT CARE) stuffed with Bic pens, the caps chewed like doggie treats. Halls branched to right and left, and another windowed door stood open directly behind the desk.

Lulah led the way through the second door. Down each wall were two more doors, with signs projecting above them. RECORDS and PRIVATE were on the left; on the right, PHARMACY and a surprise.

"Cryopreservation?" Holly frankly gaped.

"Later," Lulah decided, long-legging it down to RECORDS.

Holly followed. "Why isn't anyone here? And why are the doors mechanical and not magical?"

"Do I look like the Oracle at Delphi? There's no magic in here that I can sense at all. It stopped at the entry." Switching the overhead lights on, she paused before a desk. "We're at least fifty feet underground—and it's fifty feet of solid rock, so forget about me trying to get through it. You fiddle with that machine, I'll check the paper."

Seating herself obediently at the desk, she clicked the computer on and started exploring. Lulah was opening filing cabinets, and by the increasing vehemence of her cussing was having no luck at all.

Holly accessed folder after folder, wondering why nothing was password-protected until she realized that anybody who could get down here would be in on the whole thing and thus trustworthy. She found inventories of bedsheets, blankets, pillows. There were charts detailing orders and deliveries of drugs to the pharmacy (but no lists of drugs delivered). Someone was writing a novel in his or her spare time—a medical thriller by the look of it, in French.

"Nothing," she said over her shoulder. "Let's try the door that says PRIVATE."

For the first time, they encountered a lock. A mechanical one; nothing magic about it, according to Lulah. But she used magic to open it.

"More of Leander's work?" Holly asked as Lulah rolled a smooth wooden marble between her palms. This, too, was a half-and-half construction, sealed by Jesse McNichol's metalcraft in silver.

"Oak," she affirmed. "And some of its own mistletoe. Struck down by lightning, which is why Leander was able to use it. Hush, now."

Holly waited, incapable of sensing the power Lulah called on, even though she knew the power inherent in oak and mistletoe. Sometimes she thought it was astonishing there were any oaks left, for the Druids' sacred groves had been chopped down and burned all over Europe from the time of Julius Caesar onward. No Witch killed an oak tree; nature had killed this one, enabling Leander to use its wood, which was the more profoundly powerful for the lightning that had felled it. Mistletoe, aside from the frivolous tradition of kissing, had much more critical associations; the one Lulah was after right now was obviously its ability to open locks.

A few minutes later Holly was seated at another desk, this time with a laptop coming to life before her. Lulah stood behind her, watching.

"If this one is password-protected, we're screwed," Holly warned. "Unless you've got a way of getting a computer to rat out its owner—"

The computer was not password-protected. Dozens of file icons appeared. In German.

Fourteen

EVAN WATCHED HOLLY AND LULAH start down the stairs, speculating for just an instant on what life might be like if his wife were the type of woman to go home and stay there. Had he given such an order, she would have told him to go to hell at his earliest convenience. In fact, he had once contemplated giving that order—back when they were first dating, the night of a triple homicide. In the years since, he'd been occasionally tempted but had never followed through. Which made him, he supposed, just as pussy-whipped in his own way as Gib Ayala.

"Onward and upward?" Nicky asked.

"Onward and upward," Evan agreed.

The thing of it was, he mused as they climbed, you had to love a woman for what she was, not what you thought you could make her do or be. His mother had married his father planning to be the wife of a police captain. Lachlan had no way of knowing if ambition had been part of his father's psychology; by the time he was old enough to question, observe, and understand, all that was left was the nagging and the sneering. Seeing potential, encouraging the work, supporting ambition—those were things you did when you loved someone. But trying to control and manipulate—it lacked respect, he decided. To use one of Holly's favorite words, it wasn't honorable.

"Why decorate?"

"Huh?" He glanced over his shoulder at Cam.

"Why the chest of drawers and the flowers and the footstool with the needlepoint cushion?"

A step ahead of them, Nicky said, "My dear boy, please don't start being a cliché at this stage of your life. 'Why decorate?' Could you possibly have asked a gayer question?"

"Nick!" Lachlan exclaimed. "I'm shocked. The *really* gay thing to do would be to criticize the color scheme."

"Oh, shut up, both of you," Cam suggested.

The poor guy was taking hits from all sides tonight, Lachlan reflected. And from Holly, regarding Jamey, it would only get worse—probably because she wasn't gleefully exercising all her control-freakishness on her characters. It was Cam's misfortune to have been caught when she had nothing else to occupy her. Lachlan didn't know damn-all about Cam's history with Jamey, but it seemed to him that Holly wasn't so much trying to manipulate Cam as she was trying to shove him in the direction he wanted to go anyway. And there was the difference: she'd seen what was true about him and Jamey—anybody with eyes could see it—and she'd pester them until they resolved it themselves. They'd have to be the ones to do it; after all, it wasn't as if she could lock them in a bedroom together and—

"All right, all right," Nicky said as they reached another small landing. "Why *are* there cabinets and footstools and bowls of flowers?" He pointed to the squat cut-glass vase stuffed with blue violets and white and lavender rosebuds.

"Well, we're supposed to be exploring. . . ." Cam crouched beside the cupboard. It was a pretty thing, Evan noted, carved with an owl on one door and a peacock on the other. Cam opened the doors and pulled out what looked like a portable DVD player. There was no cord for plugging it in—and no wall sockets to plug it into, Lachlan noted with a quick glance around. But there was a cable with another kind of plug.

Nick was frowning again. "If this staircase is bespelled, and we know it is, why don't they just have a magic window in the wall?"

"Maybe they don't have the chops," Evan said.

The older man gave a disdainful sniff. "Amateurs."

"Not necessarily." Cam sat cross-legged on the floor and hit the button that activated the screen. "Dad used to say there was only so much magic you could fit into a certain space before you got overload. It's like this negotiation that goes on between Witchcraft and the real world. Give-and-take. You can tweak things just so far, you can use only so much power, before it stresses real-world physics—"

"Theorize later," Lachlan told him. "What I'd like to know is what they want to look at. Do you see anyplace to hook that thing up?"

They set about exploring the nearby walls with eyes and fingers. Nothing. Then Nicky got down on hands and knees and started inspecting the carpet and the border of wood on either side—and there it was, a little outlet one step down from the landing. The plug fit perfectly.

Onto the screen sprang a neat, spare menu of numbers: *102, 105, 208, 210, 314, 315.* Cam called up *102.*

It produced, as Lachlan had immediately suspected, a view of a hotel room. In the elaborate bed—canopied and curtained in lace with heavy velvet swags—were a man and a woman, sound asleep. Five seconds of this, and the angle switched to show the bathroom, and after another pause a different view of the bed. Then it was back to the original picture before it cycled through again.

"Three cameras." Nicky reached over and pressed PAUSE, and the rotation obediently stopped on the second perspective of the bed. "Very well, I bow to modern technology. This must be set up to record, yes?"

"I'm in 314," Cam mentioned with studied casualness.

Crouching beside him, Lachlan asked, "Did you do anything weird?"

"I took a nap. I took a bath. I got dressed."

"And we changed shirts. I hope it gave somebody besides Holly a thrill. Is there anything in the memory?"

It turned out there wasn't. And there was no DVD in the drive.

"I guess they don't expect to record anybody tonight," Evan decided.

"Why did they put me in a monitored room? Do they know I'm gay, and were waiting for me to seduce one of the busboys so they could blackmail me?"

"Possibly," Nick said. "But I think you've hit on a very interesting idea. Six monitored rooms, with viewing and recording—it may not be just the spa that is, shall we say, full-service."

NEITHER HOLLY NOR LULAH knew German.

"We'll have to take this up to Nicky to figure out what's in it," Holly said. "Damn. I was looking forward to learning *something* about this place!"

"And you with a husband whose favorite composer is Mozart!" Lulah pointed a long finger at one of the icons.

Holly thought for a moment, then said in a resigned tone, "Shocking degeneration of a formerly competent brain. *Die Zauberflöte*, okay, I get it. *Zauber* is 'magic' in German. That's likely to be an interesting file, though I doubt we'll be able to read it. But what the hell does '*∂er Puff*' mean?"

"Let's find out."

Within the file were documents, clearly labeled, readily understandable: the months of the year were almost all the same in German as in English. Holly opened up November 2004, the month Westmoreland had opened for business.

There were six columns to the page. First came the day of the week, then the date. On some days there were no entries, but on others there were as many as a dozen. Each entry in the third column was a man's full name, most of them obviously American—which meant everything from Smithfield to Valenzuela to Van Slyke to LaPierre to Goldberg. The ones that were not obviously American were the ones with three names—like the excruciatingly Russian Vladimir Vladimirovich Mironov—or the ones with the umlauts and tildes and circumflexes still attached. Most people who'd been in the United States for more than a generation, or who weren't snottily precious about the ancestral spelling (Denise Josèphe came to mind), had discarded accent marks long ago. The fourth and fifth columns were numbers. The last was reserved for a given name only.

"Adela, Kurt, Evva, Sofiya, Franciszka, Katya, Ruzena, Vilmos—"

"Not a Chuck or Mary Jean in the lot." Lulah shook her head. "Jurek, Magda, Raisa—am I being xenophobic, or am I hearing Eastern Europe in all these?"

"And the other names are all male, there's not a woman on the—oh, Aunt Lulah, this can't possibly be what it looks like."

"Tell me what you think it looks like and I'll tell you if I think it's possible."

Holly opened up more monthly records. "Here's Bill Smithfield on November 8 and December 28, 2004. Evva, then Katya—" She flicked back and forth among documents, doing a find for Smithfield in each. "January, nothing . . . February 4, Katya again . . . skips March, but twice in April, Katya and then Raisa . . . May, June, July . . . here he is again in August of last year, with Katya."

"Keep going," Lulah said grimly. "Find another name."

"Last year, Myron MacGowan in May with—with Kurt, in July with Vilmos, September—here's a new name, Rafaello—how the hell did he get in here? MacGowan with Rafaello in October and again in November—what are the numbers for? Twenty-three-dash-twenty-four, twenty-dash-twenty-two—"

"Date, customer, girl—or boy—"

"And a time!" Holly exclaimed. "The dates are European style, month second—so the times must be on a twenty-four–hour clock!"

The two women looked at each other for a brief, silent moment. Then Holly went back to the book and picked out a name she recognized.

"Grant Newbury. September 24, 2004, Raisa, 21-22, which would be nine to ten in the evening, 105—"

"Room number?" Lulah hazarded. "Wait a minute—didn't you go out with Grant Newbury in high school?"

Holly nodded. "A few times. Voice like an archangel. He soloed in the choir at St. Andrew's."

"Damn. All right, where were we? Room numbers?"

"If so, only six of them are used—the same numbers recur. Okay, Grant Newbury. October . . . November . . . the tenth, Magda, 23–24. Again in November, the thirtieth, 19–20. Nothing in December. Nothing in January. February 19, 2005, Adela, 17–19. May 22, Evva, 18–19. April 8, Evva again, 21–22." It went on. And on. While tracing Grant Newbury she saw names she recognized from five different counties and as far away as Richmond and Washington. The foreign names—Dutch, French, Italian, German, Russian—she was willing to bet would line up with the guest register upstairs at the front desk, and the spa appointments book, and flights into and out of Shenandoah Airport.

But as she went through the months, something else began to niggle at her mind. Something about the dates. It wasn't magic, it couldn't be magic—she didn't have any magic to quiver a warning or wave a red flag. It was just her brain making extra work for itself, grinding gears because she didn't want to acknowledge what was becoming more and more obvious with every name she saw written over and over again.

"Pillars of the community," she said at last, leaning back and folding her arms, glaring at the laptop screen. "Respectable, hard-working, church-going men—Cornell Hendricks, famed in song, story, and the Mormon Temple, on the same night and at the same time right next door to his good ol' fishin' buddy Norm Valenzuela—who went to Confession the next morning, I'll bet you anything, and said his Hail Marys and heard Mass—"

"You can't be forgiven if you haven't sinned," Lulah commented acidly. "Hasn't been a real brothel in this county for fifty years. The men have to drive over to Miss Follett's in Glenrose for their diversions."

"Let's get Louvena to print a special edition of the *Record*," Holly suggested.

"And ruin how many marriages?"

"Like they don't deserve it!"

"Their families don't. Who says prostitution is a 'victimless crime'? And what about these girls? Evva and Ruzena and Sofiya—not to mention Kurt and Vilmos. When they were little kids did they say, 'My friends all want to be teachers or firemen or farmers when they grow up, but I want to be a whore'?"

"Oh, God," Holly breathed. "Prostitution. The names. Eastern European names." Something went very hollow inside her chest and for a moment she couldn't breathe. "Lulah . . . Evan and I went to Reverend Deutschman's meeting at Calvary Baptist. Remember we brought the flyers and handouts home with us?"

Holly could see the printed pages as if she held them once more in her hand. In the 1970s, human trafficking had focused on Southeast Asia, mostly Thai and Filipina women. The second wave, in the '80s, had been centered in Ghana and Nigeria. Then had come Latin America's turn, especially Colombia, Brazil, and the Dominican Republic. But these days the nations no longer behind the Iron Curtain, the places where free-market capitalism had replaced communism with often disastrous results, were prime hunting grounds for traffickers. The girls were young, comparatively well-educated, pretty, and with no future at all in their homelands. Easy prey for anyone willing to sell them—including the administrators of orphanages, the girls' own relatives, and the village priest.

They vanished from Russia, Ukraine, Moldova, Hungary, Romania, Poland, Albania, the Czech Republic—with names like Evva, Ruzena, Sofiya, Kurt, Vilmos . . .

She didn't believe it even when she said it aloud. "They've been trafficked. Like the ones the Calvary Baptist ladies found in New Orleans, and the ones Poppy was bringing back here."

Calvary Baptist . . . second of the seven church fires . . . Poppy and the Calvary Baptist ladies had found trafficked children in New Orleans after Hurricane Katrina . . . there were trafficked children here at Westmoreland . . . Grant Newbury, Hugh Chadwick, Norm Valenzuela . . . church-going men with wives and families . . . seven burned churches since last September . . . beginning with Old Believers right after Hurricane Katrina and then Calvary, before the Baptists had started the anti-trafficking campaign . . . and not all the churches had been Baptist . . . the Lutheran church in December, the Episcopalian in April . . . St. Andrew's, where Grant sang in the choir. . . .

She knew then what had been gnawing around the edges of her mind. The twenty-four–hour clock times had addled her, but the connection had finally clicked. Stabbing at the keyboard now, she opened April 2005, and found the entries for the date St. Andrew's had been torched.

Grant Newbury, nine to ten, 105, Evva.

"Lulah, is there any paper? Find some paper and write this down. Make columns for date, time, church—"

"Don't you mean 'customer'?"

"No. Just stay with me on this, Lulah, please—I think I might be right but I need you to see it, too. Date, time, church, ignition point. Another chart—date, time, and *now* a column for customer."

She started with the Episcopalian fire in April. It was the only one with a narrow range for a starting time: between eight-thirty, when a Bible study group had gone home, and nine forty-five, when the call had come in to the fire department. The ignition point was a cupboard where hymnals were stored.

"April 8, 2006," Holly said again as Lulah started the second chart. "Nine to ten. Grant Newbury. You know what else? The Episcopalian wish list for tonight's proceeds includes hymnals to replace the ones that burned—they were brand new the very day of the fire. Maybe Grant hands them out every Sunday, maybe he ordered them, or unpacked them, or pasted in the bookplates that say 'Property of'—"

"Holly, honey, slow down."

"Nobody turns out to be what you thought they'd be, do they?" she asked. "They always disappoint you. The fire at the choirboy's church and his recreational hour with Evva coincide very nicely." Holly pushed the cuffs of Cam's shirt up toward her elbows. "God, how I hope the rest of these don't match."

"Let's start with the first fire and see how it goes. September 9, 2005. Old Believers."

She squeezed her eyes shut and visualized the reports Evan had strewn across their partners' desk, swearing steadily as he tried in vain to make a pattern out of them. She pictured each one in her head, and rattled off the particulars of each. When all seven fires had been listed—including the Methodist, even though that one did not involve magic—she went through the files once more.

"September 9 last year was a real party," she growled. "Chuck Driscoll was here from ten to eleven—"

"Peggy's gonna pan-fry him with plum sauce."

"I thought you didn't want any of this known, so their families are spared?"

"I said I didn't want Louvena to publish it," Lulah corrected. "I didn't say these men's wives shouldn't find out."

Holly eyed her for a long moment. "Tallulah Eglantine McClure, are you going to use magic to out all these men to their wives?"

"If they went to one whorehouse, they've gone to others. That puts their wives at risk."

"That doesn't answer my question."

"Noticed that, did you? Who was getting himself serviced that night?"

Holly returned to the screen. "Jacob Feuerstein, whom I don't recognize but sure doesn't sound like a Baptist-type name. Floyd Beaudry . . . no, he's eight to ten, and Evan says the fire couldn't have started before eleven." She paused. "Although with magic, how could anybody tell? They're going by how hot a fire usually burns when they estimate the time—Lulah, am I crazy to be thinking any of this? I mean, Grant may be a jerk, but—"

"Just keep going. September 9, 2005."

"Judge Rausche—big surprise—from eight until ten. Hugh Chadwick, midnight to one in the morning."

AFTER CHECKING OUT the other rooms and finding two more occupied—210 by a couple watching a movie while sharing champagne and chocolate truffles, 208 by a middle-aged man taking a shower—Nick told Cam to put the DVD player back where he'd found it. Not waiting to watch, he continued up the stairs. The part of his brain that craved logic and tidiness—that had kept thousands upon thousands of books organized for over forty years—told him that because the door into this place had been halfway up a flight of exterior stairs to the second floor, and this last landing had been the second they'd seen, they were inside the walls of the third floor. The part of his brain that was an accomplished practitioner of magic told him not to be an idiot. These steps would go where they had been spelled to go.

So he wasn't all that surprised when a third landing appeared, with its now expected footstool and chest and flowers, and another flight rose above it. One more half-flight, one more landing—he stopped short.

End of the stairs.

"You don't magic up something that goes nowhere," Evan remarked.

"Maybe what they're hiding is downstairs only," Cam offered.

"Cam, you said the stairs weren't originally magic?" Nick asked.

"No." Cam was definite. "They're built into the fabric of the house. It's the ninth window that nobody notices because the architect was clever and who counts windows, anyway?"

"Ninth—?"

Evan said, "Eight to one side of the doors, nine to the other. The front suites have six windows—three for the sitting room, two for the bedroom, one for the bathroom."

"And two for the main staircase," Cam finished. "Which leaves this ninth one—" He pointed to the windows, one beneath the other, and very far away now that they were at the top of the stairs. "—to light this place."

"But the magic is new?" Nicky persisted.

"Yeah. Before you ask—none of the Nevilles was a Witch, and none of them married into the local Witchly families. If there'd been any magic here before, somebody would've sensed it in the last two hundred or so years. I mean, it can't have stayed hidden all that time."

Evan was dividing a frown between the two side walls, with their cabinets and flowers. "Why do you build one of these, anyway? Aside from the fun of it."

"Smuggling," Cam said. "To hide money or moonshine, or some other contraband. I'd bet that guns and ammunition were hidden here during various wars—maybe soldiers, too."

"And of course," Nick added, "there's always the simple desire to get into and out of one's house without anyone's knowing about it. That catch in the wainscoting can't be original, though."

"But the doorway was there, so they used it," Cam replied. "Whatever mechanism was already there, I mean. Only they also disguised it with magic."

"There must be at least one other way out," Evan said, still scrutinizing the walls. "This has to lead *somewhere* besides two blank walls at the top."

"Well, where are we right now? This has to be the attic. Same thing at Woodhush. There's an entry there, so—"

"You're applying logic to magic," Nicky said with a tight smile. "You should know better than that."

"But there *is* logic to it," Cam protested. "Otherwise none of it would work!"

"Fascinating as this is," Evan drawled, "it's not getting us anywhere."

Cam was peering down the stairs to where Jamey stood guard. "Maybe they sealed up the original entry to the attic. Maybe the important stuff that the magic is hiding really is downstairs, not up."

"I repeat," Lachlan said, "you don't bother to spell something useless. *That's* logic. Find the door, Cam."

Reluctantly dragging his gaze to the walls, he started to explore as he had earlier. He had neither the bloodstone nor the holly-rowan talisman, but he knew now what to feel for. Or so Nicholas surmised—correctly, as it happened, for within a few minutes he had found a pressure-sensitive panel at a juncture of wallpaper stripes, and a quite ordinary door swung open.

"Cam, Evan—down the hall."

The young men set off obediently, and Nick pondered the pleasures of being old enough to issue orders that were obeyed without question. He recalled very clearly a time when he and Alec had been the ones deferential to their elders—and how much trouble they sometimes got into when they weren't. He looked out a dormer window that proved they were indeed in the attic, seeing but not hearing the rain. He missed his partner, missed the immediacy of their bond. There was a sense of Alec remaining, like a memory—nothing like the solid sense of his presence that Nick had known for so long that he had, he realized, become complacent. And he wondered, with a sudden unwelcome chill, if this was what it would be like if he outlived his lover.

"Uncle Nicky!" Cam was beckoning. "Man, you gotta see this."

He left the dormer window and hurried down the hall. The room was painted in sunshine yellow and leaf green. A stationary bike, a treadmill; blue exercise mats rolled up against the wall; a soft-cushioned green chaise framed by a pair of sunlamps; a hospital bed; a crash cart.

Cam braced his fists on his hips, head cocked to one side. "What're the statistics on people croaking during a stress-test?"

"I may become such a statistic if I don't find something that makes sense," Nick snarled.

Evan spoke from down the hall. "You may want to check out who's behind Door Number Two."

"Don't you mean 'what'?"

"Come see for yourself."

Two girls, maybe fourteen years old and maybe not, were sitting up in twin beds. Both had blond hair, blue eyes, and sharp, sloping Slavic cheekbones. They wore plain blue flannel nightgowns and their braided hair was tied with blue ribbons. Neither reacted to the appearance of three strangers in their doorway. They didn't look as if someone had given them drugs. They looked as if someone had taken their souls.

HOLLY GLARED AT LULAH'S two charts, feeling as if someone had just told her the jigsaw puzzle had 1001 pieces. Hugh Chadwick was the right time for the fire at Old Believers, but after some thought Lulah recalled that he was heading up the rebuilding committee for Calvary Baptist. Tom Van Slyke, whose visit to Westmoreland coincided neatly with the Calvary Baptist fire, belonged to Old Believers.

They looked at each other with frustration carving identical furrows in their foreheads. Lulah yanked the clip from her ponytail and looked for a moment as if she might start kicking things. But all she did was begin gathering her gray-streaked russet hair up again to knot at the back of her head. "Start again," she said.

"For the sixth time," Holly muttered. "Old Believers. Wooden front door burns like a son of a bitch, the fire's so hot that even the bricks melt—"

"Bricks?"

"Evan said they looked like clinkers—black, even shiny in places, like obsidian."

"Hugh Chadwick," Lulah declared.

"He's Calvary."

"What does he do for a living?"

Holly sighed. "Construction. He put in a bid for the brickwork at your house. Does that make a second connection, or—"

"Let's just keep going and see what happens. There's no link between Van Slyke and Calvary. Let's move on. First Baptist . . . the only one who fits is Jack Wheeler—"

"—who manages that home-improvement monstrosity out on Route 12!" In the next instant Holly's excitement drained away. "But even if his store has a gross of the same varnish that was the accelerant, we don't know if he belongs to the church, or has any kind of association with it, or—"

"The Lutheran is next," Lulah interrupted. "December tenth, early morning, the closet where the pastor's vestments are kept—dammit! It's not at night, and there's no customers here that day until nine that evening. The Methodists, which started about five in the morning—"

"That one doesn't figure into it. Louvena told Evan tonight that it's the only one that didn't have any magic about it." When a look of exasperation was leveled at her, she added, "Sorry. Forgot to mention it. Okay, after the Methodists were the Episcopalians, and that's Grant. Last one—"

"Wait a second, this thing just died on me." Lulah tossed the pen over her shoulder and grabbed one from another CryoCache coffee mug. "Okay."

"Gospel Baptist, sometime before midnight, in the church office. Ignition point was a metal chair, which is really bizarre."

"We've got somebody called Valentin Maximovich Saksonov—isn't that Nicky's patronymic?—anyway, he matches the timeline but can pretty much be crossed off, unless you can think of a reason why a Russian would be in the office of a Baptist church. The only one that really fits is Louis LaPierre, in Room 208 with Vilmos from nine until ten. But he's Catholic."

"Saksonov—that name comes up a lot. And regularly."

"Focus, please. Louis LaPierre, Gospel Baptist—"

Holly ruminated a minute or two, knowing she'd heard something about— "Got it! Gospel Baptist is in the process of suing him for installing faulty fire-alarm equipment!"

"Well, of course they're suing," Lulah observed tartly. "Their church burned down!"

"Evan said that the very afternoon before the fire, LaPierre swore uphill and down dale that everything was fine. But of course it wasn't." She grinned. "What do you want to bet the conversation took place in the reverend's office?"

"All right, I *might* be convinced that you're right. But it doesn't explain the magic. Nobody on our list is a Witch. Whatever magic started these fires, it didn't come from any of them."

"So whose magic *was* it?"

NEITHER GIRL SAID A WORD.

It took a couple of tries, and a clearing of his throat, before Nicky could speak. But then he couldn't think of anything to say. Evan was at the closet, dragging out a pair of blue terrycloth bathrobes, and over his shoulder said, "The nametags read 'Marika' and 'Agrafyna.' Russian?"

"As good a guess as any." So in Russian he told the girls that no one would hurt them, they were safe. Telling them they'd been drafted as power forwards for the Lakers would have had much the same effect. Coaxing them into the bathrobes proved no trouble. Cam, knotting the belt around one girl's waist, cast a frustrated look over his shoulder at Nick.

"They're in a walking coma. Magic or drugs?"

Evan said, "They've been so scared for so long that I don't think anything will ever scare them again. They don't know how to feel anything else, but they don't even feel *that* anymore."

One of Nick's specialties was what Lulah called Come-Hither; with a little tweaking it became Go-Thither. The only way he knew the spell had taken was that both girls looked him in the eyes. But just for a moment.

"Take them downstairs," he said, "and get them out through that threshold."

"Uncle Nicky—" Cam looked like a spooked colt. "There's too much magic here. Don't you feel it?"

"I'll take your word for it. Go on. I'll go take a look into the other rooms."

"I'm serious. It's not these girls, it's this whole set-up—"

"Theorize some other time," he snapped, wondering why he was so irritable. Perhaps Cam was right, and there was a surfeit of magic here.

Or, more likely, he was simply missing the solid support of his partner. "Take those children somewhere safe."

He watched them descend the first few stairs, the girls moving placidly enough as Cam encouraged them with the occasional *"Horosho"*—good. Then he turned toward the next room, and opened the door.

It was a trivial place: bed, dresser, easy chair with a basket of folded sheets and towels beside it, shelves clogged with books. The bathroom door was open, the closet door was closed. But it was a room lacking shadows, and even without extending his senses Nick felt the magic spark and quiver like tiny resentful flames. He shouldn't have snarled at Cam; the boy was right. There was too much magic in this place.

And there was a girl. She was very young, dark-haired and blue-eyed, huddled uncomfortably in the easy chair with a hardback book propped on her very pregnant belly. Squinting, he read the words printed in silver on the spine of the dust jacket.

Jerusalem Lost

McClure

Fifteen

SHE HAS ALWAYS BEEN SMART. School was always easy, although her real education came from the books old György dug out of his vegetable garden after the Communist government fell. Hundreds of books, wrapped in oiled cloth and packed in crates for more than fifty years; books in Hungarian and Russian with leather covers, paperback books in English and French and Italian; novels, history, poetry, myths and legends, plays. She is one of a score of village children who have worked their way through this long-hidden library since its unearthing. Everyone else must work the land. Decades of mismanagement have, incredibly, wreaked less devastation on this country than other former Soviet satellites, but capitalism has been cruel in its own ways and there is as fine a line as ever between survival and starvation.

But she is smart. She is also pretty. The Magyar genetic mix has given her the thick black hair of the steppes nomads, the blue eyes of the Greeks, and the pale complexion of the Slavs and their distant Nordic ancestors. She looks her age—not quite fifteen—but she is poised beyond her years and she is in many ways better educated than a graduate of college. She believes herself to be as sophisticated as one of those girls, anyway, and longs for the greater world outside her village, where she knows that being smart and pretty are formidable advantages.

It is a spring day, warm and soft, and the man and woman have stopped to have a picnic lunch. She is idling her way back home from György's house, taking her time, for her father has a fresh bottle of vodka this afternoon. As she passes, the woman calls out and invites her to share some lemonade. She joins them beneath the roadside tree. The woman is Hungarian, but the man is Ukrainian, and she is proud to show off her command of his language. Before very long, conversation turns from their trip to the woman's ancestral village, somewhere a hundred miles or so from here, to the paucity of opportunities there, to the kind of life a smart, pretty girl might enjoy as a governess.

France. England. America. With her education, they tell her, she could have her pick of positions with rich families, and send staggering amounts of money back to her family. The man's own sister and two cousins, he says, are at this very moment working in Amsterdam, Tel Aviv, and London—perhaps he has their postcards—no, he must have left them in his other jacket. The girls are having a wonderful time, the work isn't too hard, and only last week his aunt received 500 euros from a London bank.

She gulps lemonade from a plastic cup, thinking what 500 euros could buy.

After a year or two, she could return home—or, the woman says with a wink, a girl might attract the attention of a wealthy young man looking for a smart, pretty wife.

She has read hundreds of books, and school was always easy for her, and she is acknowledged as the smartest girl in the village. But she is still only a fourteen-year-old from an impoverished village in Eastern Europe, with no future except a lifetime on a subsistence farm with a husband gradually succumbing to liquor (like her father) and a houseful of children to raise (like her mother).

So she accepts the scribbled note the man gives her, and agrees to consider contacting the agency that placed his sister and two cousins in their foreign jobs.

The next Wednesday, very early in the morning, she returns the last of the borrowed books to old György and takes the bus all the way to the city. That afternoon, at the address on the note, she is warmly welcomed into an office. A middle-aged woman with a kind, round face gives her tea and buttered bread, and tells her that she would take her application right now but the chief agent himself will want to interview such a lovely and intelligent girl, to make sure the placement is just right. She is embarrassed when the warm tea makes her sleepy, but the woman only smiles and says that she must be exhausted after such a long trip.

She wakes in a dim, airless room, rank with the sweat and urine and feces of the dozen other girls who are in here with her. She knows without even glancing at the door and windows that they are all locked in.

DURING THE NEXT TWO DAYS—she thinks it's two days, but there is no way to be sure; the windows have been painted black—more girls are brought to the room. Some are feisty and fighting; most are carried in drugged, as she was. Occasionally there is food. Twice the slop buckets are taken out and emptied. It is unspeakably hot and from somewhere flies have sneaked in. Their erratic buzzing bothers her at first, but then becomes just another annoyance to be ignored.

There are twenty girls now. She listens to their quick, whispered conversations, but offers nothing herself. Their stories are sometimes like hers, sometimes worse.

One girl says she is supposed to be in Greece right now. She was to meet her fiancé at a café and they were going to Athens so he could introduce her to his family. She was to stay with his aunt, and begin the process of converting to the Greek Orthodox faith. It was all very correct and proper. But just as she was stepping down from the bus in front of the café, two men grabbed her and forced her into a car.

Another girl, proudly asserting that she can speak Russian, French, English, and even a little Arabic, says that she will be a translator, that she is very valuable, especially because of the Arabic, because of Bush's war.

Another girl has a photograph of the family whose nanny she is to be. They are very rich. They live in a castle in England and have a house on a beach in Spain.

There is a much-folded paper gripped in one girl's hand. It is a restaurant menu. She was given it to study by the recruiting agent, so that she will be able to describe everything the cooks make and thus be ready to step right into her new waitressing job at a Russian restaurant in Israel. One girl proclaims herself a singer. Another is a dancer. They expect to work in theaters, nightclubs, hotel shows.

From the far corner of the room a girl says quietly that her father is an alcoholic who sold her. She watched them hand over the money, saw him stuff it into his pocket. The protests are immediate—and frightened. This can't be right, there were promises made, pictures, letters, the menu, the fiancé waiting in vain—

Someone else says that as she was taken out the kitchen door, through the front door two men brought in a new color television. She is accused, loudly and vehemently, of being a liar. She doesn't seem to care. She knows what she saw.

A fist pounds on the door, and a man yells for silence.

It is a long time in the darkness before another girl speaks. She knew what this would be. There is no money in this country, no work. At least if she must sell herself, it won't be where people might recognize her and shame her family. At least if she must sell herself, it will be to rich men in countries where her blond hair and blue eyes will bring premium prices. She will earn enough to find somewhere nice to live, and nobody will ever know what she had to do. Her family will believe she is dead.

Someone begins to cry. The weeping spreads like a disease. The man shouts again, and the girls hide their faces in blankets, in mattresses, in each other's necks for comfort. She feels the girl next to her shudder with sobs, and turns her back. She isn't nearly as smart as she thought she was, but she learns quickly. At least, she tells herself, at least she can blame no one but herself. These others, so many were betrayed by people they knew. No one will betray her. Not again. She will not permit it. Shaking off her neighbor's beseeching hand, she curls around herself and closes her eyes and finally her mind, and sleeps.

That night—or at least what she assumes is night, for there is something about the quality of light not coming through the papered and painted windows that has changed, though she isn't sure exactly how—when she gets up to use the bucket, she does not return to the mattress she shares with the needy, graspy girl. She hollows out a position near the door, earning herself grunts and an angry elbow or two. She pays interested attention to the pain in her ribs for a while, deciding it isn't bad, knowing there will be worse to come if she is not careful. If she does not do as she is told, if she displeases anyone in authority, if she so much as looks anyone in the eyes who does not wish to be looked in the eyes, they will deal out pain much worse than a bruise.

She is close enough to the door to hear some of what is said outside. It takes her only a moment to determine which side of the wall she should choose. The door opens inward, and whereas there would be momentary comfort in being hidden behind it, she would rather not attract the kind of attention that must come when the girls there are dragged from its shelter. These are not things she has ever thought about before, but she finds no surprise within herself that she should be considering them now. If she has not been smart, at least she is not as stupid as some of these girls.

What she hears, those next hours, is interesting only for one thing: the men guarding the door are Hungarian, but those giving the orders are Ukrainian. The latter speak their own language with each other, but issue their commands in Hungarian.

The door opens, and the girls behind it are jolted awake. Three more girls are shoved in. They look stunned, and one of them seems angry. But the door does not close. Instead, a tall, fat man fills its space. In Hungarian he says that two at a time they will be taken to wash up. He then speaks in Ukrainian, in Russian, in English. And as he talks, he watches intently, dark eyes scanning every face.

She realizes what he is looking for: any reaction, anything that would indicate understanding. For what he has said in Hungarian does not match what he says in the other languages. In Ukrainian he says they will be taken four at a time; in Russian, that they will be having breakfast; in English, that they will be released.

She keeps her face a blank mask as his eyes strafe her side of the room. Several girls stiffen as he speaks in Russian, for it has been a long time since the last bread and cheese and basket of grapes was shoved into the room. The Russian-French-English-and-a-little-Arabic girl bleats softly, like a goat, when she hears the words "release you." He grins at her, and points. She wobbles to her feet. He grasps the arm of a girl cowering nearby, hauls her up, and within moments the door has slammed shut again.

Throughout the next hour, those girls whose faces revealed comprehension of languages other than Hungarian are taken away two at a time. None of them come back. This confirms her wisdom, and begins to restore some of her confidence in her intelligence. She wonders if languages make a girl more valuable, or less. An understanding of orders would be advantageous—but an ability to plead for help would not. She decides it doesn't matter for now. She will listen, observe, learn, keep her silence, and respond only to Hungarian.

There are twelve of them left now. At almost fifteen, she is in the middle age range. One of the girls cannot be older than eleven.

An unknown amount of time later, the door opens and two men enter. One of them hauls a dark-haired girl to her feet and makes a gesture.

She cowers, terrified. He rips her dress from neck to hem. The second man walks slowly around the room. Anyone looking away is forced to turn her head, open her eyes, and watch.

The dark girl is shoved onto a mattress, face down. What the man does then makes her scream. The second man shouts at any girl who turns her face away, and everyone understands that they must watch or be punished. She manages all the same not to look. She finds a stain on the floor beside the mattress and gazes at it through her eyelashes. All she sees is movement, not specifics. The screaming is bad enough.

When it is over, both men leave. This is surprising; she would have thought the other one would take his turn. The girl lies on the blanket, sobbing in great convulsions like an epileptic. Eventually someone goes to help her.

The next time she sees the outside world, it is night. She and the other girls are tied with twine around their wrists. They are taken down five flights of stairs and through a kitchen where a pot of stew and a plate of bread and a pitcher of wine have been left out on the table—a deliberate cruelty, she thinks, for there has been no food upstairs for quite some time. Out the back door, she smells exhaust fumes and gets a brief glimpse of the city's night glow above the rooftops and down at the end of the street before being pushed up a steeply sloping ramp into a truck. When all the girls are inside, the ramp is removed. Metals doors are slammed and locked.

At each of four stops within the city, ten to fifteen more girls are loaded in. After a long drive, there is a fifth stop. Six boys are flung inside. It is too dim to see their faces, but their voices are shrilly adolescent. She wonders why the others are so shocked. Can it possibly be that they still don't understand?

Along with the boys, two cardboard boxes are tossed in: one-liter bottles of water. An older girl takes charge of distribution, and says that it would be best to drink slowly, conserving the water, because they don't know how long they'll be traveling. When most of them ignore her, she shrugs and mutters that they'd all better keep hold of the bottles after they finish, because they're going to need someplace to pee.

She stays awake, sipping rarely from her bottle of water, forcing herself to ignore the smells. If she is to survive this, she reasons, she must learn to shut down her senses.

The journey lasts a significant fraction of forever. Finally, slowly, her nose stings with scents she has never smelled before: the salt and fish and dampness that must be the ocean. They have not been traveling nearly long enough to reach the Black Sea. The Baltic could not possibly be this warm, not even in summer, and it is only May. This must be the Mediterranean, then—perhaps the Aegean Sea, or the Adriatic—

The truck comes to a halt. Now that the engine noise and the road vibration is gone, she can hear a little of the outside world.

A muezzin is calling the Faithful to prayer.

Turkey? Albania?

Several of the girls and two boys cry out with a frantic babble about which direction they must face in, where is Mecca, which way should they kneel?

When the doors open, the brilliant daylight spilling across huddled bodies reveals that during the night one of the girls managed to crack a plastic water bottle and use it to slit her wrists.

"SOME OF THEM might be Jewish," says the woman. Her thick false eyelashes look like clippings from the fur vest that buttons tight under her breasts and pushes them toward her chin. "If we can pass them off as Jewish, it will be easy to get them into Israel. It's the Law of Return or something. I know several houses in Tel Aviv—"

"But will Jews buy Jewish girls?" This from a very young man, perhaps not even twenty, who is thin and fair and looks very stupid.

"I didn't say they had to *stay* Jewish," she snaps. "Just long enough to get them into the country. What about her? Does she look Jewish to you?" She points at a girl who is so obviously Romany that she could never be mistaken for anything else. "Too bad we can't take any of the boys," she continues, then laughs through her nose. "It's much easier getting girls into Israel as Jews than it is to try the same with boys!"

Her companion doesn't understand. She reaches over and takes a handful of his crotch. He winces away and takes several steps back, out of her reach.

"How about it, little one?" she says to the Romany girl. "How would you like to go to the Promised Land?"

They are speaking Italian. They arrived this afternoon at the warehouse by the docks where the truck disgorged its cargo. Waiting had been a real toilet over in the far corner, and a table with loaves of bread, rounds of cheese, and more bottled water. There are crates and boxes scattered about, all of them stenciled with the word VLORË. She thinks this might be the name of the seaport they are in. It isn't that she needs to know this, or wants to; she merely wishes to exercise wits growing stale and stiff from lack of sleep and lack of food. If she keeps thinking, she has a chance.

What this chance might look like, when it might come, and what it might lead to, are things she meticulously does not think about.

A side door slams inward and a darkly mustachioed man makes his entrance. "*Mi scusi!*" he calls out. It is the same cheery, carefree voice her father uses when he's had enough liquor to make him jovial and not enough to make him morose. "I had to go find another two *scafisti*—I had only two, and you have brought me such riches!"

Scafisti is a word she does not know. She finds she is irrationally angry because of it. How dare he use terms with which she is unfamiliar? How is she supposed to survive this, to recognize her chance, if she can't understand what's being said?

Moments later she recognizes the fury for what it is: exactly like all the crying and wailing and moaning the other girls have done. It is hysteria. Fear. Horror at what is happening to her, at what will happen to her.

The four *scafisti* turn out to be motorized rubber boats. Mustache tells his "captains" that across the Straits of Otranto it's only forty-four nautical miles (how these are different from miles on land, she does not know and decides not to care), so hurry but don't be in a hurry, yes? If they spot the Italian Coast Guard, throw the merchandise overboard and speed off. While the Italian authorities scramble to rescue abandoned girls and boys from the sea, the boats will return to Albania.

"Use the Cape lighthouse as your guide—and remember we're going to Mestre this time!" he finishes, and leaps into the boat like a pirate king.

The woman has added a wool coat to her fur vest, but still she huddles shivering in the boat as if she were wearing only the spring cottons of the merchandise. Her companion whines about wanting to drive the boat; Mustache tells him to wait for open water. The engine coughs, roars, and the boat tilts as it gathers speed, and soon the wind is flaying skin from bones. She hunkers down as best she can to shelter from the cold. Someone vomits; the wind lashes the stink away. The young man drives the boat for a time, and his reckless bravado—steering from side to side, making it rock and sway while he laughs and the girls scream—earns him a snarl from the woman.

After a long while, the boat slows. The woman snaps an order, and the young man distributes dark blankets. They are not for warmth; they are spread over the girls so that light will not find them. This must mean they are nearing shore. The word *silence* is repeated in several languages. The engine is muted to a soft purr. Bouncing atop white-crowned waves has given way to sliding through black water. Someone else is sick, and the smell this time is caught under the blankets. At last the motor cuts off. The boat lurches up onto sand. Everyone is hurried ashore. The Mustache waves a merry farewell, and leaps back into the boat for the return trip to Vlorë.

She stumbles up the slope, the blanket wrapped around her like enfolding wings. Up a hill there is a road, and a van, and everyone is shoved inside.

The woman, who is behind the wheel, lights a cigarette and starts the engine. "Can you do this by yourself next time, Gianni, without fucking things up too much?"

"I was fine!"

"You nearly dumped us all in the sea! Do you have any idea how much money is sitting back there? On my first shipment, I paid two thousand five hundred American—each—for ten girls. I made it back in a week."

"None of them were fat or ugly?" he sneers. "Not even one?"

"My suppliers know better." She drives fast, and the girls collide with each other at every corner. "I tell you, Gianni, it's the perfect investment. No government in the world is serious about rescuing whores."

"But if you get caught?" he wants to know.

"Sometimes there is a fine, sometimes a month in jail. Usually the charges are dropped—can you guess why, smart little boy?"

"My father says it's because the girls won't testify, and without testimony there's nothing they can hold you on. But what happens to the girls?"

"They get thrown out of the country as illegal aliens—or sent to prison for being prostitutes. There *are* laws!" She turns her head to grin at him, and the car swerves, and she throws her cigarette out the window.

Gianni lights the next one for her. "So you will be my father's partner in this," he says. "His houses, your merchandise."

"Half the whores in Italy are from Eastern Europe. That's not a guess, that's a fact. What other commodity is so plentiful? So cheap? So easily replaceable when it wears out? Much easier than smuggling guns or drugs—"

"And you can sell a gun or a kilo only once," Gianni muses.

One of the girls starts to cry. Perhaps she also understands Italian. The language of Dante. Appropriate: the language of hell.

The house is massive. There are fluted white pillars and cool marble floors and glasswork chandeliers hanging from the foyer ceiling like gigantic garish spiders with orange, blue, and yellow globes dangling from each leg. There is a deep blue carpet on the curving staircase, and the next day her bare feet luxuriate in the softness when they allow her and the seven other girls in her room to come downstairs. The grass outside is very nearly as soft: warm where the sunshine drenches it, wet further down toward the turf. Surely this place is too grand to be a whorehouse. But finding and selling whores would seem to pay very, very well.

The valuable merchandise is escorted down the stairs in groups of twenty or so, and let out into the open air. Men with machine guns watch, simultaneously alert and bored, as clusters of girls and boys shift nervously across the grass. She wants to stay aloof and alone. But she knows better than to attract attention by detaching herself from a group. So she huddles with a little knot of terrified girls. Well aware that the small pleasures of sunshine and fresh air are not intended as pleasures, she guesses that the hour outside is meant to keep them healthy. So is the food. So is the warmth of her bed, and the uninterrupted quiet from twilight to dawn.

So is the attention of the man addressed as *Dottore* who comes to the house the following day. She is twentieth in the line of girls that stretches from the top of the stairs down to the foyer, along a back hallway, and into a room. The line jerks forward at irregular intervals, for some girls emerge quickly from the room while others are kept for quite a while. Each girl emerges visibly undamaged, but some come out weeping. That no one limps or curls around bruises or cradles a twisted arm reassures her. That some are crying moves her not at all. What puzzles her is the change in their clothing: gray sweatpants and either a green or yellow sweatshirt. The girls in yellow are directed down the hall; the girls wearing green cross the corridor to another room.

She hears whimpers from behind her on the staircase, and shifts impatiently forward. She doesn't understand how some of these girls can still be afraid, how they can be so stupid as to show it. Anything other than silence and an expression of blank lifelessness attracts notice. Sure enough, she hears the slap of an open palm across an unprotected cheek, and resists the impulse to shake her head with disgust as a wailing cry of protest results. And, of course, another slap. She knows better than to turn and look. Curiosity is dangerous, and defiance is insanity.

It is her turn. A woman wearing a hideous polka-dot blouse addresses her, trying different languages. All of them are spoken badly, and none of them are Hungarian, so she does not respond. Short, hangnailed fingers clasp a clipboard and a pen, and when no response comes after two more enquiries, the woman writes on an index card and hands it to her. She is Number 353/2005. This year—and it is only May—have there truly been three hundred and fifty-two others before her in this house? Probably so; she is twentieth in line today, and at least fifty more girls line the hall and stairs behind her.

She walks in the direction the woman points, carrying the index card. At a closed door, another woman in nurse's whites takes the card and says, "*Dottore*" as she swings the door open. Within is a tall, reedy man with a balding head and a look of lifelong aggravation. He snatches the card, turns it over, and begins writing on the back. The woman leaves, and the door snicks shut.

She stands silent while he mutters in Italian. He makes a series of gestures, and after a moment she pretends to catch his meaning. She has learned to mime initial puzzlement so she has a little time to think. A little time to school her reaction. A little time to steel herself for whatever might happen.

He wants her to take off her clothes.

She does, folding them neatly as her mother taught her. He indicates an examining table. She sits on the hard surface covered by rough white paper. The nurse opens the door and says, "*Dottore* Santangelino—" but retreats when he snarls. She tells herself that she must remember the name—and then wonders why she thought such a foolish thing. Remember it for when? As if there will be a time when she is free to speak this man's name to the authorities. As if there will ever be such a time.

As if any authorities will be interested.

As the examination proceeds, as her knees are bent and her thighs parted and her most private places painstakingly explored, she stares up at the painted ceiling with its garlands of flowers held by smirking cherubs. When the *Dottore* pokes her belly and handles her breasts, a small gold crucifix on a chain around his neck swings into her view. She wants to squeeze her eyes shut but keeps them open: she has endured without reaction all this time, surely she can last a little longer. His fingers slide down her ribs to her hip, and this is no longer a medical examination.

He is careful not to leave any evidence or do any damage. He is just as careful not to make a sound. All he does, really, is fondle her with one hand and himself with the other. But the child's crucifix on its gold chain sways with his rhythm, and her world abruptly contracts to nothing but the tiny, smooth, naked gold feet folded one atop the other. She thinks that she ought to be able to see the nail. Light pulses with the cadence of his hands, and for an instant, as he cries out softly to Jesus, she feels dizzy and tiny flickering flames spread up the naked legs to the twisted body, the spread arms, the lolling head. She is mesmerized by the imaginary fire.

After, the nurse gives her the card and gray sweatpants and a green sweatshirt, and she is sent to another room. Her blood is drawn by a young man who says, "So you're a 'type and test,' are you? Lucky girl!" The testing must be for diseases, but she doesn't understand why her blood will be typed.

When she goes upstairs, the waitress is back in their room, wearing a yellow sweatshirt, with a new menu to study. She plods mindlessly around the room, mumbling, memorizing English words for sex acts, and the price in dollars for each.

Late the next afternoon, as lazy rain taps on the roof and soaks the wide green lawn, the girls are taken to a large room with a carved stone fireplace and more ugly glass globule chandeliers. More than sixty girls and at least a dozen boys line up, cards in hand. Each is told which of three new lines to join. She glimpses the tall woman and the stupid young man out the window. He is holding her umbrella as the van is loaded with their new merchandise. Among the girls—all wearing yellow—is the one who was traded for a television set.

The line she is directed to is the shortest. She wonders what it is about her and the nine other girls in green that makes them special. She wonders what she has in common with them. Not height, not age, not coloring, not nationality—

Blood type?

She is still trying to puzzle it out when she is taken to another room, given clean denim trousers, a white blouse, a black sweater with big gold buttons, tennis shoes, a cheap leather purse, and a passport. She has become a Russian named Natasha Ivanovna Slutskaya. She knows the English word. Someone has a sense of humor.

Natasha and the other seven are directed back into the foyer. The *Dottore* strides through, shouting furiously, something about why didn't someone tell him earlier? Another voice attempts a soothing tone; he is having none of it.

"—helpless old woman at Mass in our village church—a miracle she wasn't burned alive! Why didn't you tell me yesterday, when it happened? She's my *mother*!"

As he passes, Natasha sees his hand clutch the crucifix at his throat. She remembers how she saw it aflame yesterday, while he was handling her. He repeats, "My *mother*!" and yells for his raincoat and his car keys.

Natasha is put into a car with three other girls, and two men she has never seen before drive them to an airport. They stay together, the four of them and their escort, through the ticket line and the security line and the boarding line. Natasha never even considers crying out for help. She heard and understood what the woman said the night of the trip across the Adriatic: she will be deported as an illegal alien if she is lucky, and thrown into jail as a whore if she is not. She has not been lucky so far.

From one airport to another, and yet another; Natasha spares only a tiny smile for the dreams she once had of world travel. Then, after a very long flight, the ten who were selected back in Italy are reunited. The ensuing drive is interrupted only by rare stops for food and the toilet. The men don't bother to watch the girls anymore; the landscape is bleak and empty, and only a suicidal fool would attempt to escape now.

Natasha sleeps with her cheek pressed to the glass of the van window. When she wakes, the road signs are all in English and she realizes she is in the United States. She has heard that after September 11, American borders had become more difficult to cross. So much for that conceit.

When they cross a river, for the first time her interest sparks: a sign says it is the Mississippi, the river of Mark Twain. She feels foolish for being disappointed that there is so much industry along the river, so much concrete and steel. Did she really think to spot Huck Finn on a raft, or a fleet of white paddle-wheel steamboats? She confines herself to observing what is actually before her, and eventually a sign welcomes her to New Orleans.

The house is tall and narrow, painted mustard yellow with white trim. There is a wrought-iron fence, also painted white, all around the yard. It is at least six feet high, with spikes. The gate to the driveway squeals as a young boy shoulders it open.

Within, the house is simply vulgar. Natasha has a glimpse of a large front room with padded black leather furniture and chrome-and-glass tables, gold velvet curtains swagged back from panels of black lace coyly shading the windows. But up two flights of stairs, everything is hospital prim. She is given her own small room. Locked inside it, she finds clean clothes in the closet, fresh sheets on the bed, and books on the shelf.

Tired, alone for the first time in forever, nonetheless she cannot sleep. She selects a book with an interesting title and curls into the overstuffed armchair patterned with overblown roses. At last, eyelids drooping, she crawls into bed wearing a cotton nightgown from the chest of drawers. She sleeps until someone unlocks the door.

She doesn't know how the man discerned her understanding of English; at first she thinks that because she is still half asleep she made some slip of expression or movement. But it remains that he tries no other language on her. He merely begins speaking in English, explains that she is one of the lucky few who will not be living down one flight on the floor reserved for working girls. He tells her that cooperation will be rewarded and defiance punished—then smiles and shrugs a little, as if to say, *I know you're smart enough to have learned that already, but it's part of the speech, something I tell all the girls.* He says that she has been chosen for a very special purpose, and that once it is fulfilled, she will be taken to a country of her choosing, given a job and an apartment and money for the rest of her life. He fastens around her wrist a bracelet made of dozens of tiny silver links and a small plain disk, and smiles. He has thin lips, and an excess of large white teeth.

"Have you any questions?"

She doesn't move. She hardly dares to breathe.

"Come now, Natasha. I know you understand me."

She says nothing. She doesn't even blink.

He smiles again. "Enjoy the books," he murmurs, and leaves her alone.

That's when she sees it: the book she picked out the night before, left open and face-down on the arm of the easy chair. Of all the languages represented—German, French, Russian, Italian, Spanish, Greek—she had chosen one in English.

Dragon Ships, by H. Elizabeth McClure.

With an intriguing title and a beguiling tale of a world a thousand years gone, a woman she has never heard of has betrayed her.

THERE IS NOTHING to do except read. She reads voraciously—only in English—and almost every day there are new books waiting beside her door. They've tried to trick her by including things in Russian and French, but she separates those out and puts them aside, taking only the English books.

The ten girls have their meals together. After the first few days, nobody bothers to talk to Natasha. She still has not uttered a single word, a single sound. She has not yet conceded that she must communicate with anyone—not even the tall, elegant man who knows that she knows English.

At the top of the house, at the very back, there is a little balcony. It is the only place where fresh air is to be had. The window of her room is sealed shut, though sunlight enters freely through clear panes of glass. The balcony, with its wrought-iron chair and soft cushions, is hers for a half hour every day. She is left alone. The balcony is enclosed in chicken wire; she assumes that at some point in the past, someone jumped. From what she can see of the brick walkway below, escape could not have been the result—but then, perhaps it was not meant to be.

In a room down the hall are two stationary bicycles and two treadmills. The first few moments of the daily hour in the little gymnasium are a scramble for the bikes; no one likes the treadmills. After a few days, a sign-up sheet is posted that makes sure everyone has a fair turn.

In June she undergoes the procedure for the first time. She knows enough to know what they are trying to do. It is not a success; she bleeds as usual two weeks later. In July they try again. This time she doesn't bleed on schedule. She feels . . . odd. Not sick to her stomach, not dizzy, not any of the signs she has heard about. Just . . . odd. They begin to watch her. Three other girls are also being watched. By the last week in August, they have bled again.

Natasha has not.

SHE WAKES TO A DIM roaring sound that comes closer and closer as the minutes pass and she lies there in bed, trying to understand the noise. Gradually, as a composer might layer instruments and phrases beneath and on top of each other to create an ever-more-complex piece, other noises are added: the creaking and banging of wood, the scraping and whining of metal, the rasping of concrete and the smashing of glass. The lashing of the rain seems almost calm by comparison. The air becomes dense, thick, almost too heavy to breathe. It smells strange—as if it has escaped from some deep fetid hole in the earth. It is tremendously hot; she realizes there is no more muted whoosh of air conditioning, and the lazy rotations of the ceiling fan have stopped.

She gets out of bed in the darkness, makes her way to the window, parts the curtains. She watches for a long while as the rain beats against the glass. Slowly there comes a little light, and she can see beyond the window. The world is painted in grays and browns, as if the air itself has been bruised.

"Stand away!"

She spins around as the tall man shouts at her from the doorway. For the first time he does not seem in control of everything; he is barely controlling himself, she thinks, for his hands look a little trembly and his face is flushed.

"Natasha!" he snaps. "Move back!"

She pretends not to understand. It is the same game they have played for months now. He strides over and hauls her away by one elbow. He pushes her onto the bed and she is suddenly, irrationally terrified. The fear seeps through her like poison, hot and shivering through her belly and thighs. But he turns for the closet, pulls out clothing, and throws it at her. She doesn't move because she truly can't.

He grasps her shoulders in his big, thick fingers. "Dress yourself.

Keep away from the window. I know you understand, so do as I tell you. *Now!* Or I'll leave you here!"

But he won't. She knows that. Everyone has been far too careful of her, now that she is pregnant. She will not be abandoned. The fear washes out of her. She takes off her nightgown—she has long since shed modesty, there have been too many people who have seen her too intimately naked—and pulls on a shirt and jeans. As he hovers in her doorway, calling orders down the hall, she sits on her bed to pull on socks and shoes. The wind and the rain shriek, and her window explodes inward.

BY LATE AFTERNOON, the worst has passed. But then the water begins to rise.

It is slow and inexorable and it is worrying these men who thought that a few broken windows would be the extent of the damage. There has been argument all afternoon among them as they sit in the horrid gold-curtained room. Some want to load up the cars and the van, find safe ground, wait out the storm. Others scoff, saying that the levees will hold—and if they leave here, how will they keep track of their whores?

"I paid good money for these bitches—of *both* sexes," one man snarls. "I'm not losing a single damn one of them!"

"And what happens when the police come by again?" another man asks. "There was a mandatory evacuation order that you ignored—"

"They'll probably be tired, and needin' a little relaxation. I've had twenty houses in nine cities in four countries, and all cops are the same. You pay them, mostly in freebies—" He gestures with his cigar to the nearest cluster of girls. "—and they protect you. The ones who want money, unless they got a sick mother or they're saving up for a new boat, their buddies call 'em queers. So the payoffs usually don't cost a thing."

"I get it," another man says impatiently. "But why worry about escapes? They don't speak no English. They got no ID—"

"Because it disrespects me! If these little whores even begin to think they could get away from me—" He glares across the room and the whores shudder.

At irregular intervals the argument continues. Natasha is puzzled, not sure why the tall man, who seems to her so much in authority, does not simply give the order that will load them all into cars and take them away from here. There are things she does not know, of course, and they are unlikely to tell her, so she gives a mental shrug and curls deeper into the corner chair. The other nine special girls are talking quietly with each other, inspecting their fingernails, fiddling with their silver bracelets. They take no notice of the whores. These cluster together, clinging to each other. They sit in dull-eyed silence, and flinch at sudden noises.

It is dreadfully hot and humid. She wishes she had something to read, something to take her mind and imagination far away from here. She has read so much in the last months that she is beginning to think in English. She wonders idly how many words she will mispronounce for never having heard them aloud. She should have indicated weeks ago that she wanted a dictionary—

"*Scheiss!*" The tall man is on his feet, pointing at the water seeping from the hallway rug onto the hardwood floor.

There is no more discussion.

The tall man fixes his gaze on Natasha and is about to say something when there is a pounding at the door and someone yells, "Anybody in there? Department of Wildlife and Fisheries—we've got boats, come on!"

One of the men begins to laugh, a high note of frenzy in his voice as he says, "Wildlife? By damn, now *that's* funny!"

The door is kicked open. Water gushes in. Three young black men slog their way into the house. Their faces are tense, but their voices are kind and reassuring. Soon Natasha is crowded onto the porch. The house next door, lacking so lofty a stance, is awash to the windows.

Someone is lifting her in his arms. She is told, "It's okay, *chère*, you be safe in no time." She is put into a boat that reminds her a little of the *scafisti* in Italy. The tall man is arguing with someone wearing a green nylon jacket with some kind of logo on the breast. His pale eyes widen as the motor is gunned and the little rubber boat chugs off down the river that was once a street.

Natasha watches him until she can see him no more. Very quietly, she laughs.

THE SHELTER is in a home more or less undamaged by the hurricane. There is bottled water, sandwiches, cookies. And cots. Natasha eats, lies down, sleeps for many hours. She wakes up smiling.

"Yes, honey, you're safe now," murmurs a soft voice, and she opens her eyes to see a caring coffee-brown face. "Your friend Marika says your name is Natasha. That's awful pretty. My name's Poppy."

There is something watchful about the dark eyes that puts her on the alert. But in the next moment she realizes there is nothing malignant about this woman, nothing that wants to take and own and use. There is concern, curiosity. And some sort of knowledge that she can't identify. Best to stay silent.

"Miz Bellew?"

Poppy turns her head. "Miz Lachaille," she acknowledges as a young, weary-looking white woman approaches.

"This the little girl you were lookin' for?"

Natasha feels her blood freeze solid in her veins.

"This one and these other poor children. You know what the one of them said about that house they were in, don't you?"

The second woman nods, her lips compressing into a thin line of disgust. "Don't take much English to communicate *that*. Will y'all be takin' them with you?"

"I hope to do that, yes, if they want to come. Virginia's a long ways—but I can't imagine they'd mind being as far from here as they can get."

"Amen to that. Well, let me know when you decide to head out—we'll load up some food for your trip."

"Thank you so very kindly, Miz Lachaille." When the woman has gone, Poppy says softly, "Child, I'll be honest with you. I did come lookin' for you in particular. Sensed you halfway across New Orleans. You don't know why, I'm sure. But you have nothing to fear anymore. I can help you. Do you believe me?"

Natasha looks at her with the empty expression perfected these last months. It has worked with everyone but the tall man. It does not work with this woman, either.

"You have a secretive face, and there's quite a lot you're hiding behind those lovely blue eyes, but the air around you tells the truth. I'm no expert in that kind of reading, but I know enough to know you can understand me. If you don't want to talk, that's fine. I propose to take you and your friends back home with me to Virginia, where the people who kept you will never find you. Once you're there, you can decide what you want to do next—go back to your home, stay in this country, whatever it is you want to do. You'll make the decision. You'll decide if you trust me."

Against everything she'd learned since waking up in the blacked-out upstairs room in Budapest, she does trust this woman. Something stirs inside her, vaguely recognized from odd, isolated instances in the past—things she can't remember with any real clarity, the way images in dreams are vivid one instant and mist the next. But it is something, it is familiar, and it makes her trust this woman.

At length she gives a short, sharp nod.

"Good girl." Poppy smiles and gets to her feet, chair scraping the concrete floor. "You just rest, honey, and when we're ready to leave I'll come get you. All right?"

She doesn't respond again—after so long forbidding response in the muscle and skin that could betray her with a movement or a flush of color, she cannot release control so quickly. But Poppy only smiles again, and walks away.

THE WHOLE WORLD is a soggy mess. It takes hours to drive past the debris strewn through every street—trees, cars, bits of houses, furniture that floated out and flowed along with the water and then sank into the sucking mud. At last the car reaches an area looking slightly less like a war zone.

Poppy hasn't said much. She has the radio on, listening to news reports. Everyone is angry. The incompetence of the government is the only topic. People are being blamed and other people are defending them, and themselves, and quite often the "discussions" become shouting matches. At this point Poppy usually changes the channel. There are appeals for food, clothing, water; phone numbers and addresses are recited; people read out lists of names of missing persons. Natasha finds it interesting, in a remote way, that Americans are so eager to help, rushing to give money and collect clothing and offer shelter to total strangers. To other Americans. Not to her.

The other passengers are silent. Natasha recognizes them. Marika is "special," like her; the other girl and the boy are whores from downstairs. She doesn't know and doesn't care if they understand enough English to follow the news on the radio. The hours pass, the sunlight dims, and Poppy pulls the car into a lot with a sign that says REST STOP. She points to the bathrooms as she begins talking into a cell phone.

Natasha thinks for a moment about slipping away. That Poppy doesn't accompany them to the bathroom means she trusts them to return—or perhaps she simply knows that they have no other choices, nowhere to go. But Natasha speaks English. She might be able to—

There is a smear of blood on her underpants. She takes them off, puts them in the metal box labeled DISPOSAL, and walks back to the car.

She is half-dozing in the darkness when she feels a sharp cramp in her abdomen. Someone on the radio is complaining again about *feemuh*. Natasha sits very still and stares unblinking into the swath of road illuminated by the headlights, bordered by metal railings and languid trees. When the pain returns, her whole body clenches.

Glaring headlights shine directly into her face, startling her. Poppy pounds a fist onto the horn, hits the brakes, wrenches the steering wheel, loses control of the car. It slews toward the metal barricade, smashes, skids sideways, skitters to a stop. Poppy curses furiously. One of the girls in the back seat is crying in huge terrified sobs.

The seat belt traps her. She struggles to find the release catch, and her stomach cramps again.

"You idiot!" Poppy yells out the open window. "You ran me off the road!"

"My apologies." He leans down, and all his white teeth are shining as he smiles. "Hello, Natasha."

She feels a warm gush of liquid between her legs.

Poppy's breath catches. "You know this girl? How do you—"

"Now, madam, if you—" He falters, and suddenly looks at Poppy as if he recognizes her. "Ah! No wonder you found her. You will be so good as to restore to me my property."

"Your 'property'?"

"I know what you are. I know how you found her. And now I will take her back." He gestures with one thick-fingered hand. "It's a strange location, this. Here for a very long time, invisible except to those with capacity to see."

All at once Poppy mutters something under her breath, and her right hand rises from the steering wheel to trace a brief pattern in the air.

"No, do not trouble yourself. It will not work here. Can't you feel it? The power that prevents power's use. Someone was creative, and deeply skilled."

"How did *you* find her?" Poppy asks, her fingers stealthy, sliding toward the door handle. "How did you get ahead of us?"

"You stopped, and made a phone call. I must ask you to stay still. Put both hands on the wheel. Marika, get the other girl and that boy out of the car. Carefully."

It hurts now. It hurts very much. In a blackened haze spiked with acid, it hurts.

"Slowly now, Natasha," he says, and she flinches, for he is right next to her, leaning in the open car door. "I found her the same way you did," he tells Poppy, flicking a finger against the dangling silver disk of the bracelet.

Poppy looks startled, then shaken—and then she says with terrible contempt, "You're a parasite. You have nothing of your own, so you—"

"Enough," he says softly. "Enough."

It is the last thing she hears before the pain overwhelms her.

Three days later, she wakes up in Virginia.

IT'S A STUPID BOOK.

The others—about Viking conquests, a queen who stitched an endless tapestry, a poet, an artist, the mistress of a king—were interesting at least for the history. This one drones on and on. France is always cold and rainy, Palestine is always hot and sandy. Guillaume keeps galloping his horse into battle and waving his sword at Saracens and whining about Elisabeth. Elisabeth is forever tending her castle and fending off suitors and whining about Guillaume.

A very stupid book.

But she has folded the last load of sheets and pillowcases, bedspreads and towels, and she has nothing else to do.

She thinks for a moment about sneaking down the stairs, just for a change of scenery. But in the last weeks she has grown so big and so ungainly that it's a chore just to walk down the hall to the therapy room. She hasn't been on any floor but this one, in fact, for five months—not officially, anyway.

A few days after she woke up here, he took her down the stairs to sit on a footstool with a screen on her lap, and made her watch while a girl spent an hour with a man in a bed. In all this time, from Hungary to Albania to Italy to Mexico to New Orleans to Virginia, she has never watched the act. He did not allow her to look away, his fingers like thick claws at the back of her neck. She watched as the girl's mouth gaped wide and the man filled it. She saw the man's face contort as he shouted the name of the Son of God, over and over and over again.

"Be a good girl, Natasha, and that will not happen to you."

As hard as she worked not to feel anything, learning to ignore and repress her senses, she could not control the anger (triumph?), the helpless panic (ecstatic power?) that flared along her nerves as he screamed Jesus again, and Jesus, before slumping back across the bed.

But she had no time to sort out these feelings, for the heavy fingers shifted to her shoulder and wrenched her around to face him. He was blatantly shocked. Then he laughed low in his throat. When he spoke, his words were German. She understood every one of them.

"Of course. I was right. It needs the place and the air and the water and the magic all together—I told them it would, I *knew* it would." More laughter. "You, little one, you will be the success. I would have brought you here before, but I didn't want to risk the child—and now that I know you *can* conceive, in this place you will be my success. And you don't even know what you are!"

He has not taken her back to the landing and the chair and the screen since then. She has gone back by herself.

The first time, it was very late at night, and completely quiet. She sat with the screen on her lap and her eyes on the screen and watched the man and the girl in the bed. She was ready that time for the response inside herself. She recognized it now. She had first felt it in Italy, when the *Dottore* had groped and pawed at her, and the gold crucifix glinted with fire. She knew, with a stinging in her blood that she later decided must be how power felt, to anticipate the surge of energy racing along her own nerves.

She cannot call up that power on her own. She has only the memory of it, and at times the desire to feel it again is so sharp that she risks leaving her room and seeking out the screen where she could watch. Usually she is disappointed: there are no people in the rooms, or only people who were alone, or couples doing ordinary things like getting ready for bed, or talking, or showering, or simply sleeping. But three more times she is rewarded for daring to descend the stairs.

Now that she is too heavy and awkward to move with the stealth required, she quite often calls up the images in her head for cold analysis. She dissects the sensations, the timing, the images. The *Dottore* with his golden crucifix. The first man, calling out to Jesus. The second had begged to be forgiven, raised his hands into the air and begged God to forgive him. One of the men sang. He actually *sang* to the rhythm of his own body. Another had included the name of a woman in his litany. Not Mary or a saint; someone called Lisa. And then he started to cry. The last one she'd watched had cried, too, because he was scared. He hadn't even caught his breath—and she hadn't even felt the whiplash of power begin to fade—before he was muttering to himself about someone would find out and he was in so much trouble and Jesus God Almighty what was he going to do?

She hoards these memories for their evocations of power. She sorts and categorizes, hungers to feel it all again. Except for the books, and the daily walk down the hall to the therapy room, and the baskets of clean linens that are brought to her each morning and afternoon for folding, she has nothing else to do.

There had been another time of power for her, a time that had nothing to do with watching the screen. Downstairs, all the way down where the surgery and examination rooms are, he had been waiting with his little vial and his long syringe. He sprinkled white crystals of salt in a circle around the bed, lit four candles of varying colors, then changed into a pristine white lab coat. "My vestments," he told her with a smile. And though there was no culmination of sexual energy, she felt the now-familiar surge and quiver and burn. That there is something besides sex that kindles power intrigues her. What the salt and candles have to do with it, she has no idea.

The only thing she knows for certain is that she has a baby in her belly. And from the restless twitches that started this morning, she thinks that perhaps it will not be inside her for very much longer.

She has a healthy body, a certain blood type, a fertile young womb. These things make her valuable. Whatever she might feel—and she doesn't feel much anymore, except that fretful craving for power—whatever she might think, whatever else goes on inside her, none of it means anything. In the last weeks she has come to feel that there is a frozen crystal skeleton inside her that the birth of this baby will either melt or shatter. She contemplates both endings with no more than casual curiosity. She does not matter. The baby matters. When it comes, he will have no more use for her. And it may be that she will become one of those girls in one of those rooms.

And so, when a man appears in her doorway, even though she has never seen him before she sees him without fear. She still has value; the baby is still inside her. Perhaps he has come for the child—which is moving now with intent, kicking and poking painfully. It suddenly hurts so much that she is startled into an uncontrolled reaction when the blond man blurts out a soft exclamation.

"Te jó Isten!"

Her eyes widen as she hears her own language for the first time in longer than she can recall. He flinches as if in pain. As if he is hurting for *her.*

Sixteen

ONE OF THE THINGS Jamey Stirling most appreciated about Pocahontas County was that he could campaign for office without having to organize an actual campaign. He'd seen enough of such things to enjoy their absence. There was no manager to tell him where to go and what to do, no finance guru soliciting funds and doling them out one grudging dollar at a time, no scheduler or press secretary, not even a gofer to get him coffee. It was all on him. He did his job during the day, and on evenings and weekends accepted invitations to speak at events like tonight's, to dinner in people's homes, to coffee and pie at meetings of various county social and charitable organizations. Some nights he just hung out at one of the watering holes or diners, or Mrs. Paulet's hardware store. It was the kind of politics everyone pretended still obtained all over the country. It was really possible only in places like this, where billboards and yard signs were considered bad taste and no one would dream of airing a commercial on the local radio station. A candidate declared, spent time getting to know people not already encountered in the course of his job and life here, sent out one or two mailings, printed up a few window signs for people who asked for them, and that was it.

His father and brother had offered to come run his campaign. He'd declined with thanks, knowing how difficult it would be to explain PoCo political customs to men who hadn't worked on a level below governor or senator in twenty years.

Running unopposed, he wasn't worried about getting the votes he needed to claim for real the job he'd been doing for almost a year now.

He knew he'd done good work for this county. People knew him and liked him. What he worried about was what he hadn't done yet. He'd spoken the exact truth this evening: the church fires were really pissing him off. And now he had something new to be really pissed off about. Whatever Bernhardt Weiss was up to in his magic-infested Westmoreland Inn, Jamey was going to prosecute him on as many counts as he logically could.

His problem was figuring out what constituted "logical" when one was dealing with Witchcraft.

Gotta have a talk with Evan about that, he decided as he leaned against the wall and kept glancing back and forth, downstairs and upstairs. *A very long talk.*

But before that happened, he had to have an even longer talk with Cam.

He'd told the truth as well when he'd said he'd taken this job because he was sick of cities. But always in the back of his mind had been the notion that one day Cam might show up. Not mentioning him, especially to Holly and Lulah, had been almost intolerable. The closest he'd ever come to it was admitting that he'd been at Yale Law around the same time as the cousin they adored. He tried not to be obvious, whenever he went to Woodhush, about going into Evan and Holly's shared office to look at the family photos strewn across the walls. Once or twice he'd sat casually down at the upright piano where Cam had learned to play. And Kirby, with his bright blue eyes, really did look a lot like Cam. . . .

In short, he'd had it bad for twelve solid years, and he knew it. And now that Cam was finally within reach again, Jamey decided he was tired of waiting.

Except there was more to talk about now than just them. There was magic.

Standing here with a Glock in his hand, he examined the wall with the door he couldn't see. Nothing magical about it. It was a wall. It had silk on it. It had wainscoting. It looked exactly like the wall on the other side had looked. Turning, he frowned at the wooden chest and the fresh flowers, just as innocuous as the wall. The cabinet door was carved with various things: single keys at each corner, and a castle gate below the huge central griffin. For obvious reasons, he had long ago looked up pictures of heraldic griffins. The body of a lion, with the head, wings, and talons of an eagle; a fierce and mythical animal, and the only part of anything in this hallway that even hinted at magic. Certainly the flowers were innocent. He recognized rhododendrons and sweet peas amid the lavender roses, and thought the tall plant must be papyrus—yes, had to be, although whether it was the symbol of Upper or Lower Egypt, he couldn't recall. The point was that none of it had anything to do with magic—

No. The point was that the papyrus was *symbolic*. So were the keys, the griffin, the gate. Everything in heraldry meant something—each color, each geometric design, each animal or bird or flower or creature that didn't really exist. How many times had he walked into a Southern home to find it rife with carved and painted pineapples, emblem of hospitality? And Justice, blindfolded, carried sword and scales. Nobody in this modern world thought in symbolic terms. But when the vast majority of people had been unable to read, images and all their associations had taken the place of words. About the only thing Jamey could think of that was comparable these days was the red octagon that everywhere meant STOP.

Rhododendrons and sweet peas, roses and papyrus; keys, castle gate, and griffin. He had no idea what any of them meant in the language of symbols. But he was entirely sure the Witches would know.

Even the wood that the cabinet was carved of—hadn't Lulah McClure handed her nephew a little wooden charm to help him find the doorway?

As Jamey stood alone and alert on that landing, he believed and not believed and believed again about twenty times. Every time he decided it was all perfectly insane, he looked at the wall again. Every time he recalled that one minute he'd been sopping wet with rain and the next he'd been warm and dry, and told himself that "the laws of Nature and Nature's God" didn't work that way, he looked at the wall again.

Now he looked at the cabinet and its bouquet of flowers. A wooden cabinet. A vase of flowers. How could anything so utterly commonplace be at all magical?

He looked at the wall again. The shape of a hand indented the silk. Pushing, prodding, testing. It didn't come through. He couldn't remember what movie it was where somebody's face had done pretty much the same thing—as if it had been wrapped in plastic, or was pressing outward against a balloon that wouldn't pop.

He could stick around and wait for the hand and the person attached to it to come through the wall. This was a non-starter; whoever it was knew about the magic, and therefore quite probably could work magic. Glock or no Glock—and he was fairly certain Evan had handed the gun over just to make him feel better—he had seen enough tonight that he really did believe that he didn't want to pit one or even ten bullets against whatever it was Witches could do.

That left downstairs or upstairs.

He stuffed the Glock into his waistband at the small of his back and quietly moved the footstool so that anyone coming through the wall would trip over it. The sound would warn him to make some kind of noise that would turns heads upstairs, not down. Down was where the women were. Upstairs . . . okay, he might as well admit it. Upstairs was Cam.

He took the steps two and three at a time. As he climbed, logic nattered an irksome reminder that there were only three floors to Westmoreland, that if he counted landings he would know where he was—and that adding together the number of steps he had taken thus far would put him at the top of the Washington Monument.

"Jamey—? What the hell—?"

He looked up and saw Cam, Evan, and two girls in nightgowns and bathrobes.

Curiouser and curiouser? Alice hadn't known the half of it.

LACHLAN HAD TO ADMIRE JAMEY'S sangfroid. Instead of gaping like the village idiot, stuttering out questions, or just plain failing to react altogether, he got to the important part with the first words out of his mouth.

"Somebody's trying to get in. They're not succeeding. And I'm assuming you want to get these young ladies out."

"That's the idea." Evan shepherded his charge gently down the steep stairs to the next landing. "And since that's the only entrance we know about . . ."

"Do you think they might give up and go away?" Cam asked with no real hope.

Evan shook his head. "I think they might go find another door into this place—one that Cam didn't lock. There's gotta be more than one, right?"

This did not fill the younger men with delight. Evan shrugged and kept descending the stairs. He let Cam explain where they'd found the girls, and listened while the two speculated about finding a place to stash them. But when Jamey, alluding to Nicky's suggestion about the "services" provided at Westmoreland, asked if they might possibly be working girls, Evan interrupted with, "No. There's only two of them, and they were hidden away with magic. And there wasn't anything in that closet but the bathrobes and some plain shirts and things."

Cam feigned astonishment. "No black leather boots? No fringe and sequins?"

Lachlan flashed him a look that warned against further one-liners. This stairwell was finally having the same effect on him as the rest of the Inn; every step he took rasped from his boot heels up his spine, grating his nerves like Tillamook cheddar.

So when a figure came into view far down the staircase, his hand was halfway to his Glock—which wasn't there—before he recognized his wife. She blinked at him, knowing the aborted move for what it was.

"Hot damn," she murmured. "I finally got to startle somebody tonight. Stand down, Sheriff, it's only me." Gaze sweeping over him, Cam, Jamey, and the two girls, she said, "You found company upstairs, but we found an operating theater downstairs."

Evan countered with, "Exercise room, sunlamps, and a crash cart."

"Cryogenics." She held up a laptop computer. "And an appointment register—not, I make haste to add, for massages at the spa."

Lachlan upped the ante. "Portable DVD player that hooks up to six different rooms for observation and recording at the Westmoreland Inn, Spa—"

"—and Whorehouse," Lulah said as she joined them.

"And Home for Expectant Mothers," came Nicky's voice behind them. "Lulah, there's a girl upstairs in labor."

"Hell and damnation." She pushed past them all, tossing over her shoulder, "Anyone who does a Butterfly McQueen impersonation will be lancing boils in embarrassing places for the next month."

"Did I also mention," said Holly, "that I think Lulah and I have figured out the church fires?"

"*Now* it's a party," Evan murmured.

GETTING MARIKA AND AGRAFYNA to safety was their immediate priority. Mindful of Jamey's description of a hand trying to push through the wall, they waited a few twitchy minutes on the landing of the papyrus and rhododendrons. Absolutely nothing happened. Evan traded shrugs with his wife, reclaimed his Glock, and gestured with a flourish at Cam.

"If you'd be so kind as to open the door?"

"But of course."

Evan took a long stride through the wallpaper. A moment later he was back. "All quiet. I can't guess for how long, so let's get them out of here."

Holly stayed with Jamey, counting off minutes in her head. When he spoke, she flinched.

"Tell me about the fires."

She held tighter to the laptop. "In here are names and times that coincide with some but not all of the arsons—it's weird and it's complicated, but I think it might end up being right."

"Convince me," he said.

"Okay, Counselor. Men who were here on the same nights and at around the same time the fires started have ties to the churches that burned. Example: St. Andrew's, April 8 of this year. Start time between eight-thirty and nine forty-five p.m. Grant Newbury was here from nine until ten, in Room 105 with a girl named Evva. The fire was ignited in a cabinet where they kept their brand-new hymnals. Grant is a member of the St. Andrew's congregation."

"Not buying."

He sounded like Elias Bradshaw at his judgmental worst. Well, she had to admit that the first example was a little thin. "On September 29, 2005, Hugh Chadwick was here from eleven to midnight. He's a contractor specializing in brickwork—and the newly completed front steps were the ignition point at Old Believers Baptist."

"Still no sale."

She glared. "What do you want, signed confessions?"

"Evidence would be nice."

"Jack Wheeler," she said through gritted teeth. "November 8, one to two in the morning—"

"That was the First Baptist fire, with the varnish and the benches?"

"Yeah. Wheeler is the manager of that hardware emporium—"

"—where that brand of varnish is sold?" He shook his head. "I've met Jack Wheeler several times. I've had dinner with him and Lisa. He coaches soccer, she teaches dance, they have two great kids—" He broke off suddenly, frowning.

Holly shifted impatiently from one foot to the other, wriggling her toes within Cam's wool socks. "I'm sure Lisa's just swell, but she's not equipped with what Jack Wheeler was here for that night."

The silver-gray eyes widened, and he actually blushed.

"Damn it all, Jamey! These men were here for sex, and churches they're associated with in one way or another burned down those same nights, in fires that started at the same times they were here!"

"It doesn't tell me how."

"Magic. The Methodist fire was the only one with no magic involved, and don't ask me how I know that, but I do know it. That's what was in one of the faxes that came in tonight—not about the magic, I mean, but there was actual forensic evidence of how that fire started. Which there isn't for any of the others."

"So which of the good gentlemen of Calvary Baptist was getting a blow job on October 9 last year?" he challenged.

"None of them," she had to admit. "The only one here at the right time was some guy named Van Slyke, and Lulah says he belongs to Old Believers."

Jamey said nothing for a moment. "All right. You've got me."

"What? Why?"

"Calvary invited the Old Believers to join them that Sunday. My secretary told me all about it. Lots of arm-waving and praise-the-Lord. One of the Old Believers got up to witness to the combined congregations—"

"From the pulpit? Where the fire started?"

"From the pulpit," he confirmed. "Where the fire started. Anyway, the service was such a success that a committee is ironing out doctrinal differences so they can become a single congregation. Ginny gives me regular updates." He smiled slightly. "Ever since she learned that 'Stirling' was originally 'Silberman' she's been gently evangelizing me. This year I may have to observe Yom Kippur for the first time since the rabbi's wife said something about my *bar mitzvah* speech that my mother didn't cotton to and we stopped going to temple."

Holly sighed. "And I thought *I* could wander off on tangents."

"Sorry. The Old Believers witness from the Calvary pulpit—and subsequently a member, with Ginny, of the amalgamation committee—was Thomas Van Slyke."

"So you think I'm right?" she ventured.

"I think what I was about to say earlier, before you interrupted, is that Lisa Wheeler not only teaches dance, but she does it in the basement rec room of First Baptist. So I'm willing to entertain this—"

Cam stepped back through the wall.

"—concept that having sex at Westmoreland causes churches to burn down."

Holly bit back an untimely giggle at the expression on her cousin's face. Evan, right behind him and with his mouth open to say something, stopped short at the spectacle of Jamey's cool self-possession, Holly's incipient hilarity, and Cam's wide-eyed suspicion that not only was Jamey not in his right mind, he didn't even know its ZIP code.

"Uh . . . we found the maids' break room," Evan offered after a moment. "Cam locked the girls in. They're safe enough for a while." He waited. Holly grinned at him. A frown knitted his eyebrows together. "I'm not gonna ask. I've had it with encouraging you people tonight."

She stubbed a toe against the cabinet and swore softly as she started after him up the stairs. *"Éimhín, Éimhín,"* she called, "there's an explanation, truly there is!"

"Yeah?" He stopped, looked down at her, and blew out a long sigh. "Y'know what? This whole thing is making me crazy in ways that probably aren't good for society at large. Okay, so tell me about sex and church fires."

FLATTENING HIS HAND AGAINST the wall as he descended, Cam sought the sensation he'd found before. Nothing. There had to be more than one way into this place. Prudence alone dictated it. Unable to get in through the door from the outer staircase, Weiss—assuming it was Weiss—would seek out the other. Or others. But where? Was there a legitimate, non-magical way up to the attic? And if this had indeed been used for smuggling, there must have been an outlet at the ground floor, or maybe the basement—

Jamey interrupted his thoughts with, "Aren't you going to cross-examine me about—"

Cam shook his head. "Jamey, at this exact moment I don't want to discuss churches, or fires, or church fires, and I sure as shit don't want to discuss sex. Not with you, not right now."

"Later, then."

"No." He shook his head again, feeling like a dashboard Dodger with a negativity complex.

"Don't be such a jackass. We have to talk sometime, you know. I'll bring roses and champagne and a Sinatra CD if you want, but we *are* going to talk—" He broke off. "Cam!" And he was spun around as Jamey grabbed his elbow. "This is probably crazy, but take a look at the flowers and the cabinet, okay? What do you see?"

"Flowers. A cabinet."

"Don't things *mean* things in magic? That amber necklace of yours—you said it symbolized—I don't remember, but it *means* something, right?"

"Confidence, luck . . ." he said absently, concentrating on the cabinet and the bouquet. The former was carved with three large keys and a portcullis. The flowers were more lavender roses, more sweet peas, and others that startled and then worried him. "Enchantment. Departure. Lust. Pleasure and pain—"

"I'm guessing the obvious for the cattail," Jamey said. "But what's the green stuff, and the little white rose?"

"It's a dog rose, and that's the 'pleasure and pain,'" he responded dully. "The other is lemon grass."

"Which means—?"

"Let's just say that Morgan's parents—or Erika Ayala—would never grow it in their gardens. I don't like this, Jamey. If I'm reading this right, this is another doorway. Keys indicate guardianship, but they're also as obvious as the cattail. The portcullis—"

"I knew it had a name. It's on the cabinet where the doorway was. So were the keys."

"Of course. But the flowers were different."

"There was a griffin up there, too."

"Vigilance," Cam said shortly. "Stand back." He felt the silk wallpaper smooth and slick beneath his fingertips. It had to be here, another door had to be here someplace. Hands exploring, eyes squeezed shut, Cam sensed more silk wallpaper, more wool—and beyond it more silk, and some leather. "There *is* a door."

"Where to?"

"Do we really care all that much where it goes?"

"Not so much, no."

So they walked through a wall again. Wool: the Persian carpet on the floor. Silk: black sheets, crimson velvet upholstery and bed curtains. Leather—

A quantity of cheap black leather decorated with silvery studs and festooned with a few chains encased the meaty form of the man from the shower in Room 208. The chains rattled as he turned, and what was visible of his face through a leering leather mask was startled, then curious, and then intensely interested. In Jamey.

Teeth gleaming like searchlights from the black mask, he said something that sounded Russian but wasn't; Cam knew that much. He also knew he was less than thrilled by the way Jamey smiled back and walked toward the bed, an atypical swing to his hips that earned a distinct reaction within the black leather codpiece.

"Cam?" he said in a sugar-soaked voice as he unbuttoned his shirt. "Get your ass over here, please."

"You're doin' just fine on your own," he snarled back.

"He outweighs me by about seventy pounds and I don't have the proverbial blunt instrument to hand," Jamey answered in the same sweet tone.

"You—oh. We're gonna double-team him, right?"

"Not in the way he thinks, no," he purred. "But that's the general idea."

Cam began his own approach, knowing better than to mimic the swish. Instead, he made a bid for the man's attention by stripping off his shirt. He wasn't in Jamey's league, of course, but the dark gaze crawled over him like spiders.

The man cooed something in not-Russian. Cam deployed his dimples and said pleasantly, "Your mother was the diseased mutant offspring of a bald gorilla and a camel with terminal syphilis, and I'm gonna slug you right in your black leather jaw in about two seconds."

"If that's your idea of verbal foreplay," said Jamey, "I have to tell you it really isn't making me swoon."

They hit the guy at the same time. Cam took the more direct route, slamming his fist into the man's chin. Jamey, executing a graceful half-turn, drove an elbow into his stomach, and stomped on his foot for good measure. He whooshed sonorously, like a deflating bagpipe, as he went down.

They used the sheets and pillowcases to tie him up on the bed. Cam got creative with the chains, unhooking them where he found fasteners and looping them around the bedposts, then reattaching them to the leather.

"Hurry up," Jamey said.

"Sorry, no experience with Bondage and Discipline."

"Pity. You'd look good in black leather pants."

He decided he really couldn't afford to react to that, and stuffed about a square foot of sheet into the guy's mouth.

"Not that I'm really into that sort of thing," Jamey continued. "No silk neckties around the wrists and ankles, no fur-lined handcuffs, and certainly no whips, not even the feather kind. About as kinky as I'm ever likely to get is silk sheets—blue, I think, to match your eyes—oh, and maybe some sandalwood massage oil. By candlelight."

The images this conjured up—*Nope, not going there,* Cam told himself. "Hand to God, Jamey, if you don't shut up—"

He mimed astonishment, eyes dancing. "Don't tell me I'm finally getting through to you! Was it the candles or the sheets? I could think up some other stuff—whipped cream is even more of a cliché than leather, but I could definitely entertain the idea of chocolate—"

Cam choked on slightly manic laughter. "Oh, God—M&M's—a mouthful of M&M's—"

They stood there staring at each other across the bed, grinning like mental patients, until the ripped sheets rustled and a moan issued from their trussed-up victim. Cam wondered how hard you could hit somebody over the head without causing permanent damage, then kicked himself mentally.

"I'm always forgetting," he mourned. "I spend so much time not doing magic that sometimes I forget that I *can*."

EVAN HEARD OUT HOLLY'S EXPLANATION, and shook his head. "How many points do I get if I don't make the obvious comment about you, me, and religious experience?"

"Oh, wipe that smirk off your face. In a lot of the old religions, there were temple prostitutes—male *and* female—it's what Leviticus is about. The passage isn't about executing gay men—and why is nothing ever said about lesbians? If same-sex sex is wrong, then why point at men and not at women?"

"And she's off and running," he commented, tempted to time the tirade by his watch.

"It's one of the Clobber Passages. Two different words are used for *male*—one means an ordinary man, but the other is almost always applied to a man or male animal dedicated to a god for a sacred ritual. What it means is that Jews become unclean if they go to temple prostitutes, because that's worshiping somebody who isn't Jehovah. Deuteronomy forbids the daughters and sons of Israel from *becoming* temple prostitutes. And—"

"Just for the sake of intellectual curiosity, what about St. Paul?" he asked as they climbed the stairs.

"Mangled in translation," she told him. "Plenty of Greek gay erotica survives, and none of it uses the term Paul uses for 'homosexual'—and why anybody takes his word for anything, he didn't even *know* Jesus of Nazareth, who said absolutely nothing about gay people at all—anyway, the word Paul uses has to do with homosexual acts in connection with religious worship—just like in Leviticus, only this time it's in Greek instead of Hebrew. Ritual sex in honor of a god or goddess—which is what I was talking about in the first place." She slanted a look at him. "Do I flatter myself, or do you recall our first Beltane celebration?"

"Religious experience," he grinned. "The very definition of."

"Denise Josèphe was pretty much the ritual prostitute at The Hyacinths that night," she reminded him. Neither of them said anything for a few moments. "And remember Hallowe'en, what Noel said about sex, death, the primal power of orgasm—" They had reached the top of the stairs. "What happened to Cam and Jamey?"

CAM COULD FEEL JAMEY WATCHING him as he prowled the room looking for anything he could use. But he wasn't at all prepared for the sudden question.

"Is this how life goes with you people?"

Cam turned slowly. "'You people'?"

"Weeks and months, maybe years, of being ordinary—taking care of the kids or the farm, going to work, out to dinner or a movie—and then all at once the magic starts up again?"

"'You people'?"

Jamey had the grace to look slightly abashed. "Well, yes."

"We're not normal, is that it?"

"Oh, for Christ's sake, Cam! I never understood why you're so paranoid about being gay, but now I do. It just gets reinforced with you constantly, doesn't it?"

Cam grabbed a crimson silk pillow, tearing at its fringe. "Did you know that the Congregation for the Doctrine of the Faith—that's Vaticanspeak for the Inquisition—still has an Index of Prohibited Books?"

"This isn't Salem in 1692, or Madrid during the reign of Ferdinand and Isabella."

"No, it's the good ol' U. S. of A. in 2006, where Erika Ayala can threaten blackmail if Holly won't make her son straight. And there's very little difference between bashing a queer's brains out on a curb and piling up the faggots for the auto-da-fé." He tossed a black velvet pillow at Jamey. "Rip off the tassels, will you? I need the gold threads."

"You want me to react to that word, don't you? Faggots."

"Look, Jamey, most of 'us people' have things we want to do with our lives that have nothing to do with magic. When I was a kid I spent time studying with the man who probably made that wooden talisman Lulah gave me to use tonight—yeah, another cousin, Louvena Cox's nephew. Leander's bowls and plates and cups are in museums—the ones he doesn't sell to collectors, anyway. That's his real work, and it doesn't have anything to do with magic."

"But he *does* do magic. And I'll bet he selects those woods as carefully as those he makes into bowls and things, when he's making wands."

Cam set aside the strands of red silk and started shredding the white roses from the bouquet on the bedside table. "As you've learned by now, like just about everything else, trees have magical associations. In Wales, it's unlucky to cut down a juniper. Juniper is said to be protective. Is that because when a fox shelters beneath a juniper, the stronger scent of the tree confuses the hounds? Black locusts grow from Georgia to Pennsylvania. Legend says they're the burial place for evil—but could that be because they're incredibly poisonous?"

"Folk magic—" Jamey began.

"—is something people say in the same tone of voice as 'superstition.' But it's different. It's learned wisdom, reinforced over centuries. And it's all over the place in everyday life. We live with magic all the time." He went on plucking and tearing velvety white petals. "For instance—did you know that meeting Holly was very lucky?"

"Well, I knew right off that I liked her, but—"

"Meeting a redhead is good luck. A redhead on a white horse is even better."

"But if she'd been riding sidesaddle she'd just be somebody who got lost from the Shenandoah Ridge Hunt Club?"

"Oh, quick—write that one down," Cam said sarcastically. "With red-haired men, it's the opposite. We're incredibly bad luck. It's said that Judas Iscariot had red hair, but personally I think it comes from the English, Scots, Welsh, and Irish being terrified of the Vikings—"

"Erik the Red," Jamey interrupted. "I can see that there would be reasons for traditional beliefs like that, but—"

"Can't quite get your head around real magic, huh? How about this, then. Uncle Nicky is part Gypsy, and Gypsies believe that a lock of hair from a redheaded woman on a pregnant woman's belly ensures an easy delivery and a healthy child. I'd bet the dollar amount of every contract Halliburton has with the U.S. Government that a lock of Lulah's hair got clipped tonight. Tell me if it's coincidence that Lulah's a skilled midwife, she's here, and she's got red hair."

"It *is* coincidence."

"*And* there's a Gypsy helping her get that child born." Cam shrugged. "But you're right, it's all folk magic. *Ritual* magic is the heavy lifting, and most of us don't do it that often. Most Witches very rarely Work that way for themselves. They're usually up against somebody else's magic and have to counter with their own."

"Like now."

"Like now," he agreed. "The roses and the threads are going to help me make bindings that are way better than handcuffs."

"What happened to 'Magic is within—the rest is just props'?"

"I don't know who told Evan that, but he's right and he's also wrong. It's associations—what I was saying before—that connect up with magic inside. Gemstones, flowers, trees, scents, colors, directions, whatever—all of them have multiple meanings. We learn them, and learn how they trigger certain things inside our heads—where the magic is. I want the flowers for secrecy and silence, with a nice dose of fear mixed in, and all of those things are evoked by a white rose. But they also call up things I have no use for right now, like humility, innocence, purity—"

"You?" Jamey interrupted. "Humble?"

Ignoring the jibe, Cam went on, "You have to separate out things that might interfere with your intentions. Now, if I had some vanilla or cinnamon—"

"And those evoke . . . ?"

"Magical powers." All at once he grinned. "Why do you think you like the smell of sandalwood so much?"

"Because the cologne you used to wear had sandalwood in it, of course," Jamey answered at once. "Why did you change it?"

He considered a long-ago afternoon spent in a Paris boutique having a cologne created for him by a meticulous *maître de parfum*—at the insistence of a fascinating but ultimately transitory Australian lover who scorned even the most expensive of designer label colognes. Perhaps he should go back to what he used to wear; he was almost out of the expensive stuff, anyway. "No reason. Can you check the bathroom? There might be something in there I can use."

"Such as?"

He rattled off the list of spellcasting aids that Clarissa had made him memorize. "Basil, patchouli, peppermint, rosemary, cinnamon, rue, sandalwood, lavender, lemon peel, wormwood—just go look, okay? Soap, bath salts, shampoo, stuff like that."

"Your wish is my command, O Master Mage."

His own search of the credenza's coffee-making paraphernalia was interrupted when Jamey returned holding aloft a tube of toothpaste and a bottle of mouthwash.

"Peppermint and cinnamon!"

"Candles and a bag of Earl Grey tea." He displayed his own finds. "Yank off a few threads from the fringe on the rug, will you? They don't have to be long—maybe four or five inches, so I can tie some knots. And don't cut them. The wool has to come apart where it's weakest."

"The weak places won't absorb magic?"

"Smart man."

Ideally, the red, black, and yellow threads for this spell should all have been the same material, preferably wool. On the other hand, the ancient Silk Road ran right through the region this magic came from, so the silk of the fringe and tassels wouldn't have been unknown to the local practitioners. The real problem with gathering textiles at random was that one could never be sure what had been used for dyeing. He experienced a moment's longing for the spools of thread Lulah kept for quilting, the bright skeins of weaving and knitting yarn. Those he could have used with perfect assurance. But a mark of the true adept was an ability to work with what one had.

So. Black for binding negativity, control, sleep, defensive magic. Red: power, pure and simple. Now, were the tassel threads technically gold or yellow? Cam decided not to worry about it. He could conjure strength from the former, though he preferred the breaking of mental blocks he would get from the latter, because he was quite certain that Leather Guy on the bed would not be the only beneficiary of some nice, restful, magic-induced sleep tonight.

"Will these do?"

"Yes. Thanks." He accepted the thick threads, wondering why anyone would fringe an expensive wool rug—no matter how garishly woven—with black. "Tear open the tea bag, please. Earl Grey is scented with bergamot, which is good for restful sleep. I was taught a long time ago not to make any spell needlessly cruel."

"Couldn't prove it by me. I seem to remember freezing my ass off with that afghan around my shoulders. And all the way back to my place that day—"

"—all you could feel was disgust at what a worthless person I was, and that you had absolutely no desire to be around me ever again?"

"I got over it."

"Once you took your coat off."

"I got over it," Jamey repeated. "Did you?"

"You know what? Let's fight about it some other time." Dumping packets of sugar, fake sugar, nondairy creamer, salt, and pepper onto the credenza, he swiped the bowl clean with a finger and placed within it the loose tea, silk and wool, rose petals, a little salt, a few drops of cinnamon mouthwash, and a squirt of peppermint toothpaste. All of this he mashed together with his knuckle.

"What—" Jamey began.

"Quiet." Cam lit one of the candles from the credenza. Purple was the traditional color of royalty, but it also signified justice, success, and power. What he was interested in most right now, though, was its quality of banishing evil.

He'd forgotten that Jamey had never seen fire lit without benefit of match. The muffled exclamation startled him as he sank cross-legged to the floor; he glanced up and nearly lost his balance at the wide-eyed shock on Jamey's face.

"Come on. You saw me walk through a wall."

"Somebody else's wall."

"Oh." And the shirt cuff had been partly Holly's doing. This was just him and a flame that was suddenly *there*. "This is as spectacular as it gets, y'know."

"Fine with me."

Arranging candle and bowl in front of him, he said, "Stand back. I have to draw a circle around myself." He did so, using the packets of salt. There was barely enough.

He had learned this spell in Lebanon years ago from a woman whose Assyrian ancestors had originated it. The magic was very old, and very adaptable. And because he was in spite of himself all too mindful of his audience, he felt a certain pleasure that the chant that went with the spell, as he tied knot after binding knot in the threads, was, even in English, pretty cool.

I shall twist the threads into a cord, a strong and mighty cord,
A cord to knot and bind up evil, with my own hands I knot this cord.
By tying knots, the evil is bound, and sorcery is brought to nothing.
I bind therewith the head, the mouth, the limbs, the fingers.
I cast the water of incantation, the smoke of incantation,
I cast the flame of incantation, the flower of incantation,
That evil may be bound, that it may not escape my knotted knots,
That there may be no evil spirit, nor demon, nor djinn,
That there may be no evil fiend, nor ghoul, nor phantom,
That there may be no evil sorcery, nor magic, nor spells.
By these knots I bind and command, and evil is brought to nothing.

THE UPSTAIRS DOOR WAS WIDE OPEN. Lachlan had watched his wife go through the process of childbirth and had absolutely no inclination to watch it happen to somebody else. From the look on Holly's face, she was of the same mind. They went inside anyway.

Lulah glanced around. "Busy," she said succinctly.

Nicky left the bedside and joined them in the doorway. "She hasn't reacted at all since I came in swearing in Hungarian. Not a cry, not a whimper."

Evan took a step closer to the bed. The girl was no older than sixteen, probably younger, with dark braids and blue eyes and a face that would be pretty if a smile ever touched it. But she looked as if she didn't even know how to smile. And when she caught sight of Holly, her face simply contorted, from a flinch of recognition to a furious snarl. *"Fapicsa!"* she screamed. *"Baszódj meg!"*

It took Nicky and Lulah both to keep her on the bed. She shrieked and clawed until he took her head in his hands. A moment later she sagged, unconscious.

"I don't like doing that to a pregnant woman," he said, standing back, shaken.

"She doesn't seem to like you," Lulah told Holly, breathing hard with effort.

"Not conspicuously, no," Nicky said, rubbing both hands over his face. "Don't ask for a translation."

"I thought the tone of her voice was fairly explicit," Holly said, eyeing the girl warily. "But why me?"

"Literary critic?" Nicky shrugged. "She was reading *Jerusalem Lost* when I found her."

She digested this, then wandered over to the easy chair—stained with amniotic fluid—and picked the book off the floor. Righting the crumpled dust jacket, she held it up to show the back: a photo of her wearing a dark shirt and her mother's pearls. "I never did like this picture," she said, and placed the book on a shelf. "And while I have no idea what's going on around here, I'm reasonably sure I don't like it, either."

"That makes it unanimous." Evan reached for her hand and tugged lightly. "We'll leave you to it," he told Lulah, who nodded distractedly.

Outside, they sat on the steps, Holly leaning close to him. He waited a few moments, then nodded at the laptop beside her. "So what exactly is in that thing?"

"It's not real evidence, you know."

"I'm thinking Homeland Security, for one thing, and Immigration and Customs Enforcement. Some of these names might be interesting to them, if only to put on a watch list. In fact, I don't know that Jamey and I will be able to do anything at all."

"What about the clinic?" she asked. "OR, exam rooms, records, cryogenics—"

He held an inner debate, then said, "What gets cryogenically frozen?"

Her eyes narrowed. "Filthy rich people who want to be thawed out when the cures for their diseases are found sometime in the future."

"And what else?"

"I don't know—blood products, I suppose."

"Come on, Holly." But she wouldn't say it, so he did. "Sperm and ova."

She huddled in on herself, arms wrapped around her knees. "If I'm right, and the girls were trafficked, then it wasn't just to become prostitutes."

Surrogates were used all the time by women who couldn't carry to term or whose lives would be endangered if they attempted it, or male couples who wanted to raise a child and for whom adoption was impossible. Somehow he couldn't see Herr Weiss as a benevolent and compassionate patron of gay or infertile couples. More likely he catered to rich people—extremely rich people—who wanted a kid without the bother and inconvenience of enduring a pregnancy and undergoing childbirth. The kind of people who hired two live-in nannies so they wouldn't have to deal with diapers and three a.m. feedings. Baby as status symbol, or heir to the family fortune. The essential accessory for the perfect American life.

"Brood mares," Evan muttered. "Jesus."

Holly raked her fingers through her hair—dry now, curling around her neck, threaded with white. "It's horrible, Evan. That girl in there—hidden away like this for who knows how long—and those two other girls—"

"But why hide them inside all this magic? Can magic influence a pregnancy? I don't recall that Lulah was careful around you, but—"

"I'm not a real Witch, remember? I'm not sure if a pregnant Witch is supposed to swear off working magic, like it's alcohol or something."

"So what's being hidden around here? The girls—at least one of them about to deliver—the medical clinic downstairs with the cryogenics—"

"Why down there and not up here?"

He shrugged. "How big is the clinic?"

She considered, then nodded. "You're right, there wouldn't be room for it all up here. But why hide everything with spells?"

"Which brings up another question. Why here? Why in Pocahontas County, where they've got to know about the population of Witches?"

"Well, I'd ask Lulah and Nicky, but they're a little preoccupied right now."

Seventeen

ONCE CAM'S LITTLE LASSOS were finished, he and Jamey returned to the stairwell. Cam kept popping back and forth into the room as if to reassure himself that the door was still there. Jamey occupied himself with not watching this ridiculous little dance, and picked at the mud beneath his fingernails. He glanced up as Evan called out from the stairs above him.

"I was starting to think you'd gotten lost, except there's nowhere to go but up and down—" And, as Cam stepped back into view, "—and through that wall."

"You found another door!" Holly beamed at her cousin, who paused in his two-step to scowl. "Clever boy."

"I'm a fucking genius," he snapped. "Whatever locking spell Lulah put on the hotel rooms, it's going to get unlocked pretty soon. There's a guy in there—"

Jamey interrupted. "We took care of him, Evan; flip the safety back on that cannon."

"—who was expecting a visitor. The kind you pay for. My finely honed sense of sense suggests that when the visitor couldn't get in, he went looking for a night manager. Or security. Or Weiss. Take your pick. But somebody's trying to get into that room—they've been knocking for a couple of minutes now."

"So why didn't you tell them to go away?" she demanded.

"You didn't tell me that," Jamey said at the same time.

"Like you could do anything about it? And how am I supposed to talk to somebody who can't hear me because of a spell *I* cast?"

"And he scores—twice," Evan remarked.

"How did you hear the knocking?" Holly pressed.

"I didn't. But I could see the door rattling."

"Hat trick," Jamey said sourly. "And the crowd goes wild."

"At least I've been doing something useful with my time." Cam dug two bits of knotted wool out of his jeans pocket. The threads still smelled of roses, peppermint, cinnamon, and Earl Grey tea. "Tied around a finger, they're good as handcuffs plus about twenty milligrams of Ambien."

"That's why Leather Guy in there won't be any trouble," Jamey added. "But somebody's going to get through that outer door somehow, and fairly soon."

"Reinforcements," Evan announced with a sardonic smile, "have arrived." He arched a brow at his wife. Her lips compressed and rebellion flared in her eyes, but then he touched his chest near his heart. Evidently it was some sort of private signal. She plopped herself down on the footstool, the laptop cradled to her chest. "Good choice," Evan approved.

"May I point out," she said, like a professor with a trio of none-too-bright students, "that if they're trying to break the door down physically, it means they haven't got anything magically. I would also remind you that the carry permits for their firearms are in your office files, Sheriff Darling."

"I remember. I signed them. Gentlemen," he said to Cam and Jamey, "stay behind me."

Through the wall and inside the room, Jamey was just as happy to have six-foot-four of sheriff with Glock between him and whoever was trying to get in that door—especially when the door crashed right off its hinges to reveal two strapping specimens of security guard (it said so right on their pale blue windbreakers). Both stumbled into the room, caught their balance, and brought up their pistols.

"Down!" Evan yelled.

Jamey lunged and tackled Cam too high, catching him in the ribs rather than around the thighs. They both crashed to the floor, the noise of an overturned table nowhere near loud enough to drown out four quick gunshots.

Cam was squirming out from under him, cussing creatively. Jamey rolled onto his back. Something twinged above his left knee. He looked down his own body to where Cam was pressing both hands against his thigh.

"Evan— Jamey's hit—"

It wasn't painful. Just stung a little, at a remove, as if he knew it really ought to hurt like a motherfucker but the signal hadn't quite gotten through yet. He propped himself on his elbows and looked curiously at the blood now covering Cam's long fingers. He did have the most beautiful hands. . . .

"Stay with me," Cam ordered.

He wanted to tell him not to be a jackass, of course he wasn't going anywhere. He'd been shot, for Chrissakes. But his brain was finally catching up with things, and his leg was starting to hurt, and he lowered himself carefully down to lie flat on the rug. He watched Cam drag the heavy crimson velvet bedspread down.

"Jamey, don't you dare zone out on me," Cam warned.

"Damnation!" This from Holly. There were more hands now, and a pillow under his left knee, and he could smell his own blood. It sickened him a little, and he closed his eyes.

"Artery?" said Evan from very high above him. Pretty close to the ceiling, actually.

"Nope," Holly replied. "No pumping blood. And a clean exit wound."

Well, that was good. His first big case had been a gang murder in Richmond, and the only person who'd survived had been the one with a through-and-through gunshot wound.

"Press harder, Cam. Are they dead?"

Of course the other four kids were dead, they'd been shot point-blank and there'd been no exit wounds—

"Nah. Kneecap and shoulder. They'll bleed, but they'll live."

Wait a minute. That hadn't been in the file. Nobody had said anything like that in the depositions. Was there a new witness? New evidence? He needed the medical reports, and the ballistics—

No, he'd won that case in Baltimore . . . or had it been Richmond? . . . four dead and one survivor . . . six gang members would never breathe free air again . . . it was over and done with, and he didn't have to worry about surprise testimony or overlooked evidence or anything but the smell of his own blood and the pain of—

But there was no pain.

And that made no sense.

"Can you stop the bleeding, Cam?"

"I kept it from hurting. I don't know about the blood. I've never tried anything like that before."

"Let's get him onto the sofa. Holly, grab the blanket, that bedspread is soaked. Wrap him up—yeah, Jamey, you're gonna be fine, just relax. You take his feet, Cam."

"I'm fine," he mumbled. "Never better. . . ."

"Of course you are," Holly said in a humor-the-children tone of voice that he found both tactless and irritating. He was about to tell her so when he felt himself being hoisted up, and the nausea got worse, and the fabric shifted off his leg, and pain roared up from his thigh and his brain said *Oh, the hell with it* and he passed out.

CURSING HIS AGING KNEES, Nick stopped abruptly as Holly came through a wall. It took him a moment to find his voice. When he did, he was dismayed to find himself yelling. "What in the unholy hell have you been doing? We heard the gunshots all the way at the top of the house!"

"Well, Uncle Nicky," said Holly, "not to put too fine a point on it—Weiss knows we're here, Jamey's been shot, and we found a way out but it's bound to be guarded from now on. I was just coming to get Lulah."

Processing this as they went into the room beyond, Nick decided he really, truly needed his partner right now. Some leather-clad personage was trussed up on the bed; Cam was on his knees beside the sofa, on which Jamey reclined, wrapped in a blanket, pale and oblivious.

"Know anything about gunshot wounds, Nicky?" Cam's voice was quite calm; all the frantic worry was in his eyes as he looked up, silently pleading. "I spelled against pain, but I set it into the bedspread and it fell off when we lifted him and his face sort of twisted up. I could work it again on the blanket—or maybe we ought to stitch it up, and I could do something to the suture thread."

Nick winced a little at the bloody mess of the two wounds. Far enough from the bone; muscle fiber obviously damaged; blood seeping, not pumping. "A painkiller in a nice, tight bandage would be a better idea."

A moment later Cam snarled, "Shit! This blanket might as well be plastic! I can't get into the fibers!"

The sound of ripping cloth distracted Nick, and Holly said, "Here," pressing a rag into his hand. He accepted it with an unthinking nod, staring at the dark green material, identifying it as torn from the shirt Holly had changed into earlier.

Cam asked, "Should I try something to soak up the blood?"

"The state you're in," Holly said, "it might end up rather vampiric, don't you think?"

Nick stared at the cloth. Cam's shirt. One hundred percent cotton—the boy hadn't worn man-made fibers since discovering his talent for textiles, be damned to being teased about the fortune he could save on dry-cleaning if only he'd allow some wrinkle-resistant polyester fibers anywhere near his skin—

Fibers.

Holly crouched beside him, already squeezing a drop of blood from her thumb.

Nick seized Cam's wrist. "You work with cloth. You weave magic into the threads. Threads are woven of fibers. So are muscles."

Cam gaped at him. "You can't be serious!"

"A fiber is a fiber. Cotton, silk, wool—"

"That's not living tissue!"

"At one time it was. Cotton grows on plants. Silk is made by worms and wool by sheep—"

"You worked on my shoes," Holly interrupted. "Sluiced the mud right off them. They're leather. That's skin."

"It wasn't still attached to the goddamned cow!"

"Do it," Evan ordered. "He needs a surgeon, and what he's got is you. And whatever you're gonna do, do it now—somebody might've heard those shots through an open door, silence spell or not."

"Come on, Peaches," Holly murmured, and pressed her thumb to each of Cam's fingertips in turn. Cam placed his Blooded fingers to the bloody wound and closed his eyes. Nick watched with commingled anxiety and pride, sensing the magic, wishing Alec was here to see what their boy could do. Evan crouched behind Holly, steadying himself with a hand on her shoulder. It troubled Nick that he looked in need of steadying—his eyes were dark with some unidentifiable emotion, and the fingers that twitched the otherwise useless blanket closer around Jamey were shaking.

With the movement, Nick caught a glimpse of a silver chain at the neck of the plum-colored sweater, and then he understood. On that chain was the St. Michael medal that Evan never took off, spelled by Holly almost three years ago. He and Alec had watched her sit before the hearthfire of her New York apartment while she did it. *Flesh and blood, breath and bone/No harm shall come to thee, my own—*

The magic had worked for him. But Jamey had gotten in the way.

SOMEONE WAS CRADLING him close and warm. She smelled good—clean and fragrant with a perfume he recognized as Holly's. One arm held him snug against her chest. Her other arm circled his ribs, fingers rubbing soothing little patterns, as if writing some archaic script. He grasped that her right hand was monitoring his heartbeat, but there didn't seem to be much reason for what her left hand was doing. Something Witchy, maybe. No, hadn't somebody said that she didn't have any magic, just blood? He could smell blood, and for a moment wondered why. But it was too much effort to think, and her embrace was gentle and comforting, and there was a cheek nestled against his hair.

"Will you go, already?"

"He'll be okay?" Cam's voice, thin and worried.

"You stopped the bleeding, repaired the muscles, closed the wounds, and he probably won't even have scars. If there's anything else that should have been done, I'm not aware of it."

"You're not a doctor."

"Neither are you, but you did just fine. Peaches, my darling, you did for Jamey exactly what Jamey needed you to do. We still need another way out of here. I'm useless. Go."

Peaches? Before he could gather breath enough to ask a question, footsteps receded somewhere to his left. And despite the arms securely around him, he suddenly felt very alone.

"I know you're awake, Jamey," Holly said softly. "It's all right. Just relax. Cam will be back, I promise."

He burrowed closer to her warmth.

After a time, she spoke again. "Whatever else you remember about tonight, this one thing I want you to keep clear and absolute. Listen to me now, my dear, and believe that what I'm telling you is as real as the sunrise tomorrow morning. Cam loves you. He always has and he always will. No matter what he might say or do or pretend, he belongs to you as surely as your own heartbeat. Do you understand?"

He managed a nod, and her arms tightened a little around him.

A while later he was roused from something like sleep by another voice, deeper and accented with New York. "Hey, lady, how come you're gropin' the kid?"

"I'm only human, my lord," she answered lightly. "After all, he's got quite a body on him."

"And here I thought I was the only one you groped nowadays. He's gonna be all right?"

"Yes. And before you start, this wasn't your fault. It was mine."

A pause.

"My work," she said more softly. "My responsibility."

"My choice to take advantage of it," Evan replied. "But we can fight about it later. It's a girl, by the way."

"Really? That was fast. Everything okay?"

"Fine. Lulah's coming down to take a look at Jamey. Nicky's magic wall holding out in here?"

"So far. I haven't heard anything, anyway. Evan, what the hell are we going to do? There's that baby upstairs, the girl who just gave birth to her, Jamey's not going anywhere under his own power for a while, Weiss is probably prowling around, and—"

"And? There's an 'and' on top of all that?"

"—and you're laughing!"

"So will you when I tell you that Alec finally got here."

Jamey stirred. "Who's Alec?"

"I am."

Holly caught her breath. So did Jamey, as the movement shifted him against her. She smoothed his hair by way of apology.

A voice redolent of Beacon Hill said, "Holly, you're looking less than radiant, but so is everybody else tonight—including that young man you're cuddling. Jamey Stirling, I take it? Formal introductions later. Right now I'm well into my *deus ex magica* act. Unlatch yourself, Holly, Evan and I can carry him—"

"Oh, for Christ's sake!" she snapped. "You're supposed to be protecting my children!"

"The estimable Tim and the delightful Laura are doing that—ringed in by more wards, charms, and enchantments than I've ever managed before in the course of an hour. Nobody gets into or out of that house unless I say so."

Jamey decided that he'd probably lost too much blood to have enough for his brain cells to sort all this out with any degree of reliability. He kept his eyes shut and let things happen, reasoning quite correctly that he didn't have much choice—still thinking, *Peaches?*

"BIG KID," EVAN REMARKED.

"Nine pounds if she's an ounce." Lulah held her up for inspection: a plump and yawning little face below a full head of waving reddish hair. "I'd say she's full-term and then some. Which makes conception the second week of December."

Not conception—implantation, Evan didn't say. He knew what he knew, but he'd have to confirm it in various ways—including the testimony of the girl. That, however, might prove problematical. Nicky had told him that aside from shrieking at Holly, she hadn't uttered a sound. Not even during labor. Lachlan didn't make the mistake of thinking that maybe childbirth didn't hurt that much after all. A kid this size, half again as large as either of the twins? He wasn't about to mention that, either. The implication that Bella and Kirby had perhaps been a little scrawny at birth would not go over well with their mother.

"I hate to wake her," Nicky said. "But if you've really found us another way out of here . . ."

"I found another way *in,*" Alec corrected.

"In, out—don't be pedantic."

"They are occasionally not the same."

"You guys ought to take this act on the road," Evan observed. "And I mean that literally, pedantically, and urgently."

They were all gathered in the bedroom, which, like the stairwell, lacked shadows. Every time lightning flared outside the dormer window, sometimes brightly enough to delineate every leaf on the huge old oak nearby, his brain expected the light in the room to change. It didn't. Neither was there any thunder, and although he could see the rain he couldn't hear it clattering against the window or the roof.

The girl lay sleeping in the freshly made bed. With her round cheeks, soft mouth, and her hair in two loose braids, she looked hardly more than a child herself. Nick had also mentioned that halfway through the proceedings—which had proceeded rapidly indeed—he had stopped translating Lulah's instructions into Hungarian. The girl obviously understood what was required of her by way of breathing, pushing, and so on. But it had been *his* eyes she watched, *his* hands she clung to.

"I'm not sure if it was because I was speaking her language, or if it was my tone of voice—"

Evan grinned. "Probably she just fell helplessly in love with your adorable face."

"Remind me again why we allowed Holly to marry you."

"She and I deserve each other?"

"Ah. Of course. How silly of me to forget."

Alec was busy putting clean sheets from the laundry basket onto a pair of thin mattresses taken from the gurneys down the hall. It was his plan to use them as stretchers for the girl and for Jamey. Somebody would have to carry the newborn. Her mother wanted nothing to do with her.

Nicky had described how shocked he and Lulah had been when she refused to hold her child, refused even to look at her. Lachlan gave him a brief, low-voiced explanation of how she had probably come to be pregnant. After a few choice Romany oaths, Nick had muttered that one could hardly blame her.

Cam was seated on the floor, watching Jamey sleep. The blood-soaked blanket that had replaced the blood-soaked bedspread had itself been replaced by another blanket, taken from the closet. It would take Jamey a few days to recover from the hemorrhaging—but that was all he would have to recover from. Lulah was adamant about getting him and the girl to Dr. Cutter, a fellow Witch to whom they could entrust the whole story, but Nick's instincts had been correct. A fiber was indeed a fiber.

Evan supposed he should be able to accept things like this by now. But the chain of causation—from gunshot, to whatever the St. Michael medal had done to keep it from harming him, to the wound in Jamey's leg—had shaken him. He took advantage of what Holly had given him, he admitted that. He'd be a fool not to. He just didn't think about it all that much. And now this had happened, and if not for Cam—

What Cam had done tonight was staggering. Well, Evan told himself, from a non-Witch's point of view, what else was magic but the determination to accomplish wildly improbable things?

A lot else. For the moment, it was getting eight adults and one infant the hell out of Westmoreland. Improbable, to say the least.

As Alec was finishing up the mattresses, he began describing the route they would be taking to get outside. "I came up through a little door at the back of the kitchen pantry. It was protected magically—rather recently, too, not more than a month or so—but not that difficult to open. Through that door, along about six feet of brick hallway, and right through a sliding wall panel. Easy as calling fire to a candlewick."

"I'm absolutely thrilled to hear it," Holly said dryly. "How did you know where to look for a staircase, and how come Lulah didn't sense this door while we were on the way down to the clinic?"

He didn't answer immediately, and Evan half-turned to look at him. Alec had always been the embodiment of debonair charm, with a twinkle in his brown eyes that mocked the Boston Brahmin sophistication of his upbringing. Right now he looked shaken as he glanced over at his partner.

"I lost Nicholas," he said at last. "He wasn't *there* anymore. That hasn't happened more than twice in the last thirty-four years. I couldn't sense him from the front of the house, so I walked around to the back. The kitchen door was open, nobody was in there, and I did some exploring. As for why Lulah didn't find the door—it's not spelled. The kitchen entry is, but the way into the staircase isn't. So there's nothing to be sensed—just a mechanism with weights to slide the panel aside. Once I was in—"

"—I nearly fell over with the shock," Nick finished for him.

"We must've just missed you in the stairwell," Holly mused.

"Quite likely."

Lachlan reflected on something Louvena had said tonight—that life was all in the timing. A few minutes, an hour . . . twelve years. . . . He glanced over at Cam and Jamey, noting with a slight smile that Holly wouldn't have to push anymore. Catching her eye, he nodded at the pair, and she winked, rocking slowly from side to side with a tiny grin teasing her lips, the laptop clutched to her chest.

Timing. The church fires. Westmoreland Inn, Spa and Whorehouse.

Trafficked children. He walked over to the bed, where the new mother lay sleeping. When Nick touched her shoulder she came awake very suddenly, like one who has trained herself to instant alertness. She sat up, biting her lip, and then her expression smoothed into blankness. She looked up at Nick for a moment, but if she was reassured by his calm smile it didn't register in any muscle of her body.

She glanced around then—and reacted violently at the sight of so many other people in the room. Scooting back to cower against the headboard, she groped for Nicky's hand. He took it, murmuring soothing things that made no impression. Lulah brought the baby over. The girl shook her head, long dark hair coming loose from the braids. Lulah backed away, frowning.

"Make yourself useful," Alec said, tossing a pillow at Holly. She relinquished the laptop and climbed to her feet, scrounging in the basket of clean sheets. The girl's eyes lit on her—and she didn't stop shouting until Holly threw the pillow and pillowcase at Cam and retreated into the hallway outside.

Cam gave a muffled yelp. He flung the pillow away and stared down at his hands. At the pillowcase, crumpled onto the rug. At the girl.

"Jesusgoddamn," he breathed. "It's her. It's the same magic. Burns like a sonuvabitch—"

"Cam?" Jamey's voice was weak but clear. "What's wrong?"

"Nothing." He returned to Jamey's side. "Just relax. You're gonna be fine."

"Evan?" Alec insisted. "What's he talking about?"

Something was putting itself together inside Cam's head. What he wanted was to talk with Holly, trade ideas—however outlandish—argue it all out. But that couldn't happen here. "We need to leave. Now," he told Alec. "Can you set up a ward or something on her?"

Dark eyes searched his for a long moment. "I'll take your word for it. *Miklóshka?* A hand, if you please."

He meant it literally, of course. Jamey had struggled up onto his elbows, despite Cam's worried urging otherwise, and Lachlan could identify completely with the bewilderment in his face as Nick and Alec clasped hands and started to Work. In fact, Evan would have bet good money that by now Jamey was starting to recognize the difference between work and Work. He'd have to, if he wanted any kind of life with Cam. A long talk would be in order, Lachlan thought idly, regarding the ins, outs, ups, downs, and especially the sideways jolts of marrying a Witch—

"Evan—!"

He swung around to the door as he heard it slam shut. Holly leaned back heavily against it, shaking a little. The girl cried out fretfully, waking the baby, and Lulah began murmuring what Evan recognized as quieting spells used on his own children.

"Footsteps," Holly told him. "Coming up the stairs. Just one set. I didn't stick around to find out if it was Weiss or not, but—"

Was he arrogant enough to approach them alone? Was he powerful enough to take them on? Lachlan glanced over at two of his secret weapons. Alec and Nicky were oblivious in their own silent magical communion. Whatever they were doing to or for or with the girl, it wasn't happening fast enough.

"Cam—those handcuffs—"

"What?"

"The strings, dammit! Hand one over! The thing with the knots!"

"She's not evil," he objected, even as he delved into his pants pocket. "This is for silence and sleep against somebody who's—"

"I don't give a shit if she's the reincarnation of the Virgin Mary!"

Holly grabbed Cam's elbow and yanked him to his feet. "I'll distract her. You tie it around her finger. Jamey, stay put."

She moved to the far side of the bed. Fury gushed from the girl like a broken dam in full flood. Total silence during childbirth, but the sight of Holly caused *this*? Lachlan pushed the thought aside and kept his gaze from flickering to Cam, who approached the bed with one of the knotted strings looped to tie around a finger. Holly was babbling something about settling down, not going to hurt you, everything will be all right, will you for the love of everything holy shut the fuck up—

Cam pounced. There was an abrupt, blessed silence.

Except for the voice echoing up the stairwell.

"Sheriff Lachlan! There is no escape! You are surrounded!"

Alec rubbed his forehead, grimacing. "What do you want to bet the next thing he says is 'Come quietly and you won't be harmed'?"

Nick also looked tired and headachy. "I vote for 'It's your only hope.'"

Jamey was swaying to his feet, crawling up the brass handles on the chest of drawers. "Weiss! What do you want?"

"Only the child! She's all I want!"

"How did he know it's a girl?" Holly asked.

"Why doesn't he want any of the rest of us—meaning *you*?" Evan countered.

"Give her to me and you'll be free to leave!"

Jamey laughed, his face ghost-pale. "I don't think so!"

"Amniocentesis, I suppose. Still—"

"Shut up, Freckles," Cam said. "Jamey, whatever stupid idea is going through your mind—"

"But if he's alone, like Holly said—"

"Shut up, all of you." Lulah marched over and handed Cam the sleeping baby. "Don't drop her." She beckoned Alec and Nicky with an imperious gesture. Lachlan found it reassuring that age and magical gifts had nothing to do with whether or not men obeyed this woman.

"Just the child, and you will walk free," Weiss said from much closer to the door.

"Why her?" Jamey called out. "Why not me, or the sheriff, or his wife?"

Evan shot him an angry glare.

"Eloquent as you are, genial as the sheriff might be, and even taking account of Mrs. Lachlan's unique qualities—all I want is the child."

The three Witches held a hurried consultation, nodded agreement, and laced their fingers together in some complicated arrangement that left only Lulah's right hand free. In the open palm she held the little rowan-and-holly talisman. The two men disentangled their fingers to cup their hands around Lulah's. They seemed to be pressing inward, keeping something invisible squeezed tight around the wooden token.

Lulah caught her breath in a wounded little gasp, then reached blindly for the doorknob. Neither Alec nor Nicky could help her—their hands were pushing still against the power focused on the talisman. At last she got the door open and flung the thing into the hall, shoving a shoulder against the door to slam it shut.

The lower two feet of it splintered inward, with a blast of fierce white light that brought tears to Lachlan's dazzled eyes and made Holly moan in pain. Cam cried out and slipped to his knees, the baby howling in his arms. The girl gave a muted whimper, then settled against the pillows again.

"Evan? Evan!"

"I'm okay." He knuckled his eyes and peered down at Holly. "You?"

"Yeah. It hurt like hell for a second, though."

Jamey was holding up Nicky—or perhaps it was the other way around. Lulah was slowly sitting up, Alec beside her, picking bits of the door out of her pant legs. Cam staggered to his feet, the child securely in the crook of one elbow.

"That wasn't supposed to happen," Lulah said shakily. "That just plain wasn't supposed to happen."

"I told you there was too much magic!" Cam pointed to the wall. It was . . . rippling. So was the floor beneath their feet. "*Now* can we get out of here?"

"Herr Weiss may have other plans," Holly warned.

From her seat on the carpet, Lulah squinted through the hole in the lower section of the door. "I don't think he's going to be a problem."

Jamey reached to open the door, snatching his hand back when the knob sagged like soft dough. The wooden doorframe shrank, expanded, warped to the right. The door cracked and popped open with the pressure.

Down the corridor, Weiss lay crumpled and stunned, rising and falling with the undulations of the floor. The wall near him developed a blister that grew bigger and bigger until it nudged him over onto his back. He groaned and turned onto his side and vomited.

"It really wasn't supposed to happen like that," Lulah muttered again. "Really. It wasn't."

THE MATTRESS/STRETCHERS WERE NOW out of the question. They kept swelling and deflating. The easy chair, the bed, the dresser—all grew lumps and bulges that quivered for a moment and then collapsed, only to puff out somewhere else, like allergic hives. Holly decided that was probably a good image: the place had been glutted with magic and was going into anaphylactic shock.

She'd felt exactly two earthquakes while in grad school at UCLA. One had been a short, sharp shock, there and gone in an instant. The other had been a surging wave, seven endless seconds of nausea-inducing rock-and-roll. Going down the stairs took much longer than seven seconds. It took forever.

Nicky carried the girl. Alec grunted as he dragged Weiss—around whose left thumb Cam had tied a bit of knotted string. Cam supported Jamey with one hand and tucked the infant close to his chest with the other. Holly had wedged the laptop under one elbow and kept the other arm around Lulah, who was still shaky from the force of magic she hadn't expected to unleash. Evan preceded them all, his Glock drawn, while they bounced off the stairwell walls and slipped on sudden bumps and hollows in the steps. The walls bulged their silk stripes, and the vases undulated, some of them shattering, as the flowers turned red, yellow, orange, blue, purple—any color but what nature had intended.

Abrupt shadows appeared, bled into each other, turned to dark bruises on the floor and walls. A bulging stair underfoot made Holly leap for the next one—which chimed like a silver dinner bell as she landed. Colors wafted through the air, whispering as they passed, or whizzed by with the roar of miniature jet fighters.

"The stairs may be real," Alec gasped as Weiss nearly slid from his grip, "but so is the magic—and it's not happy."

"Átkozott!" Nicky spat, ducking a swirling blur of magenta and black. "Just get us out of here!"

"If I could identify where 'here' is—" Hoisting Weiss up again, he went on, "Cam, where's the place where you got into that room?"

"Find me a sign on the wall that says 'This Way to Room 208,' and I'll show you."

"Why that room in particular?" Jamey asked with splendid irrelevance.

Holly glanced over her shoulder at him, staggering a bit as the carpet bulged and surged beneath her feet. "Room 208 is the one always used when the customers hire boys."

"Judging by what that guy had on," Cam muttered, "it's probably stocked with more than Earl Grey tea."

"I didn't like to mention what else was in those bathroom cupboards," Jamey admitted. "But you could get into that room, so how about the others? There was more than one listening post, right? So maybe those rooms are accessible, too." The wall beside him spasmed outward to knock him in the shoulder. "Or maybe not," he finished weakly.

Holly dragged her attention from the flowers—which were now mimicking the stripes of the wallpaper in a vase a foot wide that had grown spikes like a frenzied cactus—and stumbled into Lulah when the step sagged beneath her. Alec was tapping the wall with his fingertips, mumbling that it had to be this spot, he'd made particular note of the cabinet, and since the door was mechanical and not magical, he should be able to—

His thumb slid into the wall just as a ripple coursed through it. There was a brittle snapping of bone. "Son of a bitch!" He wrenched back his hand and stared at the second joint of his thumb, crooked at an unnatural angle.

"Alec!" Nicky lurched toward him, awkward with the girl in his arms.

"Don't drop her. I'm all right."

"No, you're not," Lulah said, detaching herself from Holly. She dug in a pocket and came up with a handkerchief. "Wrap this around it, good and tight. We'll splint it later."

Jamey asked, "Maybe Cam could—"

"It's bone, not soft tissue or muscle fiber," Lulah told him as she wound the linen around Alec's thumb. "But if you could stiffen the cotton a little—"

"Like a cast?" He nodded. "That I can do."

The cabinet rocked forward and the roses crumbled to dust. Beneath them, all around them, the stairwell shuddered and groaned and warped itself almost into a spiral, then settled again.

"I can stop it hurting, too," Cam offered.

"Feel free," Alec invited, breathing hard.

As Cam handed the baby to Jamey for the few moments he would need for the work, Holly met Evan's bleak gaze. They understood each other perfectly. *We're fucked. Completely, totally, absolutely, categorically, monumentally fucked.*

"This place is coming down around our ears," he said quietly. "We can't get out through these walls."

"I refuse to be a featured performer in a Jean-Paul Sartre play," she retorted.

"You'd prefer to take our chances with a Salvador Dali staircase?"

"What about the downstairs clinic? It's built into solid rock. Even if wood and plaster and even brick aren't strong enough to hold up against an overload of magic, maybe a few tons of granite might."

He nodded. "I'm liking this theory. Mainly because it appeals to the ordinary, everyday kind of guy I am."

"*That,* love of my life, you never have been and never could be. Let's get these people downstairs."

WITHIN THE DOORS of the medical clinic, the torture of the walls and floors finally stopped. Holly sank into a chair behind the desk and let out the breath she seemed to have been holding for the past ten minutes. She hadn't felt this queasy since the morning she got married, when the combination of nerves and pregnancy had nearly resulted in the ruin of nine thousand dollars of Vera Wang bridal gown.

Still, as she watched Weiss and the girl placed on gurneys and everyone else find chairs—or in Cam's case, just wilt to the floor with the baby in his lap—it felt as if the floor still swayed a bit. She recognized the sensation. Part of her trip to Europe with Susannah long ago had been a five-day cruise through the Cyclades, and back in Athens it had taken almost a whole day to convince herself that there was nice steady pavement beneath her, not a deck.

Fingering the diamond bracelet on her wrist, she studied the walls. No, not a quiver, not a wrinkle. Solid concrete within solid rock. The relief on other faces, beloved faces, made her smile. Real magic was beyond her, but at least she had a useful idea every so often. For the moment, they were safe.

The creaks and shatters of the disintegrating stairwell were muffled here. During their headlong descent, the noise and the distortion had gotten worse. Holly wasn't sure if she wanted the sounds to stop or not: quiet would be welcome, but quiet would mean the magic had finally given up and the stairwell might collapse altogether. There was a chance that once the spells had sputtered out, the real staircase would still be there and they could use it to get out. But when she thought about the tortured brick and wood, she rather doubted it.

Evan raided the fridge behind the desk and distributed bottles of water. Jamey chugged one down and asked for another, then fixed his gaze on the laptop in Holly's embrace. She took the hint and handed it over.

"Try the files marked *Zauber*. And I'd be obliged if somebody could tell me what *der Puff* means."

Without looking up from the child in his arms, Cam replied, "Brothel."

Well, that made sense. Holly tilted the chair back to regard her husband, who had hoisted himself up to sit on the high counter. He surveyed the room, a rather brooding sort of frown on his face. Holly waited him out, and at length he said, "So the girl and the baby both have magic."

She thought that over. "If the day ever comes when I can predict what you'll come up with next, please divorce me. How do you figure?"

"All you Witchy types yelled when Lulah's little flash-bomb went off. Jamey and I didn't."

"But the baby and the girl did. I do wish we had something to call her other than 'the girl,' by the way."

"She only talks to call you nasty names."

"I'm still working on why."

"She recognized you from that book jacket photo, but why react like that?"

"Well, let's stick a pin in that one for a minute." Bending to roll up her pant legs yet again, she snarled a curse at them, reached for the scissors on the counter, and starting cutting. "You deduce, Sherlock my love, that she and her daughter are both Witches because all the other Witches were traumatized to varying degrees. I'll go along with it. She's found in a room at the top of a staircase that's real enough, but guarded by things that don't officially exist according to the laws of physics—which are taking their revenge, according to Cam. Weiss got knocked out by whatever it was Lulah did, so that's confirmation that he's a Witch, too."

"Unless that was an all-purpose—hey, Lulah!" he called. "Would that wooden thing have worked on just anybody?"

She glanced up from splinting Alec's broken thumb. "I don't follow."

"To get knocked out like that, does Weiss have to be a Witch?"

"Yes and no."

Holly rolled her eyes. Evan grinned down at her.

Alec elaborated. "It was phasers on stun—well, with some oomph we didn't expect. He'd go down if he was magic-blind or second cousin to Merlin himself."

"So why don't we wake him up and ask?"

"Not a chance," Nick said. "He stays knotted up until he's got wards on top of wards and a pair of double-lock handcuffs, the real kind. Besides, I can tell you a few things about him right now."

"This oughta be good," Alec muttered.

"He's East German."

"And you know this because—?"

"His dental work is Russian."

"Stop smirking," Alec chided. "You're insufferable when you're being clever."

"I should have said *some* of his dental work," Nick went on. "His accent is from East Germany. But at some point he lived in Russia. Their dental work is unmistakable."

Cam nodded agreement. "One might even say 'inimitable.' But why would he have been in Russia?"

"His parents. I judge this by the age of the dentistry, which is at least forty years old. He looks to be around fifty, fifty-five. This puts us in the early '60s. A young East German boy would not be in the Soviet Union on his own—"

"He might have been in school," Evan said.

"Possibly. But I believe his parents were posted there to receive training from the KGB."

Holly had been following all this with growing impatience. "Next you're going to tell us he has a tattoo identifying him as a member of the secret brotherhood of—"

"Stasi agents?" Nick interrupted. "Nothing so trite. I haven't been playing quite fair, I'll admit. I recognize the name."

"'Weiss' is as common as Wiener schnitzel," Alec scoffed. Nicky smiled. "You just went from 'insufferable' to 'intolerable.'"

"Weiss. Plus magic. Plus East Germany. Plus the Soviet Union in the '60s. Add it up—then divide by 1995." He met Holly's gaze, no longer smiling.

"And the hundred miles of a drive to Delphi?" She scarcely recognized the thin voice as her own. "Is that how he knew about me, Nicky? Is it?"

"I believe so. Hanna and Eckhardt Weiss were not the people behind the plot against you, but they were the perpetrators' contacts within a group of former Stasi, East German Secret Police. Trained in the Soviet Union by the KGB, parents of a son. They were, of course, Witches."

Jamey was looking desperately confused, but stayed silent. Evan had no such compunctions. "I thought you took care of them."

"I did. But it was a difficult time. The reunification of Germany had occurred only about five years earlier. All the former Warsaw Pact countries were fumbling their way toward democracy—"

"Thereby giving me a lot of work," Cam remarked. "You don't have to explain that part, Nicky. It's more than fifteen years by now, but all the old secret police guys—they've changed license plates but not make and model. I remember when they went after Holly and her friend in Greece. They were dealt with. But if Weiss is who Nicky thinks he is, he knows Holly is a Spellbinder. So what he's after—"

"—is still the baby," Jamey reminded them. "He's been in Pocahontas County for almost two years, right? He's had any number of chances at Holly. He didn't take them."

"She's pretty well-protected," Evan observed mildly.

"I'm sure she is. But he knows what she is—he called her 'unique,' and from what little I understand—"

"Oh, I think you understand plenty," Holly murmured.

"But all he wanted was the child."

Refusing to think about that terrifying trip back from Delphi, when she and Susannah had damn near been run off the road, Holly got to her feet and went over to look at the baby. An unremarkable infant: larger than her twins had been at birth, but otherwise she was just a newborn like any other. Except, if Evan was right, she was born a Witch.

Holly wasn't the kind of woman to go all gooey over babies. She adored her own, but was just as glad to hand back everybody else's once due appreciation had been expressed. This one was a fine specimen, robust and healthy, but she had to remind herself that to look at her as a mystery to be solved was to regard her as a thing, a commodity, the way Weiss did.

"Why you, little one, and not me?" She stroked a silky cheek with her fingertip. "I'm used to it by now. I don't think about it much, but at least I know the score."

"Right now we're losing," Cam said. "This whole discussion has been very interesting, but we need to have the talk about getting out of here. Or do we just wait until somebody comes to dig us out?"

"Lulah said there's no magic around these rooms. She also said we're way below ground and surrounded by solid rock."

"Terrific."

"You should be ecstatic," Holly complained. "It validates your theory, doesn't it? That there was so much magic in the staircase that there wasn't room for any more?"

"Validating my stupid theory is what got us stuck down here, when there was more magic thrown into the staircase than it could hold—"

Nicky held up a hand. "Enough! *O shoshoy kaste si feri yek khiv sigo athadjol.*"

They looked at Alec, who sighed and translated, "'The rabbit which has only one hole soon is caught.' Obscure Romany Saying Number 346. He's getting back at me for believing that a way in could also be a way out."

Holly had been watching Cam, who was chewing on his inner cheek so vehemently that she was worried he'd gnaw right through the dimple. "What?" she demanded.

Both dimples—undamaged—appeared. "We don't need a way out. We need a way up."

Nineteen

THERE BEING NO JACKHAMMER, power drill, blowtorch, or similar contraption available that conformed to the already outraged laws of physics, they were stuck with magic.

Among the Witches, a lot of thinking was going on. Every so often one of them would say something, they'd all cogitate for a while, frowns would be frowned or nods would be nodded, and then they'd do some more thinking.

Lachlan had seen it all before. He busied himself with the baby, making sure she was warm and dry. She wouldn't be hungry for a couple of hours yet, and how they were going to get her mother to provide if she wasn't willing to do so was something nobody had mentioned. The girl was still peacefully asleep, Cam's knotted string around her finger. So, too, Bernhardt Weiss—although one could wish his sleep wasn't so peaceful.

Alec, with his uncanny instinct for identifying what kind of Witch a Witch might be, had studied Weiss for several long minutes before shaking his head. "He isn't. There's not a quiver of magic about him."

Lachlan glanced around. "Well? Who's gonna say it?"

"What?" Jamey asked.

" 'That's impossible.' "

"Evan, you cut me to the quick." Alec shook his head mournfully. "To think that my very own nephew-in-law doesn't think I can—"

"Oh, do hush," Nicky told him. "It isn't impossible at all. We've only been assuming he's the source of the magic around here—the stairs, the barriers—"

"—the fires?" Jamey looked from one face to another. No one was willing to speculate. "Well, then, what about the girl?"

Alec stood staring and clenching his fists beside her gurney for an even longer time. At last he shrugged. "Whatever she is, I've never seen such a tangle of impulses and distortions. My apologies, Evan, this one really is an impossibility. For now."

So they'd given up the idea of tapping either or both for some extra power.

Jamey stood around looking as useless as Lachlan, also watching all that thinking going on. The kid was as disoriented as if somebody had moved his food dish. Lachlan wondered if his own expression had been as helpless and befuddled the first time he'd witnessed a full-on ritual Working. Compassion—and knowledge that he needed the man sharp-witted, not confused—sent him to his friend's side as the five Witches made their preparations.

"This is the 'Gathering the Goodies' part," he said. "Alec or Nicky could give you a whole series of lectures about associations of one thing with another, how this corresponds to that—"

"Cam mentioned a bit about trees."

Lachlan kept half an ear on the consultations going on nearby. "Water is a good, steady Element," Nicky was saying, "but it would take forever to work on all that concrete."

"Trees?" Evan repeated.

"Traditions of folk magic—I kept waiting for him to mention willow bark and salicylic acid—"

"That's folk medicine, not folk magic. And whatever he said, you didn't especially believe him. No, it's okay—I've been watching this kind of thing for almost five years now, and there are times when I still don't believe it, either. Even if you're part of the Working, it's pretty unreal."

"It *is* real, though."

"Oh, yeah." Evan hesitated, then reached into his shirt and brought out the silver medal. "St. Michael, patron of law enforcement. Blessed by Pope John Paul II his very own self, or so I'm told. Holly got it for me in Rome a few years back. And then she spelled it, with some help from Nicky and Alec, and—"

"Evan?" Holly called out. "Lighter?"

He dug into his jacket pocket and produced a silver Zippo. He let

Jamey take a look at its engraving: a five-pointed star encircled by the words UNITED STATES MARSHALS SERVICE—FOUNDED SEPTEMBER 24, 1789. Then he tossed it to his wife.

"Fire?" Lulah scoffed. "Against all that concrete you just mentioned?"

Jamey's eyes widened a bit at the prospect of a general conflagration. Lachlan told him, "She's kidding, trust me. The lighter will do duty as the Element of—wait for it—Fire. Normally it'd be a candle—in fact, a whole bunch of candles, one for each of the cardinal points of the compass, another one to represent the person standing there, a couple-three on the altar—"

"Altar? How deep does the religion part of it go?"

Lachlan grinned. "Well, I'm Catholic, so technically I'm supposed to run screaming from the room. But it's not as peculiar as you'd think. The air-fire-earth-water thing is all over the Mass. Incense, Presence Lamp—"

"—body and blood of Christ?"

"Think of the Virgin Mary as the Great Goddess. It's all very feminist—by the way, if you value your sanity, don't ever get Holly started on the patriarchy."

"Lulah!" Alec wore an exaggerated look of surprise. "I've been known to make the Earth move, but only for Nicholas, and only in private—"

Evan snorted. Jamey blushed and said, "I was kind of wondering . . . I mean, Alec and Nick . . ."

"Yeah?"

"They're gay."

"Yeah?"

"So is Cam."

Evan shrugged. "So is Professor Dumbledore."

Jamey gaped. *"What?"*

"Damn. I shouldn't have said that. Don't tell Alec and Nicky I told you, okay?"

"Is it—give me a break here, Ev, these are the first Witches I've ever met!"

"Oh, you mean do you have to be gay to be a Witch if you're a man?" he laughed. "Hell, no. You're born the way you're born, gay or straight, Witch or not." Then, raising his voice a little: "That's expensive incense, Cam!"

He glanced over and grimaced. "Don't remind me."

Jamey blinked. "They're using—"

"You work with what you got. At least it won't make Holly sneeze. It's Native American tradition—and the Flynns have some Cherokee in them, so it's appropriate." He eyed Jamey sidelong. "You didn't know?"

"Another bullet point in a long list."

"You already knew everything important about him. I knew everything I needed to know about Holly way before I found out she's a Witch."

"And it didn't make a difference?"

"Get real. Of course it made a difference."

He shifted restlessly from foot to foot. "In how you cared about her, or in why?"

"Both. In some ways, Shakespeare was wrong, Jamey. Love does alter when it alteration finds. People change, and it's not just wrong to think they don't, it'd be cruel to expect them not to. To tell somebody that you love her just the way she is, and don't ever change—" He shook his head. "You accommodate each other, because the ways you both need to be loved, that changes, too, over time. If you're lucky, it just gets stronger. Deeper."

"Better," Jamey contributed.

"As good as it was, it's better now. And there's no reason to think it won't get even better in the future. You gotta work at it, yeah, but part of it has to do with never running out of things you want to say to each other. Things you can't say to anybody else, and don't want to. You don't *have* to, do you see what I mean? Because she's there." He watched her pace and mutter, rake her hair back, ask Nicky something, start pacing again. "I've never seen her do this, for instance. She doesn't take the central role in a Circle."

"Dux femina facti," Jamey murmured. "'The leader of the enterprise a woman.' Do you ever participate?"

He gave a reminiscent chuckle. "Ask Holly sometime to give you her notes on how to do a real old-fashioned Beltane—which is not, in fact, a high-octane fuel additive."

"A what?"

"Sorry. There's a game they play around here, along the lines of 'Men are like.' You know—men are like snowstorms, you never know when they're coming or how many inches you'll get. This one is 'You may be a Redneck Witch if'—"

"A *what?"* Jamey repeated, staring.

"You may be a Redneck Witch if you think Beltane is a high-octane fuel additive. If you use an engine block for an altar. If your wand is a sawed-off twelve-gauge shotgun."

"You may be a Redneck Witch—?" Jamey echoed faintly.

"—if you call the four quarters North, East, South, and that way over yonder." Evan patted his shoulder consolingly. "You'll get used to it."

"You keep saying that." But a smile ghosted across his face, and one or two of the frown lines vanished from his forehead.

Judging that he had distracted Jamey enough to ease a little of the tension, he turned once again to the pending ritual. He'd been where Jamey was right now; he knew how unlikely the whole scene looked. "This will be pretty basic. She doesn't have a whole lot of toys to play with. If they were doing the whole big production, there'd be candles, robes, special jewelry, a cauldron, a chalice, and everybody'd have a wand. I'm not sure if it's easier with all the goodies or harder to concentrate. All that stuff has meanings—"

"But they have to be separated out from each other, and selected for a specific association."

"Whatever Cam told you, you were listening," Evan approved. "For instance, Alec will be in the North, element of Earth—did you see him picking mud off his shoes? That's all he'll need. But he'll have something else to use as a focus—they all will."

"Lulah just took off her silver bracelet."

"Did she? I was wondering what she'd use. She doesn't usually take the West—that's Water, by the way—she's more comfortable in the East, where Cam's going to be."

"Why?"

"Because that's Air, usually denoted by smoke." He chuckled. "You may be a Redneck Witch if—"

"—if your incense smoke comes from a Cohiba?"

"Well, more like a Marlboro."

CAM LIT UP, taking one wistful draw, savoring the luxuriant taste. Then he handed the cigar to Holly and tossed the lighter to Nicky. He watched his cousin go over the tokens one last time, and wished she'd just get on with it. Aware of Jamey's presence—and his perplexity—as a twinge along every nerve, he craved the familiar procedure of ritual to quiet himself down.

At long last Holly began. Lacking a wand or athame—and having firmly turned down the suggestion of a scalpel as substitute—she had nothing more arcane than her own index finger with which to delineate the Circle. As they took their places—himself in the East, Nicky to the South, Lulah in the West, Alec as North—she went around once to cense them all with expensive cigar smoke. He might have found it funny if it hadn't been *his* expensive cigar.

He heard Evan's voice murmuring what he hoped were explanations, and then low laughter from both men. His muscles untwisted a bit. Jamey wasn't completely freaking out, anyway.

Holly stood before him, edgier than someone casting a Circle ought to be. Yet it had to be her: power, real power, belonged to the four of them. Her blood would be its catalyst, and she would be its focus.

From her outstretched palm he accepted his own amber pendant, newly Blooded, and closed it tight in his left fist.

"Smoke is the prayer of Fire," she said softly. "I summon the spirits of the wind, and entreat them to share with us their powers, that we may perceive truly."

"So mote it be," he replied, and the ceremonial formula had its desired effect. He felt his pulse slow down, his breathing ease.

Holly pivoted and went to the center of the Circle, balancing the smoldering stick of tobacco across a clean petri dish.

To the South was Nicky. She gave him back his own gold wedding ring; he gave her Evan's lighter. The wick ignited without her having thumbed the flint, and Cam was suddenly reminded that calling Fire was something she could do as easily as any Witch ever born.

"Fire is the spark of life. I summon the spirits of flame, and entreat them to protect and bless us, that we may be strong."

As she returned to the center and placed the burning lighter beside the cigar, Cam was puzzled by the appeal for protection. Oh, of course: it was Evan's lighter, and on it was a five-pointed star.

Lulah was next, standing in the West. Holly let the silver bracelet flow into their aunt's waiting fingers, accepting in return a sealed bottle of water, saying, "Water is the blood of every living thing. I summon the spirits of Water, and entreat them to guide us upward, toward the rain."

She twisted the cap off, moistened her fingertips, and sprinkled a little water on the floor, careful not to douse the lighter or the Cohiba. Then she turned toward Alec in the North. A pause while she squeezed up another drop of blood, and then she opened her hand so Alec could reclaim the oval of polished green jade given her earlier. Cam smiled slightly. Other men kept everything from spare change, string, and Swiss Army knives to subway tokens, breath mints, and condoms in their pockets. Alec Singleton never left home without his collection of gemstones.

"Earth is the Mother of us all," Holly said quietly, as Alec let fall into her hand a little clump of mud. "I summon the spirits of the stone and soil above our heads, and entreat them to let us pass."

Holly's range of tokens now complete, the Quarters called, the Guardians invited, Cam expected the magic fully awakened within him to respond to the other three and focus on her.

But Holly wasn't finished, and what she did now surprised him. She knelt before the four tokens, the nearest approximation to an altar they had, and spoke a fifth time.

"The voice is the sound of the spirit within. With my voice I have summoned, and with my voice I entreat and beg. Free us from this place that entraps us. Free us from this place that imprisons us. Free us from this place that confines body and spirit. Listen! *Sgë!*"

The smoke swirled upward—thicker, more pungent—as she exclaimed that final word. He had never heard it before. He knew what it meant. He felt his own tongue and lips form the word, again and again. He heard his own voice calling out, compelled from deep in his lungs and deeper in his mind. One word, in unison with her, each time she spoke it.

"*Sgë! Una'lelü' eskiska'l'tasï'!*" Listen! Give me the wind!

Music, it was music—it was every note in all the world, merely air, only air.

"*Sgë! Ha-nâ'gwa hatû'ngani'ga, Agalu'ga Tsûsdi'ga!*" Listen! O now you have drawn near to hearken, O Little Whirlwind!

Songs he had never heard before echoed all around him, familiar as his own heart pulsing blood in primal rhythm through his veins.

"*Sgë! U'ntalï udanû'hï tsägista''tï.*" Listen! The clotted blood is your recompense.

Her blood, binding the Fire and the Earth and the Water and most especially the Air to her need—he felt its intricacy of heat and substance and liquid, and the cells richly red with oxygen, with life-giving Air.

"Sgë! Nâ'gwa tsûda'ntâ talehi'sani'ga!" Listen! Now let your spirit arise!

His portion of their heritage met with hers, supported by the steadiness of Earth, the quick power of Fire, the subtle magic of Water. Alec, Nicky, Lulah: they were familiar comforting presences from childhood. This was the first time in his life that he could sense what Holly was, the bloodbeat inside her, the elegant double helix that had given him the magic but her the Spellbinding blood. A twist, a turn, a subtle chemical variation, and it would have been him.

He chanted with her, both compelled by power and willingly using it, and thanked whatever Powers had found them tonight that it *hadn't* been him.

JAMEY THOUGHT HE MIGHT be starting to understand. There was everyday life, when small magics existed but to use major enchantments was somehow cheating, and there was a night like this, when the heavy artillery was necessary. A Witch's reluctance to deploy the big guns made sense to him. He just wondered how the hell anybody was going to explain any of this once they got out of here and explanations became necessary.

Well, he'd trusted these people to this point.

Studying the four who guarded the quarters, and the subtle changes that shifted across their faces as Holly accepted and then gave tokens, he saw them as *these people* again and that disturbed him deeply. He had a clear view of Cam when Holly moved to kneel in the Circle's center, and to look upon him as an Otherness was a terrible thing. This was *Cam*, not some stranger whose smile he had never seen, whose lips he had never tasted, whose mind and heart were unknown to him.

Cam, who had never trusted him with what he truly was.

It did make a difference. Of course it did. But was this—this *magic*—was this a newly discovered aspect of him to be learned and loved, or a disparity in their natures so immense that understanding and acceptance were impossible?

But this was *Cam*. Jamey had learned other new things about him tonight—his work during the past twelve years; his love for his family; the love they and the two honorary uncles had for him. He wondered suddenly why he wasn't seeing Holly as changed, why he could watch

Lulah cast a magic spell on a little talisman made of wood and not think of her as someone completely different than she'd been yesterday.

Well, he wasn't in love with either of them, was he?

He'd tried very hard for a very long time not to compare every man he met with Cam. Even knowing how ridiculous and adolescent it was, still he'd always found a lack of one thing or another that soured any initial attraction. It was stupid, it was self-defeating, and it was always there.

What Jamey was seeing now was what Cam really was: a man unlike anyone he'd ever known, a man possessed of power and that elusive trait usually termed *presence.* Air was his perfect Element: light and gentle one moment, a fierce tumult the next, filling the space around him with a bright profusion of warmth and laughter and music and the demands of a ferocious intelligence. Watching him now, knowing this incredible new thing about him, seeing it in his eyes and even in the balance of his body—no wonder Jamey hadn't been able to hang onto him. Calm repose, restless energy, a sudden hurricane—

"Yeah, that's me, all right—a whole lotta wind, keeps goin' around in circles." He could almost hear Cam saying it, with a tilt of his head and the hint of a dimple, wry self-mockery in his eyes.

"You already knew everything important about him."

Maybe he did, after all. It was just Cam. His face, his fine bones and intense blue eyes. His long fingers gripping the amber, his lips forming a single word, over and over—Cam's voice, sounding that odd word in unison with Holly, two octaves apart, then three as his voice deepened and hers soared, and the smoke spun upward. It hovered ten feet overhead, spread outward and downward in a delicate delineation of an encompassing globe. Four octaves now, that single mysterious word like a mantra: *Sgë! Sgë!* There was a sharp tinging sound, like a fingernail against a crystal goblet, and the smoke escaped the dome at its apex, a slither of white, thin as a thread and sharp as a spike.

"Nice, very nice," Evan whispered. "That's my girl. . . ."

And my guy, Jamey thought suddenly—right before a slab of concrete tore loose from the ceiling and smashed to the floor.

SOMEONE WAS YELLING HER NAME.

She felt very tired, and quite out of breath. It was nice just to rest for a moment, the lazy fragrance of one of Evan's cigars soothing her. But there was more than one voice now, most insistent that she pay attention. She blinked, surprised that she'd had her eyes shut, sank back on her heels, and looked around.

Nicky and Alec and Lulah were doing the shouting. Cam, she remembered, was behind her. He'd helped with the singing. She'd sensed his presence around and even within her, the strength of his magic and the suppleness of his mind, that impatient, impassioned intellect that had been his defining characteristic since childhood. He was so much smarter than she was, but just as stupid about love.

"Holly!"

Ceremonially speaking, they ought to have waited for her to get up off her knees and begin the closing of the Circle before badgering her with questions. Her fingers shook a little as she reached for the little clod of mud, and she watched bemused as the flame from Evan's lighter danced on her trembling diamonds.

"Holly! For the love of— Holly, will you listen to me?"

She wondered if anyone had listened to what she and Cam had sung. If they had any idea what that strange duet had taken out of her.

"Holly! Don't!"

No, it was her Circle, her responsibility. Thanking silently the spirits of Earth, she moved on to Water, then Fire, and finally Air. Pushing herself slowly to her feet, feeling a thousand years old with creaking knees and stiff muscles, she used the cigar smoke to cense her Circle again—not bothering to walk around it, unsure that she could, instead simply turning widdershins from Alec to Lulah to Nicky to Cam—

—who was on his knees, wheezing in huge gulps of air.

Now she knew what they were yelling about.

As quickly as she could without screwing up the magic, she finished opening the Circle. And was slammed to the floor and swept beneath a thunderous flood of chlorinated water.

"HOLLY? COME ON, babe, open your eyes. That's it." Lachlan smoothed the sopping hair from his wife's face. She blinked, coughed, sneezed twice, and collapsed back onto the gurney, moaning. "Oh, knock it off," he told her. "And be grateful it was the lap pool and not the Olympic you tapped into. Didn't any of you geniuses think to figure out just what you were standing under?"

"Oh, shut up," she muttered.

"All it said on the site map was 'Spa,'" Nicky defended. "And anyway, we tried to warn her."

"Never did listen," said Lulah. "Not from when she was a pup. That's the way, honey, just breathe."

"Angling for a little mouth-to-mouth?" Evan asked with a grin. Holly glared up at him. "Yeah, you're okay. But we're shin-deep in water here and you know how I hate getting my boots wet."

"Poor you," she said without any sympathy whatsoever. "Next time, *you* stand under Niagara Falls." She squinted up at him. "Why is it so dark?"

"You shorted out the electricity," Evan said. "You also brought down about half a ton of cement along with all that water, ruined Cam's spare cigar, and lost my lighter."

"Bitch, bitch, bitch." She coughed again and sat up, looking around at the tiny flames set at useful intervals by Lulah and Nicky. "Evan! The laptop!"

"Death by drowning," he replied. "Don't worry. Jamey hooked into it with his BlackBerry. The laptop told it everything it knew."

She relaxed with a sigh. "I do love having clever friends. How's Cam?"

"Wet."

Watching a hole being bored in the ceiling had been kind of interesting; realizing that the hole was being bored into a pool was not. The water had dripped, then spurted, then cascaded down the dome of the Circle as chunks of concrete broke and fell, sliding off the protective magic. Only the strength of three tough-minded and accomplished Witches had held the arc aloft. When Holly dismantled it, she and Cam and Lulah and Alec and Nicky had been swept along in the sudden flood. Fetching up against walls and various bits of furniture, soaked to the skin, they'd all taken a few minutes to recover. In that time, Evan and Jamey had lugged them to gurneys and checked for injuries—a bruise or two, but nothing serious.

Weiss, the girl, and the baby had slept through it all.

Lachlan sat beside his wife with an arm around her shoulders. Cam had enlisted Jamey to help him knot sheets together, and now stood directly below the still dripping gouge in the ceiling. Like a redheaded Irish fakir charming a white cotton cobra, he sent the spelled material coiling upward—not without a flourish of fingers or two that indicated he was mindful of his fascinated audience.

Jamey was the first to climb hand-over-hand to the empty swimming pool. Lachlan admired not only his fitness but his tenacity. Then again, maybe *he* was showing off a bit, too. After a few minutes, a pair of life preservers and a dangle of yellow nylon rope were tossed down. Disdaining the offered assistance, Cam hoisted himself up the sheets. Evan helped Alec and Nicky truss up first the girl and then Weiss. After them came the baby, then Lulah, then Nicky and Alec. Finally Evan turned to Holly. She was still pale and shaky with the pummeling she'd received, but he knew it was her fear of heights that was making her look woozy.

"Come on, lady love," he urged, his voice low and gentle. "I can't get out of here until you do."

She rallied a little, and managed a smile. "I swear on the lives of our children, if you *don't* tell me not to look down, I'll buy a ten-pound bag of M&M's."

"Deal. I think we'll have to share them with Cam and Jamey, though. Wouldn't be right not to, dontcha think?"

Twenty

THE DEMOLITION of a swimming pool—Olympic-sized or not—quite predictably attracted notice. By the time Holly was freed of the ropes and life preservers, and Evan had clambered up, someone was pounding on the outer doors of the spa.

"What'd you do with Weiss?" Evan panted.

"Deck," Jamey told him, bent over, hands on knees as he caught his breath.

"Freckles, darlin'," Cam said as he allowed the sheets to drop back down into the clinic, "you know I adore you, but—" He looked down at his Armani trousers. "What the hell did you do to my pants?"

"Oh, stop whining, and dry me off." She dug in her pockets—well, his pockets—and pulled out two strips of fabric to wave in front of his face. "See? I saved the rest so you can put them back together again."

"Two cigars and a suit," he replied crossly as he dried her off. "You now owe me two cigars and a suit."

"Thank goodness!" Alec's voice boomed over-loudly from the foyer. "You got the door open! I thought we were going to be stuck in here all night!"

Holly turned to Evan. "You guys get Weiss—let me do the talking. And make sure his hair's wet!"

"His hair?" Cam echoed.

Evan looked at her for a minute, then down at his own soggy self. "Plot away, lady love," he told her with a grin. "And douse those lights, Cam."

Holly was just as glad he waited to do so until after they'd run up the pool steps. She spared a glance for Weiss, sprawled on the deck. Cam hadn't bothered to dry him off. Good. She inhaled deeply, knotted her soaked hair at her nape in hopes it would look like some sort of over-gelled coiffure in the dimness, and switched on Helpless Female Mode.

"Uncle Alec!" she cried, running into the foyer. "He's still unconscious—oh!" She skidded to a stop, looked wide-eyed at the three guards, and clasped her hands piously together under her chin. "Oh, I'm so glad you're here! Mr. Weiss was giving us a tour—gracious, simply hours ago!—and he slipped on some tiles by the pool. The next thing we knew he was in the water! I think he must have hit his head—he's breathing okay—my husband—he's the sheriff, Sheriff Lachlan—got him out pretty fast but he hasn't woken up!"

Nick nodded his congratulations—a bit too soon, Holly was sure. She was right. She was definitely getting too old for this. Twenty or even ten years ago the big-blue-eyes act would have worked within moments. These gentlemen were quite discourteously unimpressed.

"Where's Mr. Weiss? What was all the noise? And what happened to the lights down here?"

On the other hand, maybe it was the clothes. She much preferred to blame their lack of instant chivalry on the shirt—ripped now where she'd made a bandage for Jamey—and the sawed-off pants. "I think my uncle must have done something funny to the wiring—he was—I don't know—" She turned to Alec. "What was it you were doing?"

"Hot-wiring the keypad," he said, aiding and abetting. "It would've worked, too, except it isn't wired to standard. I assume that's for your own security. It's quite common to switch the colors of the wires so that expert burglars don't know exactly how they can get around the—"

"Uncle Alec!" she wailed. "You could've been electrocuted!"

"Don't worry, my dear," he soothed. "No harm done. Except to the lights, of course. I'm not entirely sure how that happened." He turned to the guards. "You really ought to have an electrician out here to check the whole system. It should have worked."

Holly gave a nervous little fidget, looking back over her shoulder. "Oh, good—they've brought him out. Are there any blankets? That's my husband, the sheriff—Evan, darling, has he said anything? Is he awake yet?" Turning to the guard, beseeching: "You have to get him upstairs and call an ambulance. None of our cell phones worked! Of course, we must be simply miles underground here, but still—could one of you gentlemen go make the call, and you two carry Mr. Weiss upstairs? Or is there an elevator? No, things have blinked or shorted or whatever it's called—there won't be any power for the elevator, will there?"

"It's all right now, honey bunny," Evan said, patting her shoulder. "They're here and they can take care of him now. That's it—nice and easy. You guys get him upstairs and we'll be right behind you."

They did as told. Once their backs were turned and their attention entirely engaged by their prone and insensate boss, Holly hissed at Nicky, "Where's Lulah?"

"Massage room with the girl and the baby. Alec? Shall we?" And he slipped off down a side hall, Alec at his heels.

Holly peered up at Evan. "'Honey bunny'?"

"You'd prefer 'M&M Girl'?"

"I bet *you* would," Cam murmured irrepressibly.

"What is it with you people and—"

"Jamey, sugar lump," Holly purred, "consider their slogan."

"'Melts in your—'" He stopped. He blushed. "Oh."

She spent a rewarding moment appreciating his embarrassment, then turned to her husband. "Where'd you stash the cars? I want to go home, Evan." All at once she felt completely used up. "I want to hug the kids and fall into bed and sleep for a week."

"Best idea anybody's had all night. But we have to secure things here first. Where's Lulah? I want some good solid wards on the door to the pool before anybody else wanders down here."

"Oh, shit!" Cam exclaimed. "She'll have to undo the locks on all the doors—the guests are probably climbing out the windows by now!"

ALEC'S CHARM WAS DEPLOYED on the panicky guests—once Lulah had undone the magic that locked them in their rooms. Jamey took care of the staff milling around in the upstairs hall. Three astonished maids succumbed to his smile (and Holly's suggestion about a couple of strategically undone buttons on his shirt), but the two bewildered janitors were infinitely more impressed with his District Attorney credentials than his shining white teeth.

Evan unclipped his badge from its leather wallet, hung it from the silver chain of his St. Michael medal so it was nice and bright and obvious against the plum-colored sweater. Which was still waterlogged, because Holly's little impromptu fantasy story required it. Kissing the kids was first on his list, too, but before the sleep-for-a-week part, he wanted a hot bath.

He cursed the instinct that had told him to provide for a surreptitious escape. In his SUV, stashed in the bushes down the road, was a five-mile supply of yellow POLICE LINE—DO NOT CROSS tape. He had to make do with silver duct tape to cordon off the upper door to the spa. The pool entry downstairs was similarly marked off-limits. Both tape barricades sported Holly's handmade signs: *Keep Out—by order of the Pocahontas County Sheriff.* Standing back from affixing the improvised warning to the tape, he noted the tiny smear of blood on the paper that meant one of the Witches had been at work and Holly had helped. What spells had been set, he neither knew nor cared; all he wanted was to know that his crime scene, for lack of a better term, was secured.

Eventually the guests were all back in their rooms, the staff had returned to whatever duties occupied them at this insane hour of the morning, and the security guards had carted Weiss up to the lobby entrance to wait for the ambulance. This was done under Alec's suave supervision, with Nick ready to apply special persuasions if necessary. Cam carried the girl, Lulah had the baby; during the general chaos they slipped into the ladies' room down the hall. Lachlan surveyed the blessedly underpopulated lobby and trudged over to join Holly, who had just collapsed onto a chair.

She looked up at him with a wan smile. "Where'd you leave the Beemer?"

"Out back by the kitchen. I'll get the keys from Cam and drive it around."

"Remember to take an umbrella." Her voice was all sweet solicitude.

In reply, he pulled a double handful of clinging sweater from his chest and wrung it out onto the carpet. She laughed.

"Evan!"

He turned as Cam ran up, groaning at the burgeoning panic in the blue Flynn eyes. "God, what now?" Evan asked wearily.

"The girl. She's gone."

"Of course she is," he muttered. "Perfect."

"We were settling the baby down—she'd started to cry—"

"Of course she did."

"—we didn't have our backs turned for more than a minute or two—"

"Of course you didn't," Holly said.

"Will you knock it off? How was I supposed to know she'd—"

Holly pushed herself to her feet. "I'm getting too old for this shit, too. Trust me, she hasn't gone far. I've given birth. I know."

"She's about two dozen years younger than you are, too."

"Piss off, Peaches," said Holly. "It was your string thingy she got away from. Let's go find her."

SHE WASN'T INSIDE. Not in the ballroom, the manager's office, the men's room, the kitchen, the library, the restaurant, nor even hiding under the piano.

"A girl in a nightgown," Alec said hopelessly.

"Yeah, she'd really stand out among all the guests in their bathrobes." Evan paced a few steps, squelching in his cowboy boots. "Upstairs? She'd need a key—and to the supply rooms, too."

"We'll check," Nick offered.

"She wouldn't go outside, would she?" Jamey asked. "She'd need keys as well for any of the cars."

Alec turned to his partner. "Do they teach people to hot-wire ignitions in Hungary?"

Outside it was still raining. The short-outs had been confined to the spa and clinic; the outdoor floodlights were as just as bright as ever, and just as useless in the downpour. Evan went to a window and squinted out into the night, thinking that the girl must be either incredibly desperate or incredibly stupid to try escaping through this.

Desperate, he decided. If the knotted string had slipped off, as it apparently had, then it was a clever young woman indeed who had kept her mouth shut and her body limp until opportunity presented itself. So if she wasn't stupid, why would she go gallivanting out into the rain?

"She's not out there," he said suddenly. "She's still inside. Hiding. Waiting."

Holly studied his face. "For what?"

"I don't know."

"Yes, you do." She frowned up at him. "And so do I."

"Well, I don't," Cam stated. "Care to enlighten me?"

"Think about it," Lachlan invited. "You've spent the last nine months—at least—locked up in a place you can't get out of. You've just given birth to a child that probably isn't even yours—"

"But wouldn't she want to get the hell away from here as fast as she could?"

"How? Walking?" Evan shook his head. "No, she's still inside someplace."

A wailing siren and a dizzying display of flashing lights distracted them. The county ambulance—a converted 1972 Cadillac hearse—rolled out of the floodlit rain and stopped at the verandah steps. Evan was grateful to see a paramedic he knew climb out of the driver's seat.

"Go find her," Evan said. "I'll take care of this." Shouldering open one of the double doors, he walked out onto the verandah and called out, "Hey, Matt! You couldn't pedal that thing any faster?"

"The hamsters went on strike last week," the young man said, opening the back doors and sliding out a rolling gurney. "I tried squirrels, but they kept gettin' their tails caught in the treadmill. Whatcha got for us?"

"Mother and newborn." He waited, hoping he wouldn't have to suggest it himself. All unknowingly, Matt came through for him.

"Hmm. Steinmetz is physician on call tonight, but if it's an obstetrics case, we'd better take them over to Dr. Cutter. No complications?"

"None that I know of." Except for the tiny problem of having lost her.

Matt finished unloading the gurney and got out a stack of blankets, wrapping them beneath his orange raincoat to keep them dry. "Good party?"

"Swell," Evan said, straight-faced. He turned, and Bernhardt Weiss smiled at him.

"It pleases me that you enjoyed yourself, Sheriff Lachlan."

"What the—?" Matt began.

Evan hushed him with a quick gesture. Flanking Weiss in the doorway were Jamey, Holly, and two security guards. One guard was pointing an 8mm Beretta at Jamey's head; Jamey was holding the baby. A second man had Holly by the scruff of the neck, with a .45 stuck in her ribs.

"You know what happens next," Weiss continued.

If this was New York City, Evan thought, *I'd already have ordered up a hundred cops in Kevlar vests, and more firepower than fuckin' Fallujah on a Friday afternoon, and you wouldn't make it to the bottom of the steps before a sniper took you out.*

This wasn't New York City.

There was him, and that was all.

"Actually," he drawled, "your idea of what happens next probably doesn't coincide with my idea of what happens next. Why don't we compare notes? For instance, I thought all you wanted was the kid."

Weiss shrugged and made a dismissive gesture with his left hand—which no longer wore Cam's little woven restraint on the thumb. Lachlan didn't waste time wondering how he'd gotten free of it.

"That was before," Weiss said. "Now I can have the child *and* your charming wife."

"Plus she's your insurance," Evan remarked. "You can control everyone else by threatening her." Which explained where Lulah and Alec and Nick and Cam were—or, more to the point, *weren't*. Quite apart from anything she meant to them personally, she was a Spellbinder. Protecting her was their top priority.

She was his wife and the mother of his children. Protecting her was his only priority.

Yet it couldn't be. Of all the clichés he hated, the one he hated most was *I'm a cop—it's not what I do, it's what I am.* What he hated most about it were the times he was forced to admit it was true.

Weiss shifted forward. "I have no wish to harm anyone—which is more than can be said for you, Sheriff Lachlan. Take out your gun, set it down, and stand aside."

Lachlan pretended to consider as he took a step up. "Mmm, not so much, no. You could order me shot, sure. But they tried that once before, upstairs." Another step. "Anybody go take care of those two guys I left bleeding on the floor, by the way? Oh, and Leather Dude. Forgot about him."

"Stay where you are."

Lachlan forced a smile, hoping it looked convincing. "Educated opinion around here is that you can sense magic." He unclipped his badge from the chain so that the St. Michael medal showed. "Haven't you figured out yet what's hanging around my neck? Haven't you wondered why your hotshots upstairs fired three or four times—and missed me?"

"You waste my time."

"Go on," he invited. "Order your guys to shoot me." At the edge of his vision he saw Jamey flinch and frown. "Fire away," he added, and glanced at Holly.

"Tempting," Weiss replied, gaze narrowing.

"Before you take him up on his offer," Jamey said, sounding peeved, "I want to know how you intend to evade the police of about a dozen countries. We know about the prostitution, and the human trafficking, and—"

"What *I* want to know," Evan interrupted, "is what's going on with the cryogenics. Little Master Race embryos, right? But not blue-eyed blond Aryans. You're after the magic. Whose kid is that, anyway? Whose baby did you put into that girl?"

His abrupt smile made Lachlan's skin crawl. "You wouldn't believe me if I told you. No, you really would not. Mrs. Lachlan, Mr. Stirling, you will have the goodness to go along quietly to the ambulance. I'd intended to use your vehicle, Sheriff—"

"—but anything will do, as long as you can fire up the lights and siren?" He flicked his gaze once more to his wife, whose eyes widened a bit before she nodded slightly. When her fingers twitched at her sides, he knew she'd finally gotten the idea, and readied himself for some very vast shooting.

Weiss's face caught on fire.

All Evan had ever heard from the girl was furious screaming—but he recognized her laughter as if he'd heard it in nightmares all his life.

The man holding Holly shoved her down, turning to defend Weiss, and dropped his pistol with a yelp of pain as it sprouted tiny flames. Evan went for his Glock, a motion that caught the attention of the second man, who instinctively turned his gun toward the new and obvious threat.

"Jamey! Down!"

Evan shot the guard high in the chest as a bullet went past his ear and thunked into a support column. He fired again, and the first man staggered, clutching his belly now instead of his burned hand.

Weiss lurched past Evan, plunging down the steps into the rain. The fire burned even more brightly, more fiercely, spreading down his neck and chest. He tried to run, thrashing his arms, trailing horrific pennants of red and orange and gold. A single howl escaped him—and his next gasping breath sucked the flames down his throat into his lungs.

She was laughing. She ran from the shadows to the verandah banister, leaning out into the rain, raking the long dark hair from her face as she watched him burn. He staggered out onto the storm-soaked lawn and crumpled to his knees.

Evan felt a hand touch his ankle. He bent to help Holly to her feet and wrapped an arm around her as they watched Weiss blaze like a torch. At length there was nothing left to feed the flames. The rain fell, the fire withered, and the laughter faded away.

Lachlan slid his gun back into his waistband and put both arms around Holly. She clung to him for a moment, then eased away and lifted her head. He saw for an instant what she would look like when she was old.

"We need—" She coughed thickness from her throat and tried again. "We need to find Lulah. And Alec and—"

"It's all right, child," her aunt said from behind them, and they turned. "We weren't hurt. Just—we weren't hurt." *Just frightened* was something Tallulah Eglantine McClure would never say in a million years.

Nicky had approached the girl, who was leaning against the banister, surveying them all with a challenging glint in her pale blue eyes. He said something low and indistinct in what Lachlan presumed was Hungarian. She replied in English.

"I took his life because he took mine."

Her lips curved at one corner in a smile that mocked and hated. Lachlan wondered suddenly if she would ever forget how to smile that way. Somehow he doubted it.

SHE FEELS THINGS FLICKERING inside her like distant stars.

When she is finally free of the baby and the kind blond man touches her forehead and she sleeps, she wakes without truly awakening to a painful blaze that sets her whole body stinging for one endless instant. She has not truly been asleep one moment since. Conscious in a vague way of being carried, of voices, of some other man touching her without touching her—that is when the pinpricks of light flare painfully behind her eyes. Slowly, tentative and quivering, tendrils of light lace together in a complex white-gold glow until she experiences true awareness for the first time in her life. When some man's disembodied touch shrouds the lovely radiance, she hates him. When he ties the string around her finger, she gives a soundless scream.

But then the strangest thing happens. All the vivid little sparks pulse, shift, dance this way and that, seeking each other in new patterns. They settle, poised in quivering anticipation. She watches them, feels them, wondering if they can free themselves from the binding.

That thought is all they have been waiting for.

They work swiftly, merrily, finding and immolating the specks of light twined around the binding threads. Finished, they seek new work before she can fully realize she is free, before she can call them back to her. When there is nothing more for them to do, they spark and shimmer, and return. By the time she opens her eyes, and stands, and hears his arrogant menacing voice, the separate constellations inside her have resolved into a river of light as brilliant as the Milky Way.

The woman from the book cover is nearby, and for an instant she is tempted to take her revenge. If not for this woman's words, he would never have known that she understands English. But it seems a trivial betrayal now, compared to what he did to her. And he is there, so close, so unaware of her—so superbly unaware that her fire has been his freeing, and her fire will be his death.

She takes his life because he has taken hers. Sending out her little shining ones to swarm and glow feels dimly familiar, though nothing has ever felt as wonderful as this.

She smiles.

And then she begins to hurt.

CAM GRIFFEN HAD TAUGHT DEMOCRACY in countries where getting to his job required an armed escort. He had spoken for the majesty of American constitutional law in places where doing his job meant carrying a fully loaded automatic. But, damn it, he hated guns—and not just because he saw the muzzle of one tucked against Jamey Stirling's throat.

He would never know how Evan managed it; he only knew he owed his cousin's husband more than could ever be repaid. He had about three seconds to think about this before Bernhardt Weiss went up in flames.

A need to touch Jamey, maybe even to hold him the way Evan was holding Holly, got lost in dread as the girl's blue eyes rolled in their sockets and she wilted into a whimpering heap of white nightgown. Her fingers curled into her palms, the bones of wrists and shoulders and knees cracking as a spasm surged through her. Tiny bursts like firework sparklers danced around her, the kind of white-gold fire that meant magic. They flickered, died, and she moaned.

Cam knelt beside her, scarcely hearing Lulah's frantic warning. Arrogance or outrage or fear of what might come next made him weave stillness into the soft cotton threads of her nightgown. Her body relaxed, her eyes opened, and what he saw in them scared him more than Beirut or Kosovo.

"Cam—help her!" Jamey's voice, behind him, very far away.

He shook his head. "She's—it's her brain, what the magic is doing to her."

"You could do something for her—help her the way you helped me."

"It's *brain* tissue, it's neurons and electricity and—"

"And neural fibers, a fiber is a fiber—"

He tried. He tried when he wasn't even sure how to touch her. A hand across her forehead, like a nurse in a mawkish Victorian mezzotint? Fingers splayed around her face, like a Vulcan performing a mind-meld? Her head had fallen to one side, and he automatically slid a hand beneath her nape, and the anarchy within her skull brought a cry to his lips. If his weaving of silence through the silk lining the corridors was a linkage of threads of light, her mind was a weave coming apart. Every intersect point was a spurt of power, each center detonating, pulsing fire along delicate filaments that swelled and twisted and disintegrated. The magic was an uncontained nuclear reaction spreading through her brain.

He scuttled back until his spine was tight against a wall, shook his head, wrapped his arms around his knees. "No—it's not—there's nothing I can—"

"Hush." Holly had her arms around him. She stroked his hair, the frantic motion contrasting to the softness of her voice. "Shh, it's all right, you're all right." Then, sharply: "Get him a blanket, dammit, he's shaking."

"I can make her comfortable," he heard himself say. "But the kindest thing would be to let her die."

Jamey crouched beside them, gripping a blanket, his face stricken. "You don't know that for sure—"

"You don't understand. What I did for you—it was different." He met Jamey's gaze. "What's going on inside her—the magic, it's ripping her brain apart. Even if I could knit all of it back together, there's so much damage, so much that's gone black and dead—"

"I'll take a look," said Alec.

"No!" Cam seized his hand. "Don't—please, Uncle Alec—"

Nicky hushed him with a gesture. "If the boy says not, then we don't."

"We're responsible for this," Alec said. "We kept working spells on her and near her—we kindled her magic—"

"It's just as likely that the staircase was restraining it," his partner argued. "When that was gone—"

"Your 'laws of physics' dictum?" Jamey snapped.

"How the fuck should I know?" Cam cried.

"So you can't help her? Or you won't?"

Nicky caught his breath, Alec stiffened defensively, but it was Evan who spoke.

"Don't answer that, Cam."

There were angry glints of green and gold in Evan's dark eyes as he glared down at Jamey.

"You trust him or you don't."

Cam hid his face on his drawn-up knees.

"Listen, Jamey. This is the way it is with them. They have their ethics, and their codes of conduct—except there's nobody to enforce those rules but themselves. You have to decide whether you trust Cam to know what's right and do what's right."

When Jamey said nothing, Evan spoke again. "You and I, we don't know anything about how they were educated, what they were taught—but we know what kind of people they are. What honor looks like. What it comes down to is believing they're going to make the right decisions about things you and I don't understand."

It took a significant fraction of forever before Cam felt Jamey's hand on his shoulder. Warm, in the chill of the rainy night; but whether the touch was trusting or apologetic, he couldn't tell. He lifted his head.

Deep within cloud-gray eyes was everything. *Everything.* No one had ever looked at him this way, not even Jamey, years ago when they were young.

"Forgive me."

Unable to speak, Cam nodded once. Then he turned his head, resting his cheek to Jamey's hand for a moment before pulling away from Holly's comforting arms. He shifted closer to the girl, fumbling for and gripping tight the amber around his neck, and made himself look into the wild violence of her eyes. As her brain imploded, something feral glowed from her, like the eyes of a trapped predator.

He didn't dare touch her again. He wove warmth around her, and freedom from pain. It was all he could do for her. He sat beside her and watched her die.

DAWN WAS MORE an agreed-upon description of the time than an observable event. The storm sweeping in from the Atlantic had stalled against the Blue Ridge, and while thunder and lightning had died away, rain continued its unrelenting gray cascade.

From it, in a blue sedan with windshield wipers unequal to the torrent, came the manager of Westmoreland, a local woman who had no reason to think she wasn't running just a normal hotel and spa. No one disabused her of this notion. Fresh from a pleasant Sunday off, she was appalled by the heavily edited version of the night's occurrences given her by Lulah McClure—her mother's high-school classmate—and readily accepted a promise to be told later all the details of break-ins, accidental shootings, Mr. Weiss's abrupt departure on urgent business, and a slight problem with the lap pool. She took charge of the staff when the timelock freed them from their dormitory, set them to their duties, and to all intents and purposes Monday morning of Labor Day Weekend was much like any other at an upscale resort.

"Not a clue about any of the other stuff going on?" Jamey asked Lulah.

She shook her head. "And I'll vouch for her family back three generations. Not a hint of magic in any of them."

This proved to be true of the entire staff. Alec stood casually in the kitchen drinking espresso in a twelve-ounce mug as they filed past at five in the morning, and reported not a quiver that would warn either of magic or of efforts to conceal it.

Not even the security guards knew about the staircase, the clinic below the spa, or the rooms in the attic. Lulah had no idea how Weiss had done it. Neither did anybody else. Not that they had much energy left for speculation—not after cleaning out Weiss's office. Luther arrived from the Sheriff's Station with the other county SUV, into which were loaded computers, financial records, and anything else Evan and Jamey happened to feel like seizing for examination. Jamey's BlackBerry, with its download from Weiss's laptop and hard drive, was privately stashed in Holly's car.

Matt, who had watched Weiss's incineration, would never remember it. As the four men with gunshot wounds were handcuffed and loaded into the ambulance, first Alec and then Lulah and then Nicky in their varying ways made small suggestions. All these were reinforced by traces of Holly's blood. By the time he got behind the wheel for the drive to Dr. Steinmetz's office, Matt was convinced that Weiss had never been there at all.

"I hate having to do that," Alec murmured.

Cam arched a brow at him. "You'd prefer the alternative?"

"Don't tell me it's for his own good. The only people whose good it's for is us."

Cam shrugged; it wasn't an argument that interested him. "Did you take care of the guards, too? The ones who saw what happened, I mean." He took an involuntary step backward as Alec glared at him. "Okay, okay, I'm sorry!"

"You ought to be," was the sharp reply, but in the next moment dark eyes softened. "It's been a rough night," he went on. "Worse for you than just about anyone else, I'd say."

They both turned to watch as Lulah, cradling the baby in her arms, went down the front steps, the two girls in their nightgowns and robes trailing obediently behind her. Cam shivered at the sight of their apathetic faces.

"Does anybody know if they're pregnant?" he whispered. "Or if they're Witches?"

"No, and yes," Alec murmured. "Dr. Cutter will look after them."

"And you as well," Nick said, unexpectedly appearing at Cam's shoulder. "Get in the car."

"I'll drive," said Jamey, approaching with the keys in his hand.

"The hell you will!" Cam exclaimed. "I don't care how many gallons of espresso you poured down your throat. You got shot!"

"I'm fine."

"What part of 'you got shot' do you not understand?"

"I'm *fine,*" Jamey repeated. "I've felt worse after an all-nighter before a Con Law final."

Alec settled the question by grabbing the keys from Jamey's hand. "Come along, children. I am a man of many talents—I can drive with only one thumb."

"Akana mukav tut le Devlesa," muttered Nicky, and trudged down the steps to the rental car Alec had arrived in.

Cam snorted. *"I now leave you to God"* was exactly the benediction for anyone subjected to Alec's driving. But at least Jamey wouldn't be behind the wheel. He watched them load into the big green SUV, and as Alec drove off in a spraying of mud and a slewing of tires, he murmured again, "You got *shot.*" Then, aware that Holly and Evan were watching him fret, he turned and said, "If this was anywhere but the back of the goddamned beyond, there'd be a news crew out here right now."

"And aren't we glad there isn't," Holly remarked.

"Are you kidding? Film coverage of this, and they'd be begging Evan to become FBI Director! Plus John Warner will probably retire from the Senate in 2008—we could run Jamey for that seat and pull down ninety percent of the vote!"

Holly met her husband's gaze. "Did I mention that between college and law school he spent a year working for the House Democratic Caucus?"

"Can't speak for Jamey's ambitions," Evan said, "but I'd rather give myself a frontal lobotomy with a baseball bat. Can we go home now, please?"

Holly pointed to Cam, then to the BMW. "Evan can take Lulah's truck."

"Aw, come on, Freckles—you think I'd get lost going to my own ancient family homestead?"

"I think," Evan said, "she wants to have a talk with you."

Cam eyed her beneath a frown. "You can't yell at me—you destroyed my Armani."

"I'm not going to yell at you," she said with a smile that made him nervous. "And I didn't destroy your Armani. But I will admit that I owe you two Cohibas."

For the first ten minutes of the drive she said exactly nothing. That made him even more nervous.

At last she spoke, as if continuing a conversation they'd been having for years. "You don't get it, Peaches. It's as if you're—I don't know, challenging? Yeah. You challenge the caring that people give you, even the idea that they *do* care, because you don't think you deserve to be cared about. You don't believe it when somebody offers you love and support—somebody who isn't a relative, I mean, because they're *obligated* to care about you and they don't really count—"

"Holly—"

"Shut up. I'm lecturing. You know it's true, Cam. Your face is an open book whenever you look at Jamey—and I'm very well-read. I know you. I was the same way. If somebody wants to be around us, it's because we're entertaining, or because of our talents or our magic, because of what they could get out of a relationship. Nobody could possibly love us just to love us."

"And now you're going to tell me how Evan changed all that for you," he mocked.

"No," she replied seriously. "I wish I could say that, but it wouldn't be true. I'm not that smart. It kind of snuck up on me gradually, and one day reached critical mass. Oh, I knew what I'd been doing all those years. It wasn't entirely my fault that my relationships with men went sour, but I had more to do with it than I realized at the time."

"Was that when Evan came along?"

"It happened pretty much simultaneously. Susannah gave me almost this same lecture, and it was finally sinking in." She paused. "I miss her."

They were quiet for a time. Cam sank deeper into the leather seat, watching the paling clouds and the silvering rain as daylight asserted its claim on the sky.

"And now here you are, with Jamey ready to give whatever you need whenever you need it, and he's not asking for anything more than the chance to love you the way you deserve to be loved—and you're still pushing him away, convinced you're not good enough for him."

"You know him. Am I?" he asked bitterly. "I've spent my life hiding a whole lot of who and what I am—but he just—it's part of him to be honest, completely honest. About everything."

"Scary. Yeah, I've gotten to know him. He's a sweet man. And I know exactly why he loves you."

Another silence, smaller this time. Cam spent it thinking determinedly about nothing at all.

Holly cleared her throat. "I was up with Bella one night—she has a terrible time teething, poor sweetie—and I was watching a talk show. One of the *West Wing* guys was on, being rather rueful and self-deprecating about the fact that whereas his ancestors had raised cattle and worked the land, *he* had to admit to his kids that he had a favorite moisturizer. Made me want to smack him upside the head, because it reminded me of something John Adams wrote—something about how he studied war so his sons could study politics and *their* sons could study poetry. That this guy became an actor—that's *exactly* what his ancestors had in mind when they came to this country and cleared the land and fought in the wars. They did it so *we* can study poetry, and if we're lucky we get to create a little poetry of our own. Whether it's crafting a character and speaking other people's words in front of an audience, like he does, or writing books like I do, or keeping people safe the way Evan does, or making sure the law does what it's supposed to do, like Jamey—or teaching people how to get a government going that will let them live their lives—"

"Poetry?" He smiled. "I can't say that I ever saw it like that."

"You heard Jamey tonight. You think that wasn't poetry?"

"I think that's when I started thinking about the Senate seat—"

"I think you're full of shit. I think you need to stick around PoCo for a while and convince that man that you really are worth what he feels for you."

He considered his answer for a little while before saying, "*Numquam poetor nisi podager.*"

"Oh, Christ—don't you dare start! Rom and Hungarian from Nicky, Jamey with his infernal Latin all the time—"

"—when the only person worth quoting is you, right?" He grinned, and she glared.

He waited. Sure enough, within a mile or so she said, "Well? Translate it."

"Ennius. 'I only spout poetry when my feet hurt.' "

"I'll make you walk the rest of the way back to Woodhush," she threatened. "That ought to produce an entire sonnet cycle." She braked for a stop sign and drummed her fingers on the steering wheel. "Or I could let you out here, and you'd be at his house in twenty minutes."

Cam strained to see the street sign. "Where are we? I can't read the—"

"Oh, that's right—when they divvied up the Addair plantation they put in a new access road. Turn right, take the second left, and four miles later—"

"You're kidding. That's where he lives?"

Shifting back into first, she tossed a smile at him. "The old carriage house, yes. Backs right up onto Dragon Swamp. From his upper windows you can even see the chimneys."

Dragon Swamp—named not for any actual swamp on the property but because the original Bellew land along the James River had borne the same name—had been the inheritance through their mother of Thomas and Tallulah McClure. When Thomas married Margaret Flynn, he traded his share in Dragon Swamp for her sister Elizabeth's share in Woodhush. Upon her marriage to Cam's father, Lizza had bought out Tallulah's interest in the property, the McClures having their main residence in the village of Willowmere. The Griffens had lived in the five-room cottage at Dragon Swamp until Thomas and Margaret were killed, had returned there for a few years during Cam's childhood, and finally sold the land to the county in preference to selling it to a developer. It was county property still, and no one had lived there in more than twenty years.

"Want to hear something weird?" Cam leaned his head back and watched the rain. "I dreamed a few weeks ago that I was back in that house. It was empty, and needed a wash, and there were sheets on the furniture. I walk through the parlor and into the kitchen, and then open the door to the cellar stairs."

"But—"

"Yeah, I know. That house doesn't have a cellar. But there it was, and it didn't seem weird at all, I just accepted that now there was a cellar. No sense of disorientation or anything. There was a lot of stuff in storage, things I didn't recognize, boxes, some furniture. Then this iron door, the kind you see in a loft apartment, with a security bar that swung down. This didn't strike me as strange, either. I didn't wonder what needed to be locked in like that. I was just wondering what was on the other side of the door.

"So I open it and inside is this twenty-by-twenty room, really high ceiling, no windows. There's a bed, a dresser, a microwave, a frosted glass door into a bathroom—like a studio apartment. But the incredible thing is that the walls are covered in a painted forest. Somebody had drawn trees on each wall, connected up by ivy and Spanish moss meandering all over, and on every branch was a scene of something or somebody. Imaginary stuff, all painted like those early American portraits. The ones where the painters would travel around with the background already done, and then they'd paint the kid's face or the lawyer's face onto it—I forget what that school of art is called. American Primitive or whatever. But that's how all the people were—"

"Without faces?"

"Yeah. Landscapes and interiors—somebody was getting ready to put people into whichever scene they'd chosen and paid for. I'm walking slowly around the room, peering at all these little paintings—there are hundreds of them, like on one of those family tree things with spaces to put photos. Then this voice says, 'Well, it's about time you got here!' The guy is—I don't know, just ordinary. Maybe thirty, maybe forty, hard to tell. Not thin or fat or tall or short, just a regular ordinary man, the kind you pass on the street a thousand times a month and don't notice. He's sitting in this armchair, and he's smiling at me like he's been expecting me. I'm the one who's there to let him out. He's been living in this little apartment and painting the walls with trees and faceless portraits and landscapes, just waiting for me to come and let him out. He's not angry, and he's not in any hurry. It doesn't occur to me to be surprised, even by the implication that I'm the one who put him in there. I know I wasn't, that's the thing. It wasn't my doing that he was there. But I was the one who'd come to let him out."

Cam half-turned in the seat to look at Holly's profile. She was smiling a little.

"So you're wondering," she said, "if you're psychic, psycho, or truly psychotic."

"Can we leave Freud out of this? I know what the stupid dream means."

"It'd be pretty hard to miss," she acknowledged. "We're almost home, so tell me just one thing: did you let the man out and take up residence yourself?"

"No. I went back up the stairs and out the front door. I decided not to reopen the house after all, I guess. I don't know what happened to the guy."

"Did you leave the door open?"

"Yeah." He peered through the rain at the familiar outlines of Woodhush—smiling in spite of himself, as always, at the preposterous pillars-and-portico out front. "Should I have gone back and dragged him out?"

"I think it's his choice, now that the door's open, whether he wants to stay or leave." She parked the car and switched off the engine. "I'm so tired I don't know if I can even sleep. Is there a level of exhaustion beyond exhaustion?"

"If so, I'm right there with you, Freckles."

"Not too tired to do something about whatever Uncle Alec did to protect my kids, I hope. I mean, it'd be nice to be able to get into my own house."

He gestured with one hand, then the other. "Your wish, my command—sometimes I get them mixed up."

It amused him, once they were inside, to watch her turn into Lady of the Manor. Tim and Laura, splendidly ignorant of what had surrounded them for the past few hours—and Alec had learned a couple of new ones, Cam had discovered while untangling the layers of Wards—required nothing more than thanks and a crisp fifty each for staying until dawn to watch the kids.

"You might want to go pick up your brother Matt, by the way," Holly added as she saw them out. "He should be over at Dr. Steinmetz's place—he can tell you how much fun we all had tonight."

"That was just evil," Cam chided as she closed the front door.

"Not my problem," she said serenely. "Come upstairs and meet the twins."

On their way past portraits familiar to him from childhood, past the gorgeous antique quilts on display that he had helped to preserve, he said, "You'll have to come up with a story sooner or later for what went on. You might as well try one out on me."

"I assume you're referring to what we called up by way of your cigar."

"Was that what did it?"

"I don't know." She linked her elbow with his as they climbed. "I'm just the Spellbinder, all I ever do is stand around—"

"—with your thumb in the air. Yeah, Evan said. You did a lot more than that tonight."

"Not on purpose, believe me. But when you think about whose land this used to be—all of it, from Virginia down to Georgia—and whose blood is in our veins, it's not terribly surprising that to summon Earth, Air, Fire, and Water brought that particular magic. If we were in Ireland, or Wales—or even Portugal, where the Madeiras line comes from—"

"Because of who we are? Or because the *genius loci* can hear us better there?"

"Again with the Latin. And come to think of it, the last time anything like that happened to me, I was on Long Island, which isn't exactly Cherokee territory. So it's probably all bullshit." She opened a door—her old room, he noted—and conjured a tiny flame to a candle high on a shelf. "I don't believe it," she whispered. "They're asleep."

They tiptoed over to the beds. Kirby sprawled on his back, black hair curling around his forehead and cheeks, mouth open, one arm tight around a stuffed panda bear. He looked ridiculously like his father, even at two years old. Bella was a little curl of clenched fists and hunched shoulders, as though she went about sleeping with the same determination she would bring to anything else in life. Though she had inherited the Flynn dark auburn hair and pale complexion, she had exactly three freckles that Cam could see—one on her left cheek, two on her right. He touched the long widow's peak—also Evan's—with one finger, smoothing back her hair.

"Gorgeous," he murmured.

"They are, at that," Holly replied complacently. "I'm completely without prejudice, of course."

"And so am I." He hesitated, then asked in tones more wistful than he'd intended, "Lend 'em to me every so often?"

"You say that now, when they're silent and immobile," she teased. "Wait until they wake up."

CONSIDERING THE HOUR and the events of the previous night, Lachlan thought it might be rational for everybody to go to bed until noon and start the inevitable discussions after everyone had slept. The only rational person proved to be Nicky. Growling something about being too old and feeble for this nonsense, he disappeared upstairs into the Wisteria Room. Cam was too wired and too worried about Jamey to follow his uncle's example—and when Holly made noises about making breakfast, he barricaded the kitchen door with his own body and threatened to dissect her with a rusty hoof pick if she so much as looked at an egg.

"You don't know where anything is anymore," she protested.

"I'll figure it out." He turned and let the door slam behind him.

Evan grinned his congratulations at his wife. "Give him something to do? Nice. Gets us all fed, too."

"And lets us hole up in the office with Jamey's BlackBerry." She produced it from the pocket of the abbreviated Armani trousers.

"You're a devious bitch, and I'm glad you're on my side. Come on, let's see what we can get out of the thing."

Downloading into his computer was the work of ten minutes. While he watched the screen pop file after file, not knowing yet if any were as incriminating as he hoped, Holly went on-line for information she eventually shared with him.

"The first thing we do is have all of them tested."

He looked up from financial reports he didn't want to slog through anyway. "HIV?"

"Sex trafficking is a driving force in the global spread of AIDS."

"We can't test without consent. And the results are privileged information."

"We have the names of all the johns. We'll make some discreet phone calls." She rolled her chair over to the printer and snatched up some pages. "Listen to this. 'The younger, the better,' this one pimp says. 'At ten or twelve, they're free of diseases.' And how about this one—'If a man isn't getting it at home, what's he going to do? They come to a house, buy what they need, and you know what? When men pay for it, the nice local girls are safe from getting raped. Better the foreign whores than our own girls.'"

"Holly—"

"This is from a law enforcement official in a country that shall remain nameless. 'The prostitution takes place in the other countries. We have no responsibility for it. No crime has been committed here. The rights organizations scream at us for not protecting these whores, but who's buying them? Germans. Italians. Greeks. Israelis. Arabs. Americans. Every country in the European Union. Every country in the Middle East. Every state in the United States. These places are where the crimes are being committed—and they blame us for them!'

"But this is my favorite so far. Listen: 'They send money home, the family survives. It's survival sex, that's what it is. At least with me, they get a cut. I'm helping feed their families back home. Besides, they know what they're getting into—how stupid do you have to be to realize that being hired to go to another country as a waitress or a nanny isn't prostitution? Any girl that stupid, she has only herself to blame.'" She glanced around as if looking for something to throw—and someone to throw it at.

And then Evan saw something he'd never witnessed before, not in the almost five years he'd known her. He watched her find a book.

Or perhaps he was watching the book find her.

All she did was sit in the chair. She hardly seemed to be breathing. But the very stillness of a woman so constantly in motion told him everything he needed to know. He couldn't have said exactly what it was that changed in her face, in her eyes. He only knew the changes were there.

He wondered how Erika Ayala could begrudge her husband moments like this. Yes, Holly was far away from him right now, deep inside her mind's twists and spirals of knowledge, intuition, instinct, talent, experience, and the wealth of words and yet more words. What she felt, what she was thinking, were only shadows to him, fleeting traces around her mouth and brows, sparks that lit her eyes. She had gone where he couldn't follow. Moreover, she neither needed nor wanted him there.

She came back to him. She would always come back to him. He smiled at her across the partners' desk, and her consciousness of having been gone made her give a rueful shrug and say, "Sorry. Zoned out."

"Caffeine?" Knowing it wasn't.

"Flash of insanity." She picked up a pen, set it down, glanced at her computer keyboard. "I got snagged on something E. L. Doctorow said. Something to the effect of, the historian tells you what happened, but the novelist tells you how it felt."

"It's more work, though, in a way," he mused. "Being a novelist. You have to be accurate with the dates and places, like the historian—but you have to get inside people's heads, imagine exactly how life feels to them."

"Each is difficult in its own way, but a novel hurts more."

"What would that matter, if it made a good book?"

Sinking back in her chair, she swung it from side to side for a few moments. "You realize, of course, that you'll have to live with me while I'm writing?"

"Did I marry a writer, or just somebody who types a lot?"

"I get crazy," she warned.

"This would be different from usual?"

"I mean it, Evan. All I've done for the past couple of years are short stories and some articles. This *would* be different. I've always lived alone while I was working on a book. I never had to worry about anybody else being around, or how late I stayed up, or what might or might not be in the fridge for dinner."

"So you'll be hell to live with, you'll neglect the kids, and deprive me of regular mind-blowing sex? I have to say, lady love, that these last couple of years while you've been jonesing for a book to write, you've had your moments. They're my kids, too, and I won't let you neglect them. As for the sex—"

She was laughing. "If you tell me you don't really need for me to be awake—"

"Nah, it's usually more fun when you're conscious." He grinned back. "As long as you're not doin' a Denise, with the reanimated corpses and the zombie sex, I can handle it."

"You've actually read one of her tomes?"

"I've read the reviews. They usually make me want to use disinfectant on my brain." He spared a glance for the list of files taken from Weiss's computer and the laptop, then decided to save it all for later, when he could go over it with Jamey. "By the way, I'm guessing this isn't going to be the long-awaited sequel to *Jerusalem Lost*."

"No."

"No medieval stuff? No swords and castles?"

"This will be contemporary. Even topical." She paused. "People won't be very happy."

He grinned again. "Fuck 'em."

A weary sort of commotion at the front door turned their heads. A minute later Holly laughed silently as Jamey's voice called out, "Cam?"

"Honey, I'm home?" Evan winked at her.

"It should be that easy. Peaches wouldn't know 'easy' if it kneed him in the balls."

A few minutes later, the baby was put to bed in a cradle brought down by Cam. Alec sported a cast, Jamey wasn't even limping, and nobody said much of anything besides "Pass the butter" for the next fifteen minutes during a mass plundering of scrambled eggs, andouille sausages, corn muffins, mandarin orange slices, and gigantic mugs of coffee just this side of lethal.

And then the twins woke up.

Twenty-two

KIRBY AND BELLA'S SHYNESS with Cam lasted about as long as it took him to flip the lid open on the old upright piano. That this was Jamey's suggestion startled him; that the twins were thrilled when actually allowed to touch the hitherto forbidden keyboard was less of a surprise. The racket they made learning "Chopsticks" brought Holly to the parlor door, her whole face a desperate plea. Pausing in his placement of four small index fingers on the appropriate keys, Cam concentrated for a moment. All noise ceased beyond a ten-foot perimeter of Persian carpet. Holly mouthed a heartfelt *Thank you!* and returned to the office.

Fourteen renditions later, some of them very nearly right, Jamey prevailed on Cam to play something else. He seated Bella in his lap while Kirby stayed beside Cam on the bench, watching fascinated as first a Chopin nocturne and then a Scott Joplin rag emerged from the piano with the touch of fingers on black and white keys. A glance down at the boy showed awestruck, worshiping blue eyes, as if this was magic beyond even Aunt Lulah's.

"Haven't you ever played for them?" Cam asked Holly later, when Nicky had taken the kids upstairs, putatively for room-straightening but by the sound of it for the War of the Stuffed Animals. "I know you're not any good, but at least you could've shown them how the thing works."

"You taught them 'Chopsticks,' you despicable man. I was hoping for at least another six months or so of peace and quiet—" She paused as shrieks and growls filtered down from upstairs. "Relative peace and quiet," she amended. "Come into the office, both of you. Thoughts have been thunk, and we need your input."

Lulah had returned to her own house to sleep. With Alec sacked out in the Wisteria Room and Nicky looking after the children, Cam, Jamey, Evan, and Holly sat in conference around the big double desk, supplied with yet more coffee.

Evan got down to it. "I did some checking with an old buddy of mine at the Marshals Service—man, he was pissed off when he called back. Even a year later there's still twenty different agencies you gotta go through to find out what's goin' on in New Orleans. Anyway, this spring somebody finally took one of the trafficked boys around and found the house Weiss used. Same kind of thing on a smaller scale. Dorm rooms and a medical setup. All abandoned, though, dammit—though the kid did give descriptions, and one of them sounds a lot like Herr Weiss. I sent copies of the passport photos from Weiss's safe. He says he'll get back to me if the kid recognizes anybody."

"Not to malign my new home," Jamey said, "but why did Weiss move here? What's the attraction?"

Cam exchanged looks with Holly. "Witches."

Holly refilled her mug, then passed the carafe to Jamey. "Lulah says the old bloodlines are dying out. Originally there were five or six Irish families—realizing that this comprehends a vast cousinage—they all knew each other back in the Old Country, they all settled around here for mutual aid and protection. The population grew when more Witches moved here—Welsh, Scots, Breton—they even allowed the English in!" She winked at Cam, who made a face at her. "But one way or another they heard that Pocahontas County's a good place to live if you're magically inclined."

"Some of my father's people came here from Salem in the late 1680s, just before the Witch Trials," Cam said to Jamey. "Holly never lets me forget I'm part English."

"Not your fault, dear," she soothed. "Anyway, by the mid-1800s, the area's lousy with Witches. But that's also when the country really opens up. People leave, other people come here to live, kids who went away come back married to persons who are not, shall we say, of the same faith. The percentage of Witches born to each generation goes down. But there's still a lot of us in PoCo, compared to the general population."

Evan took up the story. "I called Elias Bradshaw in New York. He's promised some definite numbers to confirm, but the sense is that no other community that started the way this one did—the German immigration into Pennsylvania, for instance—still turns out the number of Witches PoCo does."

Jamey stirred sugar into his coffee—deosil, Cam noted, wondering if he'd always done it that way or if somebody had explained a few Witchy things to him—and mused, "Is there something about the environment, the air, water, soil, vegetation, whatever, that makes for magic?"

"That's the theory." Evan leaned back and propped his feet on the desk. "It could be one reason Weiss set up shop here. Of course, there's also Holly. I'm still wondering why he didn't take a sample somehow when she was there that time." He picked up his coffee, shook his head, and set it back down. "I might as well mainline this stuff. You're looking thoughtful, Counselor. Full of thought. Overflowing, one might say."

"You're blithering, *a chuisle,*" Holly said with a sympathetic grimace. "That's my department."

Jamey smiled tiredly. "Cam said there was so much magic in that staircase that it overloaded. But the clinic downstairs was free of magic. It was all technology."

A white cat, sleek and arrogant, jumped up onto Jamey's knees and settled down to supervise. Cam realized he didn't know if this was a Bandit, Brigand, Butch, Sundance, or Pretty Boy Floyd. Geeze, even the family cat was more comfortable with Jamey than with him.

"If environment counts," Jamey continued, long fingers smoothing the cat's lush fur, "when you're trying to breed a Witch—" He broke off. "Christ, that sounds cold."

Holly nodded. "Science usually is. There are a lot more warm fuzzies in thinking that God made people specially and specifically than in our being a product of six billion years of genetic mutations."

"What I was getting at is that you say the girl was a Witch. She was an environment, too. And that sounds colder than ever."

"Both my parents were alcoholics," Evan said slowly. "My mother more than my father—I don't know, are there degrees of being an addict? But chances were good that my sister and I would be alcoholics as well."

"But you're not."

"Neither of us, that I've ever been able to tell. So, yeah, genes are important, but environment might play a big factor—"

"Like being gay," Holly interrupted. "There's no piece of DNA people can point to and say 'This person is homosexual.' Identical twins can turn out one gay and one straight. Is it a predisposition triggered by environment or experiences? The very fact that identical twins occupy separate places in space and time—"

Evan cocked a brow at her. "I draw the line when the lectures start getting Einsteinian. We'll agree that genes and environment are both important factors, and leave it at that, okay?"

"So stipulated for the record," Jamey put in.

"Thank you, Counselor," Evan said.

"I'm still back on the question of who spelled the place," Cam said. "And why Weiss could sense Witches but—"

"—but wasn't any more a Witch than I am?" Holly smiled ruefully. "I think that may factor psychologically into what he was doing."

"Wait a minute." Jamey sat forward, gray eyes alight. "Part of the environment around here is magic—all the Witches you were talking about earlier—and if it's not some deep dark forbidden secret, might I get a list one of these days?"

"Sure. You're family now," said Evan. When Cam frowned, he widened his eyes, the portrait of innocence.

"Thank you," Jamey replied, blushing a little. "Where was I? Oh, yeah. Environment. Witches are part of this environment. Weiss would be the perfect project manager. Like putting a teetotaler behind the bar in a roomful of alcoholics."

"You can't sense magic that isn't there." Evan nodded. "I like it. But that still doesn't tell us who put it all together for him in the first place."

Holly swirled coffee around in her mug. "If we posit that this person or persons stayed here at Westmoreland very early on, to set the spells, then we may find a name or two in the guest register that Nicky or Alec would recognize. Start with 2004, when Westmoreland opened—" She bent over her computer and began tapping keys.

Cam poured and gulped black coffee, scalding his tongue. "As far as the unwilling 'guests' are concerned, I've got a friend at the INS. I can give her a call and we can start tracing how these children got here. We might be able to shut down a trafficking ring or two, if we're lucky. If the victims will talk to us."

"I called Reverend Deutschman on the way back here," Jamey said. "He'll assume responsibility for them, place them with foster families. I think that maybe after a while, they'll be convinced that they're safe, and be able to tell us something of what happened to them."

"What do you want to bet not a one of them wants to go home?" Holly stabbed a key and sat back. "I saw a piece on-line a little while ago about Iraqi girls who fled to Syria and ended up in the sex trade. A Muslim girl who goes home is killed. It doesn't matter if she was kidnapped, threatened, drugged, tortured. She's been defiled and for the sake of the family honor has to die. And don't tell me that Europeans don't do such things. These girls—and boys—might not get killed for what happened to them, but would any of them have a life?"

"Ironically circular, isn't it?" Lachlan murmured. "Part of the money raised last night goes to rebuild burned churches, part to combat trafficking. And Weiss stood there, smiling and welcoming everybody, when the source of the church fires was a Hungarian girl he trafficked."

"Whoa," Cam pleaded. "I'm not current with this."

"And I'm not understanding it," Jamey said. "What do the church fires have to do with—"

Holly was typing again, so Evan answered. "The match-ups aren't perfect, and I don't understand a couple of them yet. But we think the girl was responsible for all but the Methodist fire."

"Here's what the ledger said about those nights." Holly turned the laptop so Jamey could see the screen. Cam pushed himself to his feet and went around to the other side of the desk.

"Either she was watching it happen on the screen, or she sensed what was going on, I'm not prepared to say which. And it doesn't matter." Holly pointed to an entry. "November eighth, 2005, Jack Wheeler was with Jurek in Room 208 from one until two in the morning. The fire at First Baptist started between midnight and three—but I'm going to pinpoint it at the moment of Wheeler's orgasm. Hang on a minute and I'll tell you why. The fire starts in the vestibule, in a stack of benches that are being revarnished. Wheeler not only manages the store where the cans of varnish were bought, but his wife teaches a class at the church. There's the association—and I'd be willing to bet they were together, at the church, painting those benches that very afternoon. So that night he's doing whatever it is he's doing, or having it done to him. I don't know and I don't care. He yells out 'God' or 'Jesus' or 'Holy shit' or whatever he yells at times like that. His neurons are all firing, it's power and chemicals and all the physiological things that go on with orgasm. I had it explained to me once that it was sort of a vision of eternity." She traded glances with her husband, who frowned down into his coffee mug. "Think about St. Theresa and her raptures, all the saints who described visions. They use words like *ecstasy* and *ravishment* and *bliss*—and don't they call nuns the 'Brides of Christ'?"

"Now, that's just kinky," Cam objected.

"Yeah, kind of makes me feel squirmy, too," Evan admitted. "But if the physical sensation is pretty much the same, then Wheeler's brain is both completely focused and totally open—and the association of physical release, yelling out to God, and the place or thing he most recently associates with church—"

Jamey was shaking his head. "And benches catch on fire miles away?"

"You won't get any forensics to play with," Cam said. "But I know the feel of her magic. I'd—"

"The feel?"

"When I was playing the piano, I felt the same magic as I did when I bumped into the grand piano at Westmoreland. It's like a signature, a fingerprint. What I was going to say is that if I take a field trip to the final church-burning—"

"You're sure Gospel Baptist will be the final one." It wasn't quite a question.

Cam looked directly into shadowy gray eyes and said nothing.

"Like I said, Jamey," Evan murmured. "You gotta trust them."

"Okay, then, what *about* Gospel?" he challenged. "We've got a start time prior to midnight, in the office."

Evan checked his own computer list. "August second, this year. Louis LaPierre is with Kurt from nine to ten in Room 208—and it's important that all these guys were in rooms with a view, if you follow my meaning. That's why we think this girl was actually watching and listening. That day, Louis had been in to see the minister at Gospel about the fire alarms he'd installed—"

"Irony on top of irony," Holly observed in disgust.

"—and it turned out they didn't work, as we found out when the arson guys went through it. Faulty wiring, skimping on materials—what do you want to bet he was sitting in that chair that afternoon sweating and praying that he wouldn't get caught?"

Cam was beginning to see the sense in this, and it made him feel more than squirmy. "So when he got off that night—"

"The office was his nearest and most recent association with a church. Or God."

"That's seriously sick."

Evan snorted. "Ya think? Like I said, I don't understand a couple of them, but this is the only thing that makes sense to Holly and me."

"August second," she blurted. "God *damn*!" She bent over the keyboard, typing feverishly. "The place opened in November 2004—would it be August or—yes! October! Here he is again in—February . . . in May . . . *there's* August! October again, February again, May—"

Cam jumped up to look over her shoulder. Open files cluttered the screen, a single name highlighted in each. He saw at once that she was right. "Valentin Maximovich Saksonov," he said, "avails himself of the services at Westmoreland around the dates of the Four Quarters." For Jamey's benefit: "October, February, May, and August are the big seasonal rituals."

"Hallowe'en?" Jamey hazarded.

"Also more than just a pretty face," Evan murmured. "So this Saksonov shows up regularly, huh? Definitely we ask Nicky and Alec if they've ever heard of him."

"But how does he connect with the fires?" Jamey asked plaintively.

"He doesn't." Cam glanced over as he sat back down. "He connects with the magic."

"Not my bailiwick. Can we get back to the churches, please? What about the Methodists?"

"The only fire that wasn't started by magic." Holly leaned back and pulled up one knee, resting her chin on it in a posture of convoluted gracelessness. "Who would benefit from it?"

"Weiss." Jamey didn't look up from his coffee. "It had been a while since the last fire. Another arson kept the churches nervous and gave them something else to spend their money on instead of supporting organizations that go after people like him."

"Or he was just having himself some fun," Evan said.

"Why didn't he pick a Baptist church?" Holly asked. "Most of the others were. And they were the ones spearheading the anti-trafficking campaign."

Cam could answer that one. "Because another Baptist church might have set you to thinking that very thing."

With a frustrated sigh, Jamey said, "Am I allowed to be glad Weiss is dead? Prosecuting this would have been a nightmare."

"You might be able to snare a couple of his security people," Holly comforted. "Though I wouldn't count on it."

"Me, neither. Is anybody but me wondering why there was a fire at the Lutheran church?"

Cam chewed his cheek for a minute, caught himself at it, and said, "Being a good German, Weiss was Lutheran?"

Holly folded the other knee and wrapped her arms around her legs. "Perhaps he considered his project an act of faith."

"So did the SS, when they fathered Aryan babies," Cam said. "Except that those women volunteered. Their sacred duty as Aryan Maidens. Weiss wanted—what, a Witchly aristocracy?"

"Thaumatocracy," Jamey said. "A Master Race of Magic."

The loathing in his voice made Cam's throat clench. Pushing away from the desk, he made for the door, and the stairs, and his old room at the end of the upper hall. But Holly and Evan had turned it into a second library, and there was no bed to fall across, no Star of Bethlehem quilt sewn by his great-great-great-grandmother, its colors as bright and its stitches as taut as the day it was finished because he'd spelled it himself with his newfound magic—

He stood there in the unfamiliar room, trying to swallow the nausea of disorientation. If the very notion of magic hadn't made him sick right now, he would have fled to the attic and tripped the latch to hide himself away on the secret stairs until he stopped shaking.

No, it wasn't what he was that did this to him. It was the certainty that Jamey was now seeing him and his kin at their worst, the things that had sent generations past running for the leg irons and the hanging ropes and the fire and the black-cowled brothers of the Holy Inquisition. They used to drape a veil over the crucifix in the torture chambers so that Christ wouldn't see what was being done in His name.

Could they hang him twice? Burn him in fires twice as hot? He had lived and worked in countries where a sword ended the lives of men like him who got caught.

Cam turned numbly to the window, the view outside the only familiar thing left. He knew, on a commonsense level, that discovery of his special talents as a Witch had coincided with discovery of his sexuality. Alec and Nicholas found joy in their gifts and in loving each other. Why couldn't he do the same? They didn't live their lives afraid of who and what they were.

He'd white-knuckled his way through life thus far, hoping nobody would notice—or at least that nobody would ever find definitive proof—that he wasn't normal. He *wasn't* normal, not by the standards of any society in the world—

All at once he was surrounded by Jamey—sturdy bones and strong muscles, an encompassing warmth pressing against his back, the scent of coffee and oranges and skin washed clean by rain. Cam's flinch made Jamey's arms tighten in warning.

"Hush. It's all right."

He shook his head, mute.

"It will be if you let it." Jamey clung tighter still, and whispered against Cam's nape, "Hush, love."

He turned, his body sluggish. A tiny smile trembled at one corner of Jamey's mouth. And then they were kissing each other just exactly as if they really did know what they were doing.

LUNCH. NAP TIME—FOR EVERYONE. Holly made the upstairs rounds, Brigand pacing regally beside her. Alec and Nicky in the Wisteria Room, snoring a soft counterpoint concert. Cam and Jamey in the General's Tent, wrapped in a blanket and each other, shoes neatly on the floor side-by-side. She smiled and went down the hall to the twins' room. Before she could push the door open, Evan called softly, "In here."

A few minutes later she was snug in flannel pajamas and eiderdown, gazing at her husband across the sleeping tangle of their children and a big white cat. Evan reached over and brushed a stray lock of hair from Holly's neck.

"I can't help worrying about what's going to happen to that little girl."

She searched his eyes, asking carefully, "Do you mean you want to adopt her?"

"No. I'm sure it would be the compassionate and politically correct thing to do, but our own two are enough to handle."

"She should be raised by a Witch."

"There must be at least one in this county who'd be thrilled to have her. We can keep an eye on her, of course." He turned his gaze to the sleeping twins. "God, they're incredible, aren't they? I wouldn't want them to stay like this forever, because I can't wait to see how they grow up. But sometimes it sure would be nice. . . ."

"I know. The older they get, the less we can protect them. Do you think Alec and Nicky can stop worrying about them like old maiden uncles? Danger gone, and all that?"

"They won't believe it until they bring out the shiny rocks and tea leaves again—or get good and drunk." He smiled. "Or both."

She stroked Bella's russet hair. "Did you mean that about me writing a new book? You've never seen me in that state."

"Worse than when you were pregnant?"

"You'll have to let me know."

Leaning over for a quick kiss, he said, "I know you go places when you're working. Just always come back to us, okay?"

She propped herself on an elbow. "What brought that on?"

"Not sure," he admitted. "Maybe Erika's little neuroses."

Holly groaned softly. "I swear I'm gonna have Lulah fix it so we never have to see either of them again."

"Well . . . I kind of told Troy that if he ever needs a place to stay or somebody to talk to . . ."

"Oh, that's all right. It's not his fault his mother's a psychopath."

"On several levels. How do people live like that? Or maybe it should be, how do people like that *live*?"

"I don't think they do," she mused. Then, watching his eyes, she said suddenly, "I love you."

"You'd be crazy not to."

"You egotistical bastard—!"

"Ah!" he grinned, pointing at their sleeping children. "Five bucks. Pay up!"

JAMEY HAD FORGOTTEN how lightly Cam was made, the elegant way his bones fit together, the strength of muscle curving around them. In truth, he rather missed the old Cam: a little soft around the edges, without this lean, tense abruptness. But when blue eyes blinked open, in the instant before full wakefulness Jamey saw again the young man he'd known twelve years ago. And he laughed, because as Cam realized who he was with, he looked as if he'd been simultaneously whacked over the head, drugged to the eyeballs, and informed that he'd been elected God.

"What's so damned funny?"

Jamey rolled over and wriggled himself atop Cam, who grunted but made no other protest. "Want more?"

"After twelve years, what's a few more hours?"

"Torture. Misery. Suffering. Anguish."

Wrapping him tight, Cam laughed quietly. "Enough already, Thesaurus Boy."

"We ought to wash before dinner. Want to join me?"

"Yeah, that's gonna be conducive to restraint."

"Wait'll you see my tub at home. I want to do it there, and on the rug in front of the fireplace, and definitely on the back porch at midnight under the stars, and—"

"Do any of these scenarios involve a bed?"

"*This* one would," he grumbled. "We'll probably be too tired tonight, anyway. And tomorrow there'll be more work than I care to consider. I'll be lucky if it's only a fourteen-hour day."

"What do you care, as long as you get lucky when you come home?"

"Will I?"

Cam only smiled.

After a few moments' careful consideration, Jamey asked, "Are you hinting about spells and things? I mean, I always figured that being with you wouldn't be like being with anybody else—not that there *is* anybody else. I mean, I haven't been a monk, but—"

"I've always hated the 'share the sexual history' portion of the proceedings." Cam sighed. "How about this: we both get tested, and—"

"—and we both admit there was never anybody else who was even half as important? And never could be?"

"Never," he answered quietly. Then, shifting a little, he said, "I didn't want to have this conversation yet, but I think we have to. There's a lot to consider."

"You think if we're together, I'll get crucified at the polls in November."

"Do you want to stay Pocahontas County D.A. forever?"

"What you mean is, am I still aiming to be the poster boy for gay politicians?" Jamey slid to Cam's side and gathered a pillow to wrap his arms around. "There are gay people all over government—you know there are, you've worked in Washington. With each generation that pretends to be straight, or keeps its mouth shut and hopes nobody notices, the bigotry and fear just get perpetuated. And the lies. I don't want to live like that."

"Okay."

"You'd like to be invisible. That's not possible. I want my life, Cam—our life. You're the only one I ever wanted to live it with."

"Okay."

"So you're just going to have to get used to being—wait a minute." He scrambled the blanket in his haste to sit up and look Cam in the eyes. "What did you just say?"

"Took you long enough."

"What did you *say*?"

"*Okay* is usually considered a term of agreement. Assent. Concurrence. It means *yes*. I can say it in seven or eight other languages if you want—"

"If you're joking, Cam, then so help me—"

"I'm not. I'm really not." Long fingers slid through Jamey's hair. "It's not gonna be easy. But it'll be worth it."

"Really?"

"Really."

They might have stayed like that forever but for Holly's breezy entrance without so much as a tap on the door. "High tea is being served in the drawing room. And before you ask, Peaches, all I did was slice the chocolate cake and boil the water. That much I can do without anyone's risking ptomaine." Walking further into the room, she regarded them with an indulgent smile. "You two are just too cute for words."

"We know," Jamey said.

"Do you? Come stand over here." She went to the walnut-framed cheval glass in the corner. "Take a look."

Jamey saw it at once. He'd seen it in Holly's and Evan's eyes sometimes when they glanced at each other: pride in being loved by this amazing person. It was in his own eyes now.

Holly stood behind them. "Charisma quotient, the element of sheer adorableness—" When Cam grimaced, she smacked him on the ass. "Whether they realize it or not, when people look at you they'll see that you're for real. That you aren't a couple of sex fiends who spend all their private time going at it like rabbits on Viagra."

"Elegant phrasing," Jamey noted.

"Thank you for that mental image," Cam seconded. When she slapped him again, he jumped. "How come I get hit and he doesn't?"

"I like him better than I like you. Also, he's prettier. My point is that people are going to see something that isn't a threat, or indecent, or anything other than two people who were lucky enough to find each other, even if they were abysmally stupid about it for twelve long years."

"Shut up, Freckles."

"What he just said," Jamey added. His turn to be slapped; he yelped.

"I'm trying to get it through to you that the Bible-thumping homophobes never vote for liberal Democrats anyway, so they were a write-off from the start. Plenty of people will just shrug, as long as you don't do it in the streets and frighten the horses."

"But there *will* be people who—"

"Cam." She smiled. "They'll remember you as a boy, and your parents, and our family. They'll hear about what you've been doing out in the world. They already know what a great job Jamey is doing here, how hard he's worked, what he believes in. In fact, I suspect a lot of folks will end up being secretly proud of themselves that they had the insight to look beyond the stereotypes and be nonchalant about the whole thing." She stepped away from them and turned for the door. "Hurry up, or I won't save any chocolate cake for either of you."

"Aw, Mom!" Cam whined, effortlessly accessing his inner five-year-old.

"Be nice," she advised, "or I'll glue all the keys on your concert grand."

"Concert grand?" Jamey blinked. "Where am I gonna put a concert grand piano in my house?"

"Improvise," she told him. "You want him, you get the piano. You'll get used to it."

"Why do people keep saying that?"

Twenty-three

"WE HAVE TO TALK ABOUT that poor girl," Holly said, settling into an affectionate old armchair with a third cup of tea. "We've been tap dancing like maniacs all day, trying to avoid the subject. My question is, do you want to get there by roundabout means, or do we confront it headlong?"

"There are one or two points I'd like cleared up first, if I may," Nicky offered. "I spoke with Dr. Cutter earlier. The other girls and the two boys were retrieved from Westmoreland and brought to his office around noon for checkups—he's furious, by the way, that Weiss is dead, because he wants to kill the man himself."

"'Something lingering, with boiling oil in it, I fancy,'" Jamey murmured.

Nicky went on, "Those children are terrified of everything and everybody, and a couple of them were begging to be sent back to Westmoreland so their families wouldn't be harmed. The girls in particular—" He lifted his teacup, looked into it, set it down. "Forgive me, Holly, but might I have something a little stronger?"

She went to the sideboard and poured him a stiff Glenfiddich. When he'd knocked back a large swallow he nodded thanks and continued.

"They thought Dr. Cutter was going to do what Weiss had done." He gulped Scotch again. "Evidently when Weiss didn't succeed, they were put to work. Cutter learned this from a girl named Hadwisa—once he got a sedative in her after she had hysterics at the sight of his exam room. My guess is that there are at least a few others on the staff who will tell the same story."

"What about the two girls from the attic?" Evan asked. "Marika and Agatha?"

"Agrafyna," Nick corrected. "Dr. Cutter will give them pregnancy tests. If positive, it will be up to them whether or not to carry to term."

Cam watched Holly repress a shiver—visible only in the swift, fleeting tremor of her hands as she poured herself more tea. Her voice was soft and steady as she said, "The trafficker's goal is to dehumanize. How in the world did that girl retain enough independent will to take her revenge?"

"Did it look like revenge to you?" Evan asked. "Seemed more like justice to me. She took his life because he took hers."

She mulled this over, and at length gave a slight shrug. Cam shared her doubts; Evan's was an odd attitude for a law enforcement officer who'd witnessed what was essentially a murder. But what Holly said was, "I think she might have meant that her life didn't exist anymore. That *she* didn't really exist anymore."

"I think we need to return to what Weiss evidently wanted to do," Jamey said. "What would have happened had he succeeded?"

"I've thought about this before," Evan said, producing startled glances from everyone but his wife. "Back when Alec figured out what Holly is, the technology didn't exist. They didn't have to worry about it. By the time I met her, artificial insemination, *in vitro,* all of it was pretty routine. Eggs, sperm, syringes—how long would it take to harvest her into thousands of petri dishes? Thousands of potential Spellbinders." He met her gaze. "If we'd had trouble getting pregnant, if we'd had to go to a fertility specialist, even if surrogacy had been the last resort—there's no way I would've agreed to it. There'd be too big a chance that somebody who knows what you are would find out and steal you. The only woman who'll ever give birth to your children is you."

Cam was baffled by the fierceness of Evan's determination to protect her; Holly had never seemed to need protecting from anything or anyone. Then he glanced at Jamey, and understood. It wasn't possessiveness, or the egocentric imperative that *nobody threatens what's mine*. It was simply that Evan loved her, and he trusted no one else to keep her safe. If that was even more egotistical, then so be it.

"This baby, this little girl," Evan was saying, "in a lot of ways she's that nightmare come true. She was stolen. She'd grow up thinking what Weiss told her to. Indoctrinated. Warped the way he was warped. This 'thaumatocracy' Jamey talked about—it would've been the whole meaning of her life."

"She would have had no more choice than her mother did," Alec agreed.

Nicky finished off his Scotch. "The girl had no idea what she was, of course. Any magic she worked was instinct. Which is the most dangerous magic there is."

"She got loose from all of us," Cam reminded them. "Even my knots. If her child is half that powerful—"

Jamey drew a breath, then sat back on the couch and shook his head as if reprimanding himself. Cam touched his arm. "Say what you were going to say."

"I'm not sure it's relevant."

Holly snorted. "You've spent almost a year listening to us chase off on tangents. In this house, 'relevant' is so scarce it qualifies as a trace element."

He smiled, and for an instant breathing was something Cam had to think about. Holly caught his eye and winked. It made him want to throttle her—or buy her a brand new BMW. Maybe both.

"Well, it's just this." Any hint of apology for his presumption had left Jamey's voice. "Power's a very personal thing. Political, financial, what's commonly termed 'moral authority'—basically it's the ability to impose your will on someone else, be it a single person or an entire nation."

"Or a courtroom," said Evan. "I've seen you in action."

"That's a kind of power, too, and I enjoy it." Not looking at Cam, he added, "I'm doing what I was trained and educated to do, guided by ethics and what I believe to be right. What you people have, this is new to me in theory, but . . ." He paused, not looking at any of them. "Weiss had no magic of his own, beyond an ability to sense it in others. He had nothing of the kind of power that seemed to mean everything to him. Is there anybody here who believes he wasn't acting on someone else's behalf?"

Cam leaned forward, elbows on knees, hands clasped. "All right, Counselor, build your case."

Jamey got to his feet, smoothly graceful, and for all that he was wearing jeans and one of Evan's work shirts he gave the impression of having just buttoned the jacket of an exquisitely tailored three-piece suit. "Bernhardt Weiss was an individual with a single goal. His pursuit of this goal was relentless. In psychological terms, he was a man obsessed.

He purchased human beings. He regarded them as commodities. They were bodies to be bought and sold. To be used. He did not have *contempt* for human lives. He did in fact *value* them as one would a piece of machinery, a plot of land. Rented to others for use, or planted and reaped as a crop—this is how Bernhardt Weiss regarded the people he bought. And he made a profit. Almost all of it was monetary. One thing was not. When he wanted to escape Westmoreland, the one thing he demanded was that newborn child. Other than Weiss himself, to whom would that child be so valuable?"

"He wasn't normal." Nicky set down his glass. "I don't mean that he was crazy—he obviously was, as you pointed out. Obsessed. I mean that by Witchly standards, he wasn't *normal*."

"Neither am I," Holly murmured.

Evan pointed a long finger at her. "Don't start." When she opened her mouth to say something more, he added, "I mean it. Don't you start with me."

Jamey cleared his throat. "Holly, as I understand it, or as I think I'm beginning to understand it, your gift is simply different from everyone else's. Not lesser, or weaker—from what I saw, it may be more important than theirs. I mean, they can work magic, but they need you to really make it stick. That's right, isn't it, Cam?" Not waiting for an answer, he gave a sudden smile. "And who would have believed yesterday at this time that I'd be discussing what's usual and unusual among Witches? But it seems to me that the point here is that within his own milieu—within his own family, from what Nick said—he'd be the odd one out. Holly mentioned a psychological factor in this project of his. Some people feel estranged because of what they are, but Weiss felt that way because of what he was not. This child's mother was a Witch, and the pregnancy came to term in a county rife with Witches—for whatever reasons of bloodline or environment—so chances were pretty good that this little girl *would* be a Witch. He'd raise her, control her, teach her what to think. She'd be his entrée to power."

"A commodity," Cam murmured. "Possession of which would establish him with the hierarchy of—of whatever. Nicky? Alec? Any ideas?"

Before either could answer, Holly sat up straight and said, "Valentin Maximovich Saksonov."

Alec responded almost immediately, "John Jacob Jingleheimer Schmidt."

"Oh, no," she warned. "I was so clever in figuring out when he was here—don't you dare tell me you don't recognize the name!"

"When *was* he here?"

"Every Quarter Sabbat since October 2004! Come on, Uncle Nicky, you must have heard of him—"

He was shaking his head. "Sorry. I like your theory, though. Other Witches in the area would be busy with their own observances, safe within their Circles. Anything he did would go unnoticed."

"None of the other names Evan gave us look familiar," Alec said. "But we have a few contacts we haven't talked to in a while."

"Well, talk to them soon." Holly slumped back in her chair, disappointed and annoyed. "Please," she added, belatedly recalling her manners.

Cam had kept his gaze on his plate this whole time, fingers picking at crumbs of chocolate cake. The instant Nicky put on a baffled expression, Cam had known that lies would be told. And as he listened, chasing bits of frosting around his plate, the echoing syllables of the name finally registered. But he said nothing; Alec and Nicky might be able to lie to Holly, but he'd never managed it.

Jamey had stepped into the conversational breach. "The immediate question is, what do we do with this baby? I'm assuming no one here is willing to hand her over to Social Services. Not a child you know to be—"

"Mommy!" screamed Bella from the front hall.

"No!" yelled Kirby. "*My* blocks!"

"—a Witch," Jamey finished.

Holly muttered, "Sharing time appears to be over," and went to mediate.

Lulah, conspicuously silent up until now, went around the room with teapot and cake plate. "You know anybody who works in Congress?" she asked Cam.

"I still have a few contacts."

"Reverend Deutschman's volunteers will need legal help and I wouldn't be at all surprised if they put together a delegation and headed for Washington soon."

"I'll make some phone calls tomorrow morning." Lounging back on the couch, Cam spread his arms across its back and closed his eyes. "I'm not old enough yet to feel this tired at four in the afternoon."

"It's got nothing to do with age," Nicky told him. "This was the first Grandmastering you've ever done. Of course you're exhausted."

"Is that what it's called?" Jamey asked.

Cam missed entirely their next exchange, for Jamey settled himself against his side, tugging an arm down to rest across his shoulders. Instinct screamed at him to move, escape, deny, laugh it off. But every muscle turned to mist with the gentle flow of warmth from the body pressed close to his. When Jamey's arm slid around his waist, he told himself that this "together" thing would take some getting used to.

He decided he could deal with it.

"KIRBY," HOLLY SAID PATIENTLY, "the yellow ones are yours and the green ones are Bella's. It's not cheating to take your own blocks."

"I want a wall," he insisted. "She broke my wall."

"He broke my wall, too!"

Regarding her daughter critically, Holly said at last, "My munchkin, you mustn't make up stories unless you've been paid to do so. I think what we need here is more blocks. Anybody who wants more can come with me upstairs to get them."

A few minutes later they were back downstairs and she was doling out red blocks, hiding a grin as each child counted carefully. Brilliant though her offspring were, Kirby got lost after seven; Bella made it to nine before going back to three. How "mubberteen" made it into the mix was a mystery akin to why Kirby called butterflies "nannybows" and Bella got "moosebubbles" when she was chilly.

At length the walls were back under construction. Holly sat in the dining room doorway and watched, thinking about what Evan had said. Until that moment she'd considered only what it might have been like to be forced to carry a child that wasn't even one's own; she tried to imagine how she would feel if her child was growing inside another woman's body.

The deeply personal revulsion of Holly Lachlan demanded abandonment of that line of thinking. The professional instincts of H. Elizabeth McClure felt another part of the book slide into place. Oh, Evan was going to have a wonderful year or so while she wrote this one. . . .

"I have milk and I have crackers," Lulah announced from the kitchen door. "I also have string cheese, and if you want any you'd better hurry before Brigand jumps up on the counter and eats it all."

The half-finished walls were summarily abandoned. Chairs were climbed onto, cups were claimed, and cheese was doled out in scrupulously even portions. When the kids were busy munching, Holly took her aunt aside.

"I need to know something. Poppy's car was found right around where my parents were killed. Was the location a coincidence?"

"No, honey. I doubt it very much. Jesse went down to take a look for himself. . . ." Lulah's sharp blue eyes glazed over, and a muscle clenched in her jaw. "There'd been magic done, and more magic that made a Witch helpless to use magic." She pulled in a long breath. "We thought it might've been something like that. Thomas and Marget were too good and too well-trained not to defend themselves. And Jesse found no sign of their magic at all."

"Just the magic that killed them." Suddenly she noticed what her aunt was wearing: black trousers, black sweater, and an Hermès scarf Holly had brought her from Paris long ago.

"Yes," Lulah said in response to her look. "You'd all better go get changed. Bill Cutter is at my place with the baby. And the body. We'll be burying that poor girl before sundown."

IT WAS A LONG, silent walk to the burying ground.

The coffin had been contributed by Louvena's nephew, Leander—who, in addition to his other woodworking skills, constructed caskets for those Witches who wished interment rather than immolation. The customary pine had archaic associations with immortality. The shavings and sawdust of other woods were placed in an old iron cauldron. Ash for enchantment, for the passage between inner and outer worlds, for rebirth. Hazel, the tree of wisdom and wishes. Willow for Witchcrafting. Yew for death, apple for immortality, rowan, the tree of vision and healing, and holly to ease the passage of death. Finally, birch and elder, the trees that stood on either side of the one Nameless Day in the ancient Irish calendar. That day represented the link between life and death.

The girl was no longer nameless. Going through the passports from Weiss's office had yielded the information, although Nicky doubted the name was her own. When Alec pointed out that he wasn't the only Hungarian with a Russian surname, he shrugged. But they had nothing else to call her, so "Natasha" would have to do.

Between them, Holly and Lulah carried the heavy cauldron to the head of the grave. Holly called fire to the contents as Evan and Cam dug the grave within the Woodhush family burial ground. Rain had softened the soil, and the coffin wasn't all that big, so it took only a little while to hollow out the earth to receive it. Beneath an overcast sky, with thunder in the distance, they made grave-offerings as humans had done for millennia. The ancients had given food, jewelry, flowers, weapons, carved trinkets of bone or shell, stone or antler: these things, found in graves thousands of years old, revealed that humans had developed not only an understanding of what death was but a hope for what it might be. No one knew what they had truly meant with their gifts and rituals, but that there had been rituals and that they had left gifts for the dead demonstrated their grief, and a sense of community, and a contemplation of death and what might come after. It was, in all likelihood, the beginning of religion.

Natasha's religion, if any, was a mystery to them. So they used bits and pieces of their own.

Lulah set white candles to burning, thirteen of them around the grave. Into the open coffin she let fall cedar, sage, and myrrh: purification, peace, protection, and the release of all grief. Finally she rubbed between her palms a sprig of marjoram, releasing the fragrance of the herb that traditionally accompanied the dead, and dropped it gently onto Natasha's breast. She stepped back, and nodded at Jamey.

"There are supposed to be ten adult Jewish men present, a *minyan,* to say *Kaddish,*" he murmured. "I think I can be forgiven for reciting just a little of it here, on my own. *Y'hei sh'lama raba min sh'maya v'chayim aleinu v'al kol Yis'ra'eil v'imru: Amein. Oseh shalom bim'romav hu ya'aseh shalom aleinu v'al kol Yis'ra'eil v'imru: Amein.*" May there be abundant peace from Heaven and life upon us and upon all Israel. He Who makes peace in His heights, may He make peace upon us and upon all Israel.

Alec held out a large bead of pink quartz, carved into the shape of a rose. "The stone of serenity, of joy, of peace. To comfort the heart, to calm and console the mind. The gem of forgiveness, and of love. May it protect you from the cold, child." Gently he placed the stone rose beneath the girl's folded hands.

Evan, contending that there was a chance she'd been Catholic, had insisted on what came next. He spoke the words in English; Holly recited them in Irish Gaelic; Cam had Nicky translate them into Hungarian.

"Hail, Mary, full of grace, the Lord is with thee. Blessed art thou among women, and blessed is the fruit of thy womb, Jesus. Holy Mary, Mother of God, pray for us sinners, now and at the hour of our death. Amen."

"Sé do bheatha, a Mhuire, atá lán de ghrásta, Tá an Tiarna leat. Is beannaithe thú idir mná, agus is beannaithe toradh do bhroinne, Iosa. A Naomh-Mhuire, a Mháthair Dé, guigh orainn na peacaigh, anois, agus ar uair ár mbáis. Amen."

"Üdvözlégy, Mária, kegyelemmel teljes, az Úr van teveled, áldott vagy te az asszonyok között, és áldott a te méhednek gyümölcse, Jézus. Asszonyunk Szüz Mária, Istennek szent Anyja, imádkozzál érettünk, bünösökért, most és halálunk óráján. Ámen."

Nicholas didn't use Hungarian. Rather, he chose a ritual formula from Rom tradition. *"Putrav lesko drom angle leste te na inkrav les mai but palpale mura brigasa."* I open her way in the new life and release her from the fetters of my sorrow.

The casket was sealed. The men lowered it into the grave, then took turns shoveling. By the time they finished, the white candles had all burned out.

Holly and Lulah started back to the house together. Jamey arched a questioning eyebrow at Cam; he shook his head slightly, and hung back from the others. He glanced once more at the small graveyard. Standing there, listening to his own heartbeat, he nodded slowly to himself at the implacable reminder of that new grave, of the brief time there was to love, to work, to seek happiness, to make a life and a family and a home.

He caught and held Alec's dark gaze. After a small grimace of misgiving, the older man murmured something to Nicky and approached Cam.

"Why did you lie to her, Alec?"

A sigh. "How did you know?"

"It took me a minute, but I made the connection. 'Maximovich' is 'son of Maxim.' And 'Saksonov' is really bad Russian for 'von Sachsen.' "

They walked a few yards in silence before Alec said, "I'd hoped you wouldn't recognize the name. Or remember it. Max was Mr. Scott's counterpart in Europe. I can't believe that his son would be a party to something like this."

"But Holly was right," Cam insisted. "Saksonov—or von Sachsen—*was* here at the Quarters, and he *did* work the magic at Westmoreland."

"Very likely."

"Why did you lie?"

The older man tilted his head back and gazed up at the darkening sky. "Traditions east of the Rhine are different from Celtic, or French, or even Italian and Iberian," he said. "The Germans, Russians, the Rom—you've lived in that part of the world, you know the distinct character of those magics. Max was . . . severe in his discipline. After what he'd been through during the Second World War, it's not surprising. A German Witch, living under the Third Reich—" He shook his head. "I'll admit that Nicky and I never much liked working with him, but he was a good man and we respected him."

"Have you ever met the son?"

"No. We'll make inquiries, of course. We lied because until we look into this—"

"Alec—"

"We've been at this longer than you've been alive," he said coldly. "Leave it alone, Cam."

"You'll tell me what you find out," he persisted.

"I can see we'll have to."

BILL CUTTER, who had stayed behind to keep an eye on the children, greeted them in the kitchen with a pot of hot coffee and a dilemma.

"I can fake the death certificate, no problem. 'Massive stroke' will look odd on a girl her age, but she'd just given birth so eclampsia is a possibility. High blood pressure and so on. We can leave it at that. But what do you want me to do about the birth certificate? I phoned for pizza, by the way. Should be here in half an hour or so."

"You're a scholar and a gentleman." Holly spooned sugar into her cup. "Use the name from her passport."

"And the father? 'Unknown' and 'decline to state' are the usual options."

"Use my name," Cam said.

Jamey gave him a long, slow, searching look.

"It'll settle any hassles about adopting her," Cam added.

"Sidebar, Counselor," Jamey said, grabbing Cam's arm. "Excuse us, please."

Holly watched them leave the kitchen, then traded a bemused glance with her husband. "Well, well, well."

Evan went to the cupboards for dinner plates. "It'll play merry hell with their sex life," he commented.

"What sex life?" Holly shot back. "They don't have a sex life. They haven't even seen each other naked."

"Yet."

"How the hell are they going to raise a baby?" demanded Lulah, stirring her coffee with unwarranted force.

Cutter shrugged. "The same way other single fathers manage it. The same way *you* managed it, Lulah."

Nicky gave a small nod. "The same way anybody manages it. One diaper at a time." The expression he turned on his partner was wistful, subdued. Holly realized that however many college graduation photos lined the wall of their Connecticut farmhouse, they had no children that were truly their own. She knew again how lucky she and Evan were. And how lucky Cam and Jamey would be if—

"From what I've seen of her," Evan said, with an entirely spurious expression of guilelessness, "she kinda looks like him."

"The hair color's about right," Holly mused. "And the hairline. Evan, you know that picture of Grandmother Flynn? Her widow's peak makes that baby's—and yours!—look like amateur hour."

"Nobody ever questions it when a single woman wants to be a parent," Cutter said. "Why is it different for men?"

"It shouldn't be, but it is." Holly slid off her stool and started collecting silverware. "Look at them. One district attorney, one unemployed Witch—"

"—and one baby who needs a home where she's wanted," Evan finished. "It'll be a lot to handle, when they're so new."

"New?" She snorted. "They've been dancing around this for twelve years. And from a purely practical viewpoint, as far as Jamey's concerned, there's the Family Values thing. What could be more valuable to a politician than a family?"

Alec had been listening to all this with a look of stricken incredulity. "Hello!" he almost yelled. "They're *gay*!"

"So?" Cutter asked.

"What do you mean, 'So?' They're *gay*!"

Nick paused in his gathering of glassware. Turning, he met his partner's dark eyes. Something secret and fierce passed between them. "Alyosha," he said quietly, "shut up."

There was an awkward silence. Then Dr. Cutter said, "Holly, I don't suppose you and Evan—"

"We already discussed it. It's not very warm and maternal of me, but—"

"But Cam *wants* to." Evan rescued the green beans from boiling over. "That's the difference. We could take her, sure—but he *wants* that kid."

Setting plates on the counter with a thunk, Holly turned and scowled. "Jamey has to want this, too. He can't agree to take the baby just because he thinks he'd lose Cam if he didn't."

Lulah glanced up from folding napkins. "They'd have to get an actual car. Can't strap a baby onto that crotch-rocket of Jamey's. They'll also need household help, especially after Cam finds work. He can keep all the cloth in the house clean—he can even fix it so her diapers don't stink—but I don't think he does windows."

"I don't, as a matter of fact."

Everybody swung around to face the kitchen door—absolutely choreographed, Holly thought, amused. What interested her more was the geometry of Cam, Jamey, and the child. The angle of Jamey's shoulders and elbows as he held the baby. The curve of Cam's smile, and of his arm around Jamey's shoulders. Parental architecture, she decided. A family.

"Well, Peaches," Holly said. "Bit of a glitch with the birth control, was it?"

"I promised not to be jealous," Jamey offered earnestly, his eyes dancing.

She went on aiding and abetting. "Camellius Ruaidhrí Griffen, where exactly *were* you last December?"

"Well . . ."

Jamey's gray eyes went as big and round as glass doorknobs. "'Camellius'?"

Evan arched a brow at Holly. "That was foolish. What're you gonna threaten him with now?"

She waved it blithely away. "The simple power of suggestion is half a Witch's arsenal at times." She considered, then went over to pluck aside the pink blanket Bella had come home in over two years ago. Dark red hair. Long widow's peak. With next summer's sunshine, skin that fair would without doubt acquire freckles. Very deliberately, Holly said, "She looks *just* like you, Cam."

Lulah joined them, digging into a pocket. A slight length of delicate silver links with a single plain disk was pressed into Cam's palm. "Her mother's. Keep it for her."

Cutter harrumphed. "As a physician duly licensed by the Commonwealth of Virginia, I haven't heard a word of this."

"And as officers of the court," Evan added, "neither have we, Jamey."

"I'm still back at 'Camellius,'" the younger man admitted.

"Speaking of names," Cam interrupted firmly, "what are we going to call her?"

"Elizabeth," Jamey told Cam. "For your mother. And mine, by the way."

"Really?"

"And for Holly, of course," Jamey added.

She caught her breath; Evan caught her eye. "Your reward for—well, I'm not sure exactly what it was that you did, besides embarrass them both, but you get rewarded anyway."

"Elizabeth Griffen," Cam said thoughtfully. "Okay, I like it. But she needs a botanical name, too."

"Peach Blossom," Evan murmured irrepressibly.

"Plumbago," said Holly.

"Tiger Lily," Evan countered.

"Mugwort."

"Ragweed?"

"Enough!" Cam ordered. "I need a drink."

"Bring the bottle," said Evan.

"Bring two bottles," said Alec.

Holly followed Cam into the parlor and watched for a moment as he poked through the selection of single-malts. Before she could say anything, he slanted a glance at her and smiled.

"Freckles, darlin', if you ask me if I'm sure about this, I'll do something really vile to your pillowcases."

"Save your energy, Peaches. You're gonna need it." She hesitated, then asked, "This is both of you, right? Having a gun to your neck while you're holding a baby can be quite a shock to the system. Oh, stop glaring at me in that tone of voice," she chided. "You know what I mean. Have both of you really thought this out? When you live with somebody, and you want to go on living with him—hell, if you want to go on *living*!—you don't make unilateral decisions about something as huge as this and then try to survive the fallout."

"It's both of us. Yes, I'd do pretty much anything for him. But he'd also do the same for me." Sloshing the bottle of The Macallan to judge how much was left, he added, "And the only thing that ever really made him unhappy about being gay was that he'd never get the chance to be a father."

"And then you went upstairs to look at her. Cam, that's how babies do it, how they get you to put up with the noise and the stink and the sleep deprivation. They're just so damned adorable that you can't help but forgive them for all the nasty stuff."

"Granted," he replied calmly. "But you know what Jamey said? He stood there watching her sleep and told me he didn't think he'd be able to stand watching somebody take her away from us. So don't worry about it, Holly. We don't know what we're doing, but we know what we're doing."

"The motto of parents everywhere." Then, relenting in the face of his certainty, she smiled and murmured, " 'Through love, through hope / and faith's transcendent dower / We feel that we are greater than we know.' Wordsworth." She poured two shots and handed one to Cam. *"Mazel Tov."*

"Nashti zhas vorta po drom o bango."

"Good grief!" Holly nearly choked on the whiskey. "What the hell was *that*?"

"Rom. 'You cannot walk straight when the road is bent.' " He grinned, with full triumphant dimples.

"I swear by everything holy, if *any* of you people teach my children any word in any language other than English . . ." She sighed. "Oh, what the hell. Bring every damned bottle you can carry."

THE FIRST WEEK IN DECEMBER an invoice arrived at Woodhush, detailing the annual fee for storage of cord blood cells. Appended was a letter apologizing for overcharging by one unit the year before, and a check for the refunded amount.

After several irate phone calls, subsequent investigation revealed that CryoCache Inc. had mistaken one unit for another—the difference being two reversed digits—and after inventory in July 2004 had pulled the item for disposal. Further tracking was impossible, and the company could only assume that the unit had indeed been destroyed. Deepest regrets, massive corporate abasement, and the guarantee of free storage for the remaining unit for life all added up to *Please don't take us to court.*

Evan and Holly considered it, then traded angry shrugs and hoped to high heaven that Bella would never need the medical advantages of her own cord-blood cells. Or, if she did, that Kirby's would do just as well.

Everybody said that Poppy Elizabeth Griffen looked more like Cam every day.

Author's Note

My thanks to all the usual suspects. You know who you are.

According to the U.S. State Department's 2008 annual report, 800,000 people are trafficked across international borders every year. *Every year*. It is estimated that 80 percent of trafficking cases involve women; 50 percent involve children. In 2004, human trafficking was a $9.5 billion industry worldwide. Many of the details in this novel were taken from real-life accounts found in Victor Malarek's 2003 book, *The Natashas*.

Sometimes, y'know, you're writing merrily along, having a good time, everything pleasant about you—and a character simply shows up. It's part of the fun (?) of the writing biz. It's happened to me before, most notably with Kazander in the Dragon Prince novels. It happened again with Jamey Stirling. Holly's cousin Cam was always due to be a part of the book, but when I was sketching out the party sequence (the first section to be written), Jamey arrived. I told him to go away. He wouldn't. As it turned out, he had something of an agenda—and as many times as I rewrote the last chapter, he wouldn't cooperate until it turned out the way he wanted it to. (I realize how utterly insane this sounds. But admitting it is half the battle, right?) I am told there are writers who know exactly what's going to happen in their novels, exactly how it's going to happen, and to whom. I'm not one of them.

My apologies to the citizens of the Commonwealth of Virginia (to many of whom I am related) for sneaking into their beautiful landscape a county that does not, in fact, exist. It's very small; you won't even notice it, really.

For the record: Yes, I'm Irish. Also English, German, Polish, Welsh, Scots, French, Swiss, and Dutch, plus a smattering of Portuguese, Italian, Spanish, Russian, and Lithuanian. And my great-great-grandmother's great-great-grandmother was a full-blooded Cherokee.